MOONLIGHT SHADOWS

Moonlight Shadows
by
Paul Anthony

The Right of Paul Anthony to be identified as the author of this work has been asserted by him in accordance with the Copyright, Designs and Patents Act of 1988

~

All the characters in this book are fictitious, and any resemblance to actual persons, living or dead, is coincidental.

~ ~ ~

First Published 2012
Copyright © Paul Anthony 2012
All Rights Reserved.
Cover Image by Margaret A Scougal 2012

Published by
Paul Anthony Associates
http://www.independentauthornetwork.com/paul-anthony.html

By The Same Author

~

In Fiction...

~ ~ ~

The Fragile Peace

Bushfire

The Legacy of the Ninth

The Conchenta Conundrum

~ ~ ~

In Poetry...

~

Sunset

~ ~ ~

In Short Stories...

~

Scribbles with Chocolate

Margaret - Thank you, for never doubting me.

To Paul, Barrie and Vikki - You only get one chance at
life. Live it well, live it in peace, and
Live it with love for one another.

To my special friends - Thank you, you are special.

…… Paul Anthony

*

For Jess and Rita,
Still reading somewhere...

*

PROLOGUE
~ ~ ~

Warren Point, Dromore, Newry, Dundalk, Ballynachlosha, Crossmaglen, Aughnacloy, Strabane, and Londonderry, stream from the tongue like a list of railway stations on a journey from one end of the line to another. But these names are not mere ports of call on an engine driver's list. They are just some of the towns, villages and hamlets that were once on the front line of 'The Troubles' between the people of Northern Ireland and the Republic of Ireland.

The Protestants dominate the six counties of the north in the lands they call Ulster whilst the Catholics occupy the lands to the south in the Republic they call Eire. Of course, there are places all over the island of Ireland where Protestants and Catholics live in harmony, and in some places they agree to coexist yet divide their communities on the basis of a bloody history and a perceived understanding of inherited religious beliefs. The result is a haphazard man-made border that recognises the sad ravages of time. The subsequent geographical, economical, religious, and political divide is represented by a narrow ribbon of a border threading its way across the island. This slender, cruel, wrinkled ribbon of a border provides a constant reminder of two warring communities.

And so it was that four members of an active service unit of the Provisional Irish Republican Army left their homes in the Dublin suburbs of Swords and Malahide and headed north to the land of moonlight shadows.....

*

Chapter One

~ ~ ~

Dateline: Some Years Ago
The Republic of Ireland.

Collected by a grey coloured nondescript saloon car, the four men travelled north from their homes in Malahide and Swords before entering County Louth in the borderlands between Ulster and Eire.

The friends were dedicated to the Republican Movement. It was their calling and PIRA, the Provisional Irish Republican Army, called them forward. It was their turn. Now was the time to mount an attack on a police station inhabited by the Royal Ulster Constabulary; a justifiable excuse to strike another blow for the Republican cause, an opportunity to take another step towards self-determination on an island intent on being free from the fetters of British imperialism.

Dropped off near the target zone, Shane, Ethan, Dillon and Conor approached warily on foot. Night fell and only the moon shone on the soil of Ireland and led the way forward. Making their way towards the village, they came across a telephone kiosk. Conor entered the kiosk and smashed the light bulb fitted to the ceiling. Not a word was exchanged between the men and within a few hundred yards they came to a stile by the crossroads. As briefed by Siofra, their Quartermaster, they clambered over the stile and walked precisely one hundred paces to the east parallel to a hedgerow. Here they stopped, rummaged in the undergrowth at the foot of a large oak tree, and discovered black plastic bags inconspicuously hidden by Siofra. From inside these bags, they removed dark camouflage clothing, automatic weapons, and night vision equipment. Quickly but quietly, they donned their camouflage clothing, loaded and checked their armaments, and waited for Conor's instructions.

Conor O'Keeffe was in his late twenties, proportionately built, with prematurely greying hair that often deceived those who thought they might know his age. Accepted by the others, unchallenged, Conor was their natural leader and it had been that way since their schooldays in Swords. His hair was cropped short and did nothing to hide a small jagged scar above his left eye: the result of a fall from a tree in his teenage years.

'Come, my friends,' he ordered. 'It is our time to stand for our beliefs. Stand with me as I stand with you.'

Nodding, agreeing, they crept cautiously along the side of an overgrown hedgerow. A short time later, a barn bathed in soft moonlight came into view: its silhouette murky against the background of the sinister countryside.

'Down,' ordered Conor, and as one, they melted into the undergrowth.

They sat patiently watching and waiting, scrutinising the area through shrouded night vision binoculars. Preparing themselves for the crucial task ahead, they scanned hedgerows which bordered the field protecting the barn before studying the building itself. Their eyes searched for tell-tale signs of human presence but only an intuitive night bird fluttering her wings disturbed the peaceful surroundings.

Conor whispered, 'Now,' and led his comrades towards the bleak foreboding barn.

Camouflaged, creeping low with their bellies skirting the earth, they bonded with the land as they stuck close to the dense hedgerow. Conor held them back when they neared the barn.

The wooden building had seen better days. Its doors stood wide and rotted little by little. Hinges creaking and rusty hung perilously from a handful of badly fixed screws. And there was a hole in the roof where moonlight shone down in a narrow beam of light bathing the barn's floor. The shaft of moonlight stumbled onto the rear wheels of an abandoned hay trailer and cast dark shadows on the floor and wall nearby.

'Safety off,' whispered Conor.

Conor heard the *click* when he unlocked the safety catch of his automatic weapon, indicating to the others to spread out. Cautiously, crawling on his belly to the door of the barn Conor lingered again, watched, stood up, and walked into the barn. Turning at the entrance, he raised a hand to his forehead allowing his fingers to trickle over his scar and beckoned the others forward.

'All clear, Ethan,' stated Conor. 'Shane, guard the entrance and keep look out. Dillon, load the pile. Ethan, come with me.'

The men did as they were bid whilst Conor led Ethan to one corner of the barn. Kneeling, Conor brushed away remnants of hay and dirt to unearth a rusting tin box which he opened.

'Detonators, Ethan. Go to work,' ordered Conor as he slapped a friendly hand on Ethan's shoulder.

Five minutes later, the trailer was laden with a huge pile of hay, maybe ten bales of rolled hay altogether; a quantity of fertiliser, and a lethal concoction of explosive mix which Ethan assembled.

Conor said, 'We'll roll the trailer out of the barn and across into the far corner of the field. From there, you can see the rear of the police station at the bottom of the hill. Let's get the trailer rolling and escape before they know what's happened.'

Inserting a detonator into the mix, Ethan connected it to a battery and said, 'When this hits the building, it'll blow it sky high, so it will, and the rest of the village with it. There'll be nobody left. I just need to set the timer and turn the switch then we're done.'

Conor said, 'Let's get a move on. We can be home before daybreak.'

They slung their firearms across their backs and heaved against the hay trailer. Dillon and Shane guided the trailer from the barn, led it towards a corner of the field, and looked down on the rear of the target.

'Okay,' instructed Conor. 'Line her up for the push and set the timer, Ethan. A minute or so should do it.'

Dillon and Shane put their shoulders into the front wheels of the trailer and began to turn the trailer towards the direction of the police station below. Looking downhill, they could see how easy the task would be and how the bomb was unlikely to miss its target.

Ethan moved to the rear of the trailer and carefully set the timer quietly saying, *'Aon ghéilleadh!'*

'Wait,' shouted Conor. 'Did you hear that?'

If Conor heard a noise it was obliterated from his mind a split second later when a troop of carefully concealed soldiers from 22 Special Air Service Regiment pounced and let go a long salvo of firepower at Conor and his fellow terrorists. It was as if the troopers magically materialized from the ground; as if they suddenly emerged from the wild unkempt hedgerow to surface deviously and thwart their plans.

Dillon and Shane took the first savage onslaught of bullets and were dead before they hit the earth.

There was no warning given of their presence and no indication the soldiers were there, no attempt at arrest; just a bloody repost to a planned attack on Crossnaclonsa police station.

Ethan returned gun fire but to no avail. He found it hard to find the target and couldn't accurately locate the heavily disguised SAS troops who pounded the barn and hay trailer with rounds.

'The switch, turn it on, Ethan,' screamed Conor through a cacophony of gunfire and a deluge of flying debris.

Ethan reached out as rounds screeching through the barn blasted into the woodwork from all angles.

'Ethan,' shouted Conor again. 'Turn it on.'

Ignoring the bullets, noise and mayhem, Ethan stretched out and flicked the switch. The device was live. The bomb was activated. The countdown began.

But seconds later, Ethan took a dozen fatal shots to the head and body and twisted round in the grotesque throes of death. In his final moments, Ethan tumbled backwards against the rear of the hay trailer and dislodged it slightly.

Beginning to roll towards its target, the trailer accelerated as it appreciated the descent. A rash of loose straw formed a wake behind the trailer as it hurried downhill towards the police station.

Turning to escape, Conor swivelled his torso and ran as fast as his legs would carry him towards the hedgerow. He sensed bullets zipping around him almost caressing his skin. Terrified, he dived into a ditch and struggled along on his belly.

A grenade landed ahead of him, exploded noisily in a cloud of thick grey smoke, and threw out a horrendous shower of lethal shrapnel. Then there was a starburst projectile discharged high into the sky. A soft *crack* above was heard and the sky lit up like broad daylight. Another ear-splitting chatter of automatic fire followed and another starburst projectile launched into the sky and heralded an early dawn.

Swiftly, Conor spun onto his back, stood up, flung his weapon away, and launched himself into the hedgerow. Cut and scratched, he kicked and clawed his way through the thick bracken to the open road. With tarmac beneath his feet, Conor set off running towards the stile, the crossroads, and the Republic beyond.

Bullets whizzed around him when he sprinted as never before.

There was a sudden burning sensation in Conor's upper arm. He swore when he realised he'd been hit by a bullet. The projectile tore through his camouflage fatigues and grazed his skin. It was enough to remind him of his crazy predicament but not enough to prevent his bid to escape.

Moments later, the night fell silent and all Conor heard was his heartbeat pulsating through his chest. He hit the dirt again and crawled along a ditch towards the telephone kiosk. Covering himself with foliage, he dug into the soil and shrouded himself with the dirt and filth of the land. With his heart thumping wildly, he prayed to God he might endure the dreadful ordeal. Conor O'Keeffe, the only survivor of his active service unit, lay for a while, listening, waiting, and trying desperately to get his breath back.

'Did we get him?' an English voice asked.

'Not sure,' replied another. 'We could have winged him.'

'According to the map, we're on the wrong side of the border. Come on, three out of four x-rays is a good result.'

'Yeah, not a bad night's work,' a voice said. 'Let's get out of this Godforsaken place.'

Listening hard, Conor heard their voices gradually lower when they moved away. He could hear no footsteps at all but he knew the troops wore a soft desert-type boot. There was an eerie silence as the starburst steadily faded and day became night again.

Only the moonlight shadows wavered in the breeze that wafted across the meadows and tickled the hedgerows.

Wondering, lying patiently, Conor yearned to hear an explosion, waited for the blast, but heard nothing. Bleeding from the wicked thorns and cruel bracken that had attacked his body, he could not see his hands properly. His hands were a deep black patch of night that was mud and dirt from the ditch. He trickled his fingers across his forehead and grasped the reality that he was covered from head to toe in the filth of the land, and he appreciated there was so much soil on his head that he could not feel the sometimes annoying scar above his eye. It was still intact but he knew his forehead carried a few new scratch marks and bruises. Feeling his bicep, he felt the graze where the bullet had creased his skin. Lucky man, he thought. Yeah, the luck of the Irish is what I have with me tonight.

Conor lay still, fought the tiredness enveloping his body, and tried to focus as his eyes became accustomed to the night. He concealed himself for what seemed an eternity hiding in a ditch, through a hedgerow, beyond the stile, beyond the crossroads.

His past returned to haunt him in the undergrowth in which he secreted himself. The days of reading and learning each page of the training and induction manual of the IRA came back to him. More importantly, he recalled his early days as a collaborator when he was expected to study the manual to fully understand why he was volunteering and what he was fighting for. The manual was known as the Green Book and was originally introduced by Irish Republican Army volunteers at the time of the Civil War in 1922. Turning its pages in his head, he recounted a statement concerning their military objectives, as well as tactics and conditions for a victory against the British Army, and the general philosophy and heartbeat of the organisation.

Secreted in the ditch now, wondering if a soldier was hiding on the other side of the hedge waiting for him to move first, he recalled his lessons. If he were arrested he might tell his captives he was a volunteer in a revolutionary army; that his cause was just and theirs were wrong, and being captured by the opposition might be expected of a soldier. He would not feel ashamed of being captured, he told himself. No, he would feel bloody disgusted with himself if he were captured, he decided, but then he knew he would have to keep his mouth shut and say nothing during the long inevitable interrogation that would seek to reduce him to a blubbering wreck.

Arrested previously, he remembered why he'd been locked up in a stinking cell in Dungannon. He'd been accused of following police home from their bases in South Armagh. Intelligence gathering, they'd called it: Proof of IRA membership, they argued.

And then he served time in the Maze prison for rioting in West Belfast. But those were during his formative days before he and Siofra were taken in and instructed on the Green Book. Yes, memories flooded back to him now. But Siofra, oh God, how he carried a candle for that woman. Gorgeous, she was in his eyes. Yet she resisted his suggestions, his advances, his obvious desire. Dedicated to the cause she was, he thought. Oh Siofra, what happened here tonight, he asked himself. Where are you now, my love?

Shaking himself out of his despair, Conor listened. He'd studied his enemy well and knew they might have left a *Stay Behind* to await his first move. Was there an SAS trooper on the other side of the hedge, he wondered? Waiting and listening, he tried to pick up the sound of a heartbeat or the scuff of a boot against the vegetation of the land. He listened for a finger to slide along a safety switch or a trigger guard and held his breath so that he might hear someone breathing. But only silence filled his ears.

Slowly he realised what had happened. Ethan had placed the detonator, set the timer, switched it on, and expected it to explode a minute later when the hay trailer reached the bottom of the hill and collided with the rear of Crossnaclonsa police station. The devastation would have been terrific; the result quite horrific. Yet Conor had seen for himself the detonator fixed and the timer set. It was obvious really, thought Conor. They'd been stitched up. Someone had warned the security forces of their plan. The SAS were there to waylay them, and someone either switched the explosive mix, provided dud detonators, or made sure the timer was faulty.

There was a 'tout' at work: an informant, he surmised, but which one of his friends?

When he was sure he was alone and it was safe, Conor could delay no longer. Creeping towards the telephone kiosk, he took in the surroundings. Tolerant of his predicament, Conor allowed his eyes time to become accustomed to the dark of the night. He hung on for another eternity until he felt confident he was alone. Then he entered the blacked out kiosk and searched his pockets for a coin. Conor dialled the number.

The lighthouse keeper read his newspaper, *An Phoblacht,* by the light of the moon and half a dozen candles or more flickering from the wall of his whitewashed home. His eyes were quite good but he wore reading spectacles to help him see when the light was dim.

Approaching fifty years of age, Callum Reece, the lighthouse keeper, carried a craggy face above an overweight plump stomach. He always dressed in dark jeans and a roll neck sweater occasionally covered by a thin denim jacket. He learned many years ago that if people saw him regularly wearing the same outfit they would associate those clothes and colours with him and would not expect him to wear other styles. It was likely therefore, his thinking suggested, that he would only be recognised wearing these regular clothes. It was his way of warping and confusing the minds of others. It followed that he spent much time going about his daily business wearing the same old clothes, day in and day out. It was often said he was a little weird, perhaps a tad bizarre, and he would agree that he was occasionally a little strange in his thinking. Consequently, when he needed to do the secret and covert works of the Provisional Irish Republican Army, Callum would wear totally different clothing. Unlike Conor, Callum Reece had never been arrested for a terrorist related offence but was once convicted of drink-driving and lost his licence for twelve months. Otherwise, Callum was clean with no criminal record. Now he lived in the lantern room where the lighthouse previously hosted the lamp and lens. The glass windows were storm proof but there was no inclement weather tonight, just a fine moon and a slight breeze that gently brushed the glass but dare not invade his privacy.

The lighthouse keeper set down his newspaper, stood up, and looked out from the lantern room. Unchallenged, Callum Reece was King of the sea, Emperor of the Ocean, Prince of the Moonlight, and Brigade Commander of PIRA.

Strutting out into the Irish Sea, the lighthouse had seen better days when it had once protected ships and vessels navigating the close waterways of the Republican coast. Now the lighthouse was defunct and almost derelict, or so it might seem to the casual observer on the outside. It had no lamp and when Callum turned he could look inland where he was King of the Meadows, Emperor of the Fields, and Prince of the Highways that surrounded the building and led towards the lighthouse and its secrets. The height and location of the lighthouse was not lost on the time-served Brigade Commander. Callum could see for miles around him, to the sea, to the land, to the air, in all directions. But there was nothing suspicious to see other than his black taxi parked at the foot of the lighthouse amongst a collection of dilapidated outhouses. He'd locked the taxi and that's the way it would stay until he plied his trade again.

The telephone rang three times and then went silent.

The telephone rang three times again and then went silent.

When it rang on the seventh time, Callum answered it immediately.

'Does the lamp shine far tonight, my friend?' asked Conor O'Keeffe from a telephone kiosk in the borderlands.

'The lamp will shine only for those who seek the light,' replied Callum.

'Good!' replied Conor.

'Is all well, my friend?'

'No, they were waiting for us. We collected our weapons, made the barn, primed the bomb, and were whacked by the Brits when we moved into the field. I took a hit to the arm but the others are dead.'

'Do you need a Doctor?' asked Callum anxiously.

'No, it's just a graze,' replied Conor. 'It just nicked the skin.'

Callum moved to the edge of the glass and peered into the countryside looking, scanning, and searching for his enemies. There was nothing to see.

'Sure, that's the third time in as many months that I know of,' offered Conor. 'There's a tout at work, so there is.'

'Aye, you're right. Did you strike the target?' asked Callum.

'No,' replied Conor. 'We assembled the device as usual. I think either the mixture, the detonator, or our timer was faulty. The Brits were there before us. They knew we were coming and were sat waiting to whack us. We were ambushed, didn't have a chance.'

'Siofra?' queried Callum quietly. 'Siofra O'Sullivan?'

'She planted the weapons, delivered the mix, and buried the box containing the dets. No-one else was involved. Yes, it's Siofra.'

'Sure, you're not the first to point the finger at Siofra. Where are you now?'

'I'm near the crossroads a few miles from Crossnaclonsa.'

'Take the road to Dundalk and go to Patrick O'Malley's. I'll collect you myself. Just be waiting there like I say.'

'I know the place. It's a good Republican bar, so it is. What about Siofra?

'This night is her last sleep, my friend,' declared Callum. 'These things happen in the war we rage. It's not a precise science, I'm afraid. We lost three good men tonight but we'll recruit three more tomorrow. O'Malley's bar and don't dwell on the past.'

'*Aon ghéilleadh!*' said Conor.

'*Aon ghéilleadh!*' replied Callum from the lighthouse.

The call ended.

An eavesdropping device operating against the occupant of the lighthouse captured their telephone conversation and electronically deposited it in a listening post faraway.

In an operations room on the island of Ireland, two men in naval uniforms studied a large map framed on a wall.

Oblivious to the chatter emanating from a bank of computer-linked printers belching out intelligence data from a plethora of indefinite sources, Admiral Crow meticulously observed Commander Pape delicately guide his pointer from Crossnaclonsa south towards Dublin.

Suddenly, the door burst open and Mansfield de Courtenay Baron entered in a fluster.

Shaking his head at the intrusion, Commander Pape, mid forties, slightly built and disapproving, set down his pointer on a nearby lectern and steadied his posture with a black ebony walking stick topped with a silver rose.

'Sorry, I'm late, gentlemen. Has it started yet?' asked Mansfield.

Commander Pape shifted his weight on the stick, turned, and with a forced but prudently welcoming smile said, 'Ah, it's you Mansfield. Wouldn't you know it? It's all over, I'm afraid. Pegasus turned up trumps again. I expect you'd like to hear the tape?'

'Damn! It went down earlier than planned then?'

'It would appear so but Sabre Force was waiting patiently.'

'In that case, yes, of course, if I may,' replied Mansfield.

In his mid thirties, the slightly plump Mansfield de Courtenay Baron was casually dressed in a dark blue corduroy jacket over an open necked light blue shirt, denim jeans and dark slip on shoes. Smoothing his prematurely thinning back hair; he then shrugged his broad shoulders and waited for a reply.

'Admiral?' queried Commander Pape.

Admiral Crow continued to study the map, was aware of his undisputed authority, and without losing focus replied, 'Let him hear the tape, Commander. He's entitled.'

Engaging Mansfield, Commander Pape invited him to take a seat, flicked a switch on the radio apparatus and said, 'It rolls on for a few minutes or more. In a couple of places gunfire can be heard.'

Mansfield relaxed, sat down, and listened to the commentary. There was a hint of static before the narration burst into life:

'This is Sabre One, I have control.'
'Roger, Foxtrot out.'
'Sabre One to Sabre units, I have control, stand by, four x-rays in sight.'
SILENCE
'Sabre One, I have control... Stand by.... Stand by.... Stand by..... Go!'
GUNFIRE
'Sabre Three, X-Ray Two down,'
'Sabre Two, X-Ray Three down.'
GUNFIRE
MORE GUNFIRE
SILENCE
GUNFIRE
'Sabre Three, X-Ray Four down.'
SILENCE
'Sabre One confirms device safe, repeat device safe.'
Sabre One, all units, X-Ray One escaping.'
GUNFIRE
GRENADES EXPLODING

GUNFIRE

SILENCE

'*Sabre One calling Foxtrot, reporting a contact. Three X-Rays down. Device is safe. X-Ray One has escaped across the border. Authority to pursue requested.*'

STATIC

'*Negative, Sabre One. Abort, abort, abort.*'

'*Roger Foxtrot. All Sabre Units... Abort... Abort.... Abort.... Stand down to the extraction point.*'

Commander Pape looked approvingly into Mansfield's solid grey eyes and offered, 'Congratulations, Mansfield. An excellent result, I believe.'

Tetchily, Mansfield challenged Commander Pape stating, 'With respect, Commander, X-Ray One is Conor O'Keeffe and he quite clearly escaped from right under the noses of Sabre Force. Apart from being the leader of an active service unit he has the eyes and ears of the Republican Movement. Conor is no idiot and neither is Dublin Command. It will take them only a short time to work out Pegasus is the informant. It's the third time in as many months Pegasus has provided pre-emptive intelligence allowing us to disrupt terrorist activity.'

'It was bound to happen at some stage, Mansfield,' advised Commander Pape folding both hands over the silver rose grip of his walking stick. 'Pegasus was actively involved in PIRA proceedings. It was never going to be easy.'

Ignoring Commander Pape, Mansfield fisted the solid walnut table angrily, spun towards Admiral Crow, and argued, 'Why didn't you authorise pursuit, admiral? It could have been all over in a couple of minutes. There would have been no-one left to tell the tale and Pegasus would remain unsuspected.'

Measured, deliberate, but not quite arrogant, the admiral turned slowly to reveal row upon row of alluring medals draped on his uniform. His bushy eyebrows dominated his face and his hooded penetrating eyes focused on the relaxed sophistication of Mansfield de Courtenay Baron. It was as if he sought to deny Mansfield's very existence when he cleared his throat and declared, 'My dear Baron, this organisation isn't even supposed to be here. We have formal and informal agreements with our host government. One such agreement is that we British will not carry out military operations in the Republic. It is part of the rules of engagement. According to our GPS system, Sabre Force was quite clearly inside the Republic at the time of the shooting. It was a non starter. And I, Mister Baron, do not create diplomatic incidents for our counterparts in Dublin.'

'That's not the point,' protested Mansfield.

Admiral Crow lifted his index finger, silenced Mansfield, and said, 'I have learnt over the years that today's enemy is often tomorrow's friend and a counterpart today is a colleague tomorrow. I don't expect you to understand this rather complex issue, Mansfield. Your job, my dear fellow, is to penetrate the target.'

'You and your bloody politics, I'm in the business of creating opportunities to destroy our enemy, sir,' replied Baron angrily.

'Enough!' ordered the Admiral. 'The matter is over and will not be discussed between us again. You knew the risks. You are not new to these events. It's a pity, but there you have it.'

'I am forever disappointed at the lack of intelligence in MI6, sir. The Secret Intelligence Service exists to protect the interests of the British people not to let the enemy off the hook. Or am I the only one who thinks that the 6 in MI6 is the average IQ of its senior ranks?'

'My dear Baron, you are instructed to extract Pegasus. Please act expeditiously and proceed as arranged,' announced

Admiral Crow, deadpan, unmoved, unthreatened by a man he knew to be his subsidiary.

Mansfield looked directly into the eyes of Admiral Crow.

'Thank you for delivering Pegasus. You have saved many lives as a result but there comes a time when we must protect our sources and our methods so that we can endure and move into the future,' stated the Admiral. 'Do you understand why I make the decisions that I do?'

Mansfield sighed, shook his head apologetically, and said, 'All that work ended because of stupid bloody politics, sir.'

'Incorrect, Mansfield, our work never ends,' replied the admiral.

Commander Pape tapped his walking stick twice on the carpeted floor, interceded, and handed a piece of paper containing *signal intelligence* to the admiral saying, 'Sigint from the Lighthouse, sir. It's in real time, wouldn't you know it?'

Admiral Crow perused the signal intelligence flimsy and then handed it to Mansfield who seized the paper.

A look of horror crossed Mansfield's face as he read.

Admiral Crow ordered, 'Extract Pegasus, before it's too late.'

Nodding, Mansfield approached a wall safe, dialled a number, withdrew a brown A4 envelope, and scattered the contents onto a table. A passport, driving licence, national insurance certificate, credit cards, cheque book, and various documents littered the tabletop. He examined them carefully checking off a list inscribed in his mind and then he replaced them in the envelope and picked up a telephone. Mansfield pressed a scramble button on a grey telephone and dialled a number.

After only a few seconds Mansfield made contact and said, 'It's me, Dickey Baron. You're blown. Get out, just as you are. Pack nothing, take nothing with you. Just walk away now. Meet me on the bridge in one hour's time.' He ended the call.

Collecting the envelope, Mansfield nodded at both men and then made for the door.

'Mansfield,' called the admiral. Mansfield paused and then turned to hear Admiral Crow pronounce, 'Thank you, Mister Baron.'

Mansfield de Courtenay Baron was gone from the room.

Commander Pape switched off the wireless, removed the tape, and queried, 'The tape, Admiral?'

The admiral instructed, 'Burn the tape, Commander. We do not keep history. History is for university lecturers and pub quiz teams. History was yesterday. Our business is today and tomorrow.'

'And the file on Pegasus, admiral.'

'Is still active, Commander. Pegasus is to be relocated not made redundant. The Baron will continue to run Pegasus. Good intelligence sources only stand the test of time when their handlers learn to be patient over the years. A gardener might plant a seed and the seed might bring forth a stem, but when the seed is fed and watered...'

Pape tried to understand and nodded.

Admiral Crow smiled and revealed, 'The stem becomes a bud that flowers throughout a long summer.'

'How is your rose garden, admiral?' asked Pape.

'Well cultivated, Commander Pape,' replied the admiral. 'But it does need attention occasionally.'

Commander Pape put a cigarette lighter to the tape recording and then placed a red buff file on his desk. He removed a pen, turned to an inside page, and recorded the date of the 'activity', the location, and the result. There were only three lines; enough to inform, enough to remind, enough to justify expenditure and a course of action taken, but not enough, never enough, to jeopardise.

The file bore the inscription *PEGASUS, Top Secret Omega Blue.... Eyes Only CSIS, DSIS, The Baron.*

There was no higher classification than Top Secret Omega Blue, no record of who had started the file or why, and no indication of who had read the file and why. It was restricted by its nature, by its very existence. Indeed, it did not exist. There was no computer programme waiting to be hacked into or made public in the years ahead. It was 'eyes only' and only three men knew of the file and the very briefest details concerning Pegasus. They were the Chief of the Secret Intelligence Service, his deputy, and the Baron.

The wall safe closed with an unhealthy thud.

*

Chapter Two

~ ~ ~

Dateline: Ten Years Later
Crillsea, England.

Detective Inspector Davies King isn't hankering for a return home. He's as close to home as he ever wants to be.

Home for Davies, since the drowning of his wife, is a flat near Crillsea harbour, the Anchor Pub, a local sports club, and anywhere a criminal investigation needs his expertise. Time, they say, is a great healer, but Davies still hadn't quite come to terms with Angela's death. She'd been drowned one day when they'd been sailing in their own dinghy. A wayward ocean-going yacht had brushed theirs aside and carried on without stopping. Angela was washed up on the shore some days later.

Battling grief, Davies threw himself into his work with some startling results. And that's why he'd driven from Crillsea to Police Headquarters and found himself sitting outside the chief constable's office. Davies was waiting to be seen by the man himself, and deep inside he expected to walk into the office as a detective inspector and leave as a detective chief inspector. Davies felt it in his bones. He just knew he would be made head of Crillsea's crime division. And, in his mid forties, the man was ready for it. It was his turn for the third pip on his shoulder: the one that made him chief inspector. It was his time. For today, gone were the scuffed down at heel shoes with worn out laces; the jacket with its leather elbow patches, and his shirt that always needed a fresh ironed crease.

Davies King wondered if the make-up would be worth it.

'You can go in now,' smiled Jackie, the chief's secretary.

Climbing the short staircase to a landing where the office of chief constable was situated, Davies paused at the doorway.

Chief Constable, Sir Thomas Daniels, QPM, OBE, LLB, DL, really did hold the Queen's Police Medal, was an officer of the Most Excellent Order of the British Empire, and held a law degree and a Doctorate in Law. Such high academia enabled him to deal adequately, sometimes dispassionately, with the various advocates his office occasionally required him to interact with. These included his literary agent who he was working closely with to produce a viable account of his long and varied career.

Indeed, an editor working on his draft manuscript concluded a passage in his forthcoming biography might be 'reconstructed'. Sir Thomas had written: 'The problems of being Chief Constable today acknowledge the complacency of the British public who understand raw street criminality but who are constantly perplexed by unscrupulous solicitors, lawyers, barristers, accountants, bankers, and government officials and politicians. Such people are sometimes more intent on furthering their own careers than delivering a professional service. Joe Public is ill equipped to counter such institutionalised neo-criminality and knows not where to turn.'

Following advice regarding *political correctness*, Sir Thomas changed the passage to read, 'The problems of being Chief Constable today are somewhat complex.'

The offending passage was leaked to the Press and there were few in the constabulary, and the wider public, who did not know of his *faux pas*. Moreover, some said his days were numbered. It was only a question of time before someone in the Police Authority or the Home Office slithered up to whisper in his ear, 'It's time to go before you're pushed.'

For those who knew him, Sir Thomas Daniels began his career thirty years earlier in Cumbria before transferring to Newcastle City Police where he worked the Market Street area mainly dealing with public order issues. Transferring to Strathclyde, he worked the clubs, pubs, and massage parlours with Glasgow's Vice Squad. Gradually, he climbed the ladder and switched to Lancashire Traffic Department. The West Midlands followed and he worked Birmingham CID and the Fraud Squad, followed by a spell on Special Branch in London. His first secondment to the FBI in America followed and he worked the Bronx in New York. It wasn't surprising he occupied senior management in the shire counties.

The chief was many things. He made mistakes but also made good things happen. He was known as a man who had made it to the top by a hard and convoluted route. Sir Thomas Daniels, QPM, OBE, LLB, DL, was a *Coppers Copper*, when all was said and done.

Davies knocked on the door.

Sir Thomas boomed, 'Come on in.'

Detective Inspector Davies King entered and was immediately engulfed by an ebullient Sir Thomas.

In his early fifties and sporting a greying beard, the barrel chested Sir Thomas stood well over six feet three inches tall and immediately exuded an enduring presence.

'Davies, how good to see you. Sit down, do. Coffee, tea, perhaps a brandy, what can I get you?'

Reaching inside a glass cabinet, Sir Thomas moved a couple of books and unscrewed the cap on a pill bottle. He delved inside, selected a couple of tablets, and swallowed them rapidly.

'Headache?' queried Davies.

'Yes, indeed, a blinder,' replied the chief who then produced a half empty bottle of Magno brandy which he thrust towards Davies in an inviting manner.

'I'm driving, Sir Thomas,' replied Davies. 'Coffee will be fine, sir.'

Stowing the pills and brandy bottle, the chief ushered Davies to a chair. The intercom system garbled and Sir Thomas interrogated the apparatus with, 'Jackie, a large pot of coffee for two, if you please, and hold all calls for...' The chief looked at Davies quizzically and whispered, 'How long?'

Davies held his hands in the air and said, 'Err... an hour?'

'Yes,' boomed Sir Thomas into the intercom. 'At least an hour, Jackie, I don't want to be disturbed under any circumstances.'

'And if the Home Secretary calls, Sir Thomas?' asked Jackie.

'Use your discretion, Jackie. You know what I mean. I'm out with someone from the police authority, if asked.'

The chief closed the intercom and massaged the furrows of his forehead with the fingers of his left hand.

'Well, apart from the obvious headache, you haven't changed a bit, sir,' stated Davies taking a seat close to an enormous antique desk. 'How was America? I heard the Bronx is a better place now you've given it the once over.'

'Third visit over there, Davies, I'm taking you with me next time. You'd benefit from the break, learn a few things, probably even teach a few things, and give everyone here a rest.'

Davies chuckled but Sir Thomas added, 'I can't leave you alone for five minutes. What happened while I was away? Don't tell me, I already know. Why didn't you ring me? You've got my mobile number.'

'Not my place, sir,' replied Davies.

'Well, to put the record straight, Davies. I had no idea my assistant chief, Patterson, had introduced all those new policies and I did tell him to promote you to chief inspector whilst I was away. What a cock up! Still, it's all sorted out now, isn't it? Damn bad show I say, but well done for clearing up those two murders.'

'Water under the bridge, sir,' replied Davies.

'Water crashing against Crillsea's bloody harbour wall in your case,' laughed the chief constable. 'Anyway, thanks for stopping by.'

'You wanted to see me, sir,' smiled Davies.

'Did I? Of course, I did.'

The chief's secretary walked in with a large tray laden with a cafetiere of coffee; milk, cream, sugar, biscuits, chocolates, and peanuts. She delivered a huge smile to Davies, set the tray down on a desk in the corner, far from the chief's walnut desk, and walked out of the room with, 'It's already plunged, Sir Thomas. Enjoy.'

'Thanks, Jackie,' boomed Sir Thomas. As an aside to Davies, he whispered, 'Salt of the earth that one, salt of the earth.'

'Good, such people are difficult to find, sir.'

'Davies, I said you haven't changed a bit but actually you have. You've changed. You're different. What's happened to you? There's just something...'

'Do you like my new jacket, sir?' asked Davies. He stood and turned to show off his new black three quarter length leather jacket.

'Oh my goodness,' replied Sir Thomas. 'That's an improvement on the old one with the leather patches.'

'It was time to upgrade, sir. Claudia decided I needed a new jacket and here you are, lo and behold. She thought it was time. You know, time to smarten myself in view of things. If you see what I mean?'

'Some personal assistant that one, if you don't mind me saying,' declared Sir Thomas.

'One hell of a lady, I'd be lost without Claudia Jones.'

Sir Thomas beckoned Davies over to the corner of his office and indicated a seat at a smaller desk near a window which looked out across a parade ground. In the far distance, the land dropped slowly away towards a river and the motorway which led to Crillsea, Tevington on Sea, and eventually, London.

'Great view,' offered Sir Thomas.

'Wonderful! Headache easing?' enquired Davies.

'Much better,' replied Sir Thomas. 'My turn, I believe.'

'No, Tom,' pressed Davies. 'It's my turn, if you don't mind.'

The two men looked down onto the desk and studied their chess board. It was set into the table and all the pieces were polished marble and of oriental design and origin.

'Are you sure?' asked Sir Thomas.

'Yes,' replied Davies. 'Absolutely sure, Tom. Game on!'

A fairly long period of silence followed as the two men drank coffee and studied the game.

Eventually, Davies popped a mouthful of peanuts, pushed a pawn forward, and said, 'I needn't have bought the jacket. I'm not getting promoted to head my crime division, am I?'

The chief's fingers played with his beard but then his hand hovered over the board for a moment. He clenched and unclenched his fist teasing Davies. 'What makes you think that? I've arranged for you to receive the Lord Lieutenant's High Commendation for Brave Conduct and I'm awarding you the Chief Constable's Commendation for Professional Investigation, Leadership, and Management of Serious Crime in relation to those two murders you cleared up. What more do you want?'

'Well, I never,' quipped Davies humbly. 'That's a bit over the top, isn't it, Tom?'

Sir Thomas rattled on relentlessly, 'I know you put yourself on the line during those cases and I wanted you to get the best recognition possible. I'm told the Met are sending something too. There'll be a formal ceremony, of course, the Lord Lieutenant, police authority people and such like. Drinks and canapés, smiles and chit chat. Wear a dark suit and be there. That's an order.'

'Can't you send it in the post and I'll put it with the others?'

The ebullience and joviality of Sir Thomas was gone when he withdrew his hand and snapped, 'No.'

The chief moved a castle to threaten his opponent before tormenting Davies with the twist of his tongue. 'I'd like to win a game. For just once, I'd like to beat you at chess, Davies. Think about your next move very carefully. Do you really want to be promoted, inspector?'

'Up to you, Tom, that's your decision. I've known you too long to argue with you but I can tell you one thing.'

'What's that?'

'Your chess is improving.' Davies thought for a moment and then withdrew a king a square to the left.

Sir Thomas studied the board, sneered and cracked, 'Mmm... Well, it was worth a try.' He tapped his fingers leisurely on the edge of the board before offering, 'Good move.'

Remaining silent, Davies studied the game and popped peanuts.

Sir Thomas said, 'I'm giving you Crillsea crime division, Detective Chief Inspector Davies. Congratulations! It's long overdue. Pity I had to return from America to make sure justice was done but it's your crime area now. Well done, my dear friend.'

'Fantastic,' replied Davies, 'Crillsea, Crillsea Meadows, Tevington on Sea and everything in between. That's a big area, population close on three hundred thousand I would say.'

'Yes, but listen to me, Davies. Running a crime division isn't just about supervising a couple of criminal investigation departments. In your position, you've also got responsibility for the Drug Squad, the Fraud Squad, Domestic Violence, Child Protection, Special Branch, and every other odds and ends department that comes under the crime umbrella. That's a big responsibility and I'm very conscious that in the past it hasn't been done in the way I wanted. I need you to get a grip of it all and shake it until the bottom comes out. Understand?'

Davies nodded approvingly.

'I went to America for a while, as you know, and whilst I was away everything went to hogwash,' continued the chief. 'Now I'm pulling in my best people to put the wheels back on before it's too late.'

Davies suggested, 'Drugs, Special Branch, Fraud Squad? I know a bit about all of them but I've made my career out of bank robbers, burglars, thieves, rapists and murderers, Tom. I'll have to do some homework, I reckon.'

'Make sure you do, Davies. You've a lot on your plate and I want to see some results. We're too complacent in some areas. Shake the tree and make the apples drop out, understand?'

Visibly delighted, Davies said, 'I won't let you down, Tom.'

'Your promotion is effective forthwith, Davies,' responded Sir Thomas reaching across to shake hands with his new chief inspector. 'And as a chief inspector you'll have to go to that swanky ceremony to get those commendations from the Lord Lieutenant. Won't you, Davies?'

'I'll be busy with a crime area to run, Tom,' taunted Davies.

'Make time, and that's an order.'

'Promoted ten seconds and I'm getting ordered about left, right and centre. I thought I would be the one giving all the orders.'

'You were wrong. Make sure you're at the commendation ceremony, Davies. One or two people want to meet you.'

'For you, I'll be there, Tom,' responded Davies.

'I'm also promoting Annie Rock into your position as detective inspector and Barney will be your new detective sergeant. I'm not asking for preferences. I'm telling you my decision, Davies.'

The chief moved his castle.

Moving his queen diagonally forward four places, Davies offered, 'Excellent choices, if I may say so. I'm delighted for Barney. He's a great personal friend, Tom, and that's a promotion long overdue. Annie is a shade young. One day, yes, maybe two years away but I'm happy for her.'

'I haven't got two years, Davies.'

'So I heard, Tom. You need to sack your publisher.'

'No, I need to sack my doctor. I've got about a year to live and that's why I'm doing things now.' He paused and then said, 'You only get one chance at life. I'm just polishing over some cracks I left on the wall.'

There was a long silence and the pointers of a carriage clock on a mantelpiece moved a fragment as they pushed pieces around the board. Eventually, Davies said, 'How bad?'

'Terminal,' replied Sir Thomas abruptly easing the top button of his shirt collar loose.

'Better make it a good year then.' Another peanut scuttled down Davies's throat.

'My wife wants me to retire and take up gardening.'

'Have you told her what the doctor said?'

'No. I've too much to do.' Sir Thomas attacked the peanuts.

Davies slid a pawn diagonally and removed one of the chief's pawns from the table saying, 'You can never replace the things around you that are the most important aspects in your life. I can never substitute Angela. I wouldn't want to. Get the business out of the way quickly, Tom, and then go home to garden. Cutting the grass and pruning roses is much more important than the job.'

Sir Thomas chose to ignore the inevitability of the future, stroked his beard, frowned, and said, 'The Home Office have sent me one of these whizz kids. Felix Churchill, they call him. He's on this new fangled Home Office accelerated promotion course. He's very ambitious and they are keen he is given every opportunity.'

'Ambitious, you say; a go-getter, Tom?'

'Two years as a constable on the beat, one year as a custody sergeant, one year as an inspector heading a department, and then one year as a chief inspector. From zero to hero in five years, and there's not one iota of man management training during the whole period. Felix is determined, pushy, and highly motivated.'

'Felix?' quizzed Davies contorting his face awkwardly.

'Bloody ridiculous, if you ask me, Davies; but others will point to enhanced selection procedures resulting in good senior managers. It's all by the by actually. Felix Churchill is an inspector in Ethnicity and Diversity but his year is up and he's due to be promoted to chief inspector. He starts in your crime division tomorrow. The Home Office is delighted and so is he. Felix will be working closely with you.'

'Felix?' repeated Davies exasperated.

'I knew you would say that.'

Davies pushed the chess table away, obviously annoyed and argued, 'Another chief inspector in my crime division? That doesn't sound right, and he's called Felix. Are you ribbing me again, Tom?'

Sir Thomas puffed his chest out and offered, 'He's got an Honours Degree in Social History and is studying for a Masters in Social Sciences. He's majoring in military history.'

'With a name like Felix Churchill, he'd have too. What does he know about criminal investigation?' enquired Davies.

'Next to nothing!' replied Sir Thomas.

'Has he ever been a detective?'

'No.'

'And you sent him to Crillsea?' asked Davies. 'Who's going to look after him there?'

'You,' declared Sir Thomas. 'I'm making him detective chief inspector in charge of the Intelligence Section. He's your equal.'

'My equal?' queried Davies laughing. 'I didn't know such a mortal existed.'

Sir Thomas teased, 'One minute into a new promotion and listen to you. You're so modest, Davies. No, listen to me for a moment. I want you to make Felix Churchill into a first class detective and a decent boss.'

They moved chess pieces as they talked. Split minds and split decisions ran loose across the board.

'That will depend on the man's inner fibre,' replied Davies thoughtfully. 'I can make a man a good detective but I can't necessarily make a detective a good man.'

'Interesting comment considering you haven't met him yet.'

'Don't they have detective training schools and man management courses anymore?' asked Davies.

'Oh, he's done a hundred courses and there'll be another hundred still to do but I want him to be an accomplished detective and a worthy boss in the practical sense. Five years has taught him everything he needs to know but he'll potentially grasp very little as far as street sense goes.'

'Street sense, is it that bad? You want me to put my own personal stamp on the crime division whilst at the same time wet nursing this Home Office whizz kid? I'm not at all happy with that, Tom. I want to do things my way. I don't want to spend every moment of the day explaining the job to him. That's what you're expecting from me, isn't it?

'He needs honing,' replied Sir Thomas. 'That's why you've got him. Knock him into shape. These academic types are okay but I need to see some fire in their belly and a bit of grit in the teeth.'

'And I'd rather go back to Crillsea as a detective chief inspector fully in charge of the divisional crime area. This way it looks like you've appointed another chief inspector to keep an eye on me. What next, L plates for the learner?'

'It might seem like that to you but I can assure you, that's not the case, Davies. Just give it your best shot.'

'We'll have to finish this one another time. The hour's up, sir,' decided Davies studying the clock.

'I know,' grimaced Sir Thomas. 'I've disappointed you and you've dropped Tom and started on the sir again.'

'I know my place, Sir Thomas. Work is one thing, chess is quite another. Thank you for the leg up and I'm grateful for our game but the Met's Flying Squad has offered me a chief inspector's job on one of their operational desks. I've a lot to think about and consider. The London job is pure and simple; the other involves wet nursing kids.'

'The Flying Squad?' queried Sir Thomas. 'Davies, take your time about your future but remember I have an agreement with the Home Office I cannot break. I promised them I would elevate Felix into the senior ranks and that's what I'm doing.'

Rising, Davies said, 'It's your move next time, sir. It's touch and go this one. How long have we been playing?'

'Close on twenty years.'

'Really,' said Davies amazed. 'That long?'

'Ever since we did that job together in Birmingham and we got stuck on the train going up to Scotland for three days.'

'Oh yes,' recalled Davies. 'That winter and an avalanche that closed the rail network down. You were a detective inspector then. The Handsworth murder was solved over a chess game on the way to Edinburgh. Your first ever game and you won.'

'You taught me, Davies. Now go and teach Felix Churchill.'

Davies offered, 'I've choices then: Felix or the Met?'

'Your choice, Davies,' replied Sir Thomas biting his lip.

'Oh, I'll take Felix for the moment, Sir Thomas,' said Davies looking directly into Tom's eyes. 'In any case, you'll need someone to get you through to the last move on the board.'

Smiling, the chief said, 'Let's hope the game lasts a long time yet.'

Nodding agreement, Davies turned and ambled towards the door. 'I'll be round on Sunday, sir, unless you have arrangements?'

'It'll be a roast with all the trimmings at five o'clock, Davies, followed by chocolate cake. I'll let Helen know you're coming. She'll be absolutely delighted.'

'I'll see you then, murders permitting,' laughed Davies.

Sir Thomas Daniels stood looking out of the window when he said, 'I don't want you to go, Davies, but part of me says take the Flying Squad job. You were born to be a detective; you're wasted here. Do we have a relatively low crime rate because we're in a sleepy hollow or is it because you're on top of the criminals and a fair proportion of them are informants? I don't know the answer to that one but I do know you'd be a King in London. This is a backwater in comparison. We don't do major crime really and as for murders, well, we've had two in five years.'

'Two too many, sir, I'll see you both on Sunday.'

'I'll look forward to it, Davies.'

'And don't worry, sir, you'll just have to forgive my impatience. We both know there's plenty of Davies Kings about.'

Davies King was gone from the chief's office headed for a crime division to govern in his own special way. And his brief was to train a stranger called Felix Churchill, barring a murder or two.

Marching into the car park, Davies opened the car door, and angrily threw his new leather jacket onto the back seat. The jacket hit the back of the seat with a lively wallop and then slid unceremoniously from the seat onto the floor behind the driver's seat.

A curtain twitched in the chief constable's office and Sir Thomas withdrew from the window. Speaking into an empty office, he quietly said, 'No, you're wrong there, my friend. There's only one Davies King.'

Stepping back towards the chess table, Sir Thomas smoothed his fingers across his forehead and felt the sweat returning to his body. A steady trickle of perspiration explored his eyebrows and threatened his cheeks. Then he felt an unfriendly chill invade his torso as the perspiration began to soak him.

Oh no, he thought, not now, and then he steadied himself on the side of the table and tried to catch his breath.

For some inexplicable reason, deep inside, he glanced at the window and smiled in case anyone might have caught such a movement. He knew he might be seen by the mere mortals who constantly surrounded him and strolled across the car park hoping to capture his eye and favour them with an accommodating wave. Constantly encircled by people more intent on serving themselves than the public, Sir Thomas long ago deduced the skills and abilities of those in his company. If only they knew, he thought. They watch me; smile at me, follow me like sheep. And they adore me because it suits their purpose. They worship me - but only for their own ends - they are fickle mentally maladjusted sycophants who act like misinformed commuters waiting for the first train to take them to a land of green and plenty whilst never really understanding what it takes to make the Garden of Eden. Such people are but starlings in the dusk of day: a murmuration of individuals following their leader, turning, swooping, diving, but always following. I am their leader, he thought. God help them.

And then he felt the stomach pains begin.

Toying painfully with a chess piece the chief realised he held the king in his hands. He whispered, 'Sorry, my old friend. You've no idea how sorry...'

Sir Thomas set down his king amongst the pawns and reached for a bottle of antibiotics.

The telephone rang on the chief constable's desk.

~

Chapter Three
~ ~ ~

Dateline: Two Weeks Later

Kamakura, Kanagawa Prefecture: The Archipelago of Japan.

Once the moonlight shadows slipped away, a new dawn steadily tumbled over the 'Land of the Rising Sun'.

Maureen McCluskey smiled appreciatively when the first distinct rays of sunshine penetrated the skyscrapers of the thriving bustling city that was her home, Kamakura: a city with a population of about 200,000 situated on the archipelago of Japan, in the Pacific Ocean, and located approximately thirty miles south of Tokyo.

A holidaymaker from England travelled to visit Maureen.

On a scheduled flight, he'd flown into Narita International Airport, Tokyo, stayed overnight in Yokohama, and now made his way to meet her. More importantly, she was making her way to meet him.

Conscious of the sun slowly rising and bearing down on the streets, Maureen heralded the new day as a unique opportunity to celebrate. It was the tenth anniversary of her residence in the town she'd made her home. Gradually, carefully, and as dawn grew into the fullness of day, she strode through the streets to the rendezvous.

Maureen had settled well from the outset and taken residence in a reasonably well appointed apartment close to the town centre. She found useful employment and bought herself a second hand semi-reliable car with which to tour Japan. Over the years, she learned to speak the language despite, generally, keeping herself to herself. In time, she made friends, particularly at work. Now she enjoyed pals who were Japanese, Chinese, American, Spanish, English,

Dutch and German. Most of her mates shared one thing in common: they were all whizz kids, computer geeks, and slightly bizarre brainy people. Some of her friends wondered how she had survived financially in the beginning but Maureen reminded them of the inheritance her uncle bequeathed her some years ago. Of course, she hadn't been stupid, she declared. No, she explained, an annuity had been bought with the inheritance and a comfortable amount deposited into her account every month. Maureen met most of her friends at work. And work was an electronics company specialising in making computer software for a global market. From small beginnings, she gained both respect and knowledge as she progressively climbed the career ladder.

Of course, that's why he was visiting her from England today. Maureen had found something useful, something she knew the man would be interested in.

Dressed in a dark fur-trimmed blouson, dark trousers and flat heeled knee-length boots, Maureen was single and into her late thirties. Her light brown hair was fairly long but rested easily on her narrow shoulders. Tall, slim, and self assured, Maureen was, in her own quiet way, a self disciplinarian. If she had a weakness, it would be a propensity to be occasionally naive.

There was a faint bluish mist ahead but the phenomenon held no fear for her. Kamakura was located not too far from the coast so a touch of adverse visibility now and again wasn't unusual.

Approaching the mist-shrouded Kotoku-in Temple, Maureen evoked memories of her real home and the reason she had specifically asked to meet the man who had flown from England to see her. Chuckling to herself, she read the notice at the entrance to the grounds. The words seemed so appropriate to her appointment and read:

'Stranger, whosoever thou art and whatsoever be thy creed, when thou enterest this sanctuary remember thou treadest upon ground hallowed by the

worship of ages. This is the Temple of Buddha and the gate of the eternal, and should be entered with reverence.'

When Maureen approached the ubiquitous outdoor bronze statue of the Great Buddha of Kamakura, she reflected that in Dublin, her birthplace, almost everyone was Catholic. Here in Japan, virtually all and sundry were Buddhist, and she'd decided it was time to leave the sanctuary. She was homesick. Her mother needed her and she wanted to return to the banks of the Liffey and the Emerald Isle. Maureen wanted to go home now.

Early morning tourists were filtering into the area, marvelling at the Great Buddha, touching it, prodding it, photographing it, and just enjoying its presence, its religious significance.

'According to the handbook, the Great Buddha of Kamakura is over forty feet tall and weighs over ninety three tons,' said a man's voice.

Maureen identified his voice, hadn't heard it for a decade, but recognised it immediately, and assumed he'd shadowed her for a while before approaching her from behind. He's probably followed me for the last twenty minutes at least, she decided.

Replying unhesitatingly, Maureen said, 'I didn't think you'd miss it standing that tall; the statue I mean.'

'Makes sense to meet in a place full of tourists,' said the voice.

'Are we alone, Dickey?' she asked.

'Alone as we need to be, Siofra,' he replied.

'Is anyone following me, Dickey?'

'No, should there be?' he asked.

Siofra glanced casually over her shoulder and caught sight of him standing quite close. It was Dickey: the man she called the Baron. He was dressed in a brown leather

45

three quarter length jacket that was belted but unbuckled. His belt hung loosely from the waist loops and the two ends trailed away below four dark brown buttons that might occasionally fasten his coat. The fourth button was looser than the others and about to become a nuisance. She watched him smooth his dark swept back hair as he fingered the lowest button. It was made of horn, coloured dark brown, and complimented the soft leather he wore. A tan open-necked shirt lay beneath the jacket and his sharply creased coffee coloured slacks looked down on highly polished brown lace up shoes.

'I thought you'd be pleased to see me,' she said. 'Instead, I see you're browned off, Dickey.'

'I often dress in brown. It's one of my favourite colours. Do you like my jacket, Siofra?'

'No, I don't. Funny that though, Dickey, I've waited ten years for someone to call me Siofra and when they do they can't even pronounce it correctly. *She-Fra,* say it.'

'Siofra O'Sullivan then,' he pronounced Siofra correctly as he took a quick look around the Temple site.

'Much better,' Siofra replied.

'I'm sure you didn't ask me to come all this way to give me either fashion or elocution lessons,' quipped the Baron. 'By the way, nice name you picked, Maureen, but your real name is a strange one, Siofra. Do you know what Siofra means?'

'It means peaceful, mischievous,' she declared.

'I know. I know lots of things, Siofra.'

'You don't know everything. That's why you're here,' she replied.

'Your name also means changeling,' the Baron said. 'Are you the offspring of a fairy, a troll, an elf, or another strange creature that has been secretly left in some strange place?'

'Oh, I was secretly left here,' replied Siofra impishly. She watched him looking discreetly into the faces of those close by. He was ever cautious, she thought. 'Shall we walk through the mist?' she suggested.

'If we must,' he replied moving to her shoulder. Their eyes met for the first time in a decade. He held her gaze for a moment, looked around again, and then acknowledged her properly with a smile. 'It's good to see you, Siofra. It's been a long time since O'Connell Bridge.'

Nodding, Siofra spoke softly and said, 'Walk with me.'

They set off like a brother and sister might do, not as lovers or an affectionate couple pretending to be in love. They did not hold hands or skip idly through the park. They ambled naturally, gazed at flowers and fauna, and took in the Great Buddha on occasions when the Baron produced a camera from his jacket pocket and snapped away.

'It's been a long time,' stated Siofra.

'It was the wisest course of action to take at the time,' he replied.

'I remember it just as if it were yesterday. I fast pedalled out of Dublin like a greyhound with a rocket stuck up its backside. The only things I took with me were a mobile phone and an overnight bag. Too close for comfort that night.'

'Well, that's behind you now, Siofra. It was a long time ago as you say. You've been happy here, haven't you?'

'Fine,' she replied. 'But you've put a bit of weight on!'

'Mmm...,' he responded lukewarm.

They strolled on in silence until the Baron paused to photograph the Buddha once more and suddenly declared, 'Jason tells me you've been very good over the years.'

'Oh, Jason, your man in Japan,' replied Siofra. 'Or rather, one of your men, I suspect.'

The Baron responded only with a defiant smile.

47

'What's his real name?' she taunted. 'He won't tell me. Is Jason like you and doesn't have a name, I wonder? Or are you one of his Argonauts?'

Dickey Baron looked away but replied, 'Jason was the legendary Greek hero who led a team of intrepid adventurers in a perilous quest for the legendary Golden Fleece. You know all about Jason and the Argonauts, don't you, Siofra?'

Ignoring his remark, she argued, 'Go on, you can tell me, Dickey. What's your true name? I deserve that much?'

'You can call me whatever you want, Siofra. Any name will do because I'm disinclined to disclose my true identity to you. You don't need to know. We know why we are here. You might be selling the Golden Fleece, I might be buying a pig in the poke. We're trades people. It's as simple as that. Names are immaterial.'

Siofra smiled and suggested, 'Did you know the Golden Fleece was said to afford protection and prosperity to the kingdom that possessed it?'

'Kingdoms come and kingdoms go, Siofra. Some of us make and break kingdoms for a living.'

'Ouch, if I could touch you I'd find you colder than the iceberg that sank the Titanic,' she needled. 'Is Dickey alright or have you changed it since the Crossnaclonsa incident?'

The Baron grimaced and said, 'Stick with Dickey for now, Siofra.'

They strolled parallel to a slow moving narrow stream but then turned and headed back towards the heart of the park where Dickey said, 'You wanted me to come and see you, remember? Was it for a walk in the park or is there something else?'

'Jason asked me to report on people I met,' admitted Siofra. 'Attitudes to the Emperor, opinions on the west, military people I might come into contact with, and the people I work with. Easy stuff. Trivia, not like last time.'

'Yes, I know. Thanks,' praised the Baron. 'I'm aware you work in electronics. Some of the things you've sent are quite interesting. I got your message.'

'Good, then you'll know my story,' suggested Siofra.

'Jason tells me you won't discuss the situation with anyone else but me. So I came.'

'You'll be telling me next you were just passing.'

'You've got something, haven't you?' he enquired.

'I've got something you want,' stated Siofra emphatically. 'Something everyone wants.' She allowed her words to sink in before continuing, 'I presume you know from your man in Japan what my computer geek friends have been working on?'

'Yes, indeed,' he replied. 'We've known for some time but how did you get your hands on it?'

'The Golden Fleece, Dickey?' she cracked.

The Baron laughed and said, 'If that's what you want to call it, yes.'

'Sorry to disappoint the Argonauts but it's not the Golden Fleece,' she replied.

'I didn't think it would be,' he replied.

'Oh no, it's better than that,' declared Siofra.

'Better?' he enquired.

'Yes,' replied Siofra. 'And it will provide protection and prosperity to the country or kingdom that possesses it.'

The Baron pursed his lips and said, 'I'm listening.'

'It all started shortly after I arrived in Japan. I answered an advert looking for English speaking people to test software. The rest is history.'

'I like a good old fashioned history lesson now and again, Siofra. If you've got something special for me then I want to know how you got it, understand?' he shrugged.

'Makes sense I suppose,' she said, pulling a face. 'But will you trade if the product is good?' enquired Siofra.

'It's why they sent me,' he replied.

Satisfied, Siofra nodded in a slow, measured fashion, and volunteered, 'I started in a group with five others. The company loaded software into a test box and we were each given an individual computer system to see if it worked. It was mainly games at first: Racing cars and football games, high octane kids adventure material! They asked us to make notes of how good the game was or where it wasn't working properly. Sometimes it was a disaster. Other times their stuff was okay but often it was too slow or too fast or the graphics and colour weren't right. The computer guys worked it out, made it better, and we kept testing it until we broke it or it worked. I must have played a hundred or more computer games over the years. Boy can I race a Ferrari and score a hat-trick; you've no idea, Dickey.'

'And that's it?'

'Some of the group resigned because they were bored testing the same old games software from morning 'til night.'

'But you didn't?' enquired the Baron.

'I stuck it out. I needed the job. I was bored. Late hours became the norm and I got into the habit of backing up our results onto computer tapes so that first thing the next morning the geeks had the mistakes on their system to work on straight away. They liked that, it saved them a lot of time. Eventually they put me on a *Help Desk* for a year. I took calls from other companies who were marketing their products and dealt with any consumer problems. In the end, I reached a position where I was telling the company what they needed to do to make things work better. They liked that too. The Japanese are a very respectful people, a joy to work with. Anyway, they put me in the Research and Development team and I found myself working on the deterrence system.'

'The deterrence system! Interesting, did you test that as well?'

'Of course, but by then I was well into their systems and they looked upon me as an important cog in the machine. I'm pretty sure they trusted me. They put me in charge of quality control. I upgraded and got a new car and all kinds. It was great. Bad news is I couldn't afford a Ferrari.'

'Did you find it hard work? You've no skills to speak of.'

'I know how to kill people,' she cracked as they stood by a stream bordering the park.

A twig floated past slowly with the current turning it gently downstream.

Siofra continued as she watched the twig disappear from sight, 'I know what speed a bullet fired from a Uzi submachine travels at and the range at which it ceases to be effective. Do you want me to go on?'

'Yeah, I remember,' sighed Dickey. 'I meant computer skills.'

'Every day I learnt something new. When I ran quality control they opened up all kinds to me.'

'Was that when you realised that games were only a side-line for the company?' he asked.

'My, you guys are really on the ball, aren't you, Dickey? I'm impressed. Yeah, it took me a while but I got there in the end. The games software is only a small part of the company profile.'

'Good, that's established then. What did you do in the deterrence system?'

'I broke it,' she cracked with a subtle smile.

'You broke it?'

'Yeah, I told them it wasn't that good.'

'Did they fall out with you?'

'No, they agreed with me and gave me a bigger car.'

The Baron chortled and commented, 'A Ferrari?'

'No! A big four by four!'

'Why am I not surprised at you, Siofra?' he said.

51

'Because that's why you recruited me all those years ago.'

'What have you got that I would be interested in?' asked the Baron inquisitively. 'It's not the Golden Fleece and the Crown Jewels were okay when I left London. What could it be, I wonder?'

'You know otherwise you wouldn't be here.'

'I might but I'd like to hear about it from your own lips.'

'The constellation, I copied it and stole it.'

The Baron was visibly stunned, stopped in his tracks and said, 'You stole it! You stole the constellation and you lived to tell the tale?'

'Well, so far,' she replied unflustered.

He stood his ground and peered around him. It was as if he was expecting some kind of demon or phantom to suddenly appear through the faint mist creeping along the earth. Eventually he enquired, 'How many stars are there in the constellation?'

'Five teeny-weeny ones and don't you know it!'

Walking on, the Baron glanced over his shoulder warily, lowered his voice and asked, 'How tiny?'

'You could put all five stars on a pinhead if you so wished,' she replied. 'But then the hand that holds the constellation shapes the world.'

'I know,' he said. 'Your remark could be construed as quite spiritual given these religious surroundings; mist, Buddha and all.'

'Mystical even,' suggested Siofra with a raised eyebrow and a deep frown, 'Or from the supernatural world of cyberspace and a virtual cosmos of supremacy?'

'You're dangerous,' said the Baron eyeing her sideways.

They walked on stepping through the mist that seemed to open up before them, welcome them, and then envelope them; he with his ever darting cautious eyes taking everything in; her with a quiet look of satisfaction on her face.

The mist vanished from the Temple, its task complete.

Shaking his head somewhat perplexed, he said, 'You copied it and then stole it! Why?'

'Well, it's pretty obvious, Dickey. Now I have something that no-one else has and everyone else wants. Did Jason fill you in on the technical detail?'

'To some degree,' he replied. 'I know you haven't given us everything, have you?'

'I'm no fool and I don't expect you to treat me like an idiot. But you do want it, don't you, Dickey?' asked Siofra.

'It depends,' he wrangled uncomfortably.

Walking away from him for a moment, she said softly, 'My mother is dying. I want to go back before the end. I want to return to Dublin in safety and without problems from them. You owe me that much, Dickey.'

He waited, considering his reply, and then said, 'We don't owe you anything, Siofra. You played the game, took the money, took a chance, and you're alive today because they can't find you and we've given you enough to hide away for a lifetime from them.'

Dickey smiled cheekily as he aimed his camera directly into her face and took a photograph.

Siofra said, 'There's a peace over there now. A fragile peace, yes, but a peace and it's time to move on.'

'I'll see what I can do,' he said.

'While you do that, I'll make contact with the Chinese triads,' snapped Siofra. 'Do you think they'd be interested? How about the Russian Mafia and the Taleban? Hey, how about the Colombian cartels and the Mexican drug gangs? Please Mister Dickey 'whatever your name is' Baron, don't patronise me with your 'I'll see what I can do' bullshit. Do you think I was a quartermaster because I won all the bombs and guns in a raffle in a Dublin pub? Do you think I didn't learn anything? How long do you think it would take me to rekindle some old friends from America and Libya; yeah and one or two other places, Dickey?'

He took a deep breath and slowly deflated his lungs.

Siofra said, 'You can get me back to Dublin. That's the deal: a piece of magical mystical software on a memory stick for a plane ticket, a safe ride home, and a lifelong pension. I've got the hottest ticket in town and you know it. I want out and I want out for good, and I want out in safety. You can hide me here. Hide me there if you have too.' Siofra could see him thinking, considering, wondering. 'No, don't even think about it,' Siofra advised. 'I went around the block with you Brits once before, remember? If you've got your goons going through my apartment as we speak then put them off. The software is not at home and it's not at work. And, oh, by the way, it's password protected and the whole world will want it.'

'Technical people can get around computer passwords, Siofra. They just need time and we've all the time in the world.'

'That's true, Dickey,' replied Siofra. 'But what if I told you the software initiated a self destruct corruption process in the event of its programme being interfered with?'

Dickey thought for a while considering the process. He played unconsciously with a loose horn button fastened to his jacket and replied, 'I'd think you were calling a bluff?'

'You'd be wrong,' declared Siofra. 'Oh, so very wrong, and at any rate, your computer nerds have already seen some of the technical stuff I sent them through Jason. So don't try to fool me with your out of date British Imperialism bullshit. You didn't pop over to Japan from Vauxhall Bridge to get my take on elocution lessons or the fashion police. No, you were briefed at length on what I had to offer before you left London, and you know what I've said makes sense.'

'Then I'll need the password if we're to do business' admitted the Baron forcing the issue.

'The banker is holding; the bank never loses,' she replied.

There was silence for a while as the Baron's brain went through some objective thought processes. Then he said, 'Conor

O'Keeffe will be difficult. Some of these people aren't happy with the peace process. And if I remember correctly, he lost his school pals that day. They tell me he once had a crush on you but you didn't want to know. People like him have long memories. He might still be looking for you. I don't know.'

'Find out. Sort it,' she ordered. 'You can move mountains when you want too. Now make it happen.'

'A changeling?' he mused, almost dismissively.

'You secretly left me here now secretly take me back,' she said with an impish smile.

Suddenly decisive, he replied, 'Collect your new travel documents in the usual manner from Jason in exactly one month's time. The package will be sealed. He won't know what it is and he won't ask. I'll make the arrangements but I want your so-called magical mystical memory stick when you touch down or the deal is off.'

'One of the things I've learnt about working for a global computer company is that we use couriers who transport products all over the world. I want out and I want out for good. Get me to Dublin and I'll meet you in the usual place forty eight hours after I land. Agreed?'

'I want it in my hand when you step onto the tarmac at Dublin International,' he declared.

'I don't think so, Dickey,' she replied. 'Your hearing isn't as good as it used to be.'

The Baron paused, lost in a time warp somewhere, thinking, but Siofra knew he was trying to locate where the memory stick was and she persevered, 'The software programme on the stick is worth millions, maybe billions in the right hands. It all depends on who holds the cards and how they are played. Isn't that what they say?'

The Baron remained silent.

Siofra continued, 'This software can change the world, Dickey. It's going round in circles in the sky until I pull it down and the airline delivers it to a place I choose. You've no choice.'

He thought for a second before saying, 'Forty eight hours?'

'Forty eight,' she acknowledged.

The Baron argued, 'I need something to take back to the top brass in London. I want a guarantee; a deal, an agreement, something that says we're trading and the trade is good; in short, the password.'

It was Siofra's opportunity to consider her options. She nodded her head thoughtfully and replied, 'Moonlight Shadows!'

'Moonlight Shadows?' queried the Baron with a muttered hint of derision.

Siofra O'Sullivan alluded to a sly smile and then walked away without another word.

Mansfield de Courtenay Baron watched her go, appreciated the slight swing of her hair, heard the soft scrape of her boot, and struggled to wonder why a human being hankered so much for her home.

Turning to the Great Buddha of Kamakura, the Baron aimed his camera, zoomed, and heard a dull click from its shutter mechanism.

*

Chapter Four

~ ~ ~

Dateline: Four Weeks Later,
Dublin, Ireland.

Shaped in the eighteenth century, steeped in history, and set in the heart of Dublin, O'Connell Street is the main thoroughfare running through the centre of the Republic of Ireland's capital. In 1916, Republicans seized the General Post Office and proclaimed the Irish Republic from this very street. The Easter Rising was quelled; the rebels escaped, and the street was sacked and looted by the occupants of nearby slums. These events laid the foundations for the battle for Irish independence and the Civil War of 1933. Eventually however, O'Connell Street was rebuilt and the slums banished to the past. Now it's the main route of the annual St. Patrick's Day Parade and is the place where the 1916 Rising is commemorated every Easter Sunday.

Daniel O'Connell's statue stands in the street and overlooks O'Connell Bridge. He was a nineteenth century nationalist leader who campaigned for Catholic Emancipation and was known as 'The Liberator'. The bridge spans the River Liffey and is constructed of granite with three semi-circular arch structures.

Maureen McCluskey headed for a rendezvous in the middle of O'Connell Bridge, right above the centre arch, and she knew this particular area very well indeed. Back home in Dublin tonight, Maureen McCluskey was Siofra O'Sullivan once more and she was on her way to meet the man she knew as Dickey Baron. Tonight was a special night. It would be the night Siofra walked away from Dickey Baron for the last time: a night of liberation in exchange for a piece of software everyone wanted. Within twenty four hours, she'd be living with her dying mother, under protection, in Wexford, Southern Ireland. It was wonderful, yet so very sad her mother's condition triggered such homesickness. Leastways, that's what she told Dickey.

The Baron had kept his word all those years. There was no confusion in her mind. She trusted him.

Siofra did not doubt him now, couldn't, and wouldn't. She just drove herself to believe. From the outset of their relationship, the money had always been there. He'd always made sure she was safe and secure. And when danger threatened he'd secretly uplifted her and planted her in Japan with a new identity, a huge wad of cash, and a pension for life. Yes, she trusted him. She even trusted him when he'd told her that Conor O'Keeffe was doing a life sentence for murdering a British soldier in South Armagh seven years ago. And, in a way, she was glad Conor was doing time. Locked up inside, he wouldn't be able to chase her like he had once tried so many years ago. Oh yes, she thought, she was safe. She'd played the game hard and fast and made all the running, all the demands, and she'd won. Victorious, it was her night. Nothing could go wrong, she thought, as she played her last card at the table of her own making: O'Connell Bridge.

Nearing midnight, Siofra approached the bridge. A slight mist lingered a moment and then vanished mysteriously. Pausing, she watched the moonlight cast its reflection on the tranquil waters of the River Liffey. She looked out across the river towards the bridge and studied the string of people strolling along a dark dimly lit pavement. It was a strange, eerie, spine-chilling place to meet at this time of night, she decided. The murky black river was bathed in a sinister beam of reflected moonlight and the lengthy broad bridge was inhabited with creepy, uncanny shadows that seemed to dance above the arches of the bridge as people went about their business.

A few black taxis, a couple of late night buses, and a scattering of vans drove past her and crossed the bridge but there was nothing to stop Siofra tonight. There was no sign of Conor

O'Keeffe because he was in gaol, and there was no sign of Dickey Baron because he was late again. But he would be there somewhere out of sight, watching her watching the people.

Smiling, Siofra grew in confidence, and took a step towards the bridge.

Freedom beckoned.

Siofra began to chuckle. She knew the street, knew the bridge; knew the monument, knew the history, and she giggled. As she walked, she laughed aloud without a care in the world. She knew Dickey Baron, had met him or telephoned every week for God knows how many years before Japan. And Siofra knew everything he did had a hidden meaning, always a conundrum to consider and work out. Oh you silly stupid ignorant arrogant man Dickey Baron, thought Siofra. I invite you to meet me in the front of the Great Buddha of Kamakura, where religion dominates the area, and then you respond by agreeing to meet me in O'Connell Street where the first heartbeat of the Republican Cause sounded: where the Republican Movement was born, where I am to be freed from the shackles of British Intelligence in full view of the monument of 'The Liberator'. What a strange warped sense of humour we both have, she thought. But how nice that is, she decided, in that dangerously naive way she sporadically alluded to.

Siofra walked onto the bridge towards the centre span and the monument to the Liberator, Daniel O'Connell.

A bus dove past at high speed followed by a line of taxis, private cars, and a police patrol car. Men and women, couples and singles, strolled, darted, slunk across the bridge in a never-ending promenade of human traffic. The River Liffey reflected a fractured beam of silver moonlight quivering on its surface as it lapped at the edges of its confines. The dimly lit bridge played silhouettes and shadows in equal abundance, and the statue of Daniel O'Connell cast a dark shadowy spectre towards the centre of the bridge. It was as if the proponents of the Republican Movement had assembled to observe proceedings, to witness the final traitorous act of one of their own, to congregate and scrutinize the final Dublin lockout.

The freedom of Siofra O'Sullivan was at stake. Also known as Maureen McCluskey, she was referred to in a red buff file marked *Top Secret Omega Blue... Eyes Only* as, quite simply, 'Pegasus'.

A clock struck midnight and an owl hooted in Phoenix Park.

Stepping towards the centre arch, Siofra gathered her fur trimmed blouson closer and spotted him on the other side of the road. She watched him waiting for a break in the traffic. She recognised him. Indeed, could pick out Dickey Baron from a hundred yards. He was tall and smart and strode out in an upright fashion with a strong rigid backbone.

Ambling towards the centre of the bridge at her own leisurely pace, she observed him step briskly across the road. He dodged the traffic and she felt a surge of excitement and relief ripple through her slender body.

Dickey Baron had made the meeting and he was on time.

Strolling, smiling, almost a spring in her step, Siofra kept an eye on Dickey as he approached. Yes, that's him. I can almost see the wrinkles on his forehead from here, she giggled. Dark sharp ironed trousers and a long black overcoat covering a smart lounge suit no doubt, she thought. But his hat was new.

And then he waved with the casual throw of his hand and she responded by smiling and tapping the outside of her jacket over the pocket carrying her ticket to freedom.

Siofra increased her pace as a bus and a black taxi vied for position as they approached the O'Connell Monument ahead.

They headed towards each other: he with his rigid back, conceited stride and long dark overcoat; she with her humble flat-heeled knee length boots and fur timed blouson. And the traffic flying mercilessly by as the Monuments to Republican history edged forward to witness her final audacious betrayal.

Moonlight shadows crinkled soft silver folds on the surface of the Liffey.

Siofra delved in a pocket for a memory stick.

He reached inside his overcoat pocket. He wore gloves.

Gloves, she grasped. Gloves?

'Oh no, it's you. What are you doing here? Did he send you?'

There were two gunshots fired from a handgun removed from his overcoat pocket.

Travelling at approximately 600 feet per second the 38 calibre bullets entered the chest cavity of her body, near the heart, within a second of each other. Each bullet ripped through her torso destroying ribs, lungs and the body's support structure before exiting her back and slamming into the brickwork of the bridge.

Siofra fell backwards, pushed ungraciously by the force and impact of the onslaught, and cannoned into the parapet of the bridge. Total shock invaded her face as she slid slowly onto her backside. A darkness threatened as her eyes took in a face shrouded by the rim of a black trilby.

Bending down, the man took the memory stick from her jacket and dropped it carefully into his overcoat pocket. He walked away as she slowly turned her head. Her eyes followed the receding figure then she heard a car horn, tyres screeched, and brakes squealed.

Jumping from his vehicle, the taxi driver ran towards Siofra. He looked down to see the hole blown in her chest and blood oozing from her, staining the pavement with her issue. Turning, he screamed at the receding figure crossing the bridge, 'Hey!

The gunman spun and haphazardly aimed two shots at the taxi driver who dived behind the taxi door as soon as the gunman raised his weapon. Holding his gun horizontal to the ground, the gunman aimed again at the taxi driver, but then lowered the barrel and stepped backwards across the bridge. Rounding a corner and out of sight, he was full of confidence when he casually dropped his gun into the River Liffey below.

Sensing the immediate danger had passed the taxi driver stepped onto the pavement again and bent down by Siofra.

'It's you' she said weakly. 'I thought he was… He told me…'

'Don't be speaking now, child,' said the taxi driver. 'Save your strength until the ambulance gets here.'

'No ambulance, not for me. Just like the old days, no ambulance.'

'Hold on, Siofra. Hold on!'

Siofra looked wide-eyed into the face of her saviour and said, 'It's you. He sent you, didn't he? The Baron sent you…'

Her voice trailed away into a mind confused by identity and trauma.

Promptly, the taxi driver removed his denim jacket and gathered it around her shoulders when he felt her body cold against him and saw her blood spilling from the pavement into the gutter.

'I should have known,' Siofra whispered. 'They've got the software. Tell the Baron they've got the constellation.'

'What did you say?' asked the taxi driver kneeling close to her lips, bending his ear to catch her words.

Drawing a feeble breath, Siofra uttered, 'The Dutchman, tell the Baron the Dutchman has got the constellation.'

Her eyes closed as she faded into the black.

Siofra O'Sullivan died a traitor to the cause at the birthplace of the Republican Movement, watched by a dozen statues, monuments, and unfaltering immovable representatives of a lifelong cause. She had been liberated by two 38 calibre bullets delivered by an unknown hand.

Callum Reece, former PIRA Brigade Commander, always a taxi driver, held her as she died and watched the Dutchman make good his escape across the bridge and out of sight. He recognised the Dutchman who murdered Siofra, and he knew where to find the Dutchman. The lighthouse keeper knew the courier who delivered guns, ammunition, and uncut diamonds for the criminal underworld throughout Europe and for PIRA in a war not won but not yet lost. Such knowledge was inbred: a legacy of the 'Troubles'.

Callum laid her back against the wall. Glancing across the bridge, there was no-one there.

A woman screamed and then a couple stood still, frozen to the ground, bitterly distressed at what they saw.

Casually almost, Callum climbed into the driver's seat of his taxi, turned it around, and set off in pursuit of the Dutchman.

Five minutes later, Mansfield de Courtenay Baron, Dickey to Siofra, stepped onto the bridge. A police car arrived with its siren squealing and its lights pulsating and an ambulance crew ran from their vehicle to Siofra's body.

Mansfield strolled casually by, stood unperturbed, and looked down at the lifeless body of the woman he called 'Pegasus'.

Moments passed before the Baron walked silently away.

Later, in the early hours, a computer screen flickered and fingers tickled the keyboard. Five minutes later, the hacker was into the close circuit television system governing O'Connell Bridge. Mansfield studied the meeting between

Siofra and the man in the overcoat. He saw the shooting, identified the man stealing the memory stick from Siofra's clothing, and knew the taxi driver who stopped, hid, and then set off to follow the man in black. More importantly, Mansfield examined the video footage and saw Siofra speak some words to the taxi driver. Engaging his keyboard, Mansfield zoomed into Siofra's face. He read her lips when she spoke the words, 'The Dutchman, tell the Baron the Dutchman has got the constellation.'

Mansfield de Courtenay Baron knew the man in black as 'The Dutchman'. It was his job to know such things. He switched off the computer and considered his options. Drumming his finger tips gently on the table top, a smile visited his face briefly before he chuckled softly, unloosened his tie, and unfastened the top button of his shirt.

A professional hit, mused Mansfield. A *one-time* gun dropped into the river and *a walk away* into the night. The assassin is quality but who sent him after Siofra and why, he asked himself. Pegasus was so green, he thought. All those things he'd taught her, all that training, and she was so bloody naive at precisely the wrong time.

Picking up the telephone, Mansfield dialled a number for the freephone Garda confidential line. A few seconds elapsed before the call was answered and he announced, 'A woman was shot dead on O'Connell Bridge a few hours ago. Listen very carefully because I'm going to give you information that will lead you to the gunman. Who I am is not important. What is important is the identity of the man who ordered the killing.' He waited only a short time before saying, 'Of course I know who it was. Are you ready to write it down?'

A short time later, Mansfield snatched a telephone directory from a desk. Thumbing his way through yellow pages, Mansfield followed his index finger down the contents until he stopped at the name and business telephone number. It was getting late, very late, and fatigue had invaded his body. Dawn approached and Mansfield needed a taxi ride home.

The tide was inbound. A brace of yachts fought for supremacy on the waves at the mouth of Crillsea harbour, and Felix Churchill and Davies King discussed their new roles.

Abandoning his usual threadbare coat in favour of a new black leather belted jacket, Davies carried a relaxed air about him and was laid back and groomed somewhere close to the casually acceptable mark. Felix, on the other hand, wore an eye-catching dark pin stripe suit with a smart shirt, tie, and highly polished black leather shoes that were finished off with silver buckles on the side. He looked quite suave dressed in his version of an everyday business suit. Fashion was a simple tool for Felix but the difference between the two men was quite conspicuous.

The inbound waves gathered, colluded, rushed at the harbour wall, collided majestically, and exploded into a thousand droplets of brine.

Felix offered, 'I'm really grateful to you for showing me the books, Davies. Now I can appreciate how the system of criminal administration works. It's quite complicated this crime recording scheme but I think I've got it at my fingertips now.'

'I'm pleased,' replied Davies with an encouraging smile. 'It's much more detailed than you might imagine.'

'Yes, I noticed,' admitted Felix. 'I've obviously done a lot of crime reporting whilst in uniform but when you see the system as a detective supervisor it brings a different perspective to you.'

'If you're going to run the Intelligence Department you need to be acquainted with the procedure and how to connect Intelligence with reported crime. But don't get too hung up on crime statistics. Every time we get a new government they change the recording system to make it look as if they've introduced some new initiative that has reduced crime.'

Shoulder to shoulder, they strolled along the promenade bordering the harbour wall.

'Yeah, I've heard about that but at least now I recognise there's much more to it than just writing it all down,' agreed Felix.

'The secret is where to find information and then how to protect it when you've got it, Felix. Some intelligence is easy to come by because it's in the public domain already. For example, an advertisement promoting an illegal rave might appear on the internet but the bumf announcing the party will tell you where it is, when it is, and who might have organised it. What you do with that information is up to you.'

'Can't wait,' enthused Felix. 'Let me at 'em.'

'Take it nice and easy, Felix. You'll find the really interesting material often lies in covert intelligence: surveillance and informants in the so-called criminal underworld. You know; things that only thieves know about each other.'

'Ahh,' joked Felix in a conspiratorial whisper. 'It's a world of clandestine code books and cloak and dagger meetings.' He paused; looked guardedly over his shoulder and continued, 'Stakeouts, satellite surveillance, and spooky spies with gorgeous girlfriends in tow, no doubt.'

'Oh dear me, you've watched too many Bond films, Felix. No, it isn't like that at all. It's just dealing with criminals firmly but fairly and making sure they get a good deal out of the system. You can lock them up and throw away the key but sometimes it's how you do it that counts in their eyes. The vast majority of burglars, robbers and car thieves come to our notice time and time again. They're the ones who'll tell you something useful in the future. Often when it suits their purposes but tell a toxic a lie and he'll remember you forever. Give a crook a chance and it will stick in his mind and he might just repay you.'

'Are they all like that?' asked Felix.

'I wish they were,' chuckled Davies. 'Most of the regulars couldn't care less but you'll find some of our best customers want to do business with you. You'll find them. Or rather, they'll find you if you treat people right. It's all about trust, Felix.'

'Interesting, how many informants have you got, Davies?'

'None at all,' cracked Davies.

'That's not what I heard,' replied Felix, slightly confused.

'You heard wrong, Felix,' scowled Davies.

Felix grimaced, 'Oh, I don't think so.'

'Put it this way,' advised Davies candidly. 'The first thing you learn about informants is that you haven't got any. Never admit you're close up and personal with a toxic. A grass will never forgive you if every Tom, Dick and Harry knows they are snitching for you. They'll shut you out right away. They're in danger from their own kind if it gets out they're working with you, and we have a duty to protect our sources. Don't shoot yourself in your foot. Keep things legal but say nothing.'

'Then how will a Head of Intelligence know what intelligence is out there?' asked Felix thoughtfully.

'Oh yeah, your new job,' acknowledged Davies.

'Well, it did occur to me, Davies, that as the boss I should know what's going on and as I am the boss...'

'Someone meets an informant and then writes up the product for the computer,' explained Davies. 'The system assigns a code to that information. It's then computerised so that it can be read by whoever has access to the system. You're the Head so you'll have a handle on everything. But you're the one who decides who is allowed to read the system. You can let the most trusted read everything and only grant less access to the less trusted.'

'Trusted, I don't quite understand what you're driving at.'

'Well, trust usually goes with the type of job someone does. A traffic officer needs to know about disqualified drivers. A drug squad officer needs to know about drug suppliers. Now and again they both need to know everything but the secret is to keep your finger on the pulse and make sure only those who need to know get to know.'

'Ahh, the 'need to know' principle. I've heard about that.'

'At least, that's the simple explanation but read the procedures manual I gave you. It's in there and it's easy to follow,' said Davies.

'Easy to follow, that'll be a change then! Still, I suppose it's all run of the mill stuff in Crillsea anyway.'

'Most of it is, Felix,' agreed Davies. 'But trust is a big word.'

'So I see.'

'The more important and crucial intelligence is, the harder it is to protect. That's why you need to build up a good relationship with your informants and protect them properly and legally. I call it networking but I don't think it's the kind of networking you hear about at these business breakfast meetings.'

'Thanks for that. Sounds like I need a spy case or a terrorist case to get a hold on this,' joked Felix.

'You wish,' chuckled Davies. 'You'll probably get a druggie grassing up another druggie in return for a word with the Judge and a shorter sentence, Felix, but it'll come. Don't worry. There's always a client out there waiting to do a deal when the circumstances are right.'

'Well, that's as maybe, but I'll settle for a tip off about a foreign nuclear submarine attacking Crillsea harbour, Davies.'

There was a crash of tidal water and slight spillage onto the promenade in front of them. The two men walked on unperturbed.

'I'll stop your nuclear sub with my submarine net, Felix.'

'Where you going to get a submarine net from?'

'The same place as you got your nuclear submarine from.'

They laughed.

'You just got one thing right though, Felix.'

'What's that?'

'If you want to crack Intelligence look beyond the harbour wall and see how far the horizon is. If you only cast your eyes inside the harbour you'll only find out about broken lobster pots and you'll be bored after a while.'

'Ahh, I understand what you're driving at. Thinking outside the harbour equates to thinking outside the box, yes?'

'I'll settle for that,' replied Davies. 'Remember, I'm here to help. If I'm not in Crillsea Sports Club, I'm almost certain to be in the Anchor so don't hesitate to ring my mobile if you need advice. We'll meet regularly but ask anytime if you're not sure of anything. You'll find the paper system duplicates the computer system and both Annie and Barney know it inside out. Put your trust in them. They won't let you down.'

'Thanks, I'll take that on board as they say.'

An errant wave smashed into the harbour wall, cascaded high, and doused both men with a liberal soaking of seawater.

Shaking water from his hair, Davies teased, 'Keep a sharp look out, Felix. You just never know what is beyond that harbour wall.'

'Brilliant, bloody brilliant,' cursed Felix. 'Soaked to the bloody skin; I should have seen that one coming.'

Davies doubled up laughing, walked on, and then suggested, 'What you really need to concentrate on is an interesting investigation and the ability to identify good people working for you, or not so good as the case may be.'

'What in Crillsea? Fat chance, nothing ever happens here.'

'I used to think that,' accepted Davies. 'Hey, just concentrate on being able to read people around you as well as looking for intelligence leads. I don't mean to be disrespectful. Indeed, it's a terrible thing to say, but you need a murder to get your teeth into.'

'Two in five years we've had. I'll be drawing my pension when we get the next. But, changing the subject...' suggested Felix.

'Please do.'

'Why are you always in the Anchor?'

Davies twisted a laugh and responded, 'Because they need me there. Someone has to do their bit for the licensing trade.'

'But it can't be good for you,' warned Felix. 'An ex boxer who is regularly in a sports club rather than the office; drinking all hours in a pub, and trying to lose weight at the same time, isn't quite the picture of a senior detective I expected to be working with. The Home Office would have a fit if they knew who I'd been teamed up with.'

'Mmm...,' replied Davies somewhat mystified. 'Drinking all hours? I knew there was something I forgot to mention about intelligence. Make sure your snouts are giving you the correct information whenever you can. There's nothing worse than getting false information. Look, is there anything else on your mind while you're at it, Felix?'

'Yes, well, I can understand how you're trying to lose weight and all that. You're approaching middle age and not getting any younger. It makes sense to try and lose weight and get fitter. Get rid of the paunch; kick the drinking habit, that kind of thing.'

'You're so kind, Felix,' glowered Davies.

'Oh, sorry,' tendered Felix. 'I didn't mean it to sound that way. But I don't understand what the attraction to the pub is?'

'Don't you?'

'No, I don't, Davies. I studied for my degree in a tiny squalid flat on a dinghy estate in Newcastle. I'm not used to pubs and night clubs like you. I just think it's wrong, oh so wrong.'

'Oh I don't do night clubs, Felix,' advised Davies. 'Just the Anchor, it's my office. It's where people can find me if they need me.'

'But you've got an office at the police station.'

'True, but my people know where to find me.'

Felix looked at Davies, saw the audacious look in his eye, and then glanced speculatively beyond the harbour wall.

'Oh, and by the way,' said Davies, 'Annie Rock, your new DI, does have a degree but Barney, Webby and the new trainee, Mark Tait, haven't an 'O' level between them. Mind you, Barney's investigated over fifty murders: some in London, some in Ireland. He's ex Met and ex RUC. What they all lack in academic qualifications they make up for in common sense, experience and ability. You don't have to possess a certificate to be knowledgeable, Felix. Listen to Annie and Barney and ring me when you get your first big one, whatever it is. Just for now, I'll be having lunch in the Anchor.'

'I'll not be ringing you when that happens, Davies. I can't afford to be seen to asking you for advice. I've thrown my cap in the ring,'

'What do you mean, you've thrown your cap in the ring?' enquired Davies.

'The Super's job is advertised. Bert Allithwaite retired recently and the division needs a new Superintendent. I'll be applying. We both know I'm good enough. I've got an honour's degree and I'm going places. I always interview well, you see. That's going to be my next job.'

Jolted to the point of disbelief, Davies replied, 'Is it? Don't you think you should learn about the current one first?'

'What! The Intelligence department? I'll crack that, don't you worry, Davies.'

'Well, I'm pleased to hear it but let me tell you something.'

'Go on.'

'In the matter of Claudia; I've been ordered by Sir Thomas to share her with you.'

Felix swooned, 'Good, I'm so very glad we agree on that, Davies. An eloquent decision by the chief, if I may say so. In any event, I'll need someone to tend to all my letters and my application. I expect to be quite busy with all manner of things.'

'Ahh,' sighed Davies. 'Well, Felix, I don't agree with Sir Thomas. You've yet to meet Mrs Claudia Jones: widow of this parish; but you will. Anyway, be warned and take note. She's my personal assistant, not yours. The office is mine and my safe is out of bounds. You can double up until we sort out a proper office for you but until then I'd be obliged if you didn't go ratching through my desk and no, the safe is mine and mine alone and I'm not sharing. And Claudia, she'll eat you for breakfast if you step out of line. Okay?'

Davies didn't wait to see the quiet nod from Felix as he walked away from the harbour towards the Anchor pub.

Tomorrow was another day. Davies King was making for the pub, and, in any case, nothing ever happened in Crillsea, anyway. Did it?

Removing a mobile 'phone from an inside pocket, Felix Churchill punched some numbers and waited for a reply. Looking across the harbour wall towards a pair of dancing yachts he eventually said, 'Is that Brogans Bookmakers? Yeah, it's Churchill, Felix Churchill... Two hundred and fifty pounds to win on *Dan's Quest* in the three o'clock... Yeah, on my account.'

The waves withdrew, lauded themselves, and tumbled inbound as a couple of grey broken clouds appeared on the horizon.

*

Chapter Five
~ ~ ~

Dateline: The following day, Tuesday.
Amsterdam, Holland.

An excited group huddled together like ewes being rounded up by an Old English sheepdog on the Cumbrian Fells, or perhaps it was fear of becoming detached from their party in a large unfamiliar city. Jostling, they murmured their minor irritations as handbags, rucksacks, and cameras fought valiantly for supremacy whilst they awaited her every word.

'Quickly now, quickly,' commanded Ruth, the young female tour guide, when the assembly crammed into an imaginary circle she signalled with her hands. 'Thank you,' she proclaimed. 'Yes, thank you indeed. Now then, Amsterdam is named after a dam in the River Amstel....'

Japanese tourists in the party nodded and smiled widely and a large overweight fifty something American, by the name of Brandon, wearing a baseball cap, a baseball top, a pair of shorts and sandals, stood with his hands on his hips engrossed in the tour.

'Listen up, Betty Lou,' he said to his younger diminutive wife. 'We paid good bucks for this tour now listen up and learn something and stop chewing that gum, God damn you.'

Looking into her husband's eyes, Betty Lou blew a bubble with her gum, allowed it to burst over her lips, and said, 'I'm bored, Brandon.'

Gesturing with her hands, Ruth continued, 'The dam is still here many years later except now it's called Dam Square and is about half a mile from *Centraal Station,* the city's main railway station, but about five or six miles from Schiphol Airport where most of you flew into yesterday.'

The Japanese nodded and smiled and Betty Lou, whispered, 'Like hell it was, Brandon.'

The lecture tour continued. 'The square joins the streets of *Damrak* and *Rokin*, which run along the original course of the Amstel from *Centraal Station*, to *Mint Square*.' Steering the group away from the middle of Dam Square, Ruth introduced the surrounding area declaring, 'A short walk from here finds you in the famous red light district. In this area prostitution is legalised and you will find many coffee houses where cannabis can be openly and legally smoked in the most liberal of European societies.'

'Well, I'll be...,' said Brandon tilting his baseball cap.

'No you won't, Brandon,' interrupted his wife. 'You'll stay right beside me and listen up to what I have to say.'

Looks of surprise and intrigue seemed to cross one or two Japanese faces in the group and a bespectacled gentleman in his fifties asked, 'We can buy prostitute and cannabis in coffee shop, yes?'

'No,' snapped Ruth. 'This way please.'

'How much is coffee shop tour?' asked the persistent Japanese gentleman.

'This way,' replied Ruth walking quickly. Then she stopped to point to the west end of Dam square and revealed, 'This is the Royal Palace. Close by you will find the fifteenth century *Niewwe Kirk* or New Church as some call it, and the ever popular Madame Tussaud's Wax Museum....'

Cameras struggled from their hideaways and flashed repeatedly at the various sights.

Flying low, a pigeon made a deposit on a beleaguered Japanese gentleman who was more intent on the red light district and coffee houses than monuments and waxworks. There was a faint splash and the gentlemen said, 'Damn pigeon, very funny. You understand, damn pigeon in Dam Square.'

'Quite, sir,' replied an irritated Ruth smiling insincerely. Then she escorted them towards *Rokin* whilst continuing with her lecture.

'Keep up, Betty Lou,' ordered Brandon.

'The first canals were built in the seventeenth century. *Rokin* leads us to the *Bloemenmarkt*; the world's only floating flower market situated on the *Singel Canal*. It really is the Venice of the North,' Ruth chuckled.

'Hear that, Betty Lou? Two holidays for the price of one.'

'Wonderful,' yawned Betty Lou.

'The main canals, of course are the *Herengracht, Keizersgracht* and *Prinsengracht,*' announced Ruth. Checking her watch she added, 'Oh dear, we're behind schedule. Would you please keep up and we'll try to make up some time. We'll talk about the canals when we take our cruise tonight. Meanwhile, can I remind you to watch out for the trams and please, please, please, be careful of these bicycles when you cross the road? There are literally hundreds of them on any street at any time of day.'

'Yeah, keep up, Betty Lou,' whispered Brandon.

A football, chased by a boy of about ten years old dressed in an orange football shirt and orange shorts, bounced innocuously along the tarmac to the annoyance of the guide.

'And that is Holland's football strip,' quipped Ruth becoming increasingly annoyed. 'You'll see orange flags and shirts everywhere because the nation is football mad.'

The assembly strolled purposefully south towards *Rokin* amid a hundred scattered pigeons and a dozen statues.

But the statuettes twitched slightly every now and again. Perched a foot high on small portable platforms, the statues were actually human beings and each one seemed to have a predetermined space in the broad expanse of Dam Square. They were dressed in a plethora of costumes all competing for a paid photograph; a tip, a gratuity, or a hand out, but it was a tourist spectacle to appreciate because the event display was quite amazing.

Spread out across Dam Square one could see a number of statues. They included the world famous Neptune who was undisputed leader of the pack. He was a professional live statue. But also on show were Batman, Superman, Spiderman, and Darth Vader dressed in their celebrity costumes. There were also three female statues clothed as Nuns, and a cowboy wearing boots, denims, a roll neck sweater, a bandanna across his face, and a cowboy hat tilted low across his forehead. Every few seconds the cowboy removed a six shooter from his holster and robotically aimed it at a child or passer-by. Darth Vader replied with a sudden swish of his black cloak and then Spiderman abruptly crouched lower or stretched higher as the case might be. And Neptune playfully challenged with his famous spear. Meanwhile, Batman and Superman took another pose.

When the group made for *Rokin* some stragglers took an opportunity to photograph the human statues. Cameras clicked, smiles appeared, and coins and notes fell into the statue's collection bowls.

In nearby *Damrak*, every window sported an orange banner or an orange flag flying from the upper storey windows. The street was alive with Dutch flags, banners, and bunting celebrating the forthcoming football match between Holland and the Republic of Ireland.

The Dutchman walked down *Damrak*.

Dodging the bicycles, crossing the road, he heard the approaching trams softly clanking their way towards the railway station. Football shirts, banners, flags, and bunting, had no place in his mindset. Looking dead ahead, the Dutchman snubbed the fine buildings, the posh departmental stores, a sex museum, the fast food kiosks, and the bars and cafes lining *Damrak*. He walked into

Dam Square bound for his apartment near *Vondelpark*. Tall, with a rigid backbone, he wore a dark overcoat, gloves, and a dark hat. He carried a small suitcase and strode out purposefully across the square whilst Japanese cameras snapped away.

Neptune stirred and his spear playfully menaced. A cowboy drew a bead and then lowered his silver six-shooter. Darth Vader flashed his cloak and Spiderman crouched low as two Dutch policemen cycled close to the Royal Palace to observe proceedings.

Stepping into the middle of the statues, the Dutchman vaguely became aware of Superman, Batman, Darth Vader, and three nuns.

There was a rustle of a cape, the flicker of an eyelid, and a slow hand drawing a fast gun as the statues vied for the Dutchman's attention.

A sudden gunshot ripped through the air and the Dutchman clutched his chest and stumbled backwards. Another blast rang out and the Dutchman fell to the ground. There was a sickening thud when the back of his head smashed against the tarmac,

Jumping from his platform, the cowboy holstered his smoking silver six-shooter and rushed to the man lying on the ground. Screams filled Dam Square as the cowboy kicked the suitcase away, rifled the Dutchman's pockets, pulled out a memory stick, stuck it into his jeans pocket, and strode towards *Centraal station* and *Damrak*.

'Well, I'll be...,' puzzled Brandon moving his right hand instinctively to where a shoulder holster might have been.

'No you won't,' shouted Betty Lou. 'Get inside the museum before he takes a shot at us.'

She pushed her husband through the queue towards the entrance of Madame Tussauds but Brandon shrugged her away and swivelled his cap from front to rear. Removing a tiny camera from his pocket, Brandon smoothly pointed it at the gunman, began clicking as fast as he could, and said, 'I'm going to work, Betty Lou.'

'Brandon!' shouted Betty Lou.

But it was too late. A camera was clicking and Brandon was working the shutter mechanism feverishly.

Panic took over very quickly but a Japanese holidaymaker didn't appreciate the trauma of it all and started to laugh. Eagerly, removing his camera, he ran after the cowboy killer, overtook him, and laughed aloud. Then the Japanese tourist pointed his camera into the cowboy's face. 'Very good, very funny, I take photograph,' he said.

Levelling his gun to the horizontal, the cowboy callously squeezed the trigger and slotted a bullet into the tourist's forehead. Then he fiercely smashed the camera with the heel of his boot. Striding away, he tugged his bandanna and made sure it was tight across his face.

Two Dutch policemen on bicycles heard gunshots, saw the Dutchman lying on the ground, and cycled quickly to the scene.

On the opposite side of Dam Square, a grey haired man in his late thirties stood in the doorway of a jewellers shop. Decisively, but casually, he mounted his bicycle and watched the cowboy hat moving up *Damrak* ignorant of Brandon clicking away with a tiny camera held in the palm of his hand.

Police were on the scene with their bicycles lying on the ground next to the dying Dutchman and their radios blaring from slings mounted around their necks. Neptune pointed his spear towards a disappearing cowboy hat and Darth Vader removed his cape to cover the dying man and give him warmth in his final moments. There was shouting and pointing and a few screams of distress adding to the growing chaos. And there were still a few people standing about who thought it was all part of some crazy bizarre Dutch street theatre.

They were laughing.

One of the policemen remounted his cycle and listened to instructions from Neptune and a pointed spear.

A bizarre concoction of screams, chaos and laughter provided a surreal drama that might have symbolized Dutch street theatre had it not been for the gravity of the situation.

A cowboy hat grew smaller as it bobbed along Damrak bound for Centraal railway station and Brandon stalked the action with his hand held high and his index finger working a camera cupped in the palm of his hand.

The policeman bellowed into his radio and cycled in pursuit.

Seconds later, the cowboy stepped from the pavement and jumped onto the running board of a passing tram. Again tugging his hat down and his bandanna up, he hung to a handle at the rear of the tram.

Bouncing his charge from the footpath onto the road, the policeman cycled furiously up *Damrak*. The tram was ahead of him and he joined dozens of bicycles as he pedalled as fast as he could towards Centraal station in pursuit of the tram.

Moments later, the cowboy leapt from the tram, narrowly avoided the front of another tram travelling in the opposite direction, and darted across the thoroughfare into a large department store. When the door closed behind him, the cowboy removed his hat and cheekily perched it on the head of a mannequin as he sought the rear entrance.

Outside on the street, the policeman had lost ground and was reacting to people pointing and shouting in confusion.

'Where did he go?' he shouted.

'In there, inside the shop,' came the reply.

'That way!'

A faint sound of an ambulance siren could be heard but in Dam Square it was too late. A policeman couldn't find a pulse. He nodded at Darth Vader who draped his cloak over the body of the Dutchman.

Meanwhile, Brandon lowered his camera. He'd lost the target momentarily but he rebooted his brain and recounted his training.

Inside the department store, the cowboy was through the ladies section, through the gents section, through perfumes and into lingerie and nightwear, and there was still no sign of an exit. He scampered down a flight of stairs into a basement to find himself in the children's toy section. Unbuckling his gun belt as he walked, he deliberately deposited it, and his gun, in amongst a collection of cowboy suits and plastic toy guns. Striding out, he was through bedding and soft furnishings before he saw the green exit sign. Moments later, he snatched the bandanna from his face and stuffed it into a litter bin.

'That way, he went that way,' shouted staff to the policeman.

'Which way do you mean?' shouted the policeman. 'Where is he?'

The cowboy barged through the rear exit and trotted into the alley at the rear of the store just as the policeman was running down the stairs, two steps at a time, into the basement.

There was an unattended bicycle parked against the wall in the alley. The cowboy threw his leg over the saddle and pedalled away. At the top of the alley, he turned left, crossed over a narrow canal bridge and turned swiftly into a narrow alley where he dismounted the cycle and hurried quickly away.

The rear exit burst open again when the policeman crashed through the doorway and raced through into the alley with his gun drawn and his radio blaring through a mass of annoying static.

Sirens were louder now, but they were in *Damrak, Rokin* and Dam Square, and they were too far away to worry the cowboy. He knew bicycles could negotiate the narrow streets and alleyways but patrol cars couldn't. He turned a corner, leaned against the wall, saw a wheelie bin and quickly removed his roll neck sweater and denim jacket to reveal an orange football shirt. He stuffed his sweater and jacket inside the wheelie bin and walked down the alley towards another canal bridge wearing his denim jeans and the orange football shirt. At the end of the alley, he removed an orange wig from his rear jeans pocket and placed it on his head. He saw a sign for '*Oude Kirk*' and headed deeper into the red light district.

Another canal presented itself as an obstacle; another bridge was crossed by the cowboy who turned to hurry alongside the murky waters of Amsterdam.

Back in the department store, a policeman studied a dark felt cowboy hat sat cheekily on a mannequin's head and shook his head disappointedly. Taking a deep breath, he spoke into his radio, 'I've lost him,' he admitted. 'He just dissolved into the crowds.'

Near Dam Square, a Japanese tourist took his last gasp and the blood ran a deep purple red and spoiled the tarmac upon which he lay.

Close to the *Oude Kirk*, a grey haired cyclist quietly congratulated himself for predicting the cowboy's movements by taking a back route parallel to *Damrak*. Perceptive, the cyclist had watched the cowboy don his orange shirt and wig and stride deeper into the heart of the sex industry.

Turning a corner, the cowboy walked towards a plate glass window. Behind the glass a large busty brunette, wearing red leather boots and red tassels, draped herself with a red fluffy boa and gyrated provocatively to the interest of a couple of gawping teenagers. The next window contained a quite gorgeous long haired blonde wearing high heels and little else.

Ignoring the sights, the cowboy withdrew a coin from his pocket, slotted it in a turnstile, and sauntered into a coffee shop. It was dark and dingy inside with the deep overwhelming smell of stale cannabis harsh on his nostrils. He took a seat and toyed with the menu.

'What can I get you?' enquired a waiter.

''I'll take a black coffee and some Moroccan Gold, so I will,' replied the cowboy. 'That's all, for now.'

The waiter scribbled the order, acknowledged his orange shirt and wig with a grin, and asked, 'Holland or Ireland?'

'Both!' replied the cowboy expressionless.

The waiter nodded with half a smile and turned to leave when the cowboy asked, 'Is there a telephone I could use?'

'In the corner by the juke box,' indicated the waiter.

Nodding his thanks, the cowboy eased himself over to the telephone, dialled a number, and eventually announced, 'I've got it, so I have. I'll be on the morning flight.' The cowboy listened and replied coolly, 'Problems? None I couldn't take care of myself.'

Smirking, the cowboy set down the telephone, turned, and was completely taken aback to encounter the grey haired Conor O'Keeffe.

'Conor?' uttered the astounded cowboy. 'Conor, I...'

'Does the lamp shine far tonight, my friend?' asked Conor.

The cowboy swallowed hard for a moment. Dumbstruck almost, he glimpsed over Conor's shoulder not quite knowing what to expect, temporarily lost his composure, paused, but then responded hurriedly with, 'The lamp will shine only for those who seek the light, Conor.'

'You're a long way from your taxi and your lighthouse, Callum,' suggested Conor.

'Sweet Mary, Mother of Jesus! Where did you come from? What are you doing here, so help me, God?' asked a confused Callum Reece.

Wearing a black leather jacket, an open-necked shirt, and casual trousers, Conor barred Callum's way to the door and audaciously announced, 'Oh, I'm seeking the light, so I am. I've come for the light of the constellation.'

'I don't know what you mean, Conor,' lied Callum.

'The devil you do, Callum. You know what the constellation is. Who were you on the 'phone to?'

'The phone?' stumbled Callum nervously.

'Aye, the bloody phone, Callum,' demanded Conor. 'Who were you talking to on the telephone?'

A sudden wisp of wind announced the arrival of a dozen or so males in their early twenties. They breezed into the coffee house wearing orange football shirts and jeans and within moments dominated the shop with friendly football chanting and youthful banter.

'It's time to go, Callum,' ordered Conor visibly concerned by the intrusion. 'So let's you and me go for a walk by the canal, understand?'

Unsure, Callum stood his ground but Conor declared, 'I'll shoot you here if I have to, Callum, but I'm hoping two Dubliners can come to some arrangement over the piece of software you're carrying?'

Conor flashed his eyes downwards towards his jacket pocket where a bulge suggested the barrel of a gun was pressing against the cloth.

'A walk it is then,' replied Callum fearful of the weapon. 'And a talk about old times perhaps?'

'It's loose talk that caused all the trouble, so it is, Callum. Now move out in front of me and turn right when you get outside.'

'Towards Dam Square?' asked Callum.

'That's right, where you killed the Dutchman and your oriental friend with the camera,' replied Conor. Then grinning, he cracked, 'Great cowboy suit, Callum. But what you really needed was a leprechaun to magic you out of town. Instead, you got me. Now move it.'

'Will you grant me three wishes, Conor?'

'I'll give you three seconds,' cracked Conor. 'I said move it.'

They threaded their way carefully through the high spirited youths out onto the street where they walked alongside a canal. At least a dozen bicycles were lying against the railings close to the side of the canal.

'Don't even think about it,' threatened Conor sweeping a free hand through his grey hair.

At the far end of the street, Brandon turned a corner and walked casually towards the two men with a tiny camera cleverly cupped inside the palm of his right hand.

'How did you know I was here?' asked Callum taking a clean lungful of fresh air.

Conor replied as they walked, 'I got to thinking, Callum. I got your phone call telling me Siofra was killed by the Dutchman on the bridge in Dublin, but then I got to thinking why you were so sure the police were after me. And do you know what happened next? I looked out of the window and half a dozen squad cars were closing the street down. They were coming for me just like you said. You set me up for Siofra's murder, didn't you?'

'No, no,' replied Callum anxiously. 'It was just a warning to you that you might be suspected that's all, Conor.'

Ignoring the remark, Conor continued, 'I flew here as soon as I could to find you. Who sent you?'

'I can't say.'

'Who were you on the phone to?' insisted Conor.

'You want to know what I'm doing here, Conor?' replied Callum obviously affronted but gaining in confidence. 'And who are you, Mister bloody Conor O'Keeffe? What makes you think you're so important? And, while we're on the subject, since when did the Movement send you to do its business?'

A silence shrouded the two men when Brandon approached.

Apparently unconcerned, Brandon ignored Callum and Conor as he gazed down on the dark waters of the canal. The fingers in Brandon's right hand loosed slightly as he allowed a tiny camera to slip a tad in his palm. He opened his hand slightly. The exposure was minimal. There was no discernible sound when the camera shutter mechanism operated and photographed the two Irishmen as they walked along the canal path.

Brandon ignored the pair, stared down upon a glass-topped canal boat, and pocketed his right hand. Mission accomplished, he twisted from the canal into a narrow cobbled alley. He was gone from the path.

Alert as ever, Conor slung a darting glance over his shoulder to confirm they were alone and said, 'There's a peace back there, Callum. Sure, it's only a fragile peace, so it is, but I've still got my contacts in the Movement. You're not here on business for them. You tipped me off Siofra had been killed and told me the police probably had me at the top of their list of suspects because of Crossnaclonsa.'

'Aye, that's right,' acknowledged Callum.

'But you also told them I was involved in Siofra's murder. I want to know who told you Siofra had been killed and who told you the Dutchman had stolen the constellation? The police, was it?'

There was only silence from Callum when the two men walked through *Wallen* towards a row of plate glass windows all faintly illuminated by a red light.

A small crowd of youths and older men had gathered outside one of the windows looking in. Conor and Callum skirted the crowd and stepped passed a line of windows adorned with females in various stages of dress, then Conor indicated they should walk over a narrow canal bridge and they did.

'I need to know, Callum,' said Conor. 'I must know who sent you to Amsterdam to steal the constellation from our friend, the Dutchman.'

'Aye, Yan, our Dutch friend,' pondered Callum. 'I was sorry it had to be Yan after all those years he worked for us.'

'Was it the Brits who sent you? Or was it the Yakuza? Maybe it was the police or the Provisional Irish Republican Army that sent you?' demanded Conor.

'Is there a difference?' challenged Callum.

'Oh, yes there's a difference,' countered Conor. 'If you're here because the police, British Intelligence, or the Movement back in Dublin sent you, then we can probably work out a deal once you tell me who's behind all this. But if it's Yakuza: the Japanese Mafia, that sent you, then there's no way back.'

'The guy was just a tourist that got in the way, Conor,' revealed Callum. 'Just an annoying little oriental with a camera; you know how it is. You've been there before yourself. He was in the way. The guy wasn't Yakuza and I didn't have time to pose for him.'

'No, you blew him away.'

Walking in silence, they eased their way through the growing throng of people going to the football match. Mingling with the red light district tourists and residents, Conor was always slightly behind Callum but with a gun discreetly hidden in his jacket pocket prodding squarely into Callum's back.

'What's the Yakuza got to with this all this?' asked Callum.

'Yan was a paid assassin for those who could afford him. You remember that, don't you, Callum?' said Conor.

'Oh yes, of course I do,' said Callum.

'Yan travelled from Japan to Dublin to murder Siofra.'

'From Japan?' replied Callum. 'Look, Conor, I was driving my taxi over O'Connell Bridge when I saw Yan shoot Siofra. I knew it wouldn't take long for the police and the Garda Special Branch to work out that you had a motive to kill her. After all, she worked for the Brits all those years ago and tipped them off about Crossnaclonsa. You would have been first to pull the trigger if you'd ever found her. She killed all your friends, remember? I thought I'd give you a head start before they came for you.'

'It doesn't wash, Callum. Why did you warn me when you knew Yan was the killer? No, it's like this, you told me ten years ago Siofra would sleep her last night that night, but somehow she disappeared into thin air without even packing a suitcase. Oh yes, I know you sent the boys looking for her, but she'd already gone. She'd been spirited away like all the other touts that worked for the Brits and you knew that, didn't you?'

'You've got it wrong, totally wrong, Conor. Look we're old friends. I saw the murder and thought of you. I thought you might have contracted the Dutchman to do the job for you, and I thought....'

Conor interrupted with, 'I fancied her once. Did you know that? But at the end I hated her with a passion, Callum. I would have pulled the trigger gladly had I known she was back in Dublin. I'd never have given a thought to getting Yan to do it for me.'

'I don't know anything about the Yakuza and Yan travelling from Japan, Conor, and that's a fact, so it is.'

Thinking for a moment as they walked, Conor finally responded, 'Funny how you knew where to find her when she returned to Dublin, don't you think?'

Callum didn't reply.

'And by the way, Callum,' said Conor. 'We're certainly not old friends. To put the record straight, we were once on the same team and we wore green. You're wearing orange today and I'm wondering when you changed sides.'

Callum replied, 'How do you know the Dutchman travelled from Japan to kill Siofra, Conor?'

With the red light district now behind them, they casually walked towards the National Monument and Dam Square. Police activity was obviously increasing and the sound of sirens seemed to be coming from every conceivable direction.

Ignoring Callum's question, Conor stated, 'It's always bothered me, Callum. All these years, it's worried me,' stated Conor.

'What's worried you, Conor?' demanded Callum. 'What are you talking about? Why don't you answer my question?'

'Crossnaclonsa,' replied Conor. 'I was wrecked that day, physically and emotionally. And you were all too keen to blame Siofra O'Sullivan. I fell in line with you because our attack had failed and I needed someone to blame.'

'But it's a fact, Siofra was a tout and she got what she deserved even if it was ten years later,' acknowledged Callum.

'Yes, but I've often wondered if there were two touts at work that night, not just one.'

'Don't be stupid, Conor,' replied Callum. 'You've been drinking too much potcheen. You're not suggesting I was a tout for the Brits, are you?'

'It has occurred to me,' replied Conor. 'You wandered away from the Troubles and you've never been touched by the Garda, the RUC, the army or anyone else. That probably means you're clean and working for British Intelligence. Isn't that the case?'

Callum struggled to reply.

Conor declared, 'If someone in the IRA sent you, I would have known. You and I know the Provisional Army Council have been trying to get their hands on this for years. He who holds the constellation holds the world in his hands. No, you're working for the Brits, aren't you?'

Callum asked, 'Conor, why do you think that?'

Conor replied, 'Because Siofra worked for the Brits and the constellation was stolen from Siofra when she was killed by Yan on O'Connell Bridge, that's why. The Brits sent you to recover the constellation for them, didn't they?'

'You're wrong, oh so wrong, Conor,' fibbed Callum unconvincingly. 'Why would they do that?'

'Jaysus, Callum,' swore Conor. 'You and I know the Brits for the bastards they are. They'd never get their hands dirty. Oh no, they'd rather send their touts and their agents to do their dirty work for them. That way if their agent gets caught, it's not down to the Brits. It's what they call deniable. They sent you because you, Callum Reece, are bloody well deniable, that's why.'

'We could do a deal and double cross….' Callum's words trailed away into the heavens.

'Double cross who?' demanded Conor abruptly.

Callum looked away struggling to find a meaningful response before eventually asking, 'Who told you about the constellation?'

'Take your wig off, Callum,' ordered Conor ignoring the question. 'It's time these people in Dam Square got a good look at you.'

'They won't recognise me without my cowboy suit on.'

'No, but you've got a problem, Callum,' suggested Conor.

'Which is?'

'Everyone going to the football match is walking up to the railway station to catch a train to the stadium. You're dressed to go to a football match and you're walking the wrong way. You need to be careful. It would be so easy to point you out to a policeman and ask them if they were looking for a suspicious guy walking the wrong way, wouldn't it.'

'You'd do that to me?' cracked Callum. 'Hey, you're the one carrying the gun.'

'And you're the one the police are looking for. I'm running out of time and so are you. I want answers to my questions,' demanded Conor. 'Who sent you to recover the constellation?'

A police van screeched to a standstill directly in front of the two men who stopped abruptly. But no-one rushed from the police van; there was just the sound of a handbrake being pulled on without the ratchet.

Callum felt the smooth barrel of Conor's gun pressed tight against his back and heard Conor's voice saying, 'Into the jeweller's shop and slowly does it.'

They were back on the corner opposite Dam Square where Conor had started. The police van gradually discharged a squad of heavily armed officers wearing helmets and carrying ballistic shields. As the police debussed and methodically gathered their kit together, Callum and Conor casually mounted two steps into the reception area of a jeweller's shop.

'We can do a deal?' hinted Callum feebly. 'It wasn't the police who sent me.'

'Then how did you know the police were coming for me?' asked Conor suspiciously

'Who told you the Dutchman had the constellation?' countered Callum.

Conor scowled, shook his head, and demanded, 'Hand it over.'

Callum backed away through the reception area passing the staff behind a counter, through the double doors into the main shopping area, and then glanced over Conor's shoulder.

Brandon shouted unintelligibly at police officers outside the building then he gesticulated wildly with his baseball cap and pointed inside the shop.

Two armed officers looked at Brandon, watched him quickly unfurl some kind of identity card from a trail of plastic credit card holders, and then turned to climb the steps into the shop. The older more experienced officer casually slid his right hand to a holster and unfastened the catch securing his pistol.

Hearing their footfall, Conor swivelled his head to follow Callum's gaze.

In the moment Conor peeked over his shoulder, Callum spun on his heel and headed through the shop. By the time he had taken a few strides, Callum realised the shop wasn't a shop at all. He was in a diamond factory. There were counters in what might have been a retail area; but behind each counter sat a man or a woman tending to the process of preparing diamonds for sale or exhibition. And the counters were beset by dozens of tourists studying the various processes from cutting diamonds to polishing diamonds.

Seizing the moment, Callum barged his way through the gathering of customers. In the uproar and turmoil that followed, shouts of anger and annoyance saturated the factory shop and one young man, wearing Bermuda shorts and a matching tee shirt, struck out at Callum as he pushed his way forcibly though the crowd towards a ground floor window.

Callum wobbled, momentarily lost his balance, and cannoned into a glass display cabinet laden with uncut diamonds. The rough looking dull champagne coloured stones were dislodged from their place of safety. A micro switch came into play and an alarm sounded.

Immediately, screeching, squealing counter measure alarms sounded all over the building. The noise was ear-splitting and was swiftly followed by the abrupt closure of the front and rear doors as a portcullis antitheft system thundered promptly to the ground and locked everyone inside the building.

Caught unguarded, Conor backed away from the police and watched the portcullis system suddenly drop into place between himself and his chasers. The police were on the outside; he was on the inside.

And a dozen champagne and dull lemon coloured uncut diamonds rolled scandalously across the floor to the utter astonishment of assembled customers.

Turning abruptly, Conor watched Callum disappearing from view.

The portcullis system was surely securing all the windows but Callum's speed and ferocity was incontestable. There was a crash of glass and the noise of wood splintering when he hurled himself through a window and into a rear yard. Ten strides later, he reached for the top of a wall, climbed up, threw his leg over, and dropped to the ground below. Striding out, as fast he could, he was down an alley with Conor twenty yards behind giving chase.

Yet behind Conor, on the outside looking in, one of the policemen was on his radio whilst the other drew his pistol.

A quick thinking receptionist realised what was happening and pressed a button on her console. The portcullis system came to a standstill and then retracted lethargically. Shouting excitedly, complaining bitterly at the listless portcullis, the policeman eventually crawled beneath the contraption and entered with gun drawn and radio blaring. He ran though the reception area, through the diamond factory, through the bustling confused crowd, and reached the open window. There was no-one to see; he'd temporarily lost sight of the miscreants again.

Holstering his pistol, the policeman turned but then realised how many customers were on their hands and knees scrimping away at the uncut diamonds scattered across the floor.

Outside, dodging pedestrians, bicycles and trams, Callum haphazardly traversed the street and then criss-crossed back as he made for a bridge over a canal with bicycles and pedestrians scattering in every conceivable direction, and the soft clanking of slow-moving trams outlandishly invading the big city atmosphere.

'There they are,' someone shouted, maybe Brandon again.

Drawing his pistol, Conor brandished it randomly backwards at the following police. Conor let off two wild shots then collided awkwardly with the side of a tram. There was a noisy crash and he rolled uncomfortably into the street across the tram line. Recovering his feet in a flash, he glimpsed at the two policemen taking cover behind a builder's skip. They were on their radios; he was close enough to hear their voices.

One of the policemen drew his handgun, steadied it across his wrist, and selected his target. He squeezed the trigger.

Conor hit the deck and rolled.

Callum took the opportunity and in two massive strides he was airborne from the canal bridge shouting *'Aon ghéilleadh!'* with his legs still running in mid air and his arms stretching into nowhere.

Conor watched him jump but then lost sight of him.

Running to the bridge parapet, Conor looked down into the canal to see Callum standing on the back of a long narrowboat waving and laughing at him as he cruised towards the Singel canal.

Another police bullet zipped through the air close to him but, undeterred, Conor levelled his pistol and took careful aim. He squeezed the trigger, heard the loud retort that followed, and watched Callum fall backwards against the narrowboat's cabin.

'I'll give you *No Surrender,* so I will,' muttered Conor.

However, like the meat in a sandwich, Conor appreciated his predicament. He spun round, dropped to one knee, lessened himself as a target, and rattled a succession of shots off at the police. Then he quickly crossed the bridge and scampered along the path trying to catch the fast moving boat.

Down on his rear end, Callum caught his breath and rested for a second with his back against the cabin door. The bullet had torn into the upper part of his shoulder and he clasped his hand over the bleeding mess. Yet, unperturbed, Callum was thankful the crew and passengers were completely oblivious to his presence. He glanced round the corner of the cabin towards the bow but couldn't see anyone on the long narrow vessel. All he could hear was the noisy diesel engine chugging away somewhere beneath him. Then he watched Conor striding down the pathway running parallel to the waterway.

Snatching a sigh of relief, Callum forced a smile through his pain when he realised Conor was losing ground.

On the old tow path, by the canal, an elderly man wearing a black beret, a dust jacket and brown corduroy trousers, biked towards Conor unaware of the disturbance taking place. He'd enjoyed a pleasant day by the canal outside the Tulip Museum sketching Amsterdam's famous townhouses. His easel and writing materials poked cheekily from one of his pannier's as he pushed on the pedals and cycled home.

A moment later, Conor grabbed the handlebars, twisted the bike, and pushed the old man to the ground. There was a nasty *thud* when the gentleman landed against a set of railings and rolled callously into the street.

Seconds later, Conor was cycling furiously along the path in pursuit of Callum and the narrowboat whilst an old man was floundering on his knees trying to recover his beret and easel.

High in the sky, a distant blip appeared and a policeman glanced up, shaded his eyes from the sun, and spoke into his radio.

On the path, parallel to the canal, sweat streamed from Conor's skin as he finally drew alongside Callum in the narrowboat.

In *Damrak,* the sound of sirens escalated, flashing blue lights reflected from the shop windows, and a dozen armed policemen ran south towards *Rokin.* And with them jogged an unarmed overweight retired CIA operative called Brandon Douglas who was pointing the way and shouting at the public, 'Down, everyone down!'

Callum realised he had nowhere to go when the narrowboat approached a bridge and moved slightly into the middle of the canal in order to negotiate the central archway.

Abandoning the bike, drawing his gun, Conor took careful aim.

Callum buried himself into the woodwork.

A helicopter was heard approaching the Singel canal.

A gunshot rang out, and then another. Callum took both bullets in the chest and lay writhing on the deck of the vessel.

Pocketing his gun, Conor ran along the pathway planning to jump onto the narrowboat which was gradually approaching the floating flower market, *Bloemenmarkt.*

Callum tried to pull himself onto his knees but couldn't. Painfully, he rummaged in his clothing and slumped back against the side of the narrowboat bleeding heavily.

Suddenly, the bridge was upon them. In a trice, the narrowboat squeezed beneath the central arch of the bridge with Conor bringing himself to a standstill and quivering perilously on the edge of the canal as he watched the narrowboat disappear slowly from view.

When the narrowboat passed serenely beneath the bridge, Callum removed the memory stick from his inside pocket.

The flower market came slowly and surely into view.

Gradually, struggling to the side of the boat, blood gushing from his chest, Callum used every sinew of his remaining strength and hurled the memory stick into an open marquee area of the flower market. He watched it sail through the air towards a display of colourful fresh blooms. Then he fell back against the cabin and looked skyward. Through misty, dimming, bewildered eyes, Callum glimpsed a helicopter hovering above, heard the strident noise of sirens and people screaming in terror, and with his last breath shouted, 'A*on ghéilleadh!*'

The narrowboat continued on its way steadily passing the flower market with the skipper waving happily to the police helicopter overhead whilst blissfully ignorant of murderous affairs on his long narrowboat.

Conor crossed the bridge and ran alongside the path again. His mind was set and there was too much to lose. Determined, he did not care for the helicopter overhead and he ignored the sirens and the screaming people when he jumped onto the stern of the narrowboat and dragged Callum away from the cabin wall.

Quickly, but thoroughly, Conor searched Callum's clothing.

Attracted by the helicopter crew pointing to the rear of his vessel, the skipper of the narrowboat set the wheel and swaggered to the stern with a concerned look on his face.

On seeing the skipper approach, Conor took one look at the helicopter above and another at the skipper. Then he took two strides backwards, turned, and leapt to the side of the canal using the edge of the narrowboat to lever himself into the air. Stumbling, almost falling backwards into the water, Conor stretched out and clung to the railings bordering the canal. With one final heave, he pulled himself onto dry land.

On the canal path, Conor looked skyward into the face of the helicopter observer, waved coolly, and stepped quickly into the floating flower market.

Moments later, he was in an open marquee area, across a narrow lane where the flower market berthed with the land, into a walk-through shop, and through the bustling alleyways where he disappeared.

For every citizen and tourist cowering in fear and horror, there were as many in the crowd ignorant of proceedings. Flocking to the flower market, several hundred tourists and customers admired thousands of seasonal blooms, tulips, and amaryllis on display and offered for sale.

The skipper of the narrowboat bent down beside Callum's corpse, glanced cautiously towards an empty canal bank, and then watched a helicopter gain height and veer away from the Singel.

Within minutes, the area swarmed with police.

Brandon Douglas squared way his baseball cap and punched the digits on his mobile. 'Betty Lou! I'm at the flower market. Get your sweet ass down here double time, honey. Whoa, some chase but he got away.'

Pausing to listen for a moment, Brandon replied, 'Yeah I got his photo, honey. Lots of 'em; what a story I have to tell. I'll be back in the saddle soon just you watch. Yes, siree, everyone's gonna know that Brandon Douglas is back in town.'

Melting into the crowds, absorbed by the big city life, both Brandon and Conor were totally unaware that the most valuable piece of software in the world was resting in its hiding place, a short distance away, on the banks of the Singel canal.

*

Chapter Six

~ ~ ~

Dateline: Later that Day.
The Anchor Public House, Crillsea.

The waters slapped erratically against Crillsea's harbour wall and a sharp breeze rushed into the Anchor when Archie Campbell entered and ambled to the bar. A big screen was in play on one wall and a few of the pub darts team had met for lunch and were watching one of the news channels.

Gloria, the team captain, threw a casual wave in the direction of Archie as he approached the bar. Her red haired ponytail swished from shoulder to shoulder when she turned back to the screen.

Wearing a cloth cap; tweed jacket, checked shirt, corduroy trousers, and brown laced up shoes, Archie was climbing into his sixties and carried a rugged weathered face upon his narrow shoulders. Acknowledging Gloria with a 'Yo, Glo!' he waited to be served whilst drumming his slightly arthritic fingers impatiently on the counter as he hung on for the bar staff.

Archie leaned across the bar and peeked left and right but to no avail. Glimpsing Davies King out of the corner of his eye, Archie doffed his cloth cap and said, 'Good day, Mister King. Day off, is it then?'

Glancing up from his ploughman's lunch, Davies replied, 'Hello, Archie, how are things with you today?'

'Adequate, Mister King, no more than adequate, I would say,'

'Only adequate,' replied Davies. 'What's the matter, Archie?'

'It's my dog, Yorkie, Mister King,' said Archie taking a tiny box of snuff from a jacket pocket. 'I've had to leave him at the vets. Toothache, Mister King, Yorkie's got toothache.'

'You'll be down in the mouth then, Archie,' chuckled Davies.

'I don't appreciate your humour sometimes, Mister King. No, I do not, not at all.' Archie tapped snuff from a tiny silver box onto the back of his wrist, checked over the bar again, and offered the snuff box to Davies who declined with a shake of the head.

'No thanks, Archie; mind you that's a nice piece of silver you have there. Can I take a look?'

'No, you can't. You sound like Harry Reynolds. You'll be trying to buy it next.' Archie took a pinch of snuff, hurriedly pushed the box into his jacket pocket, and said, 'Where's Bill gone to?'

Both Davies and Archie glanced along the bar to see the licensee, Bill Baxter, watching a group of youths playing a fruit machine in a corner close to the big television screen.

'Bill,' cried Davies. 'Customers at the bar.'

Bill turned and mouthed towards Davies, 'Come here.'

Shaking his head, Davies abandoned his lunch, moved along the bar, and said, 'What's going on, Bill?'

'Funny thing that, Mister King,' whispered Bill hooking his thumb towards the fruit machine. 'The little fat one there just won a tenner but I didn't hear any money drop.'

'You've lost me, Bill. What do you mean you didn't hear any money drop?' asked Davies. 'You must have heard the tenner drop.'

'It's a big pub, Mister King, I've got a function room and two bars and staff with eyes in the back of their heads but my ears are bigger than anyone else's,' said Bill chuckling. 'You see, when you play the machine, you stick a pound coin in the slot and it falls into the cash reservoir inside the machine. If the reservoir is empty you can hear the coin clatter against the tin. As the machine fills up the sound changes and you hear a coin landing on a pile of other coins in the tray.'

'And you can hear that can you, Bill?'

'It's my business to hear such things, Mister King. You might not hear it but then you're often too busy playing chess or having a drink and a chat with the locals. Anyway, I can tell you this much, there's no money going into that machine and they've won a couple of twenty pounders. Something wrong there, I can tell you.'

'When did you last empty the machine, Bill?'

'Last week, it was full. I usually empty it once a week and use the change for the till. It saves going to the bank, Mister King.'

'Last week?' queried Davies. 'So it's going to be pretty full then?'

'Oh yes,' replied Bill, 'Definitely.'

'How much is the jackpot worth, Bill?' asked Davies.

'Two hundred and fifty quid.'

'Goodness me, that's worth a crack at. Walk away then, Bill,' suggested Davies. 'You tend to Archie and get him his drink. God knows he'll wear his fingers out drumming into that bar if he's not served soon.'

Bill looked quizzically at Davies who replied, 'Go on, and leave it with me. I'll take a look.'

Reluctantly withdrawing his slightly overweight stomach from the bar, Bill eyed Davies again and then sauntered towards Archie forcing a smile. 'What can I get you, Archie? Mister King said you needed a drink.'

'Very kind of Mister King to ask,' replied Archie. 'Well, seeing as how he's asked, I'll have a pint of mild with Mister King, Bill. Top man is Mister King, top man. He's the new governor, you know. Well, nearly the new governor because there's two of them now. I don't know why there are two new governors now. I'm only a tax paying citizen of Crillsea, is what I am. Nothing to do with me why they have two bosses doing detective work but there's only one licensee in this pub, isn't there, Bill? Yes, a pint of mild, Bill, on Mister King's slate then.'

'Mmm...' muttered Bill. 'Why don't I choose my words better?'

Facing the bar, Davies studied the optics on display. Indeed, he stared directly into the mirror behind the optics watching three youths playing an amusement machine behind him. He had his back to the group and they were oblivious to his presence as they fed a slot machine with pound coins. All in their early twenties, there was a smallish young man whom Bill described as fat. He wore a brown bomber jacket whilst one of his friends wore a dark grey roll neck sweater and the other wore a checked shirt. All wore blue denim jeans and were totally absorbed in what they were doing.

There was another gust of wind from the entrance when Detective Sergeant Ted Barnes strode into the Anchor seeking Davies.

Glancing up from the beer pumps, Bill yanked his head towards Davies and said, 'Down the bottom, Barney. Good timing I think.'

A puzzled look crossed Barney's face but he unzipped his anorak as he acknowledged Bill and said, 'Thought I'd find him here; just a quick half, Bill,' as he headed for Davies. Appearing stressed, and into his fifties, he ran a hand through his balding head and shuffled onto a bar stool beside Davies. 'Davies, we've got problems,' said Barney.

'We certainly have, you got your radio with you?'

'Of course,' answered Barney. 'Why?'

'These lads behind us,' declared Davies nodding towards the mirror behind the optics. 'They're dropping the bandit.'

'Lucky people, I can't even win a bag of salt in a packet of crisps.'

'It' a long time since you've opened a bag of crisps then, Barney. No, I said they're dropping the bandit. You know, working the mechanism. It's a yo-yo job. Best call for the troops otherwise it's down to you and me, pal, and I'm on my day off.'

'No, don't move,' ordered Barney. 'Remember what happened last time? Don't move an inch. I'm not going through it all again. It took me nearly thirty years to get these stripes and I asked for a pair that doesn't have zips fitted. I don't want you involved and I don't want you fighting. Now sit still, I'll sort it.'

'Then make the call,' suggested Davies.

'How do you know they're dropping the bandit?'

'I've been watching them, Barney. Take a look yourself.'

Barney checked the mirror out behind the optics, eventually smiled in consideration, and said, 'Clever, very clever, Davies. They crowd closer together whenever he drops a coin into the machine. Problem is, of course, we know what he's doing.'

'That's right and so does Bill,' acknowledged Davies. 'They're having a go and every now and again they drop some winnings but there's no coin dropping all the way down the box into the tray.'

'I'll make the call, Davies,' declared Barney. 'I thought you said you were off duty?'

'I am,' laughed Davies looking for his meal.

Moving away, Barney spoke surreptitiously into his radio.

The crashing sound of a jackpot cascading from the mouth of a fruit machine dominated the surroundings when three golden bells appeared in a neat row across the machine's screen.

Hilarity and laughter followed the clattering of pound coins and ended with the trio reaching to collect their winnings.

'Oh no,' cracked Bill grasping a telephone.

'Prime witness again,' said Archie. 'Prime witness is what I am. I know what's going to happen next, Bill. You'd best move the good china!'

'And the peanuts,' replied Bill. 'He'll knock the peanuts over.'

'Not long,' advised Barney. 'They're on their way.'

'Oh good, I'll finish my lunch then,' replied Davies pulling his plate along the bar and helping himself to a chunk of cheese.'

The youths promptly began to fill their pockets with coins from the fruit machine but then realised they needed more space.

'I'll sort it, Pete,' said Mickey, an overweight youth wearing a brown bomber jacket.

'Okay, Mickey,' replied Pete. He wore a checked shirt.

Mickey approached the bar and shouted to Bill, 'Oy, you got a plastic bag or something behind the bar there.'

'Don't think so,' replied Bill. 'What's it for?'

'Sorry, mate, but we just won the jackpot,' announced Mickey.

'Have you indeed?' said Bill.

'Yeah, mind you, easiest thing is to swop us the pound coins we've won with notes out of the till and we'll be on our way. I'm sure you could use the change.'

'Oh, yes, I could,' replied Bill. 'But how much did you win?'

'The jackpot,' said Mickey. 'Two hundred and fifty quid; we really got lucky, man.'

'I think you cheated actually,' intervened Davies chasing a pickle around his plate with a fork. He glanced up from his ploughman's and said, 'Yes, definitely cheated.'

'Cheated? You're having a laugh, pal,' cracked Mickey. Jake and Pete slowly moved towards the bar in support of Mickey.

'What's it to you?' snarled Jake.

Barney moved to Davies's shoulder, flashed his warrant card, and said, 'Steady, boys. We're detectives and you're all nicked. Just take it easy until the uniforms get here because you're not going anywhere until the van comes.'

'Nicked? We played fair and square,' declared Mickey. He looked over his shoulder for support. 'Your local, is it? Pissed off because we won the jackpot, are you?'

'No, you've been playing Yo-Yo,' claimed Davies swivelling on his stool. 'I've been watching you. In fact, we've all been watching you.'

Suddenly, Mickey made a dash for the front door but Davies thrust out his arm and caught Mickey square on the chin with the heel of his open hand.

Falling into Barney's arms, Mickey shook his head and slid to the ground momentarily dazed.

Gloria, and the remnants of the darts team, suddenly became interested in proceedings.

'Damn you, Davies,' cracked Barney. 'I just knew it.'

Breaking the neck of a bottle on the edge of the bar, Jake moved sideways heading slowly for the front door.

'Whoa,' shouted Gloria reaching for a snooker cue lying on the nearby table.

"I wouldn't do that if I were you, young man' advised Davies. 'Just take it easy. You're not going anywhere. Glo.... Gloria.... Put that down.'

Jake thrust the jagged end of the bottle towards his antagonists, threatening, menacing, and trying to frighten Gloria, Davies and Barney as he swung the bottle from side to side.

'Careful, Gloria,' shouted Davies.

Gloria raised her snooker cue higher and seethed at Jake.

Behind them, Pete delved inside his back pocket for a knife.

Bill moved a bowl of peanuts from the bar and shouted to Archie, 'Hey, Mister Prime Bloody Witness, bolt the front door and let the police in when they come.'

Archie squared his cloth cap onto the back of his head but remained glued to the bar.

'Now, Archie,' shouted Bill.

'The police are already here, Bill,' said Archie. 'Mister King used to be a boxer and Sergeant Barney, well, Barney is...'

'Lock the bloody door, Archie,' screamed Bill.

Livid, complaining beneath his breath, Archie stole a drink from his pint, turned, and shuffled to the front door where he reached towards the bolt. There was a clank of rusting metal when Archie drew the bolt across the door and secured the entrance.

Snatching another mouthful, Archie carefully slid his drink on the windowsill behind a curtain and muttered, 'Makes no sense if you ask me. I've locked the police in and I've locked the police out. I only came for a pie and a pint and now I'm an unpaid doorman with nowhere to go.'

Jake snarled and lunged again with a jagged broken bottle.

There were cries on anguish from a darts team and a bunch of customers near the television area.

Gloria struck out with her snooker cue and connected with Jake's head. 'Double tops!' she shouted.

A second later, Jake snatched an ice bucket from the bar and flung it at the redhead.

The plastic container sailed though the air and walloped into Gloria's face. Hollering in anguish, she dropped her cue and a dozen ice cubes spilled onto the floor.

Pete pulled a flick knife from his jeans. He pressed a button on the handle and a blade shot out. Stepping forward, Pete slashed out as he bullied his way towards the front door.

'Watch it!' cried Davies. 'You're bloody dangerous, son. Put the knife down and don't be so stupid.'

Yelling from behind the bar, Bill barked, 'The police are coming. Now let's all take it easy.'

The jagged end of a broken bottle swished through the air three times in quick succession. On the last occasion, Davies allowed the arc of the blade to pass him by before unleashing a thunderous punch into Jake's face. There was a sharp *crack* on the chin; the bottle fell to the ground, and Davies followed through with strikes to the body before watching Jake slump to the ground

There was a loud continuous banging on the front door and Bill shouted, 'Open it, Archie.'

'What was that?' asked Archie.

'Open the bloody door,' bellowed Bill.

'Close it, bolt it, lock them in, and lock them out. Am I coming or going and does anyone care?' muttered Archie trundling to the door.

When Archie withdrew the bolt from the front door, Pete ran towards the entrance slashing and slicing his knife through the air at everything and anything.

Barney wrenched an expandable truncheon from his jacket pocket, whipped it through the air, and promptly whacked Pete on the leg with it. The attacker collapsed instantly and his flick knife clattered to the floor where Barney immediately kicked the blade out of reach.

'Shot!' cried Davies. 'What a cracker!'

'Concerned, Bill said, 'You've broken his leg, Barney.'

'I aimed for the common peroneal nerve,' said Barney proudly. 'I've just done the training, that's my first time with a telescopic thingy.'

'Wow,' shouted Davies. 'I couldn't hit anyone that hard when I was in the ring. What a strike. Is he all right?'

They looked down at Pete who was numbed and holding his leg just above the knee.

'Of course he is,' said Barney closing his truncheon down with a *thump*. 'It's only a temporarily disabling blow to the side of the leg. Give him a few minutes and he'll be up and running again,' explained Barney.

'Best get him trussed up for the troops then,' said Davies bending to secure the prisoner. 'Do the honours, Barney. They're all your toxics.'

'Oh yes, they are,' laughed Barney. 'Right, you're all under arrest and anything you say will be written down and given in evidence. Understood? Hello, is anyone there?'

There was only silence from three 'out of action' youths.

'You okay, Gloria?' asked Davies.

'No, I'm not. How can I play darts with a black eye, a bruised knuckle and broken pride?'

'You'll find a way,' laughed Davies.

Tom, a uniform sergeant, sauntered casually into the room with two constables and said, 'Okay, okay, who rang three nines?'

'Me,' said Bill who then pointed to Barney and Davies and said, 'For them.'

'I didn't see anything,' explained Archie retrieving his pint from behind the curtain and moving away from the entrance. 'I'm just the doorman. I wasn't here. I'm not the prime witness. Not me, officer.'

'I radioed in, Tom.' explained Barney to the sergeant. Barney nodded towards Davies and said, 'He's off duty and I'm on duty.'

'I see. Tell me then, what happened to him?' asked the sergeant looking down at a trio of causalities on the floor.

Stirring at last, Mickey propped himself up onto an elbow. He was still seeing stars when he mumbled, 'How did I get here?'

Jake and Pete were coming round slowly. Pete stared at Barney and asked, 'What did you hit me with?'

'Never mind that just now,' intervened the Sergeant. 'Why have you arrested them, that's what I want to know?'

'Simple really,' explained Davies. 'They've been using a Yo-Yo.'

'I've no bloody Yo-Yo,' retaliated Mickey angrily.

'Check his trouser pockets, Tom,' suggested Davies nodding towards Mickey.

Tom did as he was bid and Mickey kicked out to no avail.

Davies suggested, 'No, the other pocket, Tom.'

Removing a coin and thread from Mickey's trouser pocket, Tom held them up and looked baffled as he tried to make sense of the device.

'There you are,' announced Davies triumphantly. 'A one pound coin which is drilled through the centre. A thin piece of cotton is threaded through the middle of the coin and knotted at one end. You play the Yo-Yo by holding the free end of the string, which you tie in a loop for your finger, and then feed the coin into the slot. That's what our Mickey here was doing. I watched him, Tom. He's very good.'

'What did he do exactly, Chief Inspector King?' queried Tom.

'He played his Yo-Yo, Tom. The coin sinks into the machine and activates the mechanism. The mechanism then kick starts the spools inside and activates the reels. You then retract the coin by pulling the thread and waiting until the machine is ready to play again. Of course, you never let go of the thread, do you, Mickey?'

'A bloody chief sodding inspector! All the pubs in Crillsea and we pick one with two bloody jacks on the drink for the day!' cried Mickey.

Bill handed Ted Barnes a half of beer.

'Took your time, Bill,' cracked Barney. 'Go on, Davies, Tom hasn't seen one of these before.'

Barney took a drink and licked his lips.

Continuing, Davies said, 'Well, Tom, you just keep dipping the gismo like a Yo-Yo and getting free turns and then, of course, the reels eventually activate a winning line and the mechanism pays out. Play it long enough and at the right time and you get the jackpot.'

'Marvellous,' said Tom studying the coin and thread. 'So simple.'

'Well done, lads,' offered Davies. 'But I'm sorry. You're well and truly nicked for going equipped for theft, assault, possessing offensive weapons, and theft of two hundred and fifty quid. Anything else, Barney?'

Barney shook his head, 'I'm sure we'll think of something.'

'Never mind!' said Davies. 'Where are you from, Mickey?'

'Tevington, down the coast a bit.'

'A Tevvie, that explains it,' replied Davies chuckling. 'It won't be the first time you've done this. I watched you. But why here?'

'We hadn't done this one before and it's just a way of getting a few extra bob, that's all,' explained Mickey.

'It's a very clever way of making a few bob, young man. Problem is, it's illegal, and so are flick knives and broken bottles, but in a silly kind of way I take my hat off to you for trying to be modern day entrepreneurs,' said Davies.

'What's one of them?' enquired Jake.

'It doesn't matter, lads. Lock them up, Tom, please,' advised Barney. 'They're bang to rights, I'm afraid.'

Pocketing the device, and seizing the knife and broken bottle, Tom and his colleagues led the three youths away without further ado.

Clanging the door closed, Archie announced, 'That showed them. We don't take kindly to thieving toxics from Tevvie down here.'

'Toxics? That's my line, Archie,' said Davies.

'Thanks, Davies, Barney,' said Bill. 'And I suppose thank you too, Archie, but remind me never to employ you as doorman in the future.'

'I need a drink,' said Archie settling his cap squarely on his head. 'Too much excitement for me in one day, and, if you don't mind, Mister Licensee, I think we did very well in sorting that out. I'm glad I was a help to you all. If I hadn't rushed to the door like that, they'd have got clean away with all your money.'

Barney, Davies and Bill exchanged disbelieving glances.

'Oh yes, down to me that one,' snapped Archie. 'Indeed, I think I deserve a drink on the house seeing as how I saved you two hundred and fifty quid, Bill. Yes, so I do. A pint of mild and have one yourself, Bill. Barney, Mister King, will you join Bill in a drink?'

'No thanks, Archie. Next time perhaps,' said Davies who promptly turned to Barney saying, 'Drink up, I'd best come to the nick with you and write a statement out.'

Barney took another slurp and said, 'I can't believe you congratulated a toxic for being a clever thief. Are you okay, Davies?'

'Yeah, well,' chuckled Davies. 'Some people think outside the box to make money. That's all, Barney. What did you want by the way?'

'It's Claudia,' moped Barney sadly. 'She's gone and had a right up and downer with our Felix and told him exactly what she thinks of a system that has two bosses. I told her the difference between the two of you but she wouldn't have any of it.'

'Oh, no, not Claudia,' grimaced Davies.

'She's refusing to come back to work, Davies, and, frankly, we need her. She runs the ship when we're not there.'

'Yes, I know. Okay, leave it with me. I'll have a word with her.'

Archie wedged uncomfortably between the two detectives and said, 'More murders, Mister King. Have you seen the Crillsea Chronicle?'

'What? No, I haven't,' snapped Davies. 'Archie, I'm trying to have a private conversation with Barney.'

'In a public house, Mister King? No such thing as a private conversation in a public bar.' Archie spread the front page of the Chronicle flat onto the bar and pointed to the headlines. 'The newspapers are going on about murders in Dublin and Amsterdam that are connected to each other. Look, international crime this is, not your run of the mill Crillsea crime. Two Irish terrorists have fallen out over a woman by the look of it. One of them honey pot traps, I reckon.'

'A honey pot trap?' queried Davies.

'Honey pot, Mister King: a beautiful woman that baddies use to trap their enemies with. I thought you'd know that.'

'Oh!' replied Davies baffled.

'You should know things like that, Mister King. Me? A common man is what I am. What would I know about spies and terrorists and pots of honey? I'll tell you. Nothing because me, being a common man, expects people like you to know about terrorists and spies and pots of honey. Pinch of snuff?'

'No, Archie, no thanks.'

Barney followed suit with the shake of his head, pulled the newspaper towards him, and casually scanned the heavy print.

'Begging your pardon that is, Mister King,' offered Archie. 'I know we've had two minor murders in Crillsea. Not that a murder is minor but this is heavy stuff. Terrorists murdering terrorists, I shouldn't wonder.'

'Do you know them?' asked Davies. 'I mean your time in the RUC; did you ever come across them, Barney?'

Archie interfered again with, 'One woman shot dead in Dublin and a Dutchman and another Irishman killed in Amsterdam. And guess what? They all are known to the Irish police. Something funny there, Mister King; something very funny going on there, if you ask me.'

Archie delved for his snuff box again and asked, 'Try a pinch of snuff, Mister King?'

Davies shook his head.

'Barney?' queried Archie.

'No, no thanks, Archie,' Barney replied.

'It could be one of those complicated lover's triangle tiff things,' suggested Archie. 'Best thing is one of them used to be an IRA boss. I've heard the one about thieves falling out but never terrorists falling out. I thought they all wanted the same thing?'

Setting down his glass, Barney snatched the Chronicle from the bar and read the small print studiously. 'Oh yes, Davies. I know them. Not personally, of course, my old friend, but I know the score there. I'm not sure the newspaper has got it right though.'

'Do they ever?' quipped Davies.'

'Oh dear,' chuckled Barney. 'Now that's a blast from the past if ever there was one. I haven't heard about her for years.'

'Who's that then?' quizzed Davies.

'Siofra O'Sullivan. I thought she was dead.'

'Obviously abducted by an alien,' joked Davies.

'Shot dead in Dublin apparently but Conor? Well, I never. What a small world it is. It's got to be ten or twelve years ago since he reared his head. Now he's a problem as I recall: A big problem!'

'Who are you on about now, Barney?'

'Conor O'Keeffe, Davies. According to the paper, he's wanted for murdering Siofra and some guy I've never heard of. It looks like it's been a bit of a war zone in Amsterdam.'

'Conor O'Keeffe,' remarked Davies. 'I wonder which rock he's hiding under now.'

'Davies, Barney,' shouted a voice from the area of the television area. 'Look at the screen, lads.'

Barney set the newspaper down on the bar as heads tilted to engage the screen. He lifted his beer to his lips when the image of a man wearing a back to front baseball cap appeared on the screen. He was smiling.

A ticker tape ran along the bottom of the screen informing the audience.

Breaking News... Amsterdam.... Breaking News.... Amsterdam...

*

Chapter Seven

~ ~ ~

Dateline: Wednesday, the Next Day
The Singel Canal, Amsterdam, Holland.

Staring at the gloomy water below, Conor espied a fallen tree branch wedged against the bridge parapet. The trapped bough wouldn't budge despite the apparent wrath of the Singel's current.

Adjusting his sunglasses slightly, Conor whispered to the broken limb, 'No surrender.' Then he studied his quivering reflection in the canal. Now wearing a white panama hat sporting a brown and orange ribbon, a beige jacket and matching slacks, he possessed himself of a fresh image that bore little resemblance of the previous day's activities.

Looking towards *Rokin*, he eyed the path he'd ran down chasing Callum on the narrow boat. When his eyes met the bridge, he recognised that was where he'd lost sight of Callum. But on the other side of the bridge, Conor studied the flower market and its open marquees berthed along the banks of the Singel. He reworked the route from *Rokin* to the flower market trying to put himself into Callum's mind, wondering what Callum had done with the memory stick. Sighing, disturbed, Callum must have thrown it into the canal, he decided. But surely not! It didn't make sense to kill Yan, the Dutchman, and an unknown irrelevant Japanese tourist and then just throw the software into the water when he was trapped. No, that wasn't Callum, thought Conor. Callum wasn't the kind to chuck things away so easily. Not something that important.

He'd come a long way and taken a lot of daring chances for a piece of enigmatic software on a memory stick, and he'd killed a former comrade in the process. But Conor didn't intend to abandon his quest and leave empty-handed. There would be no surrender as far as he was concerned. Opportunities to change your life forever rarely cropped up but this was one of them. The constellation was hereabouts and the fact remained that he who held the constellation held the fate of the whole world in his hands.

Conor had disappeared into the woodwork for a while, booked into a run down side street hotel overnight, taken a light meal, and recounted events in his mind. Now, daringly, he was back at the scene of the crime standing on a bridge overlooking the flower market and watching police activity.

White forensic suits were taking photographs and swabbing railings for a DNA they wouldn't find there. A couple of detectives questioned store keepers and another pair seemed to be going from bar to bar along the Singel asking questions. Yesterday's excitement had disappeared, concluded Conor. All the usual activities were taking place, he thought. Detectives detecting, uniforms securing, and forensics, police, and interested onlookers abundant in the aftermath of the drama. But there was no-one looking in the water.

Maybe, just maybe, thought Conor, Callum had thrown the memory stick into the stalls. Conor allowed his eyes to study the water and the bank. If it's not in the water, decided Conor, the memory stick has to be somewhere in the flower market. There's no where else it could be.

'Press, is it? Who you with?' asked a voice at his shoulder.

Spinning round suddenly, caught unawares, Conor looked into her hazel eyes and caught his breath. 'The Times,' he blurted, flustered. He was temporarily out of control.

'The Times?' she queried with a frown.

He turned his back slightly, trying to ignore her.

'I'm sorry if I disturbed you,' she said. 'I saw you watching the police and presumed you're one of us; the Press, I mean.'

115

I wish you'd walk away, he thought. But then he tilted his head a tad and caught those hazel eyes again.

She smiled, 'My apologies,' she offered.

'Oh, I was miles away, that's all. I'm with the Dublin newspapers affiliated to the Times,' he lied pushing a forced smile between his teeth. Trying to sound convincing hadn't quite worked, he decided. He turned his attention to the flower market.

'They've shut up shop,' she said. 'The story will run a while but there's nothing much to copy to London at the moment. And there's nothing to make the editor hold the front page.'

'Oh well,' said Conor. 'These things happen, so they do. I mean the story dries up, as you say.'

'I'm with the London Standard so I don't get to work with fancy reporters from Dublin and such places very often. They sent me across to see if there was another angle and follow up anything that might rear its head but the fact is the police have closed us down. Whatever it is they were looking for isn't here.'

'Oh, I see.'

'Don't I know you?' she asked inquisitively.

'I don't think so,' he replied. Conor shuffled his weight from one foot to another trying to regain his composure.

'Avril! Avril Hodgson,' she introduced herself. 'You are?'

'Divers? Did they use divers?' he asked ignoring her enquiry.

'Oh yes, the divers were here yesterday. I watched them drag this part of the canal but other than a couple of abandoned bicycles I don't think they found anything interesting.'

'How do you know that?'

'When they packed up to leave there wasn't any excitement or handshakes. You know these guys they slap each other on the back if they get lucky. No such thing here, I'm afraid. No whatever they were looking for isn't there. Why do you ask, Mister...?'

'No reason, but that's good, so it is.'

'What's good about that?' she asked.

'Water, I suppose, lots of it,' replied Conor. 'They'll have given the canal a good clean out if they've removed some bikes.'

She giggled and her long chestnut hair flittered across her face. A dark trouser suit seemed to enhance her slim build and attractive looks.

Conor felt drawn to her in a strange kind of way.

'Sorry,' he said. 'We didn't get off to a good start, did we?'

Unflinching, Avril studied him with interest. Where did she know his face from, she thought?

Twisting away from her, Conor observed a lorry pull up in the street outside the flower market. He read the words painted in fine gold on the wagon's door: *Impex - Amsterdam Harwich*.

A weather-beaten long narrow canal boat navigated the Singel adopting the centre of the waterway whilst a glass-topped boat with a uniformed crew and well dressed passengers boomed out a cautionary *whoop* as the vessels approached each other. A tram, clanking and trundling across the bridge over the Singel, joined in with a *rattle* of a bell and a *blast* of its horn. The narrow boat diverted a degree or two to the left and cameras on the glass-topped boat clicked to capture the splendour of it all.

Life went on.

A moment later, a couple of workers from the flower market emerged from an open marquee each carrying a box of plants.

Loitering for a while, Conor studied a steady stream of boxes being loaded into the back of the wagon: plants, flowers, bulbs: all colours.

'What's going on there?' asked Conor nodding in the direction of the marquee.

'The flower market?' queried Avril. 'Well, Mister Dublin Times, they obviously export the flowers that have been bought today. That's them on the way to who knows where. The Impex company is probably the biggest company down there, certainly does most of the export stuff.'

'Export? I thought everyone bought flowers and tulips from the bulb fields, not here,' suggested Conor.

'If you're taking bulbs out of Holland you need an export licence,' replied Avril. 'A few bulbs hidden in a suitcase is one thing but the traders here pride themselves on exporting goods all over the globe. They export mostly to England and America.'

'Is that a fact, Avril?' And a slow reality dawned on Conor's face. 'Aye, that's interesting, so it is.'

'God, that was deep Irish,' she cracked. 'You're definitely Dublin with an accent like that.'

Chuckling, he asked, 'Might be Dublin, yes. But you seem to know a lot about how this flower market operates, Avril.'

'My parents have an apartment near *Vondelpark*. They're on holiday back home in England at the moment,' she divulged. 'My boss thought he was doing me a favour when he sent me across. Kill two birds with one stone, Avril, he said. Chase the news and catch up on the family at the same time. I get here and they've gone over there. Typical! Now I'm on my own in a big city with no-one to talk to except the Press Corps and that, quite frankly, is as boring as hell most times.'

'Sounds like a friendly sort of boss though.'

'He is. Anyway, to get back to your point, my parents regularly arrange for bulbs to be sent to friends back home. They've no transport here unless they hire a car so they buy the bulbs at the flower market, not the bulb fields in the country.'

'And you're telling me all those people working in the flower market have export licences?' Conor asked.

'Of course they do. You'll see the licences pinned on the stall uprights. This is a big business in Amsterdam, They do the job properly. I thought you'd know that,' queried Avril.'

'Why should I?' he laughed.

'Well, you are a man, I suppose; a man without a name.'

'Sorry, there I go again. Colin, my name is Colin O'Neil, so it is.' He stuck out his hand and she shook it limply.

'How long have you been a reporter?'

'Too long,' he chortled without elaborating.

Nodding, she asked, 'Where are you staying?'

'Close to the railway station, it's handy for the airport.'

'Have you eaten today?'

'Questions, questions, questions! Sure you're a questioning kind of woman, aren't you?'

She smiled but contested, 'Married?'

Considering for a moment, Conor offered, 'To the Times, so I am. And you?'

'No, that's two things we have in common. We're both single and married to the news.'

'Small world,' countered Conor.

'Why do you ask about the bulb market when we're interested in the murders and the shoot out?' queried Avril.

'Just interested; reporter's nose, I suppose.'

'What you looking at then?' she asked.

'Nothing specific,' he replied. Then he eyed her at length and realised she was quite attractive in a dusky kind of way. Large hazel eyes dominated a long pointed face offset by a slender nose potentially shrouded by chestnut hair. The bridge of her nose appeared smaller than one might have imagined and probably unfairly enhanced the length of her face. Maybe she was in her mid or late twenties, he didn't know. She was quite tall, her hair was long, but her skin seemed to be naturally quite dark whilst her complexion was obviously quite smooth.

'Is that the Dublin Times you work for, Colin?' she asked.

'No, I'm freelance. A lot of my stuff goes through the Dublin link to the Times and some of the tabloids. You know how it is. I sell anything to anyone who wants it.'

'I see,' she replied. 'Your face is just familiar, that's all. Hey did I see you the other day across the water? Did you cover the murder in Dublin: the one on the bridge? It's apparently connected with this lot.'

'Is it?' responded Conor nervously, and then he lied, 'Yeah, my back yard. Of course I covered it, Avril.'

Another tram clanked by and honked at a bunch of cyclists vying for a free piece of tarmac.

Avril studied Conor's face unsure.

'Can I get you a drink,' he asked. There was a pleading look in his eyes and he threw a smile in for good measure. 'Look, it's been a long day. Don't take this the wrong way.'

She moved a step away from him and favoured him with the back of her head when she said, 'Well, I don't think we should. I hardly know you, Colin.'

'Okay, that's fine. It's just that I've got some notes to write up from my interviews with the police, that's all. I need to take the weight of my feet and get my head together.'

'You got an interview?' she hollered excitedly. 'An exclusive, what did you have to do for an exclusive?'

'Nothing, I'm with an Irish newspaper.'

'Yes, of course, well maybe a drink would be okay,' she acquiesced excitedly. 'Did anything interesting come of your interview with the Dutch police?'

'Tea, coffee or something stronger?' he asked.

Avril studied him for a moment and then asked, 'Did you cover the Old Bailey trial with that Irish couple who were trying to sell refrigerators to the Icelanders?'

'Is that a joke?'

'No, it's a question.'

'Then no, I didn't.'

'Mmm.... Come on,' she said, striding away.

Conor took another look at the canal, the flower market and a lorry now fully laden with boxes for export.

'Are you coming or not?' she asked.

'I'm with you,' he replied stepping away from the bridge parapet, returning a conscious smile.

Within a few yards, Avril halted close to a row of vehicles. She approached a big red motorbike: a Harley Davidson.

'Hop on,' she instructed unlocking a pannier and handing Conor a crash helmet. She removed a loose helmet hanging from the handlebars, fixed it to her head and kick-started the engine. 'I know a bar near my apartment where we can get a drink,' she shouted above the barking engine noise.'

'Wow!' he laughed. 'Let's go.'

Conor pocketed his sunglasses; folded his Panama hat into the pannier, threw his leg over the saddle, and listened to the throbbing engine.

'Hold tight,' she ordered and then pushed her buttocks tight into him. 'No real tight or you'll fall off,' she said.

Flicking the blacked out visor down from the brow of his crash helmet, Conor tentatively stretched his arms around her waist. 'I can ride a bike,' he replied. 'But it's been a while.'

'Much better,' she said and pulled into the traffic.

Within minutes they were well south of the Singel skirting *Vondelpark* and his hands were as tight around her body as her lonely soul wanted them to be.

She swivelled her head shouting, 'Here we go.'

Avril leaned into a bend, twisted the throttle further, and accelerated hard.

Conor felt her buttocks squirming tight against him. He moved his hands, exploring, probing.

Five minutes later the red Harley Davidson was parked outside a terraced house and Avril was unlocking the front door.

'Top floor, maybe we'll have a drink in my apartment instead,' she suggested in an enticing provocative way. 'You'll find it quieter when you go through your notes.'

Stepping over a newspaper delivered to the door mat, Conor took in his image clear and perfect on the front page.

'Maybe,' said Conor closing the door behind him and bending to collect the tabloid.

Avril glimpsed at the front page and then gazed into his eyes. It was only a brief encounter.

'Maybe,' he repeated.

There was a deep blackness in the paint of the door when Conor slammed shut the rest of Amsterdam and the floorboard of a staircase creaked with the weight of two.

Early morning saw a discarded newspaper flapping forlornly in the gutter when a wagon drove carefully away from the flower market and threaded a route through traffic south from Amsterdam towards Rotterdam.

The rider on a red motor bike fired his engine and followed the lorry from a distance.

At the port of Rotterdam the lorry stopped and waited for the ferry. The driver booked the load through customs, signed the relevant paperwork, and gradually trundled his load aboard the vessel that would cross the North Sea. Upon the side of the wagon's door was printed in gold *Impex - Amsterdam Harwich*.

Within the hour, the load was bound for Harwich, just north of the town of Colchester, lying on the eastern seaboard of England, in the county of Essex.

By midnight, the wagon rolled off the vessel into Harwich and onward into the heart of England to the base of its UK distribution chain.

In the early morning, a low mist gradually rose and cautiously welcomed a consignment of Dutch blooms to the English countryside whilst a plethora of traders jostled expectantly waiting for the best buys.

Conor O'Keeffe carefully followed the load into the heart of England on a red motor bike. His was a hunch based on observations from a bridge, a throwaway comment from Avril about the biggest exporter in Amsterdam, a gut feeling wrangling deep inside, and an understanding of what his associate, Callum Reece, might have done with a memory stick when cornered in a trap. He didn't expect to find the stick on the wagon he was following but he knew his journey might lead him closer to the goal.

Conor had all the time in the world. He wouldn't surrender, not when the constellation was still to find and he who held the constellation ultimately decided on how many flowers there might be in someone's life.

There was a flash of lightning followed by a crack of thunder when he rode over a humpback bridge into the depths of English solitude. Forked signatures lit a dark cloudy sky and streams of rainwater formed uneven pools on the glistening tarmac.

Conor throttled back, hunched low, and rode into the horrendous deluge.

The morning mist was long gone back to its lair and well behind the rear mudguard which splashed dispassionately though the puddles.

A storm gathered and all Conor could hear was the devil's deep voice of tumultuous thunder crashing down from the heavens above.

*

Chapter Eight

~ ~ ~

Dateline: Later in the week.
Crillsea, England.

Solitude!

Rising early, Davies King hit the gym at Crillsea Sports Club and fiercely swung some kettlebells into the air for half an hour or more before taking to the treadmill for thirty minutes.

After showering, he stepped onto the scales and glowered at a steady unsympathetic needle between his feet. He hadn't lost any weight. Annoyed with himself, Davies genuinely reckoned he was perhaps half a stone or so overweight and no matter what he did, he just couldn't shed those few extra pounds that he badly wanted to lose. He wasn't trying hard enough in the gym; he wasn't watching his diet, he needed a personal trainer, and he knew it. Yet he loved the isolation of running on his treadmill. Such independence allowed him time to think things through and he'd resolved to visit his personal assistant, Claudia Jones.

Hence, he headed to a stall at Crillsea market.

Bustling was just one tag Davies might label the harbour area with as he negotiated a path through Crillsea's seaside market.

Fluffy pink candy floss and *Kiss me Quick* hats; sticky toffee apples, silly tee shirts, long baggy shorts, and a selection of discounted clothing vied with posters, music albums, bric-a-brac, badges, scarves, football gear, swim wear and beach toys for the attention of the undecided shopper. There was even an occasional mock auction of kettles, pots and pans to contend with, although no-one would dare accuse the stallholders of being confidence tricksters. But Davies headed for the fruit and vegetable stalls. They were all packed under row upon row of canvas that stretched right around the harbour and attracted people from throughout the region. The market was thronging with tourists, dealers, and locals alike, it was truly chock-a-block.

A flower, of course, is the way to any woman's heart, deemed Davies. And Davies understood that something unique would cheer his personal assistant up no end. He sympathised with Claudia. In her sixties now, she didn't like being messed about by a system that decreed she should have two bosses not just one. Davies recognised Claudia was the heart and soul of the department. She did all the filing, most of the typing, answered the telephone, sorted the mail, arranged appointments, organised the duty rota, and knew virtually everything that happened in Crillsea nick. More importantly, as far as Davies was concerned, Claudia was his personal assistant whom he now had to share with Felix Churchill. Poor Felix, thought Davies. He's yet to get properly acquainted with Claudia, but he'll find out one day.

Davies considered Claudia as he picked his way through the crowded market. She was the unofficial boss who floated elegantly down the corridors of power wearing a long black pencil skirt and swishing a grey cardigan in the direction of anyone who might upset her best intentions. Basically, Davies surmised, here was a lady of utmost refinement who knew precisely what she was about and woe betide anyone who got in her way, and that would include Felix Churchill and anyone that sided with him. The problem was she often felt the system expected too much and it was prone to stepping over the mark by taking her for granted. Claudia Jones: widow woman, personal assistant and chief administration officer, to confer her correct title, was a force to be reckoned with. The office would collapse without her, and that was a fact.

'Mister King, what brings you here?' asked Harry Reynolds suddenly conscious Davies was eyeing the merchandise on the store. 'There's no Spanish brandy on this stall, I can tell you.'

'Morning, Harry,' replied Davies. 'How's business?'

Harry looked every inch a spiv. Wearing a blue striped blazer and a shirt dominated by a ridiculously large old fashioned kipper tie, Harry carried his forty odd years well. Pristine trousers and black and white sparkling shoes seemed to suit him well.

'Making a crust; you know how it is these days, Mister King,' replied Harry. 'What can I get you then? Radio, vacuum cleaner, electric razor, or a new chess set? Don't tell me you're looking for flowers?'

'Yes, I am actually,' grimaced Davies. 'A bunch of flowers, that's all.'

'You got a lady in your life at last then,' cracked Harry. 'Who is she? Anyone I know? Blonde is she, or brunette? It's not the bird from the darts team, is it, Mister King? You know the redhead, Gloria, is it?'

'Just a friend, Harry. My secretary if you must know. What you got that looks nice and is guaranteed to cheer someone up?'

'Perfume! It smells lovely; very sexy, too damn expensive, and it fell off the back of a wagon only yesterday. But to you, Mister King, just a fiver for old time's sake.'

'Harry?' quizzed Davies.

'Only joking, Mister King, but I have a cracking little line in *Primrose Mystique* if she's really special. Know what I mean?'

'Just the flowers, Harry, and a quiet word,' smiled Davies.

'Well, I recommend these tulips, Mister King,' remarked Harry offering a fine display of colours to the detective. 'Fresh today, Mister King. They're imported from the Netherlands. Hey, I could have told you I grew them myself in my garden up on Crillsea Cliffs but I didn't. I'm an honest man, Mister King. You know me.'

'Oh, yes I know you, Harry,' said Davies nodding, and then in an almost whispered voice he asked, 'Anything happening I should know about, Harry?'

'Roll up, roll up,' shouted Harry. 'Come on, ladies and gents, one giant bunch of bananas for a pound and I'll throw in a couple of apples for the kids. Come on now. Let's be having you.'

Then, leaning over to speak into Davies's ear, Harry replied softly, 'All quiet, Mister King. Well, other than a bit of funny white powder going round the bar in The Rose and Thistle the other night. I'm keeping my eyes open on that one. Leave it with me. Otherwise nothing to report, guv, you'll be passing again though?'

Harry returned to the upright when Davies responded, 'I'll have to now you've gone up in the world, Harry. No more pub to pub or door to door sales then?'

'Oh, I get around the pubs and cafes with my bits and pieces, Mister King. This is her indoors idea. The wife's going to run the stall and I'll be doing my usual shuffle around town with my bits and bobs.'

'Bits and bobs, is that what you call your dubious gear these days, Harry?' suggested Davies. 'Well, good luck with it all.'

'Thanks, guv,' smiled Harry. 'Okay with the tulips are we?'

'Not really, Harry, last time I bought Claudia flowers I decided on lilies and got a right ear full from her. How about a plant? I can't go wrong with a plant, can I?'

Stowing his tulips, Harry stepped to the other end of the stall. He gathered a potted plant into his hands and presented it to Davies saying, 'Amaryllis, Mister King. She's beautiful, so she is; more expensive than tulips but a beauty when she flowers.'

'Big bulb on her, Harry?' queried Davies.

'Yeah, that's how they come. Touch of water and leave her alone. She'll be just what the doctor ordered, Mister King. You mark my words.'

'How much?' quizzed Davies apprehensively.

'Normally a tenner but today it's on special offer. Here, take it. I still owe you for the last shindig I got involved in.'

'A tenner it is then,' replied Davies examining his wallet.

'No, it's a hundred percent discount, Mister King,' said Harry quietly. 'I can't charge the guvnor when all's said and done.'

Davies rubbed the Queen's head on a twenty pound note but pushed it forcibly towards Harry murmuring, 'The Rose and Thistle, you say. It's on my board now, Harry. I'm interested. Find out who's pushing the gear and keep the change. Have a drink on me, okay?'

Swiftly pocketing the note, Harry handed the amaryllis to Davies, winked and replied, 'Beautiful, Mister King. Absolutely fabulous! You look after the plant and don't forget to check back with me next week to make sure she's doing alright. Understand?'

'Understood, Harry,' said Davies accepting his charge. 'Look after yourself, won't you.'

'Always do, guv, always do. Mind you, this Claudia woman doesn't like lilies, you say?'

'Didn't last time, why?'

'Amaryllis, Mister King, she's a species of lily. Good luck.'

There was a shuddered look of disdain from Davies and then he was gone from Harry's market stall carefully tending an amaryllis, and bound for Claudia's home.

They walked unsteadily through the broad green expanse that was *Vondelpark* carrying a holdall each. He wrecked with arthritis in the knees and making good use of a walking stick; she an ageing matriarch going to shepherd her flock.

There were no human statues vying for attention in the park. Here, the Dutch people listened to their open air music concerts and ate their crêpes. Children played hide and seek in the shrubbery and lovers walked hand in hand, and business suits lingered to impart a tale from the office. It was where flowers grew and fountains splashed.

It was Amsterdam in all its breath taking wonderful glory.

And a cynical breeze was scuttling through the green and varied splendour whipping up pockets of litter and depositing them in the verges and bushes.

Laughing, joking, dodging pedal cycles drawing home-made wooden trailers and trams carrying tired out, stressed out passengers, they returned home lugging their holdalls and stories from across the sea.

Waiting for a gap in the hectic traffic, they eventually stepped out rashly across the road and made for the top floor apartment. She scurried her elderly body down the path almost running, despite her age. She was so excited to see her again, and the older man followed hobbling quickly and fumbling for a key in his pocket.

She was thumping on the door and shouting pleasantries to her before he had the key in the lock. And then she was into the hallway and climbing the stairs shouting, 'We're home.'

He shuffled behind, last as usual, removed the key from the door, and turned to climb the staircase.

Mother's scream penetrated the apartment, rushed outside into *Vondelpark,* and exploded over Amsterdam in a fitful eternity of anguish and terror.

Father wheezed all the way to the top flight, lurched into the bedroom and saw the body of his daughter, Avril, lying with her back against the wall in a macabre display of hideous death.

Outside, a wind drew breath in *Vondelpark*, seemingly encircled the building, and bade its farewell with a rush of contempt as Mother's scream chillingly pierced the atmosphere.

Tall and slender, an attractive new inspector ran her fingers through her light brown hair using a reflection from a shop window to flick her tresses from her shoulders. In her early thirties, her promotion had been earned thanks to the Chief Constable Sir Thomas Daniels; her hard work, and a first class honours degree in economics and public administration. But Detective Inspector Annie Rock didn't suffer fools gladly.

Wearing a denim trouser suit with a blue cotton scarf draped around her neck, she strode purposefully beside Chief Inspector Davies King commenting, 'The plant suits you, guv.'

'In what way?' enquired Davies.

'Bulbous and a touch overweight,' smirked Annie.

'Ouch!' he grimaced. 'I didn't deserve that.'

'I meant the lilies,' she smiled.

'I'm sure you did,' replied Davies. 'Do you think I've made another mistake, Annie?'

'Rather you than me with Claudia,' chuckled Annie. 'She might throw the plant at you. You never quite know with Claudia.'

Moments later, they were a mere half mile or so from the centre of Crillsea but approaching a row of quintessential bungalows which faced south towards the sea.

'How's Felix getting along?' enquired Davies.

'So, so, he's finding his way round. He's very keen mind you.'

'Good! Any problems I should know about?' asked Davies.

'None that I know of,' replied Annie. 'He's settling in. The gang don't necessarily like him yet but that's because he's not been here long enough to get his jacket off.'

'The gang?' queried Davies.

'Yeah, the gang, you've got a short memory, guv. Promotion gone to your head has it?'

'I hope not. Who do you mean? Black and white and on the board, Annie; life is a game of chess and I prefer it that way, if you don't mind.'

Annie pursued her lips but then continued, 'Webby doesn't trust him and Mark Tait thinks he needs a grounding in how to deal with people, to mention just two of the gang, but other than that everything in the office is ticking over nicely.'

'Oh dear,' said Davies shaking his head. 'Am I reading a dose of jealousy because Felix is the new boy getting all the attention or is it something else?' asked Davies.

'Mark Tait is the new boy, guv. You should know. You picked him. Remember that last murder? A fairly irrelevant non reportable incident occurred and he made a note of it and then stuck it into the intelligence system and that was it.'

'Actually, he rang me and his information tied up the evidence very nicely, that's all, Annie,' corrected Davies.

'But on the strength of that minor occurrence,' argued Annie, 'You seconded Mark Tait to CID for six months.'

'What's wrong with that?' asked Davies.

'It's not really how things are done these days, chief inspector. You know that surely.'

'Yeah, well he wanted the job and my task is to work out who's right and who's not right. Mark Tait was right for the job that's why I gave him his chance,' said Davies.

'He should have applied and gone through the interview stages like everyone else. There's a procedure to follow, sir.'

'Annie, I don't do procedural things. Claudia keeps me right. I just try and detect things and captain a good ship.'

'Not anymore, guv,' responded Annie. 'You're a chief inspector now. People expect standards of honour; dignity, standing, procedure, integrity, you know all that goes with the promotion. You've got to be unbiased and without prejudice and examine all the relevant candidates from whatever quarter they come from.'

'Oh no, that wasn't part of Tom's brief,' muttered Davies quietly as they turned into a warm and welcoming sea breeze inbound from the shore.

'Who is Tom?' asked Annie. 'Never mind, tell me later. Look, to put things in a nutshell, Felix is five minutes into the Intelligence job and he's always been a boss of some kind since the day he stuck his pointed hat on. Intelligence is a top job; it's a pointer to the future. It's the kind of posting everyone who wants to be someone wants because it penetrates the entire organisation's functions. Yes, there's some resentment from the gang, even those who couldn't care one little bit about doing a promotion exam.'

Annie paused, took breath, glanced sideways at Davies and continued, 'Felix Churchill might have all the qualifications in the world but he's got less experience and less service than the rest of the gang and they're a little unsure of him. He needs a result under his belt to get everyone on board.'

'It'll come,' said Davies.

'Agreed,' replied Annie. 'He just needs time. He's like a striker struggling for a premiership side in the football league. The crowd need a goal from him every game; they don't want to wait weeks on end for the man to score.'

Davies stated, 'You and football, wow.'

'I know about football,' said Annie.

They walked on side by side before Davies said, 'Barney tells me Felix has upset Claudia and she won't go back to work as long as he's there. Hence, the amaryllis and a smile; God, I hate this job at times. I get to run my own crime division but I end up being criticised by my DI for choosing the wrong people and wet nursing office workers.'

'I didn't say that and don't let Claudia hear you call her an office worker,' snapped Annie. 'She'll eat you alive and I'll be submitting reports for the next five years.'

'Annie, I know you cracked that complicated fraud case through dissecting papers day after day for months on ends. And I know you're probably trying to keep the office together just now.'

'So?' she asked. 'What are you driving at?'

'Just thanks, that's all.'

'Don't mention it, guv. It'll all come good. Just you watch.'

Twisting a cheeky grin, Davies said, 'I told Sir Thomas you were too inexperienced for a DI's job. He told me I was wrong.'

'He was right,' declared Annie.

'Ah, here we are, Annie.'

'Guv, when you said Tom just before did you mean...'

Davies ended the conversation with, 'Wish me luck, Annie,' as he pointed the way to Claudia's house.

Turning into a short cul-de-sac, they strolled towards Claudia's bungalow. The picturesque two bedroom dwelling appeared, at first sight, to be overgrown with a mass of ivy sprouting from ground level. Yet it seemed to tumble down the walls and dominate the quaint facade. A keen eye would identify the quality couture of her plunging ivy and how everything in Claudia's garden was well cared for.

Unlatching the wooden gate, Davies ushered Annie down the flower bordered path saying, 'You go first, Annie.'

DI Rock grasped the old brass knocker and rapped the front door gently. She turned to Davies and with a satisfied smile replied, 'I'm always in the lead, chief inspector.'

The door opened and Claudia hissed, 'And what do you two want? Well, I'll tell you the answer is no. Now take the plant back to the supermarket because I'm not changing my mind until you sort that man out.'

'Just what I'm here to do,' smiled Davies ubiquitously. 'But I do need to discuss the situation, Claudia. Could we come in, even if it's only for a minute?'

Moments passed as Claudia considered a response.

'It's not from the supermarket either,' declared Davies with a cheeky smile.

'You mean you bought it from that florist in the High Street?' suggested Claudia

'The market actually,' replied Davies.

'The market?' barked Claudia. 'Cheap as usual I suppose and probably infested with bugs. Is it from someone's allotment?'

'No, but it is all the way from the bulb fields of Holland,' responded Davies. 'And I didn't go Dutch to get it.'

'Mmm... The Netherlands,' commented Claudia. 'Poor joke, chief inspector, very poor.'

'It's a beautiful plant, Claudia,' offered Annie nodding supportively.

'Is it indeed? Come in for just a moment then and we'll take a look at it,' beamed Claudia suddenly. 'It is for me, I presume?'

Davies and Annie entered warily wondering if they might be set upon by one of Claudia's many cats that overran the hallway and meandered their way through her house like mystical sentries guarding their charge. They followed the sixty plus year old widow down the hall and into the lounge.

'Tea or coffee? Make your minds up,' said Claudia.'

'Tea, please,' replied Annie eyeing a tabby suspiciously.

'Coffee,' said Davies simultaneously.

135

Claudia sighed and said, 'You see, that's exactly what I mean, two voices instead of one. Can I have a decision please?'

Davies glanced sharply at Annie and then replied, 'Err, whatever you're having, Claudia,' said Davies.

'Yes, whatever you're having will be fine,' replied Annie.

'I'm having a gin and tonic,' said Claudia. 'I'll make tea for the two of you. Take a seat.'

The tea brewed; the biscuits arrived, the cats espied the visitors suspiciously, and then cakes and conversation took over.

'I'm here to ask a question, Claudia. Why aren't you coming back to work?' asked Davies nibbling into his fruit cake.

'Felix,' snapped Claudia.

'What about Chief Inspector Churchill?' asked Davies.

'My contract says I'm chief administration officer and confidential personal assistant to the officer in charge of the crime division. That's you, Chief Inspector King. Actually, I am *the* chief administration officer for your information and there's no mention of working for the officer in charge of the Intelligence section. So according to the paperwork I have one boss, not two. Now try telling that to Chief Inspector Churchill because it doesn't mean a thing to him. It just sails right over his head. Do this; do that. One moment he wants coffee; the next it's tea, then it's iced water, then we move on to hot chocolate. He's driving me mad. He's not my cup of tea, or iced water come to think of it. He thinks I'm at his beck and call. Well, I'm not. I'm not running around for him or anyone else. My job is working for you, no-one else, and I'd thank you to attend to this as a matter of urgency, chief inspector. I don't need two bosses and it's time...'

'Whoa,' interrupted Davies. 'What's got into you, Claudia?'

'What do you mean,' snapped Claudia. 'What's got into me?'

'Settle down and I'll have a word with the chief inspector. He's new; he's learning and he's on my board. I'm watching him. Leave it with me and I'll sort it out,' smoothed Davies.

'You and your ridiculous chess,' softened Claudia. 'It's on my board indeed. Who are you playing chess with now that Max has returned to London?'

'A friend,' replied Davies non committal. 'Look will you come back on Monday morning? Your job is actually about working directly to me for the good of the department and you are such a big miss. I mean everyone is worrying about you and it's true to say you never really know how brilliant someone is until they're not there. We've taken you far too much for granted, Claudia, and you really are vital to the office. We need you, Claudia. We can't do without you. It could be the ageing process you see and...'

'I'm not old,' barked Claudia viciously.

'I didn't mean you, Claudia,' responded Davies carefully. 'Felix is rushing so fast that his brain might be ageing prematurely. He just might be learning things too quickly and it could be that all he needs is to take a week's holiday and relax. Believe me, Claudia; I admire Felix. He's going to be a great detective and a good boss. Let me sort this out with Chief Inspector Churchill. You, you're young and vibrant and all go. He could just be in need of a holiday.'

'Do you think so?' asked Claudia sneaking a glance in a mirror on the wall. 'You mean I really am important to the office?'

'Of course, you are,' confirmed Annie.

'Well, I suppose if you're going to sort it out, chief inspector, then, yes. I might be able to make it on Monday morning,' said Claudia stroking a cat that had climbed onto her knee. 'What do you think, Scooby?'

Annie and Davies exchanged inquisitive glances as Claudia smoothed the thick soft hair of a Siamese cat and then held the pet to her face and looked into the cat's eyes.

'He says yes, Annie,' counselled Claudia. 'Scooby says yes so I'll be in on Monday morning. You can be sure of that.'

'How long have you been talking to cats, Claudia?'

'Years, chief inspector, absolutely years.'

'Oh dear,' said Davies. 'Well, thank you, Claudia. Here, you'd better take a look at this beauty we got you. It's an amaryllis.'

Davies handed the plant over carefully. The base of the plant was wrapped in fine tissue paper reaching above the level of the soil and protecting the bulb which dominated the pot.

'So it is. Thank you,' replied Claudia.

'I'll put it in a larger pot for you and then water it,' suggested Davies with a growing air of ostentatious knowledge.

'No, you won't. Don't touch it,' advised Claudia disapprovingly. 'That's how the Dutch grow them. Leave it alone. In fact, let me take a proper look at it.'

'Sorry, Claudia,' responded Davies disappointedly. 'I thought my green fingers were improving but obviously not. It's a bad habit of mine thinking I know something about horticulture.'

'Bad habit?' queried Claudia. 'You need to talk to Chief Inspector Churchill about bad habits. I know you've said you admire him and obviously support him but I don't trust the man.'

'Why ever not?' asked Annie.

'His gambling,' delivered Claudia in an aristocratic abrupt manner worthy of her perceived standing in the pecking order.

'Gambling!' chuckled Davies. 'Has he been down the bookies with a fiver on the favourite in the office sweep?'

'No, he has a telephone account with a betting company and he bets huge sums of money on the horses.'

'How do you know?' enquired Davies.

'I listen to things. It's hundreds of pounds worth of bets actually, chief inspector.'

'You've been listening to his telephone calls haven't you?' surmised Davies.

'Whatever gave you that idea?' asked Claudia.

'Personal experience, Claudia,' smiled Davies.

'Well, only in the interests of efficiency. But it's not acceptable to spend hours reading racehorse papers whilst at work, chief inspector. Until this stops, I will not be able to trust the man.'

'Okay,' offered Davies. 'Hundreds of pounds, you say?'

'Yes, I do, Mister King. I'm sorry, but in his position with everything crossing his desk....'

Davies interrupted, 'I'll have a word. Leave it with me.'

And then he snatched a fleeting look at Annie who returned an undecided stare.

'What's this?' demanded Claudia twisting her head awkwardly towards Annie and Davies. 'Is this some kind of joke?'

'What do you mean?' asked Davies.

'Look what I've found lying on the top of the plant pot.'

Claudia handed over the potted plant and Davies discovered a memory stick wedged loosely in the soil close to the edges of the pot. It was held in place by the soft tissue paper.

Claudia asked, 'What on earth is that growing in my amaryllis?'

Lifting the memory stick carefully from the pot, Davies saw traces of dried blood on the rectangular memory stick cover.

'I don't know, Claudia,' replied Davies. 'But whatever it is it appears to be bloodstained. What do you think, Annie?'

Annie took closer inspection and proposed, 'I'd say that is a memory stick for a USB and it's covered in someone or something's dried blood. Wherever you got it from, guv, you need to take it back.'

Purring dispassionately, Scooby the Siamese cat, leapt from Claudia's lap, unleashed its tail ambiguously towards the memory stick, and then sauntered discourteously from the room.

'I knew it would be cheap, chief inspector,' counselled Claudia. 'Lilies, always lilies; wouldn't you know it?'

Time frittered away.

Cakes scoffed and tea drank Davies and Annie bid farewell to Claudia and set off back to the office.

'Mission accomplished,' stated Davies. 'That conversation went a lot smoother than I anticipated. But it was also worrying.'

'The blood, the memory stick or the gambling detective?' asked Annie.

'All three!' responded Davies. 'Look, I'm returning this plant to the market right now but there's something I want you to do for me when you get back to the office, Annie.'

'Whatever you want, Guv,' conceded Annie.

Davies declared, 'You heard what Claudia said, Annie; keep it to yourself for the time being. Gambling isn't a problem when it's only a couple of quid here and there but when hundreds of pounds are mentioned, I want to know what's going on. Can you arrange for an itemised phone bill for the chief inspector's phone? I'd like to know who he's talking too and which bookie he's in with. If he's got money problems, we can help him out. If he's got an addiction, we can help him out. Without knowing, we can't do anything and it's not the kind of thing he's likely to respond to if I just walk in and ask him what's going on. No, we'll do it this way. In any event, it might just be Claudia going off on a wobbler and getting it all mixed up. No, knowledge is power. We'll check it out quietly.'

'Are you sure? That's usually a job for the Complaints and Discipline Department and there is a procedure in place.'

Davies returned an icy stare.

'Okay,' replied Annie. 'I'll do every phone in the office seeing as how you want to do a check on the department's telephone budget. That way it will be above suspicion if Headquarters gets nosey.'

'Fine, just make it happen, Annie... Please.'

'No problem,' agreed Annie. 'I'll catch you later.'

They parted their ways and Davies headed for Harry's stall in the market. Clutching the amaryllis with both hands, Davies wondered where on earth the bloodstained memory stick had come from. He dropped a hand to his trouser pocket and checked that the memory stick was safely wrapped in an envelope supplied by Claudia. I should have got a bunch of roses, he thought. It would have been so much easier.

'Now then, Mister King,' said Harry Reynolds. 'What brings you back so soon?'

Davies raised the amaryllis high for Harry to see as he approached the stall.

'Oh no, don't tell me she didn't like the plant. I don't believe it, Mister King. What happened?'

Lowering the plant, Davies placed it on the table and asked, 'Where did you get this plant, Harry?'

'Usual place is where I got this plant, Mister King. Usual place, why? What's the matter with it?'

Rooting in his pocket, Davies produced the envelope, and displayed the bloodstained memory stick. 'There's nothing wrong with the plant, Harry. But can you tell me how this got into it?'

Scrunching his eyes and frowning, Harry fingered the knot on his kipper tie and inspected the memory stick carefully.

'You mean it was stuck in the plant?'

'It wasn't dug deep into the soil. It's just lodged against the side of the tissue paper but don't touch it, Harry,' instructed Davies. 'Just answer the question?'

'Looks like blood to me, Mister King. Dried blood, I'd say. Strange, it is. Very strange! I really don't know how it got there but it's a right bloody mess isn't it? It's covered with black dried blood. Course, it might not be human. It could be from a mouse or some kind of animal.'

'I know,' replied Davies. 'That's why I'm posing the question. Where did you get it from?'

'My distributor, Mister King; it's a firm called Impex UK from the Midlands. I get all my horticultural stuff from them.'

'Do they deliver or do you collect?' asked Davies.

'Both, but this consignment was delivered. Between you and me, most of the garden stuff on the market here comes from Impex. Well, tulips and amaryllis definitely, but I thought you'd know that.'

'Why Impex?' asked Davies.

'Impex is an import export company specialising in Dutch bulbs from Holland to the UK market, Mister King. This lot's from Amsterdam, I'm told. Here let me get you the address and phone number for Impex and you can have a word with them.'

'Thanks! That will be a great help, but the blood, Harry, where did the blood come from? Did you check the plants before you put them out on the stall?'

'Of course not, straight from their van onto my stall. It's the same with all these guys on the market here. All these bulbs and suchlike are mass produced. The result ends up on market stalls all over the place. Good business Amsterdam business, Mister King. Very good business, even if I say so myself!'

'Amsterdam!' exclaimed Davies. 'Interesting, I suppose it would be silly to put two and two together wouldn't it?'

'What you on about, Mister King?' puzzled Harry.

'Oh nothing, just something I read in the local rag but I think I'm being daft. Old age, I expect, Harry. It comes to us all.' Davies nodded decidedly and admitted, 'Tell you what, Harry, I'll keep the plant, and I'll take the contact details for Impex, if I may?'

'No problem, Mister King. No problem at all. I'm really sorry about that. I can't apologise enough. Wait one.'

Ducking down beneath the stall for a few moments, Harry reappeared with a postcard which he handed to Davies saying, 'Here you go, Mister King. Impex address and telephone number on the back; ask to speak to Guy. He runs the office there and will be best to help you, I reckon. It's Lincoln area, just off the A1.'

Turning the post card over, Davies studied the pencilled note and replied, 'Thanks, Harry. I appreciate your help but what's this at the bottom of the card?'

Beckoning Davies to the end of the stall, Harry glanced both ways to ensure privacy and said, 'I know you often say you like things in black and white but can you read in black and white, Mister King? It says this Friday night, about nine...ish at the Rose and Thistle. You're looking for a white van with a two black stripes on the side. The driver is a face from Brighton: well known and carrying coke to sell at the night club next to the pub. It's in black and white, that's all I know, Mister King.'

'Cocaine?' queried Davies.

Eyes darting everywhere, Harry disclosed, 'Yeah, the thing is he does the business from the pub, not the night club. He's yours, Mister King. Black and white van and we're even now.'

'How do you know this, Harry?' demanded Davies.

'Voices, Mister King. I hear them everywhere,' disclosed Harry with a mischievous grin.'

'Oh, yes, voices again. Where have I heard that before? You knew about this when I bought the amaryllis earlier didn't you, Harry? What's your involvement?'

'Me? None, I'm an honest trader, Mister King. I hear voices; I listen. I do my friends a favour; end of story. Trust me, Mister King. Trust me.'

Nodding slowly, anxious yet pensive, Davies carefully folded and pocketed the post card, stroked his face and chin, and replied, 'So, you've known about the shenanigans at the Rose and Thistle for some time by the sound of it. You're telling me this because one of your so-called trader friends is upset that someone from out of town is muscling into their parish. So you think you can do your friend a favour and clear the decks for them. What's in it for you, a nice little earner? You're using the police to remove the opposition, am I right?'

'Mister King, how could you think of me like that?'

'Because I bloody well know you, Harry Reynolds,' snapped Davies trying to control his temper. 'I know what makes you tick and, no, we're not even. I'm always ahead of the game whether it's in black or white or yellow and blue with bloody little pink stripes on it. And you still owe me. Understand?'

'What?' queried Harry.

'You've a foot in both camps, Harry,' barked Davies.

'Who me, Mister King? Nah, you got that all wrong.'

'We'll see, Harry. We'll see.'

Catching sight of a customer waiting to be served, Harry scurried nervously to the other end of the stall, and cried, 'Mind how you go, Mister King.... Now then, madam, what can I get you? Flowers, is it, or perhaps a lovely bunch of bananas?'

There was a detective's lingering icy glower upon a man selling bananas and then Davies King clung to his amaryllis and the memory stick as he pushed his way politely through the throng towards Crillsea police station.

The long journey ended.

Conor O'Keeffe reached the distribution centre and allowed the wagon he had conscientiously followed from Amsterdam to peel off into the depot. A quick scan as he passed the centre revealed a handful of large portacabin structures; a brick office building, telegraph wires, fuel pumps, a weighbridge, and little else. It was hardly the throbbing hub of a European distribution centre, he thought. But then again, it was fit for purpose, he decided.

Cruising slowly alongside the site; Conor finally twisted the throttle and accelerated smoothly away from the depot. A few miles down the road a turn off for the A1 dual carriageway presented itself but he ignored the junction and rode through a typical quintessential English village. He skirted the village green at a respectful speed noticing the post office close to a row of shops and a bus stop before he glided casually past a couple of bed and breakfast establishments serving the Heart of England tourists. But within a minute or so he was through the village and pulling into a lay by about five miles from the Impex distribution depot.

Braking to a standstill, Conor switched off the engine. He dismounted and pulled the bike onto its stand before stepping away from the lay by. The grass verge dropped away to his left and down a slope where a stream ran parallel to the road. He looked around and waited for a van to pass before removing his crash helmet. Unlocking the pannier, Conor removed a pair of black casual trousers, a dark roll neck sweater and a dark grey blouson. He changed clothing quickly. The countryside was still. Only the grass swayed quietly in the wind and there was a distant hum of traffic noise from the A1.

Conor pushed the motor bike from its stand and rolled it down the bank towards the stream. With a final push, he let go, stood back, and watched the big red machine career into the water below. There was splash and he stood for a while watching the bike submerge in the water.

Regaining the bank, Conor turned to face the direction of the depot. The sun was trying to break through the clouds but he saw smoke billowing from the chimney pots of the nearby village.

Stepping away from the lay by, Conor walked towards the village.

Ted Barnes and Davies King sat in Crillsea police station examining a blood stained memory stick and an amaryllis plant that occupied the desk before them.

'Don't water it, she said,' revealed Davies. 'So I brought it back here for my desk, but what the hell do we do with this?'

'Clean it and stick it in the computer,' suggested Barney.

'The plant or the stick?' quipped Davies. 'Never mind, what do you think it is, Barney?'

'I haven't a clue,' replied Barney. 'But I can tell you your jokes are getting worse. How about holiday snaps; music albums, spreadsheets of some kind? It's anyone's guess, I'd say. There's only one way to find out.'

A rap on the door heralded the entrance of Terry Webster. Webby, as he was known to his colleagues, stood six feet tall. With dark features, a rounded chin and a handsome cut, he was renowned for wearing flawlessly tailored pinstripe suits as well as boasting the largest collection of ties and shoes in Crillsea. Moving in behind Webby was the newest addition to Crillsea's junior detectives: Mark Tait, a country lad of similar age but slightly broader and more athletic in stature. Mark sported a ruddy complexion and swept back fair hair that accompanied his more considered and slower rustic twang.

They were a strange duo: one smart, a tad flash, with a tendency to be a man about town, and the other who liked nothing better than an afternoon's fishing or a stroll down the leafy lanes of Crillsea Meadows enveloped by his favourite Barbour jacket.

'Ah!' proclaimed Davies. 'The judging panel has arrived. What do you make of this then?'

'It's a memory stick,' declared Webby.

'No, it's a plant and a memory stick,' corrected Mark. 'Actually, that's an amaryllis and a bloody mess of a memory stick. Cut your finger did you, boss... Barney?'

'No, I bought the plant and we found the memory stick on top of the soil. The plant is from Amsterdam where all the fun and games seem to have been taking place lately. We're wondering what to do with it,' said Davies.

'Clean it up and stick it in the computer; find out what's in its memory I reckon,' suggested Mark. 'There's probably some information in there that will show who the owner is?'

'I've got a better idea,' revealed Webby.

'Oh yeah, what's that then?' queried Mark.

'Send it to forensics and get it cleaned up properly,' suggested Webby. 'Get a blood group and some DNA and then stick it in a computer.'

'Now you're being daft,' said Mark.

'Yeah, well, maybe a little bored, that's all,' countered Webby.

'Bored!' insinuated Davies. 'You're bored Detective Constable Webster. Barney, you're not working these guys hard enough.'

'Oh, but I will from now on, don't you worry,' responded Barney with an amiable chuckle.

'I bet you a pound it's human blood,' said Webby

'Okay, I'll take a pound on animal blood,' voiced Mark.

'Well, I never,' said Davies. 'A proper little betting shop isn't it. I'll put a pound in the kitty for a human. So, does that mean if the humans beat the animals the humans share the pot?'

'A pound on animal,' said Barney

'A pound, only a pound,' cried Felix Churchill from the doorway.

'Oh, Felix, do come in,' said Davies smiling. 'And Annie,' he continued politely as the two officers entered. 'Well, we're all here now. What began as a quiet chat between Barney and I is now an office conference by the look of it.'

'We've been standing at the door listening to you all,' revealed Felix. 'Looks like a job for the Intelligence Department, I would say.'

'What does?' asked Davies.

'This does,' replied Felix. 'Your bloodstained whizzy stick; but actually I need five minutes of your time. I came to see you about a raid I'm planning as a result of reading a recent intelligence report about drugs being offered in a night club.'

'We'll discuss that later,' proposed Davies. 'One of us needs to pick that one up. It's yours if you want it.'

'Can we talk through the finer points later?' asked Felix.

'Of course, but make a good job of it,' insisted Davies.

'That's it? Simple as that, is it?' queried Felix.

'Have you guys nothing better to do than mess about with Claudia's amaryllis and that bloody computer whizzy stick?' interjected Annie. 'What's going on?'

Scratching his chin, Davies pointed his finger at the table and offered, 'I know, Annie. You're right. It's the shootout in Amsterdam. It was on the telly, that's all. It's like chess you see. It's rattled me so I need to be sure this isn't an important move and isn't connected to the Dutch job. It's probably just me being me. Yeah, Webby is right. Let's have an office sweep on the forensics.'

Annie shook her head and said, 'I think one of the privileges of being promoted is to be able to speak your mind to your boss.'

'Well, that never stopped you before,' laughed Davies. 'What's on your mind, Annie?'

'Oh, nothing, Chief Inspector. I just think you're pretty nuts at times. You're the original square peg in a round hole because tomorrow you'll read about a murder in Australia and start wondering if it's kangaroo blood.'

Davies chortled and said, 'To many moves on the board, Annie, but what do say?'

'I'll go with you on this one,' said Annie. 'What do you think guys?'

There were murmurs of agreement all round.

Barney flicked a switch on a kettle and reached for an empty tin in a cupboard saying, 'Leave it with me, ladies and gentlemen. I'll book it into forensics and do the necessary report.'

Turning to Davies, Barney said, 'Ordinarily I would suggest we all just skip it and get on with whatever it is we're supposed to be investigating right now. But my job as detective sergeant decrees I am responsible for staff morale. So, come on, kitty up.'

Barney rattled the empty tin. The word *SWEEP* was printed on the side of the tin and seemed to shiver slightly as pound coins fell into its shallow heart.

Davies pointed an inquisitive unforgiving digit again and said, 'The plant is from Amsterdam, that much we do know but I'm wondering if this memory stick is from the Midlands, Amsterdam, or someplace else. So let's bet on human or animal and Amsterdam or England. All agreed?'

More mutterings of consultation followed by nods of content but then Felix took hold of the tin and said, 'I suggest we make it worthwhile. Why not twenty pounds each?'

Davies noticed an ominous look visit Mark Tait's face at such an elaborate and unnecessarily expensive suggestion.

'We'd decided on a pound. It's an office sweep,' said Barney with an air of resolve that welcomed no challenge.

'A tenner then?' quizzed Felix.

'Traditionally, the man who holds the sweep, makes the play,' disclosed Davies. 'Barney, it's down to you.'

Barney tugged the tin back from Felix and said, 'A pound will do. It's a bit of fun, chief inspector, that's all.'

'Of course,' replied Felix apologetically. 'A pound it is then.'

Mark Tait leaned close to Webby and whispered, 'Is the governor on the same planet as everyone else? This is stupid. It's not the Grand National or the Derby.'

Webby smiled, declined a proper answer, and replied, 'Good idea, Mark, let's take the tin round the nick and get a few quid in it. We could give half of it to the kid's ward at the hospital or stick it in the Widows and Orphans Fund. What do you think?'

'Charity?' queried Felix, slightly vexed perhaps as his eyebrows seemed to merge towards one another in a challenge to the onlookers. 'Steady boys, no reason to be rash when there's money at stake.'

'Excellent idea, Webby,' intruded Barney forcefully. 'And don't worry, Mark, everyone knows Chief Inspector King is an odd ball. You'll get used to it.'

Felix acquiesced with a weak smile.

'Mark, our Mister King has also got ears in all the walls,' cracked Webby. 'The governor can hear a pin drop in the car park. Super hearing, they call it.'

'Oh dear, that's me in trouble already then,' replied Mark.

The tin rattled noisily amongst the meaningless chatter and idle ribaldry of colleagues at work.

Suspicious, Davies sought Annie Rock's face. Allowing his hand to gently hover and rest over the telephone, he peered deeply into Annie's eyes to ask the unspoken question.

Annie read the movement and slowly, undiscernibly, shook her head slightly.

Davies retracted his hand warily and slowly nodded twice in acknowledgement. There was no telephone bill to discuss yet, he'd just learnt.

*

Chapter Nine
~ ~ ~

Dateline: The Weekend
Crillsea, England.

Draining his pint slowly, Mark Tait, dried his mouth with the back of his hand, slammed the glass on the bar and said, 'Fill her up, my old son, and have one yourself.'

'Oh cheers. I'll take for a half,' replied the barman. 'Haven't seen you in here before; passing through or local?'

'Crillsea Meadows,' replied Mark. 'I was in the night club next door but it's too noisy so I thought I'd try your beer out.'

'And?' quizzed the barman.

'And it's a nice drop of water mixed with the finest southern hops and a good blend of northern barley.'

The barman laughed. 'Expert, are we?'

'No, not really; look, is there any action here later on?' asked Mark.

The barman pulled a fresh pint and enquired, 'Action? What do you mean by action then?'

'Music, dancing, girls, a live band,' said Mark. 'I don't know; a magician? What else do you get in a pub on a Saturday night?'

'Ten minutes and the warm up band is due; well actually, it's just a couple of guys singing to backing tapes. They're Tevvies from up the coast but they're quite good.'

'What do they call themselves?' asked Mark.

'The Tevvies,' replied the barman placing a full pint on the bar. 'What else would they be called?'

Paying with a ten pound bank note, Mark replied, 'Of course, The Tevvies.'

Eyeing the interior of the Rose and Thistle, Mark wasn't surprised to find a dart board and a pool table. There was a big screen on one wall and a DJ unit in another area away from the bar. The disc jockey spun the discs and donned his earphones. There was the flick of a switch and a ripple of lights from the unit as he cranked up the evening. The sizeable pub was packed with pre-club drinkers numbering close on a couple of hundred. But there were a few dark corners where Mark's eyesight could not penetrate.

Moving away from the bar, Mark put his hand in his jeans pocket and found the transmitter switch. He pressed the *talk* button and reported, 'Very busy in here now; filling up nicely.' He retracted his drink as two mini skirted giggling blondes nearly trampled across his toes and then said, 'Nothing doing though, out.'

Sampling a drink from his pint, he turned and casually followed the two girls towards one of the darker corners that seemed to be poorly lit in comparison with other areas of the site.

Outside in a battered old van that bore the name of a fictitious heating engineer on its side, Felix Churchill radioed his reply, 'All quiet here, continue low profile.'

Webby winked at Felix, checked his camera and said, 'Not for long, sir. Don't you worry.'

And so the night wore on.

Across the car park, next to the pub, Annie Rock sat in a blue Ford Mondeo with Davies and Barney. She monitored Felix's transmission and suggested to her colleagues, 'If there's nothing in the next fifteen minutes, we've been sold a pup again.'

Davies smiled and said, 'Never bought a pup in my life, Annie. Have patience, you'll see.'

A white Transit van, with two black and white parallel stripes to the rear, cruised into the parking area and drove round the nightclub car park. The van rolled to a standstill in the middle of the car park but the engine kept running and a puff of grey white vapours escaped from its exhaust pipe.

Barney lifted a camera fitted with a telescopic sight and clicked away zealously capturing the Transit.

Annie pushed the radio button and relayed, 'We're on; black parallel stripes on a white Transit, standby.'

'Copied,' acknowledged Felix.

The Transit remained static save for a shiver from the exhaust and a purring from its engine.

'What's he up to?' asked Annie.

'Nothing, he's looking to see who's here and why, that's all,' suggested Barney as he triggered the camera mechanism.

'Yeah, hold tight,' submitted Davies.

Minutes grew and then the Transit trundled slowly from the night club car park into the car park of the Rose and Thistle.

The Transit stopped at a corner of the parking area and the driver got out and strolled casually to the entrance of the pub.

Barney's camera captured the movement.

Closer, much closer, Webby's hidden camera monitored every movement from the heating engineer's van

Felix seized the radio and broadcast, 'Standby all units; male, white, five ten, slim build, white top, dark trousers making towards the entrance. White on black! Wait until he's inside the pub.'

Davies grabbed the radio and advocated, 'Wait it out, let it develop. We have the suspect in sight but no visible evidence. Wait.'

'All units, watching brief only,' counselled Felix. 'The suspect is white on black.'

'Nearly lost it there,' remarked Annie.

'It's a learning process,' said Barney. 'Felix wanted to run it on his own so the governor is letting him.'

'Felix made a decision,' announced Davies. 'He could have taken the van on the dual carriageway and ended up with a prisoner denying all knowledge of the consignment. It might be a borrowed van or a hire vehicle for all we know. Chief Inspector Churchill decided to let it run all the way into the pub and see what happens. That's why he's got Mark Tait in there watching.'

Annie nodded but Barney asked, 'Now what's he up to?'

The suspect with a white top above his black trousers entered the pub alone.

Elsewhere, Webby focused and clicked.

Inside the pub, Mark was half way down his third pint and enjoying the sights and sounds of the Rose and Thistle. Sitting midway between two corners of the pub, he used the dulled reflections from the television screen to observe people moving about the floor. The door at the entrance opened and white on black walked in.

'Got him,' responded Mark on the radio net.

The night grew with rumbling rolling dark clouds and the clock moving on ten minutes.

Mark watched the white top move round the bar shaking hands with people: obviously friends and contacts, and then he approached the bar and ordered a drink. No money changed hands at the bar and the suspect in the white top merely took the drink and allowed his eyes to rove the bar.

Standing up, Mark stepped onto the dance floor.

Moments later, Mark was dancing close to the blondes he had espied earlier. They exchanged casual smiles and then one of the girls turned slightly towards him, accepting him into the company. Nodding with a smile, Mark bent his knees, swayed his hips, and watched his suspect from the middle of the dance floor.

A short time later, white on black emerged from the Rose and Thistle and leaned against the door frame at the entrance.

Simultaneously, the rear doors of the Transit opened and a hefty black male slid out of the vehicle wearing blue denim jeans and a heavy blue anorak that seemed to swallow his big hands.

Felix immediately broadcast the man's description.

'Here we go,' said Davies, 'Blue on blue.'

Barney's camera burst into life again.

The black male stepped out six feet three inches above the tarmac as the first drops of rain formed a puddle on he ground. He was broad across his shoulders and chest and swaggered slightly as he strode towards the suspect leaning against the door frame.

Inside the bar, Mark danced and watched as the two suspects entered the pub and made for the bar.

The hefty black guy melted into a dark corner whilst his mate sauntered around the bar. Except this time, noticed Mark, the chap wearing the white top was shaking hands with his right hand and holding his left hand low. Mark smiled, hugged the blonde, spun her in tune with the music, and then changed position on the dance floor to maintain his view of proceedings.

'You've got all the moves,' suggested Mark's dance partner.

Boom, Boom, Boom, crashed the DJ on his unit, twisting and spinning the discs as his head bobbed feverishly to the tempo and the atmosphere in the bar cranked up a gear.

Then Mark caught the full deal.

The suspect's right hand palmed the bank note in a shake of hands with a customer and simultaneously released the deal from the left hand held low and close to the body. Well practised, thought Mark. Quick as a flash and no questions asked. Money in, drugs out, gone, and move on to the next customer.

Yeah, that was it, reckoned Mark. He'd missed the switch between the black guy and the hustler but there was no doubt in his mind that the suspect's first pass in the bar had been to take orders. He'd just delivered. What next, he wondered.

Mark's earpiece begged for an update.

The hefty black guy stood at the end of the bar close to a dark corner with his hands deep in his pockets. The suspect in the white top closed with him. There was an exchange and the suspect in the white top moved back into the bar.

Excusing himself from the blonde on the dance floor, Mark walked towards the toilets. Depressing a switch in his pocket, he said, 'I've got enough. Do it now. The deal is going down fast. Take them both. Blue on blue is the mother ship. White on black is the hustler.'

Outside in the confines of a car, Davies muttered, 'Well done, Mister Tait, now for a result.'

Parked close to the entrance, Felix radioed, 'All received, uniforms one, two and three make ground, seal and secure.'

Half a mile away on the dual carriageway three liveried police personnel carriers containing thirty men and three dogs fired up and moved swiftly towards the site.

Moments later Felix radioed, 'All units to standby... Wait... Wait... Wait...'

The police personnel carriers swung onto the pub car park at speed and Felix shout bellowed into the radio system, 'Let's go... STRIKE... All teams... STRIKE...'

Blue uniforms discharged from two carriers at the front whilst the third swung to the back door and discharged its cargo.

They rushed into the bar followed by Davies, Barney and Annie. Uniformed officers had been briefed to do a particular job. Two secured the DJ unit and commandeered the radio system.

'Everyone standstill, this is a raid. You are not in danger. Standstill, you are not in danger. This is a raid.'

Two officers secured the light switches, two secured the counter, four made for the toilets, a dozen or more ringed the dance floor, and so on.

And then three dog handlers strolled into the bar with a Cocker Spaniel each.

Making for the hefty black guy, Annie flashed her warrant card, and said, 'Police! I intend to search you for drugs....'

He bolted.

Annie hadn't finished her sentence when the black guy turned and sprinted towards the door. Barney reached out to grab his anorak but missed; a uniform made a lunge but the suspect ducked and rushed the door.

Daylight beckoned.

'Whoa!' yelled Davies.

Bulging muscle, seething spit and venom, the black guy lashed out and tried to push Davies against the wall.

Davies responded with one well placed clenched fist into the solar plexus.

There was an audible discharge of oxygen from the suspect and he crumpled to the ground as Davies screamed in agony, 'Argh! Not again!' He shook his fist and clenched his teeth.

Up and running again!

With Davies temporarily out of action, the black gent scrambled to his feet and clambered to the door.

Whack!

An extendable baton connected harshly with the suspect's legs. The lower limbs went numb and he collapsed once more.

'You're nicked,' cried Annie.

There was the shudder of a telescopic baton closing followed by the trussing of a very large man with a pair of handcuffs

'Well done, Annie,' said Davies.

Annie swivelled her head to catch sight of Davies with his fist deep in an ice box.

Barney located the man in the white top.

Mark Tait quietly walked out of the front entrance and into the night and a police dog began meandering through the bar sniffing out the residue.

With keys taken from the black hefty, Annie opened the Transit and began rummaging in the rear to the discontent of the gent who was becoming restless. In his presence, Annie opened a sports bag lying on the floor of the van and uncovered more deals all wrapped in tiny strips of cling film.

'Barney?' queried Annie.

Barney searched the guy's anorak and recovered a dozen made up deals or more.

'Bingo!' cracked Barney. 'Is that what you're looking for, Annie?'

Annie nodded as Felix entered the Rose and Thistle, dominated the place with his presence and said, 'It's a wrap. Close it down for the night and take everyone's details. Slowly and politely. We got what we came for.'

Moments later Davies stood by the bar watching proceedings with a fist still stuck inside an icebox. 'Nice work,' said Davies. 'There's a new sheriff in town. You made the right decision, Felix.'

'But of course,' replied Felix. 'You can bet on it.'

'There's a new deputy too, actually, Felix,' said Davies.

'Who's that?' asked Felix.

'Mark Tait,' announced Davies. 'Getting his feet under the table. He kept his head, didn't get excited, blended in and pulled it off. I'm pleased for him, that's all.'

'Yeah,' replied Felix. 'Yeah, that's good then.'

There was a pat on the head and a hand tenderly brushed the hair of a Cocker Spaniel as its handler bent down to collect an abandoned wrap.

*

Chapter Ten

~ ~ ~

Dateline: Sunday
The Heart of England

There was the soft crunch of gravel when Conor took his first step from the smooth tarmac of the main road onto the parking area outside the transport cafe. Ideal, he considered. A cafe, a public telephone box that hadn't been vandalised, and a window seat across the road from the entrance to the Impex distribution centre.

Eagerly, he stepped into the 'phone box, randomly selected a couple of coins from his pocket, and dialled a number only to hear the engaged signal bleeping in his ear.

'Damn,' he uttered quietly. He tried again but there was no change and he watched another wagon trundle along the road, wait for traffic to clear, and turn into the Impex centre.

The front door of the cafe blew open when a man wearing oil-stained overalls rushed out and stepped quickly towards his articulated wagon parked nearby. The driver haphazardly deposited a worn out magazine into a nearby litter bin and then reached up to grasp the handle of the cabin door. There was a *phew* from the driver, a heave into the cab, and the slam of a cabin door closing behind him.

Seconds later, the engine burst into life and the articulated wagon dragged itself from the cafe onto the main road.

Conor returned the 'phone to its cradle, stepped from the 'phone kiosk, and thoughtfully reached into the litter bin. He swiftly grasped the magazine, rolled it in his hands, and entered the cafe.

Across the road, there was a hive of activity when another lorry load of flowers arrived and staff worked to discharge the cargo.

Moments later, Conor waited for his food order and sat watching the comings and goings at Impex distribution centre from behind a large mug of coffee and a magazine.

The waitress approached, set down a plate of bacon sandwiches, smiled as a prelude to offering conversation, and then returned to the counter when Conor spread wide the pages of the magazine in front of his face.

Once she had moved away, Conor lowered his magazine and tucked into the bacon. Wiping some residue butter from the corner of his mouth he thought to himself how long it had been since his last proper meal; yet his mind quickly refocused on the entrance to the distribution centre and an empty telephone box.

Another wagon pulled into the distribution centre; another sandwich slid into an empty stomach.

But then a medium sized van emerged from the heart of the distribution centre and braked to a halt. Conor scrunched his eyes and read the motif on its side *Impex Deliveries Nationwide.* The van was white in colour and bore the motif of a tulip on both sides above the Impex Deliveries text.

Conor observed the driver alight from the vehicle and enter a portacabin office situated in the yard.

Mmm, Conor thought to himself, a great window seat, good coffee and tasty bacon.

Moments later, the same driver emerged from the portacabin carrying a clipboard securing a wad of papers. Turning, the driver waved towards the portacabin and jumped up into the van as a girl in her mid twenties emerged from the office and stepped across the yard towards a larger office. She wore long dark trousers and a lemon coloured turtle neck top, and sported a long ponytail that flowed down her back.

Pushing his empty plate away, Conor studied the girl and watched her skip happily up a couple of steps and walk into what appeared to be the main building.

A customer in the cafe approached a juke box in the corner, dropped some coins into the mechanism, and made some selections.

The music of a rock band filled the cafe but Conor merely took another drink and considered his next step.

In another part of England, in Crillsea Meadows, Davies King was keeping an appointment with his boss: Sir Thomas Daniels and his good lady: Lady Helen Daniels.

The spacious four bed-roomed modern bungalow occupied a full acre of land and was bordered by rhododendrons and a shrubbery that deliberately funnelled the visitor towards a panoramic view over the cliffs and out to sea.

Helen opened the front door when she saw Davies striding down the garden path.

Reciprocating, Davies produced a huge bouquet of flowers and kissed her amicably on both cheeks. Then he clasped his arms round Tom's shoulders and entered the house like the old friends they were.

Standing a good six inches shorter than her husband, Helen wore her fifty years well. Matronly, would be a good description of her, thought Davies. Yes, matronly with her rounded face, stout build, and dark hair tied in a cosy bun.

He watched Helen carefully arrange the flowers in an appealing crystal vase whilst the chief took his coat and hung it on a peg in the hall. Then he was guided into the dining room.

It was Sunday and Sunday dinner could not be missed.

'Take a seat, Davies,' said Tom. 'I'm glad you could make it.'

'Wouldn't have missed Sunday dinner for the world, Tom,' revealed Davies pulling his chair closer to the table. 'How have you been lately?'

Helen entered carrying a gravy boat which she set down on the dining table and declared, 'He's not been himself all week. I want you to talk some sense into him. My chief needs a few days off; rest, and to take it easy for a while.'

'Nonsense, woman,' interrupted Tom. 'I'm just a little tired from working too hard, that's all. I'll be the judge of when I need to rest. Anyone would think you used to be a nurse.'

'I was, and you just can't accept that I'm right. You are so used to giving orders, Mister Chief Constable, that you've forgotten how to take them. won't be at work tomorrow, okay?'

'Okay!' cracked Davies. 'No problem! I'll let the Deputy Chief know. I'm sure the Force will manage without you for a day or two.'

Disagreeing, the chief snapped tetchily, 'I'll be at work tomorrow and every day next week, Helen. No reason not too. And as for you, Chief Inspector, you'll do no such thing.'

'Oh dear, shall I go out and come in again?'

Laughing, Helen said, 'Later, we'll talk about it later. Now which one of you gentlemen is going to carve this chicken?'

'Allow me,' volunteered Davies keenly. 'It's time I got the knife out for someone.'

'Ahh, a bad week then,' suggested Tom. 'Don't tell me about it. I don't want to know a thing about work until nine o'clock tomorrow morning.'

'You're always in at eight and in any case, you won't be there tomorrow,' insisted Helen. 'You'll be resting. Come on, Davies. Get cracking with that knife.'

'Unless, of course,' suggested Tom, 'It's about this absurd challenge I've heard you've set up, Davies. Animal or human, or is it animal, vegetable or mineral? You tell me!'

'Whoever told you?' puzzled Davies.

'Look, a little banter now and again in the office is fine,' reasoned the chief. 'I mean, a new pip on the shoulder and all that. It's to be expected. I understand you want to be seen as the new boss and, knowing you, you probably want to still be seen as one of the lads, Well, it just doesn't work like that I'm afraid. You can't be a boss and one of the lads at the same time. It just doesn't work. Take it from me. I've been there and tried it. In any event, involving the Forensic Science Department in a stupid office betting bacchanalia is a bit over the top, isn't it? I expected better from you, my old friend.'

'Oh no, I think someone has got their facts wrong, boss,' submitted Davies. 'Actually, I'm following up on a legitimate intelligence lead following a rather bizarre discovery of a bloodstained item at Crillsea market. The item in question is a memory stick and I think it might have arrived here from Amsterdam!'

'Are you indeed, interesting!'

'Anyway, who told you?'

'The Home Office,' grunted Tom.

'You mean Felix,' proposed Davies. 'The Home Office spy?

Helen scolded, 'It's a good job you two know each other or there'd be blood on the carpet by now.'

The two men exchanged sheepish glances.

'Are you going to let me down? Can you carve this chicken or not?' wrangled Helen.

'I do apologise, Helen. My fault entirely,' smoothed Davies.

'My fault actually I believe,' offered Tom.

'Well?' cracked Helen eyeing Davies cheekily.

'Are you losing weight, Tom? You look a little gaunt if you don't mind me saying. And the headaches, any improvement?'

'The chicken, Davies. The chicken!'

Accepting the challenge, Davies raised a carving knife from the table as if to stab, thought better of it, smiled to his hosts, and set about carving the roast chicken with a vengeance.

There was a belly laugh from the chief when the first slice missed Helen's plate.

'Sunday, it must be Sunday,' laughed Davies.

It was still Sunday at the Impex Distribution Centre.

'I didn't think you would be open on a Sunday,' said Conor.

The young girl wearing a lemon turtle neck top disciplined a loose tress from her forehead, flicked her ponytail, and replied, 'We are always open on a Sunday, sir. Twenty four seven actually. We are the biggest distributors of imported flowers, blooms and plants in the United Kingdom. The shop is closed, of course, until Monday morning. This is the trade area but how can I help you?'

'Oh, I'm sorry. I didn't realise this was just for trade. It's my wife, you see,' explained Conor. 'I need a big bunch of black tulips to make her happy. They're her favourite would you believe. Its her birthday soon and I was passing, saw all the vans coming and going, and thought to myself what kind of garden centre is this. Can you help me at all or do I need to come back tomorrow when the shop opens?'

Flicking wayward fluff from her sweater, she advised, 'We don't actually sell flowers from the trade area, sir. If you want the shop you'll have to come back tomorrow.'

'Oh, I'm so sorry, It's a great pity but I do understand.'

'We're a distribution centre. We import flowers and then sell them on to retailers. The shop is just for locals and workers here: a factory shop as it were.'

Ever alert, Conor noticed a television set on a desk. His image was on the screen and he realised it was a closed circuit television monitor. His eyes slowly scanned the office area as he said, 'Well, it's not that important since I was just passing and wondered where I could get black tulips.'

'Oh I can help you there. Would you like a catalogue, sir?' she asked with a smile.

'Would it help?' Conor enquired inquisitively.

'Where are you from if you don't mind me asking?'

'Why?' queried Conor eventually locating a camera lens straining from the ceiling and pointing into the reception area.

'I just wondered,' she said.

'Newcastle, actually,' offered Conor.

'I thought you had a strange accent,' she laughed. 'I've not heard a Newcastle accent for real before. That scar above your eye, nasty accident was it.'

'Nothing to concern you.'

'I did wonder if your accent might be Irish or Welsh with that strange twang.'

'Really,' chuckled Conor. His hand slid surreptitiously beneath his jacket reaching for his gun nestling in the belt at the small of his back.

'It's just that this catalogue covers all our retail centres; you know, places that sell our goods,' she explained. 'Florists and markets mainly. Some just sell daffodils, others just plants. Our reps like this catalogue because it tells you where all the plants and flowers come from. And they can source everything with photographs to our buyers. It really helps if you know where your flowers come from, don't you think? Some of the photographs in here and absolutely amazing. Anyway, you'll probably find a local outlet in here somewhere.'

Expressing interest, Conor nodded, allowed his eyes to follow cabling from the CCTV to a video unit.

'Are you going south?' she asked.

'Yes, I travel a lot. Can I have a look?' asked Conor.

'Of course you can,' she replied with a friendly smile

Leafing the pages casually, Conor said, 'Wow! They're really beautiful. So tell me, where can I buy them? Are all the retail shops listed here?'

'Not all of them,' she replied. 'There's a few in this one: the Bloemenmarkt catalogue.'

'The Bloemenmarkt! What's that?' asked Conor.

'The floating flower market in Amsterdam.'

'Oh, I see,' replied Conor taking a deep breath.

'Yes, there's a list of our customers inside. Not all of them will take black tulips of course but it will give you an idea of where we sell and what price you can expect to pay.'

'Wonderful,' enthused Conor. 'Can I buy one of these catalogues from you?'

'Why don't you just take the catalogue and then you've got it. We've got dozens of these for the reps and such like,' she offered.

Conor beamed a sudden smile and simultaneously felt his fingers begin to curl around and grip the pistol handle. He declared, 'That's so very kind of you, thank you.'

'You're welcome,' she chirped.

The pistol began to see daylight but then a horn sounded from a wagon.

They both looked up and saw a flat back lorry pull into the yard with its driver repeatedly sounding the horn and waving from the cab.

'It's Reg,' she announced. 'That means, put the kettle on.'

Conor smiled and rammed the gun firmly back into to its hiding place behind his back. He recovered the catalogue, turned, and was gone from the portacabin of Impex distribution centre.

'Bye,' she offered limply at the retreating figure. Then she turned her attention to an electric kettle and a jar of coffee.

Moments later, Conor was back in the telephone kiosk outside the transport cafe opposite the distribution centre.

A coin dropped and Conor made the connection.

'You're a difficult man to catch,' he said into the 'phone. 'I made it but I just ran into a brick wall, so I have. The cupboard's bare. Any suggestions?'

There was only silence as Conor listened but then he responded with, 'Yeah, I'm safe. Things could be a bit neater here and there but I'm home free so far. And you?'

There was more listening and watching from the kiosk before Conor said, 'Oh there's always light at the end of the tunnel. It's just a long tunnel, so it is, but I've plenty of time if you've a mind to play the game.'

A medium sized van with the motif of a tulip on its side and bearing the title *Impex Deliveries Nationwide* turned left out of the distribution centre and headed along the main road: destination unknown.

'No, all is not yet lost,' said Conor speaking into the 'phone. 'If the memory stick is here I've got a list of places it might have gone to. I managed to get my hands on a sales catalogue.'

Conor listened as he scanned the catalogue. He nodded before saying, 'There's lots of places listed but only a couple of pages indicating what exactly is imported from the flower market in Amsterdam. Most of the imported stuff seems to come straight from the various bulb fields in Holland and isn't of interest to us. I'm only looking at the flower market catalogue.'

A wagon driver emerged from the cafe and made his way across the car park towards a large articulated vehicle.

Conor observed the driver and spoke quickly into the 'phone, 'Yes, that's what I was thinking. Look, you make your own luck. I'm on the case. I'll ring you tomorrow - same time - I have to go.'

Replacing the 'phone onto its cradle, Conor stepped from the kiosk and shouted towards the wagon driver, 'Excuse me, driver, any chance of a lift?'

In Crillsea Meadows, Davies King carefully poured a helping of thick yellow custard onto a generous slice of chocolate cake and remarked, 'My dear Helen, that roast chicken was absolutely wonderful. I don't know if I'll manage this chocolate cake as well.'

Smiling broadly, Helen Daniels responded, 'Oh, I think you'll find somewhere in that frame of yours to hide that considerable slice of cake, Davies. You're surely not going to let me down and chase it around the dish with your spoon merely pretending to devour it, are you?'

'I wouldn't dream of it, Helen,' replied Davies. 'And in any event, this will be the best chocolate cake ever made in Crillsea.'

Sir Thomas Daniels leaned across the table and cracked, 'Flattery will get you nowhere. You're still on the list for washing up and that's a fact.'

'I thought I'd try; that's all,' laughed Davies.

'Nonsense,' said Helen. 'I'll do the washing up. We have a smart white machine called a dishwasher. It's brand new and keen to make its debut. You can both have a brandy in the lounge and finish that game off.'

'Do you mean the one we've been playing for a year?' suggested Tom reaching for a water jug in the centre of the table.

'Yes, that's the one,' replied Helen. 'I'll be able to dust the table once you've finished the game.'

'Never going to happen,' muttered Tom.

'What was that?' asked Helen.

'Water, Davies?' suggested Tom hovering with the jug.

'Yes please,' replied Davies who twisted to Helen and said, 'Tom said that sounds a great idea, Helen.'

'No, I didn't,' cracked Tom. 'I said the game's never going to end because I'm not going to let him beat me.'

Davies laughed in between mouthfuls of chocolate cake and reached to move his glass when Tom began pouring water.

There was a splash and a damp tablecloth when Davies mistakenly moved his glass and the chief poured water into an empty space.

'Oh damn!' cried Davies. 'I'm so sorry; my fault entirely.'

'Oh thank God you've spilled something at last,' chuckled Helen. 'Now I can relax.'

'What do you mean by that?' asked Davies.

'You always spill something or knock something over,' suggested Tom. 'We've come to expect it of you.'

'Oh dear, you sound like Claudia,' offered Davies.

'Ha ha ha,' countered Helen. 'How is Claudia?'

'Being a nuisance which means she's still running the shop.'

'I thought I did that,' suggested Tom.

'Only when you're there,' cracked Davies.

The bantering continued but when he had finished his meal, he stood up and began clearing the table.

'Sit down, Davies,' said Helen.

'Yes, do,' repeated Tom. 'And that's an order.'

'Tut, tut,' chuckled Davies. 'No orders in the house; your rule remember?'

'Well, terribly bad habit of mine, I suppose,' replied Tom. 'I'll pour the brandy while you help the boss clear the table… Helen?'

'Not for me, Tom. You two enjoy your game. I'll be in the garden with a pair of secateurs once I've filled the dishwasher.'

The telephone rang in the hallway and Tom cried, 'I'll get it.'

Davies followed Helen into the kitchen carrying a collection of dirty dishes. He set them down near the kitchen sink and said, 'A quiet word. If I may?'

'I know what you're going to say,' countered Helen backing away slightly.

'He doesn't look well at all. Is there anything I can do?'

'There's nothing anyone can do,' Helen replied rubbing the back of her neck with both hands.

'He's not for telling anyone about it.'

'He wouldn't even tell me but he'd no choice when I caught him with the pills. In any case, you just know something is wrong when he complains of freezing whilst sweating buckets.'

'What is it?' asked Davies.

'Some form of brucellosis,' whispered Helen.

'Brucellosis! Is it curable?'

'Possibly, it's not necessarily terminal despite what he thinks.'

'How on earth do you get brucellosis?' queried Davies.

'Generally from animals or contact with infected animals and their remains.'

'America?' suggested Davies.

Thoughtfully, Helen replied, 'He could have contracted it there but he's been to South America too and then last year he was in the Middle East advising the police in Jordan. He seems to get selected by the Foreign and Commonwealth office for all these ventures overseas.'

'Mmm,' reflected Davies. 'I don't know much about brucellosis. There must be something the doctors can do surely?'

'It's the side affects,' explained Helen. 'Back pain, fevers, chills, fatigue, headaches, loss of appetite, weight loss. It's like having influenza apparently, but much worse and at a certain age the human body can't take all those problems at the same time.'

'You mean he could take a heart attack during one of these fevers?'

'Who knows? We've just got to hope all these antibiotics work.'

'Davies!'

There was a shout from the lounge and Helen swivelled her head directing Davies to attend the neighbouring room.

'Davies, the board is set and it's my turn.'

Smiling wistfully at Helen, Davies offered, 'Fingers crossed, we'll have to watch out for him.'

Helen nodded and said, 'I don't want him to go to work, Davies. I want him to stay here and rest. I want you to put a rocket up his backside and make him see sense.'

Then a voice boomed, 'Davies.'

Taking hold of Helen's hand, Davies nodded understandingly towards her, and replied, 'Coming, Tom. Just helping out here. Anyway, it's my turn. Not yours.'

'Are you sure?'

'Oh yes, It's always my turn. That's how we end all the sessions, remember?'

'Well...'

'I'm white, you're black,' declared Davies. 'And I took one of your knights last Sunday.'

'Did you? Oh yes, I remember now. Brandy, Davies? I've poured you a large one.'

'I should think so too.'

They sat and studied the chess board, drinking their brandy and making their moves.

'There was no need to spill the water deliberately, Davies,' said Tom. 'I've got brucellosis. Helen knows and now you do too. You needn't have disappeared into the kitchen with her. I would have told you in my own good time.'

'It's not good news either way, Tom. Not good at all. You need to rest a couple of days at least, I'd say.'

'No, it's not good news but I've been advised to keep taking the tablets and there might be an improvement.'

'Let's hope so,' said Davies. 'You know, I'm serious. Perhaps a few days off would do you good after all. Let the deputy and the assistant take over for a while.'

'No, I can't do that. I am the chief.'

'For God's sake, if there's an earthquake or an alien invasion they'll ring you, I guarantee it.

'No, it's not just that. They want me to head up an international task force on crime,' said Tom as he slid a knight across the board.

'Who does?' questioned Davies responding with a bishop on the attack.

'Foreign and Commonwealth although the instruction has come from the Home Office.'

'Instruction? Sorry, but you've lost the plot. You're a chief constable,' reminded Davies. 'You're an independent body with no affiliation to any political office or party. Everyone in the service knows that really pisses the government off but that's the way it is. The autonomy of chief constables is enshrined in case law. The police are the servants of the law in terms of operational discretion, and are not subject to administrative or political direction. No-one can instruct you. You really are the chief. What's going on, my dear friend. That sounds like they are gunning for you, and if that's the case, I want to know why.'

'It's nothing to do with you.'

'Tell it to the marines!' cracked Davies.

Politics!' declared Tom quietly.

Hands on the board moved the pieces deliberately before Davies sat back and asked 'In what way?'

'They want me to head up enquiries into the murders in Dublin and Amsterdam,' confessed Tom pushing forward with his remaining knight.

'What? You must be joking. The Irish police and the Netherlands police should be able to do that. They shouldn't need a UK chief to run the show.'

'The murders are connected,' stated Tom mopping his brow.

'Yeah, so Europol and Interpol can co-ordinate the job and respective heads of detectives in each country can run it on the ground, theoretically. In practice, one of those forces will develop a natural lead when they get onto the right track and they'll push things on from there. Extradition will come into play; you know, legalities, practicalities. Stuff like that. Let them get on with it. They don't need you. Take a week off and out your feet up. You'll feel better for it, mark my words.'

'I don't need to rest I need to work. But you have a good understanding of international practice and procedures, Davies.'

'And a poor understanding of politics and why they picked you to run the show. Now look me in the eye and tell me what the hell is going on,' implored Davies.

'Hey, I'm the chief. You're an Indian. Know your place and stand there,' snapped Tom as another bead of sweat formed and threatened to ruin Sunday altogether.

'Okay, I'll tell you why,' countered Davies ignoring the remark. 'It's common knowledge your biography upset a few people here and there; most of them in powerful positions, I understand. Some of them didn't like reading the truth. And that's the rub, isn't it. They don't like you anymore so they've given you the job that no-one else wants. Am I right?'

'You're out of order, Davies,' commented Tom angrily. 'The Home Office have personally selected me for the job, I'll have you know. And that's a fact!'

'Are you sure it was the Home Office? Could it have been a Utility company personally selecting you for the most complicated gas tariff ever devised by mankind?' challenged Davies sarcastically.

'Very funny, Davies. That's typical of you. Subhuman comedy from Crillsea's best!'

'If that's what it takes to bring you to your senses, then yes.'

'Look, I was going to ask you to join my team and get on board but now I'm not so sure,' declared Tom. 'I don't need a wisecracking comic in the team.'

Sir Thomas stood up for a moment, wiped a handkerchief across his brow, and exhaled loudly. He seemed to feel the better for it and sat down again to await a response from Davies.

'Oh, I'll join your team with or without wisecracks.' sparked Davies. 'As much to make sure you don't overdo things as well as making sure you haven't been sold a pig in a poke by your so-called Home Office friends.'

'We'll see, Davies,' acknowledged Tom. 'We'll see. I might decide to take Felix with me.'

'Your decision,' replied Davies. 'You're the chief. I'm just an Indian.'

The chief pushed his knight forward into the heart of Davies's pieces but Davies immediately removed it from the board with the swift redeployment of his bishop.

'I don't want you to fall into any more traps, Tom, that's all,' announced Davies with a sly grin.

The chief looked down at the board trying to fathom the last move as he mentioned, 'I'll know tomorrow whether I'm going to start in Dublin or Amsterdam.'

'Good,' nodded Davies. 'I'm worried they've decided to pull the plug on you. In any event, I've never been to either place and I don't know whether my passport is up to date so you'd best take Felix Churchill.'

'You were quite sharp there for a moment or so, Davies,' snapped Tom. Then he looked up and asked, 'Have I just lost my best knight?'

Davies looked him in the eye and replied, 'Yes Mister Chief Constable! Oh, and by the way, Tom, you're also in check. It's mate in two!'

As Sunday grew tired in a late afternoon, Conor O'Keeffe dismounted from the passenger side of an articulated cabin, waved his thanks to the driver, and waited for the vehicle to slowly draw passed him.

Standing on the footpath of a small town in the south of England, Conor glimpsed at the page of his retail catalogue and checked the street plate nearby. Looking along the street he saw the shop closed and shuttered as he gradually strolled towards it windows.

Agreeing pleasantly with himself, Conor turned from the shop and found a discreet bed and breakfast nearby. Tomorrow, he thought. Tomorrow is another day.

Chapter Eleven

~ ~ ~

Dateline: Monday
Crillsea Police Station, England

'Morning, Claudia. Glad you're back,' said Ted Barnes dominating the outer office in his new suit. 'What a miss you've been. Tell me, is Davies in yet?'

Claudia gathered her grey cardigan around her and replied haughtily, 'The Chief Inspector has been in, as you put it, since seven thirty this morning. He's trying to get on top of the backlog his predecessor left him.' Then Claudia smiled and said, 'On the other hand, good morning, Sergeant Barnes. Thank you, it's nice to be back. How are you today?'

'Fine, Claudia, wait until Davies sees this. He'll go ballistic.'

'Just go through, Sergeant Barnes,' declared Claudia. 'Chief Inspector King always has an open door for you even when it's closed to everyone else.'

'It's Barney, Claudia. Barney,' he suggested.

'And I'm the chief civilian administration officer in this police division, Sergeant Barnes. Proceed with caution.'

Barney took a deep breath, eased past the department's gate keeper, knocked on the door labelled *Detective Chief Inspector King,* and immediately entered saying, 'Human, Davies. It's bloody human. Can you believe it?'

'Morning, Barney,' said Davies looking up from a pile of paperwork on a cluttered desk 'I presume you mean the result of the DNA check on the memory stick. Of course it's human. I knew it would be.'

'Oh, there's more, Davies. Much more,' enthused Barney.

'Coffee?' queried Davies abandoning the paper for a moment and handling a percolator jug.

'Yes please, Davies. The thing is, we've got a match on the DNA. Can you believe it?'

'A match? Now that is news,' said Davies filling two mugs. 'Where does it take us?'

'The DNA sample from the memory stick is identical with the DNA profile of one Callum Reece. He's got one previous conviction for drink driving in Dublin,' stated Barney. 'I checked his record.'

'Wow! We caught ourselves a big fish, Barney,' laughed Davies. 'A man caught on the breathalyser years ago no doubt. Never mind, can't win them all.'

Barney shook his head disagreeably and said, 'Do you remember when we were in the Anchor the other day with Archie and the news came on the telly?'

'Yes, I do. It was the day we nicked the yo-yo gang in the Anchor. I've just submitted the file through to the Prosecutions Section.'

'Well, one of the murder victims that day was Callum Reece. He used to be a top man in the IRA. He's one of the guys who was shot dead in Amsterdam. You've got yourself a lead into the Dublin-Amsterdam shoot out, Davies.'

'I don't believe it!' exclaimed Davies. 'It was just a wild stab because I bought Claudia an amaryllis from Amsterdam and… Well you know the rest. My chessboard mind again.'

'Well believe it, my old pal because it's right. Here…' Barney handed over a sheaf of paper and a plastic bag containing the memory stick saying, 'It's all in the forensic report.'

Accepting the package, Davies detached the memory stick, glanced through the report and said, 'I'll find a safe place for that. Any fingerprints on it?'

'No, hey, you can't have everything, Davies,' chuckled Barney. 'I suppose that means we lock up Harry Reynolds for multiple murders and...'

'Oh, no,' interrupted Davies. 'That's been done before and I don't think we'll be doing it again this time. No, I'll speak to the chief constable about this. Apparently he's been put in charge of a Multinational Task Force to look into these murders.'

'Has he asked you to join his investigating team?' queried Barney.

'No, and I'm not expecting him to,' remarked Davies. 'I think he'll be taking Felix between you and me. That's up to him. But it makes sense. It's a Home Office appointment so they'll be expecting the chief to take their Home Office man with him.'

Barney nodded and replied, 'It's logical, I suppose.'

Davies asked, 'Look, I need to study this forensic report at length and advise the chief on the content. I'm not allowing the boss to go into battle without knowing the facts. Do me a favour, Barney. Write it up for me please. A report for the chief would be great. It will save me some time whilst I get on top of this paper work and sort these bloody annual assessments out. Unless you're too busy yourself of course?'

There was a tap on the door and Claudia breezed in with a pile of letters and reports saying, 'Chief Inspector, you will desist from swearing however mildly that might be. Sergeant Barnes, Inspector Rock wants you at the daily briefing five minutes ago. Chief Inspector Davies, you've got all these to sign if you want them in the post by lunchtime.'

'Have you bugged my office?' asked Davies.

'No, why do you ask?' replied Claudia inquisitively.

'No reason! Well, maybe your hearing, that's all.'

'Oh, I see,' cracked Claudia. 'Sorry.'

'You're back then,' responded Davies.

'As if I'd never been away,' replied Claudia. 'What's that?' she enquired pointing to the memory stick.

'A clue to the Amsterdam-Dublin murders,' said Barney enthusiastically. 'By the way, Davies. Have you taken a look at the design on the side of the memory stick?'

Davies fumbled with the transparent plastic bag and said, 'Oh yeah, I see what you mean. What a strange design. It must be the company logo. What do you think, Claudia?'

Claudia dropped her pile of letters on the desk and said, 'I think Sergeant Barnes is still here when he should be elsewhere. Let me have a look at what you've got?'

Chuckling, Barney bade farewell with, 'I'll update Annie with the forensic result, Davies. And I'll rattle a report out for the chief for you. Catch you later.'

Detective Sergeant Ted Barnes was gone from the DCI's office bound for an office briefing with DI Annie Rock and the daily routine of Crillsea nick.

'One day, chief inspector, you'll get on top of this paperwork.' Claudia indicated the pile and instructed, 'Sign those on the top, read the next pile, and check your diary for appointments.'

'Appointments?' queried Davies.

'Yes, make sure you're free at twelve noon, Sir Thomas requires your presence in his office.'

Studying the design on the side of the memory stick, Davies replied, 'Twelve, I'll be there, Claudia.... What do you make of this?'

Claudia examined the memory stick through the thin plastic bag that enveloped the device and asserted, 'That's not a company logo. It's the image of a constellation, chief inspector. If you look at the base of the stick you'll see the name of the manufacturer. No, that's just an attractive design put there so that people will choose that one over others on sale; that's all.'

'Oh, well, well, well. What would I do without you, Claudia?'

Returning the memory stick, Claudia offered, 'You'd forget to charge your mobile and you'd need a new typist.'

Claudia tidied his mobile 'phone from his desk, plugged it into the charger, removed a diary from his desk drawer, leafed through it and declared, 'You have a meeting with the new superintendent at twelve noon but fortunately he won't be with us for another month.'

'Why ever not?' questioned Davies.

'He fell off a ladder and broke his leg,' replied Claudia.

'Painting and decorating?'

'I believe so,' said Claudia.

'Pity,' responded Davies. 'If he'd been star gazing from the roof we could have asked him which constellation was engraved on the memory stick.'

'Chief inspector!' cried Claudia. 'That is a disgraceful remark to make. You should be ashamed of yourself. Your sense of humour really needs to look at itself in the mirror.'

'Mmm....' mused Davies studying the memory stick again. 'Sorry, I hope he gets better soon. Who got the job, by the way?'

'Some Chief Inspector from Kent and I can tell you that the constellation on the side of the memory stick is the Plough. I think the Americans call it the 'Big Dipper.'

'Nah, it's not the Plough, Claudia. That's got seven stars. This one has five.'

'Well, there you are then,' decided Claudia. 'It's a company logo after all.'

Davies King looked at his wristwatch and said, 'Twelve noon with the chief, you say. I'll be back in time.'

Pocketing the memory stick, Davies said, 'The paper can wait. I'm playing chess with an unknown opponent and the answer might lie in the library. Where's my mobile?'

'Still charging,' cracked Claudia.

'Whatever,' remarked Davies with a cheeky grin.

Davies King was gone from the office of Crillsea police station, bound for the harbour and Crillsea library.

As the door closed behind him, Claudia Jones: widow of this parish; gatekeeper to all things sacred and beyond reach, chief administration officer and personal assistant, shook her head, pulled her long grey cardigan tight about her, and quietly said, 'One day, Mister King, you really will get into trouble.'

In a town far away, Conor O'Keeffe spent the day in and out of florists, featured in his catalogue, looking at plants and bulbs that had been imported form the floating flower market in Amsterdam: The Bloemenmarkt.

Of course, he didn't really know what he was looking for in some respects. He hoped to find a memory stick but thought the chances of such good fortune were pretty slim. But then it was a chance in a million and people bought lottery tickets every week to try and win that million.

With a cheeky Irish smile, a bucketful of charm and sophistication, Conor looked, prodded, examined, turned over a leaf or two, and listened as he questioned the shopkeepers about the authenticity of the Bloemenmarkt products.

'It's not easy doing door to door surveys for the Netherlands Bulb Society,' he argued.

'The Netherlands Bulb Society,' the shopkeeper responded. 'How unusual. If we have any problems, I normally just ring our agent and he fixes it.'

With equal measures of charisma and a bewitching smile borrowed from the school of enlightenment, Conor reacted with. 'But someone has to do it. So tell me, sir,' spoken with a gentle amiable lilt in his voice, 'Have you had any problems with the import service from the flower market?'

'None at all,' was the answer. 'Not that I can think of that is.'

'What about deliveries?' asked Conor.

'Always prompt within an hour or two,' the shopkeeper replied. 'Never had cause to complain.'

Conor pushed on with his questions.

'Do they arrive on time and in good order?'

'Yes,' was the reply.

'Let's talk about the last delivery you received,' suggested Conor and then he probed deep with, 'Any problems with that delivery? Was the product good? Was it delivered on time? Was it well packaged? Was it damaged at all?'

The shopkeeper responded by tending his display in the bay window and imparting, 'Wow, you bulb people are really intent on making sure things are okay, aren't you!'

'We try our best,' returned Conor beaming a smile as his pencil scribbled replies on a clip board bought for the purpose of falsehood and prevarication and his machine-made identity card hung loosely from a cord around his neck.

Minute by minute, Conor was turning the pages, ticking the boxes, shortening the odds. Getting closer, forever getting closer, probing and delving with his spurious smile and fake personality.

'Thank you, Mister Leadbetter,' cried Davies walking down the steps of Crillsea library with a couple of books tucked under his arm. 'I'll have them back to you by the end of the week.'

'It's Cyril, Mister King. Cyril! And there's no rush with the books. Take your time.'

Davies threw a grateful wave in the air, checked his wristwatch, and made for the Anchor round the corner.

As he strode out towards the pub, Davies glanced at the front of the book covers and thought, medical science and astronomy, now that's what I call a good read.

He turned the corner by the harbour and entered the Anchor.

'Coffee, brandy, beer or lager?' asked the licensee, Bill.

'Coffee has too much caffeine in it, brandy too much alcohol, and beer and lager just make you podgy,' replied Davies. 'What else do you recommend?'

'A strawberry milk shake, Mister King,' suggested Bill. 'It has to be good for you surely; fruit and milk?'

'Only if you have a straw, Bill,' chuckled Davies. 'And throw in a sandwich, won't you?' suggested Davies.

'On the slate is it, Mister King?' enquired Bill.

'Please, end of the month as usual, Bill.'

'I'll rustle something up, Mister King. Cheese and pickle okay with you?'

'Fine! No Archie today?'

'Haven't seen him, Mister King,' said Bill fixing a milkshake and setting it down in front of Davies. 'And he's usually in by now. He won't be far away and I suspect we'll know it when he arrives.'

'Too right there,' chuckled Davies.

Turning his attention to his literary finds, Davies leafed through the books, drank his milkshake, and devoured one large cheese and pickle sandwich before there was a tap on his shoulder and he swung round to see Barney.

'Thought you'd be here, Davies. The chief has just arrived at the nick in his Jag. He's asking for you.'

'Damn! I forgot all about that. Did you cover for me?'

'Yeah,' cracked Barney. 'I told him you were meeting an informant but I think he sussed me.'

'Oh dear, come on, let's go,' said Davies. 'Bill, I'm off. I'll catch you tonight, okay?'

'Take care, Mister King,' responded Bill waving from the end of the bar.

Collecting his books, Davies advised Barney, 'I've been thinking, Barney. I reckon our memory stick might just be central to this Amsterdam-Dublin thing. In fact, I think it's so important that I'm going to put it into one of the local bank vaults.'

Pausing at the door, Barney remarked, 'You're the boss, Davies. Well, at the moment you are but I don't think the chief will take kindly to you being late. Come on, let's step it out.'

The two men walked along the pavement beside the harbour wall where Barney asked, 'What's so special about the memory stick, Davies? Do you know something that I don't? I mean, at the end of the day, it's just an item that's heavily bloodstained. It's not going to prove central to the enquiry, is it?'

'I don't know, Barney. I just don't know,' replied Davies.

'Time you had a game of chess, Davies,' suggested Barney. 'Your mind is in another place again.'

'Yeah, I know,' replied Davies. 'But we need to be at the nick and we're not.'

Lengthening their stride, they soon found themselves in the police station car park. Before climbing the stairs to the office complex Davies remarked, 'Do you know something, Barney. I think we'd better keep that memory stick under lock and key. It's bothering me and you know what that means.'

Barney pursed his lips and nodded, 'I do indeed, Davies.'

Moments later, the two men walked into Davies's office to find Chief Constable Sir Thomas Daniels sat at the desk scanning through the paperwork.

'Ah, Davies!' exclaimed Sir Thomas abandoning a crime report of some description or other. 'Your friend, Sergeant Barnes found you then. The Anchor was it?'

'My apologies, sir,' replied Davies. 'I had some research to do at the library and...' Davies set his books down on the corner of his desk and continued, 'And I got carried away in the reading.'

Sir Thomas uttered, 'Mmm...' and then swivelled the books so that he could examine the covers. 'Taken up astronomy and surgery have we, Davies? Not a bad time to consider an alternative income stream when you're late for an appointment with the boss.'

'You called; I answered, sir,' revealed Davies. 'One of the books has a chapter about brucellosis in it; the other contains images of all the star constellations. Depends what you're reading interests are, doesn't it?'

'Medical books, Davies?' queried the chief. 'Surgery and sorcery?'

Davies quipped, 'I have a friend suffering from the disease, sir. He might need help or someone who knows what to expect, that's all.'

Barney threw a sideways glance at Davies but did not speak.

'Mmm...' mumbled Sir Thomas again as he drummed his fingers on the table.

Leaning back into the chair, Sir Thomas allowed his beard to threaten his barrel chest. He gently combed his beard with his long fingers and said, 'Mmm... Well, it's official, Davies. I've been appointed by the Home Office, in consultation with the Foreign and Commonwealth Office, as task force commander. The government have instructed me to take the lead in the murder investigations relevant to Dublin and Amsterdam. I am to protect British interests and liaise as appropriate with relevant enforcement agencies taking the lead in enquiries as approved by other European governments.'

'Congratulations, sir,' remarked Davies. 'Well done indeed.'

'Yes,' mentioned Barney. 'Many congratulations, sir. That's a feather in your cap, isn't it?'

'I don't know, sergeant,' replied Sir Thomas thoughtfully. 'It's a soft shoe job apparently and I'm not at all sure what it's all about.'

'Soft shoe?' queried Barney scratching a bald patch on his head. 'You mean it's a bit dodgy, sir?'

Sir Thomas replied, 'I don't know what to make of it at the moment but I want you two on board and in the team. Davies, I've selected you as my senior investigating officer. Sergeant Barnes, you have experience of Dublin haven't you?'

'From my RUC days in Northern Ireland, sir,' replied Barney. 'I went to Dublin a couple of times but I wouldn't call myself an expert by any means.'

'Mmm...,' remarked Sir Thomas. 'I want the two best detectives in the force and that's you two. I'm leaving Felix and Annie in charge of your division and I'm not taking the head of CID with me since he'll be acting assistant chief constable in my absence. Any objections or do I need to make this an order?'

'We're with you, sir,' replied Davies. Glancing at Barney, Davies offered, 'All the way, sir, actually.'

Barney nodded and agreed, 'All the way, sir. Thank you. An international task force? Wow! I've never been in one of those before.'

'Davies, I want you to ring your friend in London: The one in the Flying Squad,' instructed Sir Thomas.

'Big Al Jessop, sir,' replied Davies. 'Detective Chief Superintendent Alan Jessop.'

187

'Yes, that's the man, yes. According to the Home Secretary I can co-opt anyone I want into the task force. I've already spoken to the Met commissioner but if you speak with Mister Jessop, I'd be obliged.'

'He's a chief superintendent, sir,' remarked Davies. 'I'm a chief inspector and the senior investigating officer? Doesn't make sense if you ask me, sir.'

'I'm not asking you, Davies,' responded the chief. 'And you're right. Nothing makes sense at the moment. One more thing; I want you to ring Commander Pape on this number. The commander is my primary link to all government departments and will oversee the political interface necessary.'

'Political interface?' probed Davies.

Ignoring the remark, Sir Thomas slipped Davies a piece of paper with a telephone number on it and advised, 'I'll handle the politics, Davies. I'm sure we're going to ruffle some international feathers. Look, a friend of mine told me recently that I might have been selected because of an impending argument over extradition, sovereignty, who knows what. He might have been right. I don't like the way this has fallen out of the nest. It just seems odd, that's all. International task force indeed. There's something amiss.'

Reading the slip of paper, Davies remarked, 'Well, at least there's one good thing here.'

'What's that?' asked Barney.

'Commander Pape! He'll be a Met police commander, I expect. Probably one these double degree boy wonders going places faster than an express train and leaving us all on his wake. I wonder which department he heads up?'

'Mmm...' said the chief. 'I should perhaps mention that Commander Pape is not a police commander, Davies. No, he's a naval commander and he's the deputy head of the Secret Intelligence Service. And that stays within these walls.'

'MI6?' quizzed Barney.

'Indeed,' acknowledged Sir Thomas.

'The plot thickens as they say, sir,' puzzled Davies.

'Martial arts, judo experts, fast cars, fast women and fast guns,' cracked Barney. 'Can't wait to meet him.'

'Too many James Bond films, Barney,' suggested Davies. 'More like linguists, mathematicians, surveillance experts, living undercover and....'

'Chess players?' intruded Barney.

Tom Daniels lifted his hand like a mediator and advised, 'Make the arrangements with Commander Pape, Davies. Find out what's going on, lay out your plan of investigation to him, and ask him what his role in this affair is. I need to bring some officers into the team from other countries apparently and that's what I'll be doing today. You're my right hand man on this one, Davies, so I expect you to use my authority to open the doors if you need to.'

'You're not telling us everything, are you, sir?' suggested Davies exchanging concerned glances with a puzzled Barney.

'I don't know if Commander Pape plays chess, Davies, if that's what you mean?'

'No, that's not what I meant, sir.'

'I didn't think it was,' replied the chief. 'No, I'm not telling you everything, but then I'm not sure of things myself. I've never met Commander Pape. Indeed, I've never heard of him before today. It seems he might be a government man put in to keep watch over us. What British Intelligence has to do with these murders, God alone knows?'

'I'm guessing he's on board in order to report back to the government?' suggested Davies.

Sir Thomas smiled slightly and declared, 'I need a close team, gentlemen, tight and security conscious and I have to start somewhere.'

'Sir,' interrupted Barney. 'If we're going to be close....'

'What's on your mind?' asked Sir Thomas.

'Two things really, number one - I seem to remember the Provisional Irish Republican Army might be involved in this: the IRA. That might explain the MI6 man.'

'Agreed,' cracked Sir Thomas.

'Number two - If we're looking for a close team and good security then can I suggest you accept that I've known you and Davies have been close friends for many years? It's common knowledge in some places, but not all.'

Sir Thomas studied Barney, looked at Davies, and then said, 'Friendships at different levels in an organisation can upset people at different ranks, Sergeant Barnes. How did you know?'

Barney shook his head slowly and eventually said, 'Chess... it's a give away, sir. And a few of us have seen the chess table in the corner when we've been called up to your office.'

'Oh dear,' uttered the chief. 'That obvious, is it?'

Barney replied, 'We haven't spotted the brandy yet but I expect that's under lock and key.'

'Humph!' grunted Sir Thomas. 'What did I expect of a man I have just described as one of my best detectives.'

'Apart from that, sir,' offered Barney, 'There's only two men in the force play chess badly: you, and Chief Inspector King.'

'Badly? Badly?' quizzed Davies.

Sir Thomas gradually beamed a huge smile at Barney, thrust out his grizzled huge hand, and said, 'Of course, Barney! Of course! Welcome aboard.'

'Thank you,' replied Barney. 'Got that off my chest then.'

Sir Thomas laughed aloud and said, 'Make those calls, Davies. Make the calls.'

'Tomorrow morning; same time, same place,' said Al Jessop into the mouthpiece of his telephone. 'And do me a favour,' he hinted. 'Don't be late.'

Thoughtfully, Jessop placed the phone on its cradle, kept his hand on it, and then lifted the apparatus again. He dialled a number quickly and said, 'Jim, I might be a little late in the morning. I'll be with my personal trainer.'

Laughing at the reply, Jessop said, 'We'll see about that. It might be something. It might be nothing. But don't worry; he'll do things my way or not at all. Just mind the shop for me until I get back, Jim.'

The line went dead and Detective Chief Superintendent Alan Jessop stepped casually to the window and looked out across the immense panoramic view his open plan glass domain allowed him.

He brushed an imagined speck of dust from his dark pinstripe Saville Row suit and fettled his matching silk tie as he studied the office blocks rising into the sky and the cathedrals and churches throwing their spires and domes into the pot in a worthwhile challenge for supremacy. The sky was a deep azure blue with only a smidgen of cloud coming in from the west. Down below at street level, he could see the traffic and pedestrians threading their way through the thin ribbon of streets that lead from here to everywhere.

Smiling, happy, he thought to himself, London... This is my London.

The telephone lines were busy.

One hundred miles away, in a market town on the hinterland of the south coast, Conor O'Keeffe lifted the handset, dropped a coin into a public telephone, and said,

'I'm checking in. I've hired a car and I'm shortening the odds. The list is getting smaller.'

A heavy goods vehicle passed the kiosk and Conor felt the shudder of the beast as it shook his hire car parked on the nearby lay by.

'Oh, it'll come,' said Conor into the mouthpiece. 'It's just a question of time, that's all.'

*

Chapter Twelve

~ ~ ~

Tuesday.
Central London and Crillsea.

Detective Chief Superintendent Alan Jessop was taking an early morning jog in the park before going to work.

His problem today was that work was an office situated on the north side of the River Thames and the park he was jogging in was south of the river. There were no skyscrapers to admire and no miniature traffic systems to appreciate from on high.

Dressed down from his normal attire of significant distinction and elegance, he wore a dark blue tracksuit and grey-white training shoes, and he was taking his time as he stepped out carefully along a path bordering the park.

Vigilant! He felt vigilant this morning as his eyes darted from left to right, from the hedgerows to the bushes and back again, as he mentally made safe the way forward. The stab proof vest was a hindrance to him. It was light enough to wear and carry but awkward enough to snag in all the wrong places of his body. Sure, it would hold back and deny the penetration of the knife, but it wouldn't stop a bullet. The vest would surely slow such a missile down but he'd been set up before on jobs like this, and had attended to many police funerals not to learn the lessons of those *killed in action* before him.

This detective chief superintendent was an exception to the rank. He was still a grounded jack: a hands on detective, jack the lad, a Mack the knife type character, a policeman's policeman - God how he hated the term *Copper;* and he knew every snout in London by name and profile because he was the Head of the Flying Squad and it was his job, his calling in life, his profession, to penetrate the target, to penetrate the very deepest evil heart of the criminal profession in London.

Al Jessop was a legend in the corridor he walked, but nowhere else.

Big Al was in the park, on the streets. This was his office and this was the place he carried out his primary business.

He put the discomfort of the stab proof vest to the back of his mind and concentrated on the path ahead and the slightest movement that might catch his eye. One man's walk in the park was another man's alley of death.

On his second circuit of the park, Jessop became aware of another jogger on the route in front of him and he increased his speed to match his adversary: shoulder to shoulder.

'You're late,' quipped Jessop from the side of his mouth. 'I don't pay you to be late. I pay you to be on time.'

'I made it,' replied a slightly overweight middle aged runner. 'Stop complaining, governor. I made sure no-one followed me. In any case, they all know I'm on a health kick so this makes sense, okay?'

'Okay, but what you got for me?' asked Jessop. 'It had better be good and before I have a heart attack.'

'It's my brother, guv,' cracked the runner.

'I thought he was on remand awaiting trial for that post office job in Southwark?' replied Jessop.

'He is, guv,' admitted the jogger. 'But he was only the lookout. Can you put a word in with the man in the wig?'

'Doubt it at this stage,' cracked Jessop.

The two men ran on, slowly, casual, shoulder to shoulder through a sparsely populated park.

'Depends what the trade is?' suggested Jessop.

'A raid on a security van!' offered the runner.

'When?' puffed Jessop beginning to labour slightly as the path twisted and began its uphill climb.

'A week today! Twelve noon, three shooters involved, two lookouts and two drivers,' advised the runner who was feeling the ascent.

'Where?'

'Ilford High Street!'

'Who?'

'Geordie Joe's mob.'

'Geordie Joe! I thought he'd gone off my radar. You sure?'

'Yeah, of course I'm sure, guv.'

'You involved?' queried Jessop.

'I went visiting my brother on remand the other day,' offered the runner when the climb ended and the path levelled out long and level in front of them. 'He tells me they wanted him to drive one of the getaway cars but he can't now, can he?'

'Anything else?' asked Jessop, glad of the easier going.

'I'll have more for you later in the week when I know who they got as the replacement driver.'

'Okay, only next time make it the cafe. I'll be knackered if I have to do another circuit.'

'I don't want any cash this time, guv. The trade is for my brother. It's his third conviction. He'll go down for a long stretch.'

'I'll see what I can do. No promises but I'll speak with the right people, okay?'

'God bless you, guv. You keep fit, okay?'

Suddenly, the runner set off at a sprint striding out from Jessop and through the park gate and into the main thoroughfare.

Al Jessop came to a standstill and placed his hand on his hips. He bent down and then stood up again taking in the air, filling his lungs, feeling energised with the thrill of it all.

Meeting over, Jessop began a slow walk as he composed himself and got his breath back.

Then he left the park by a side gate, crossed the dual carriageway using a pedestrian crossing, and disappeared into the tube station.

Nearby, on the footpath, a traffic warden was writing out a ticket for an illegally parked Volvo when he glimpsed a view of Jessop disappearing into the tube station.

Jessop, thought the traffic warden. Wasn't that Big Al Jessop from the north side, he thought. No, it wouldn't be a chief superintendent jogging in the park down this way, surely.

The traffic warden shook his pen expecting the last drop of ink to flow into the ball point before he dispensed his duly assigned form of British justice. He glimpsed again at an empty park and the entrance to a busy tube station before concentrating on his duty and the slow scribbled scrawl of his pen nib.

Penned in, Bill Baxter was trapped in a corner of the chess board trying to defend his honour from the marauding white knights of Davies King's onslaught.

'Wish you'd never taught me this game, Mister King,' proposed Bill. 'Remind me, it's the knight that moves diagonally, isn't it?'

'No, that's the bishop that moves diagonally, Bill,' responded Davies moving his mobile phone across the table out of the way. 'The knight can move forwards, backwards or to the side one square, and then one square diagonally. A total of two squares. Don't worry, it's only your first proper game. You're going to lose to begin with but you're also going to learn how the game is played properly.'

'Yeah, heard that one before,' cracked Bill.

'Well believe it because it's right,' announced Davies. 'Do you want to start again? You're never going to get this one back and you didn't even try to take the four squares in the middle of the board.'

'I forgot,' replied Bill. 'He who controls the centre of the board controls the game. Isn't that what you said?'

'More or less,' said Davies. 'Ah, here's breakfast.'

Bill's wife appeared with a tray containing a pot of coffee and two huge cooked breakfast which she placed on the table set for two nearby.

'Brenda!' cried Davies. 'Where am I going to put all that lot. There's enough there for a ship's company.'

'You'll manage, Mister King. I'll put it on the tab, shall I?'

'If you don't mind, Brenda,' replied Davies. 'Where did you find this lady, Bill. She's a star!'

'Behind the bar one morning, Mister King. Found her, decided to keep her. Never regretted it since.'

'Cheeky,' cracked Brenda. 'I'll be in the cellar sorting out the orders. I'll catch you both later.'

'Thanks,' cried Davies as he stood and removed his new black leather jacket.

'What's on today, Mister King? The last time you wore that jacket you got promoted. They're not bumping you up again are they?'

'Busy day, Bill. Conference in London!' cracked Davies.

'Sauce?' asked Bill offering a bottle of ketchup. '

'No thanks,' answered Davies. 'Oh no, here comes Archie.'

Wandering into the bar like a lost sheep, Archie Campbell pulled up a chair beside the two men, doffed his cap and bid good morning to his friend before launching an attack at Davies.

'Not impressed, Mister King?'

'What? You'll not get a better breakfast anywhere else in Crillsea, Archie,' responded Davies slicing into bacon.

'Mmm....' muttered Archie.

'Mmm...' muttered Bill.

'God, it's a disease,' declared Davies. 'What's up, Archie?'

'You know me, Mister King. I don't speak publicly of the flaws apparent in others but I'm not impressed and I'll be keeping it to myself, if you don't mind.'

'That'll be the first time then,' cracked Bill.

'Pardon? I can soon take my business elsewhere, so I can,' countered Archie.

'Good,' replied Davies to a startled look from Archie. Davies chased his food, loaded it onto a fork and took a mouthful followed by a gulp of coffee. 'No, I mean it's good you can keep a secret, Archie,' explained Davies. 'Very good indeed.'

'It's your new boss, Mister King,' cracked Davies. 'That Churchill man. He's one to watch he is.'

'One to watch?' queried Davies. 'Explain if you please, Archie.'

'Mister Discretion is what they call me, Mister King. I cannot divulge a distraction from the legitimate.'

'Now, I'm confused,' remarked Bill. 'Look, I'll go and help Brenda for a moment while you are legitimately discreet, Archie.'

'No need,' replied Davies. 'We've all known each other long enough, Bill.... Archie, get it off your chest before I lose my temper and stab this fried tomato to death.'

'I was at the dogs last night, Mister King,' explained Archie. 'And so was your new man.'

'Which new man?' asked Davies.

'The one that had his photo in the Crillsea Chronicle, Mister King. Felix Churchill, they call him... Funny name if you don't mind me saying so.'

'Is that it? He went to the dog track at Crillsea. Wow! Is that the whole story, Archie?'

'Yep!' cracked Archie chuckling.

Davies exhaled loudly and threw an exasperated glance at Bill before Archie returned with, 'I took twenty quid and made a couple of bets. Lost a tenner and had a couple of drinks. Your man Churchill lost a few quid, so he did.'

'And how do you know that, Archie?' asked Davies.

'He was standing in the queue in front of me. I saw him. Is that tomato going spare?' asked Archie.

Reaching across, Archie swiftly snaffled a tomato from the plate and gobbled it down in one swallow.

Looking shocked, but unperturbed, Davies said, 'And?'

'And he was betting in hundreds of pounds, Mister King. I reckon he must have lost about ten grand last night... Yeah, ten thousand pounds, I reckon. Tell you one thing...'

'What's that?' questioned Davies.

'Your man Mister Churchill didn't back any winners at the dogs. No, sir. No winners last night. But he lost a packet and I'll tell you something else.'

'What's that?' asked Davies.'

'I'm thirsty, Mister King. Ready for a liquid breakfast this morning, I think.'

'It'll be a mild, Archie. Bill here will put it on my tab,' offered Davies. 'But what else is there to tell me?'

'It'll be a pint, Bill,' clarified Archie. 'Thank you very much, Mister King. Very thoughtful of you if you don't mind me saying so. Yes, a pint because Mister King needs to know that his man Felix has a very bad temper when he's losing.'

'A bad temper, Archie?' probed Davies.

'Oh, yes, Mister King. He was livid when he lost. He turned away from the track so very annoyed when his dog was third. He pushed me flat against the wall in a fit of temper, he did. And then he barged passed me like I wasn't there. Needs watching if you ask me, Mister King.'

'Really?' cracked Davies.

'Really,' agreed Archie before mustering his tin once more and offering, 'Snuff, Mister King? Pinch of snuff to set you up for the rest of the day?'

The mobile 'phone on the table rang and a hand stretched across the chess pieces, snatched it from its resting place and duly answered the call, 'Davies King!'

Bill and Archie exchanged glances as Davies listened with the phone pinned to his ear.

'It's me... Annie,'

'Morning, Annie,' snapped Davies. 'I'll be in the office shortly. Is everything okay?'

Annie replied, 'I don't think so, chief inspector. I've got hold of the 'phone records. Chief Inspector Churchill seems to spend a lot of time ringing the bookies. In fact, to be honest with you, it adds up to about an hour a day.;

'How many calls?' asked Davies.

'Depends,' replied Annie. 'But at least a dozen a day by the look of it. What do you want me to do with the 'phone bill, sir?'

'Keep hold of it for now, Annie. I'll take a look myself shortly.'

'There's another thing, Barney's approached me and expressed concerns that Mister Churchill is in charge of the shop whilst you two are gallivanting on this hush-hush enquiry that everyone knows about, sir. He's worried the wheel might fall off while you're away.'

'I'll talk to him, Annie. You can run the place without help from anyone,' said Davies. 'I have total confidence in you but you need to make a big decision now.'

'Yes, I know. I've been thinking about it. I've done it. The report is ready for you. I thought you would want it before you went on your jaunt with the chief.'

'Good! I'll be across shortly, Annie. There's a couple of things I need to do in the office.'

The 'phone went dead and Davies closed it into his trouser pocket. Then he reached for his leather jacket and slid into it preparing to leave. Thinking hard, oblivious to his surroundings, Davies was playing chess in a far away place in his mind. He was planning the moves, chasing the pieces in his mind, and deciding what to do next.

Glancing up, Davies looked directly into the eyes of Bill Baxter and Archie Campbell.

Ignoring them for a moment, he selected a slice of bread, chased round the remnants of his breakfast, and enquired, 'I need to be back in the office pretty soon. All kinds of stuff to sort out. I'm off to the big city with the boss.'

'Mmm...' responded Bill. 'Enjoy.'

Davies leaned across the table and captured Archie's attention with, 'Now then, Archie. The dog track, what exactly happened at Crillsea dog track?'

That afternoon, Ted Barnes drove Tom's sleek-looking black Jaguar to the outskirts of Epsom with Davies in the front seat and Tom in the rear.

Dressed smartly in his uniform, Tom handed over an email to Davies who read aloud the directions to Barney. It wasn't long before they were close to the M25 motorway and the network of roads that led to the heart of the capital: London.

Steering the chief's Jaguar down a long red gravel drive towards a large detached country house, Barney mentioned to his passengers how the house was more akin to a large country hotel than a domestic residence. The house looked compact but it soon became apparent it was much larger than first thought.

Here and there, they could see the occasional couple strolling with dogs, or was it patrolling with dogs, suggested Davies.

But, nearer to the entrance, two men dressed in grey suits and equipped with radios stood in a parking area and directed them to a vacant space.

The chief opened his door to step onto the colourful gravel when one of the men in a grey suit welcomed him with, 'Sir Thomas, Commander Pape awaits you in the drawing room. My colleague will escort you and your party, sir.'

'Thank you,' replied Sir Thomas as the three policemen allowed themselves to be ushered into the large imposing building.

Commander Pape, perhaps mid forties or thereabouts, slightly built with a deeply furrowed brow above a pointed nose, steadied his posture with a black ebony walking stick topped with a silver rose as he stood waiting for his guests.

The room was decked with fine leather armchairs, a deep pile carpet, and a bay window that looked out across an expanse of lawn inhabited by a gathering of secret squirrels. But one part of the room was given over to a sizeable mahogany table surrounded by upright contemporary office chairs that signified business. Upon the table was set a tray laden with glasses and a crystal decanter full of water and there were a series of ink blotters and lined paper evenly spaced where the assembly might sit. A huge television set occupied one end of the table and, on the wall above a resplendent Adams fireplace, a portrait of Her Majesty Queen Elizabeth the Second hung from a velvet cord. And to finish the decor a fine walnut table adorned the area beneath the bay window. Upon the table sat a chess board and all the pieces positioned ready to play.

When the men from Crillsea entered, Commander Pape stepped forward, extended his hand in warm welcome, and declared, 'Ahh! Chief Constable Sir Thomas, how good of you to come at such short notice.' Gesturing Barney and Davies, Commander Pape continued, 'And your colleagues, of course. Please do join us. Sherry gentlemen or would you prefer coffee? Tea perhaps?'

Davies swapped an approving glance with Barney whilst Sir Thomas responded, 'Coffee by three will fine, thank you, Commander.'

'Of course, wouldn't you know it,' smiled Commander Pape.

'And iced water, sir, if that's possible,' intervened Davies.

Sir Thomas threw an enquiring glance at Davies who responded with a low whisper, 'To keep your temperature down, Tom.'

There was a double tap of a walking stick on the carpeted floor and a white-coated steward appeared at the commander's shoulder within seconds.

'More coffee all round, Jeremy, if you please,' instructed the commander. 'And some ice cubes, wouldn't you know it.'

Jeremy nodded and retired as silently as he had arrived whilst Davies took in their prestigious surroundings.

There was a quietly discerning wave from the immaculately dressed Al Jessop sat in an armchair by the window sipping his coffee and Davies smiled in acknowledgment.

Unusual, thought Davies. You can usually hear Al Jessop before you see him. I wonder why he is so quiet.

In the time honoured traditions of a working partnership, Davies glimpsed at Barney and threw a slight nod in the direction of Al Jessop.

The acknowledgement from the balding Barney was barely noticeable.

A man in a grey suit tapped Commander Pape on the shoulder and whispered in his ear causing the commander to address his guests.

'Please forgive me, gentlemen,' advised the commander. 'The admiral requires my presence. Please excuse me for a moment, won't you. Help yourselves to savouries. The briefing begins in five minutes time.'

With a pleasant smile, Commander Pape left the room.

'You'll be the Chief of Detectives,' boomed an American voice emanating from a huge man who appeared to be in his early fifties.

'No such rank in the United Kingdom, sir,' offered Davies. 'I am, however, appointed senior investigating officer under the command of my chief constable. And you, sir, you are...?'

'Brandon Douglas! C.I.A. Recently retired but recalled out of Langley, Virginia: the good old U. S. of A. I'm senior field agent, Europe, by the way. And you are...?'

'Detective Chief Inspector Davies King,' announced Davies before introducing his colleagues. 'And this is Detective Sergeant Ted Barnes and, of course, Sir Thomas Daniels: our chief constable.'

Brandon shook hands vigorously with everyone present and stated, 'You Brits are last to arrive to see my peep show. The police from France, Holland, Italy, and Germany are already here.'

Sir Thomas said, 'Good, as arranged. And the Garda Síochána from Dublin?'

'Those Irish guys are playing small talk with Mossad in the next room,' revealed Brandon.

'Mossad?' queried Sir Thomas, visibly astounded. 'Mossad? You must be joking?'

Brandon explained, 'HaMossad leModi'in uleTafkidim Meyuchadim to be precise, chief. Or if you prefer the Arabic, *al-Mōsād lil-Istiḫbārāt wal-Mahāmm al-Ḥaṣṣah*. Either way, it's the national intelligence agency of Israel. They're responsible for intelligence collection and covert operations.'

'Covert ops?' remarked Davies. 'I thought this was an international task force set up to co-ordinate enquiries into a couple of murders in Dublin and Amsterdam. What the hell has Israel got to do with all this?'

'No idea, but that's on my board, Davies,' advised Sir Thomas. 'And I didn't invite them. I'll deal with the politics, you investigate the murders. As agreed!'

Davies nodded but Barney ran his hand through thinning hair and intervened with, 'Bizarre start to a weird day if you ask me. Mossad, as far as my limited experience is concerned, is suspected of targeted state sponsored killings and paramilitary activities beyond Israel's borders.'

'I'm beginning to understand why Al Jessop is watching and not speaking,' said Davies.

Nodding and smiling conspiratorially at the same time, Barney replied, 'That might explain why the deputy of MI6 appears to be adopting the political interface.'

'Why's that?' asked Sir Thomas. 'I'm not with your train of thought, Barney.'

'Oh, nothing to worry about, sir,' offered Barney with a demur smile. 'But Mossad are committed to protecting Jewish communities worldwide. Did you know the director of Mossad reports directly to the Israeli Prime Minister?'

'Mmm... Politics!' mused Sir Thomas.

Brushing past the three police officers, Brandon offered, 'Well someone invited them to the show, Mister Chief Constable, because they were here when I arrived this morning and they've been with Commander Pape and the admiral all day. Good friends by the look of it.'

'The admiral?' enquired Sir Thomas.

'Who's the admiral? Another seaman with a rusty boat! What's going on?' asked Davies.

'My cinema show is going on, Mister King,' disclosed Brandon. 'In five minutes. Come on. Take a seat.'

'C.I.A.! Central Intelligence Agency?' probed Davies. 'Tell me, Brandon, what does the C.I.A. do when it's at home?'

'All kinds of everything,' cracked Brandon attempting to break free from the group.

But Davies caught his elbow politely and said, 'No, tell me. I really need to know you see.'

Responding with a glance at his wristwatch, Brandon replied, 'We're responsible for providing national security intelligence assessment to senior policymakers mainly using covert psychological techniques, cyber methods, and social warfare. That's what the good book says. In a nutshell, we carry out intelligence gathering operations and report to the Director of National Intelligence.'

'But why are you here, Brandon?' enquired Davies. 'You introduced yourself with the revelation that you were recently retired and had been recalled to duty, as it were. Why is this, Brandon Douglas?'

'They couldn't find anyone better,' chuckled the American.

Intervening Barney suggested, 'Whilst away from home the C.I.A. oversees and sometimes carries out covert activities at the request of the President of the United States, isn't that correct, Mister Douglas?'

'Well...' began Brandon.

'If I remember correctly,' continued Barney, 'The C.I.A. is often used for intelligence-gathering instead of the American military. You guys succeeded the Office of Strategic Services: the OSS, which was formed during World War II to coordinate espionage activities.'

'Do you know something, Sergeant Barnes,' suggested Brandon. 'You're absolutely right. Will you excuse me for a moment?'

Brandon Douglas was abruptly gone from the control of Davies King, gone from the discussion, gone from the trio gathered with their questions and puzzles.

A moment or so elapsed before Sir Thomas quietly declared, 'Spies everywhere! Not what I ordered. I don't like this one little bit, gentlemen.'

'Are you thinking what I'm thinking?' asked Barney.

'Is the sherry bugged?' suggested Sir Thomas sarcastically.

'Probably,' replied Davies. 'We're being set up!'

Al Jessop looked across the room into the eyes of Davies King and then lifted his right hand to his face and caressed his earlobe three times.

Davies nodded his head in silent acknowledgement.

The hands on Brandon's wristwatch ticked on.

'Joking apart, be careful what you say,' smiled Davies to Sir Thomas and Barney. 'There's bugs everywhere apparently.'

The coffee arrived. Iced water was taken. A sherry or two was poured and delegates took their seats at the table when Commander Pape returned with a small group of men, and a particular man who was dressed in a naval uniform.

The naval man had grown to be of average height and was of slim build. His hair was greying and swept back in a well groomed manner. Perhaps he was approaching his sixtieth birthday, it was difficult to tell because his face was tanned and he seemed physically fit and well kept. The most prominent thing about him, thought Davies, was the row upon row of medal ribbons adorning his uniform. And the uniform worn was that of a naval officer of the rank of admiral.

The admiral's bushy eyebrows dominated his face and his hooded dark eyes automatically discreetly scanned the room and penetrated each face as he took a seat close to the table.

The man with the crow like face bobbed his head to Commander Pape who took centre stage and spoke to his guests.

'Thank you. For the purposes of our conference here today, I will be acting as the political interface between this task force and your various governments. Sir Thomas will lead and head the enquiry and, when and if appropriate, will deal with press and media enquiries and will co-ordinate all actions by police services throughout Europe and elsewhere. He has selected Detective Chief Inspector King to lead the criminal enquiry and this will focus specifically on the gathering of evidence for respective coroners and the formulation of legal proceedings should that prove to be the case. You will see that the case is well and truly solved, wouldn't you know it, gentlemen. It is merely a case of locating the offender, assisting Sir Thomas and Chief Inspector King in securing evidence for the coroner, and ensuring that any political problems brought to our attention are dealt with expeditiously.'

Davies shuffled uneasily on his seat and felt Sir Thomas's eyes engage his as the chief's desire for discipline became apparent.

Barney scowled, wiped an imagined problem from his face, and allowed his hand to massage the point of his nose and the curve of his chin as he listened curiously to what was being said.

There was a shared glance of displeasure between Barney and Davies and then Commander Pape stepped aside and introduced the American.

'Gentlemen, I now hand you over to Brandon Douglas who is an American law enforcement officer who was in Amsterdam when one of these murders took place, wouldn't you know it. With the help of colleagues from Ireland and the Netherlands, and together with his own footage taken on the day, he has prepared this presentation for you.'

Ushering in Brandon, Commander Pape stepped away leaving the American in charge.

Barney whispered to Davies from the side of his mouth, 'If he says, wouldn't you know it, one more time I'll...'

Nodding, Davies raised a finger to his lips.

Brandon continued his spiel, 'Beside each blotter on the table in front of you is a file containing the current state of play. Times, dates, places, primary eye witnesses, secondary witnesses, forensic reports, details of the policing enquiries to date. I'll run through this film coverage we've put together and then we'll focus on what we need to do to find this man.... Conor O'Keeffe.'

There was a murmur of approval and Brandon continued, 'You'll find his photograph on the front page of the file and we need to find him as soon as possible and before he commits another murder.'

Switching the television on, Brandon mastered the remote control and waited for the picture to flicker onto the screen.

Then, sliding onto a seat, Brandon sat down and in silence the gathering watched a mixture of CCTV images, still shots and video coverage of recent events in Dublin and Amsterdam showing a lady from Eire, a Dutchman, a Japanese tourist, and a Dubliner shot down in cold blood at various locations.

The minutes flew by and the images trickled across the screen before Brandon stood and said, 'There we have it. Any questions?'

An Italian policeman asked, 'All the murders seem to have been committed using handguns, 38 or 45 calibre, I presume?'

'No,' asserted Brandon. 'They are all 22 calibre, sir. It's the preferred close quarter assassination weapon and ammunition of our enemy because of the accuracy gained from the weapon. A 38 or 45 might go right through you and out the other end. A 22 from a close distance will explode inside your skull and blow your brains to pieces.'

The Italian policeman nodded and said, 'Thank you for the graphic detail. I just wanted to raise the question of what our adversary might arm himself with; thank you.'

Al Jessop raised his hand and acquainted the audience, 'For the information of the gathering, I'm Detective Chief Superintendent Al Jessop, Metropolitan Police Flying Squad. Mister Douglas, if you were so close to the action with your camera in Amsterdam, why didn't you make a challenge? I presume you were armed at the time?'

'No I wasn't armed, Mister...

'Jessop! Al Jessop!'

'Mister Jessop,' continued Brandon. 'I was on holiday with my wife and I sure as hell didn't want to become the one hundred and third star on the Memorial Wall at Langley.'

'That makes sense, Mister Douglas,' responded Jessop. 'But did I hear you say you were retired and recalled?'

'It's Brandon, and you know how it is. It's often a case...'

Interrupting swiftly, Commander Pape was suddenly up on his feet and dominating with, 'Chief Superintendent Jessop, sometimes the best man to do a presentation is the man best in place to explain things as they happened. And, in any event, Mister Jessop, I'm sure you'll agree that law enforcement officers never retire. They just take the occasional long holiday. Can we move on to the capture scenario we need to discuss?'

'No,' persisted Jessop. 'Watching the television confirms your man, O'Keeffe, is definitely wanted for questioning in connection with the killing of Callum Reece but we're talking about four killings in total. And the man you're trying to hang out to dry didn't commit all four murders. Yeah, four murders, and I want to know what the motive is for each one.'

'Hear, hear!' added Davies standing in support. 'It's not just about who did it, Commander Pape. It's about why they did it and fancy films, covert cameras and public CCTV don't give you those answers. It might be what your so-called American law enforcement officer does back home in the States but it's not how we do things in England.'

Commander Pape declared, 'I agree but Mister Douglas is a world authority in tracking offenders down using profile techniques and a network of highly specialised and exceptional informants. You see, we need to find our offender first and then soak up the evidence left behind him. Sir Thomas, don't you agree?'

Analysing the question for a moment, Sir Thomas studied Al Jessop's posture and then shared a quizzical look with Davies.

There was a tiny overt threat of an unknown kind twisted in the commander's voice when Pape challenged, 'You are the Home Office appointee in this matter, aren't you, Sir Thomas?'

Slowly, but deliberately, Sir Thomas rose to his feet and answered, 'No, I don't agree with you, commander. Using my contacts in Europe, I have assembled a team of hand-picked police officers experienced in murder enquiries.'

He nodded to officers from Italy, Germany and France then continued, 'You appear to have invited one or two others from, shall we say, government agencies. Government agencies that have a completely different idea of policing to the majority gathered here. And, with respect, I intend to run a murder enquiry properly....'

With an ironic rebuke in his voice, Sir Thomas added, 'Or not at all.'

There was a sideways glance from the commander to the man dressed in the admiral's uniform but the admiral remained as a statue, stern and unmoved, cold, and unapproachable.

'Very well,' considered Commander Pape. 'A murder enquiry it is then, wouldn't you know it. But let us move on and assign each other some tasks that will lead to the man's arrest and...'

'In that case, I will take the floor,' intervened Davies King. 'For I am the senior investigating officer here and I will make such decisions...'

The man in the admiral's uniform raised his hand, stood and announced, 'Detective Chief Inspector King, please sit down a moment and let me come clean with you.'

'About time,' remarked Davies giving way. 'And you are?'

'Who I am is unimportant, Chief Inspector King. I am the man who is charged with the prevention of the assassination of the Head of our Sovereign State and the Commonwealth of Great Britain.'

There was a ripple of astonishment and shock through the room before the admiral continued, 'Yes, we are looking for a man whom we believe to be in possession of plans to assassinate our royal family. That is why Commander Pape wishes to focus specifically on the capture aspect of this investigation. I suggest we take a short break for coffee before turning our attention to the matter in hand and addressing the implications of our immediate requirements.'

Al Jessop protested. 'You mean we've all been brought here under false pretences?'

The admiral replied, 'Not quite, Mister Jessop. You've all been invited through a form of selection that has taken place.'

'How strange,' uttered Davies.

'Yes, we need professionals who can extract information... Steward!' cried Commander Pape.

The white-jacketed Jeremy moved in smoothly with a fresh trolley laden with hot coffee and another jug of iced water. The trolley seemed to force a wedge between the parties and Davies retreated to his seat.

Once the coffee was poured and shared, Davies used his eyes to engage and enlist Barney and Al Jessop to his side.

Jessop imparted to Davies, 'They'll never find him like this. There's something wrong here.'

'Agreed,' side-mouthed Davies conspiratorially.

'I think they want to know where he is, that's all,' declared Jessop.

'Agreed again!' declared Davies.

Finishing his coffee, Davies crept up to the shoulder of the admiral and quietly demanded, 'Why didn't you tell us the truth from the word go?'

'We need you all here and we don't want any intrusions or leaks to the press,' explained the admiral as he delicately stirred his coffee. 'The world and his dog will be all over us with their cameras and microphones irrespective of any legal powers we may invoke to try and prevent them. Can you imagine the mayhem this news is likely to cause to the royal family to say nothing of the reaction that can be expected from the British people and the media?'

'Depends on whether the British people are interested in the monarchy, sir,' suggested Davies. 'Some people couldn't care less about the royals. Your job is saving the royal family from an assassin. My job is saving the British people from themselves.'

'Sir Thomas!' called the admiral.

Commander Pape stepped carefully to the admiral's side.

Distracted for only a moment, Sir Thomas glanced across and then connected with, 'Can I help?'

The admiral explained, 'I left instructions with the Home Office that I would only deal with people of senior rank who had high level security clearance. This man obviously hasn't!'

'Oh dear,' smiled Sir Thomas. 'The flippant, Davies King, I suspect. Do forgive me, Mister.... Well, that's the difference between us, isn't it, Mister.... I really am Sir Thomas Daniels and you... Oh, you haven't a name, have you? You see, you and Commander Pape know who we are but we don't know who you are so when asking questions of us one needs to get a grip of reality.'

'Crow! Admiral Crow!' He snapped, offering his card. 'I am the head of British Intelligence. My card!'

'I would never have guessed,' smiled Sir Thomas wryly. 'And I can't believe you guys run around with business cards.'

'We don't normally,' confirmed the admiral. 'Indeed, we don't even carry identity cards but on occasions such as these there is always a use for them.'

Davies snatched the card from the chief's fingers, read the words, and passed it down the line to Barney and Jessop.

'This was dropped on me recently, gentlemen,' explained Admiral Crow. 'It's a hogwash of a job I can tell you. My problem is I don't actually have any political masters although my service is generally seen as having a tad degree of responsibility to the Foreign Office and the government of the day as opposed to a political ideology or party. In this case, Whitehall are all over me, and some. This is a fast mover and we need to be ahead of the game, not behind it.'

'Royal family assassination bid you say?' enquired Al Jessop mooching into the group. 'Sorry, I've been eavesdropping - a task you will be well aware of - but tell me this if you can?'

'Go on,' responded Admiral Crow.

'Where's the Royalty and Diplomatic Protection Group? Where's the Met Special Branch? The anti terrorist branch? MI5 for that matter? Some of my colleagues in Scotland Yard work with British Intelligence every day of the week. Where are they?'

Admiral Crow fell silent but sparked back to life when Davies King said, 'Seems to me, Admiral Crow, that someone is leading somebody up the garden path. It's not time for a coffee break. It's time for some home truths and I want to look at the source of your television documentary.'

Glancing at those around him, the admiral announced, 'We need to find Conor O'Keeffe before he destroys the world!'

'Not just the royal family?' queried Sir Thomas.

There was a shake of the head form Admiral Crow.

'You said this O'Keeffe man had plans,' reminded Davies.

'Correct,' acknowledged the admiral bluntly.

'Who put this party together the Home Office or yourselves?' asked Davies.

'The Cabinet Office - C.O.B.R.A.,' replied Admiral Crow. 'The Cabinet Office Briefing Room.'

'Who runs the show there?' asked Barney.

'The make-up of the Cobra committee depends entirely on the nature of the issue,' disclosed the admiral. 'The name refers to the location of the meeting, not a particular set of people.'

'We know well of Cobra,' intervened Sir Thomas. 'Who sat round the big table, admiral? The prime minister and...?'

Admiral Crow fell silent.

'Were you there? Did you take part in the meeting?' asked Sir Thomas belligerently.

Only closed lips from Admiral Crow.

Davies challenged Crow and revealed, 'Watching Brandon's film we saw the helicopter images of a canal boat approaching a flower market and then the man, O'Keeffe, doing the shooting and escaping into the alleyways of Amsterdam.'

'Correct again,' confirmed Admiral Crow.

'As a result of information received and enquiries made, I can tell you, Admiral Crow, that I have a memory stick recovered from our police area and I can positively link the memory stick to Conor O'Keeffe. Interested?'

Visibly shaking with relief, Commander Pape intervened and instructed forcibly, 'I'll need details of your source; the full circumstances involved, and the memory stick in our possession before the day is out.'

'Really!' remarked Davies.

'Who is your source? Human intelligence, I presume?' persisted Commander Pape.

'Oh just a network of highly specialised and exceptional informants, commander. Nothing to write home about.'

Al Jessop tried to hide his smirk, Barney smoothed the hair that wasn't there and the chief stood like an iceberg.

'Where's the memory stick now?' demanded the commander.

'Memory stick!' said Davies. 'I don't know what you mean. I didn't mention memory stick, did I, chaps?'

The chief constable's head shook negatively from side to side quickly followed by the heads of Al Jessop and Ted Barnes.

'Silence, commander,' ordered the admiral. 'You have us under the cosh, Mister King. Please proceed with your interesting departure relative to found property, and your obvious panache in dealing with informants.'

Davies declared, 'You've wasted all day messing us about and leading us up the garden path. Now chill out, Mister Head of MI6. Someone, maybe you, maybe one unknown to us at the moment is giving us the run around. Well, I don't run around for you or anyone else.'

'Davies!' warned Sir Thomas.

Ignoring the intervention, Davies continued, 'The memory stick is under lock and key and that's where it's staying.'

'Have you interrogated the stick?' queried Admiral Crow.

'No! Not yet, but I will,' explained Davies.

'Don't, it will self destruct,' informed the admiral. 'No, let me have it now and we'll take it from there.'

'The hell you will,' interjected Sir Thomas. 'That is completely out of the question. Davies King is in charge of the evidence. I'm running the show and you are the political interface. Butt out, Admiral Crow. Butt right out. Report that to Cobra if it ever existed today.'

The admiral moved a step away thinking but then turned and said, 'I owe you the ability to take control of the memory stick and secure it for eternity.'

'No,' responded Davies. 'It's an exhibit in a multiple murder enquiry and I'm in charge. I'll take responsibility.'

'Then may the Lord help us,' replied Admiral Crow. 'I do not think we can do business with you, Mister King.'

'Not my problem,' replied Davies, 'Yours! But tell me this, how do you know the memory stick will self destruct if it's tampered with?'

A question ignored and an uneasy shuffle divided the group.

'I can arrange a court order to secure the evidence to my custody,' warned the admiral.

Ignoring the threat, Davies casually turned to Barney and instructed, 'Barney, do me a favour. Ring our contact in the Crillsea Chronicle and issue a press release. Tell them our chief constable, Sir Thomas Daniels, has been appointed head of an international task force assigned to investigate a significant international criminal offence following the discovery of a mysterious piece of computerised software in Crillsea. I want it in the evening editions tonight and the morning nationals tomorrow. Let them speculate as much as they want. No admissions, no denials, just mystery. Once the press take it the radio and television will soon follow suit. No-one wants to miss out. Barney, tell them the software has been placed in a bank vault in Crillsea. Then leak that it's a memory stick. No further details will be given to the press.'

'Will do,' acknowledged Barney. 'We playing chess again?'

'Oh, and Barney,' said Davies. 'Get Felix on the 'phone. I want armed surveillance teams on the banks from tomorrow morning. First thing until further notice.'

Admiral Crow nodded understanding.

'That's Crillsea covered, Admiral Crow,' suggested Davies. 'Now I want to see the tapes that were used to make up Brandon's television show. I want to see, touch, and read all the statements made by witnesses in Dublin, Amsterdam and anywhere else that's involved. And I want a major incident room set up right here right now.'

Davies glanced at Al Jessop who nodded in satisfaction.

There was an exchange of glances before Admiral Crow suggested, 'Perhaps I was wrong about you, Mister King. Maybe we can do business with you after all.'

'That's good to know,' countered Davies. 'I'm used to dealing with people who don't play by the book... Al?'

'I'll set the Incident room up. We'll need readers and screens and...'

'That won't be necessary, chief superintendent,' interjected the admiral. 'We have those facilities here already. I'll take you there soon.'

Nodding, Al Jessop smiled in appreciation.

Carefully studying his audience, the admiral suggested, 'Gentlemen, I do believe that one of the privileges of my station in life is the ability to open the bar here when necessary. Would anyone care to join me in a drink? I think it's time we dispensed with the pleasantries and got down to business. Put simply, we've made a complete cock up of this conference and set off completely on the wrong foot. It's time to make amends and put the record straight.'

'Who's round is it?' enquired Davies.

'Oh for you, Mister King, I think we can even rustle up a glass of Magno,' chuckled the admiral.

'You've done your homework then,' suggested Davies.

'Have we indeed, Mister King? We seem to have made a mess of things so far, and you are right...'

'Right about what, admiral?' queried Davies.

'Things are not always what they seem to be. Come, gentlemen, follow me.'

An adjournment followed; a bar was opened, an incident room was revealed, and the business of the conference began.

That night the printing presses rolled.

Paper was selected, cut, sized and schemed to the last fraction of an inch, planned to perfection with its computerised system and text box headlines in varying coloured texts and fonts. And the Crillsea Chronicle computerised library of images was opened and a suitable photograph of the chief constable chosen and uploaded to the file. Then the ink was transferred to paper and the process gradually but deliberately became a newspaper.

The Chronicle was folded and stacked to await collection and delivery by the network of wholesalers who carried the news to the retailers of Crillsea, and beyond.

A telephone call was made from one editor to another; an investigative journalist was queried, questions were asked, telephone calls were made. And then the matter was discussed with a broadcasting company. The story was rewritten and images of Crillsea and its chief constable were sought and brought to life on a television screen.

Suddenly it was news. It was open news and possibly a long running developing story because the police source didn't want to be drawn on the subject, and didn't seem to object to the mounting speculation.

And somewhere in the south of England, Conor O'Keeffe caught sight of a bill board and bought a newspaper.

Moments later, Conor stepped into a telephone kiosk, dropped a coin, dialled a number, and spoke into the mouthpiece, 'Crillsea! It's in the news... Crillsea!'

*

Chapter Thirteen

~ ~ ~

Wednesday.
Crillsea.

The deserted car park heard only the soft slither of her shoes treading on the dry tarmac leading to the entrance of Crillsea police station. With a slight push, Detective Inspector Annie Rock was through the revolving doors and inside the building.

The station sergeant merely waved nonchalantly as she stepped across the concourse and into the depths of the office block. 'Where is everyone, Tom?' she enquired.

'Job on!' hailed Tom, the sergeant. 'Claudia has the details but I can tell you what's going on and...' The telephone on Tom's desk rang and he answered it immediately whilst articulating, 'Sorry, ma'am. I've got to take this.'

Waving in mild understanding, Annie offered a slight grin before bounding up the stairs, two at a time, into the Criminal Investigation Department. The sound of a dozen telephones ringing on empty desks welcomed her in unison. Shaking her head dispassionately, Annie rattled a door and promptly burst into Claudia Jones's office.

'The office is deserted, Claudia. What the hell's going on?' she enquired feverishly.

'You mean Chief Inspector Churchill didn't inform you, Inspector Rock?' asked Claudia peeking from her computer screen.

'No! Not a phone call. Not even a note on the desk. Is it a murder? Has everyone been called out?' probed Annie anxiously.

'Goodness gracious, no, inspector,' answered Claudia reaching from her desk to switch the kettle on.

'Sergeant Barnes telephoned last night and on the instructions of the chief constable every bank in Crillsea, Crillsea Meadows and Tevington must be watched from nine this morning.'

'The whole division?' quizzed Annie.

'Yes, indeed. The balloon's gone up, as they say,' replied Claudia. 'All the firearms officers have been called out.'

'Firearms? Oh dear! It must be a bank robbery? Is it a tip off from one of Barney's snouts?'

'Now how would I know that, Inspector Rock?' chastised Claudia. 'All I know is that Detective Constable Webster is with Chief Inspector Churchill and Constable Tait is your only detective source today because he's not yet firearms trained is he.'

Gathering mugs, milk and sugar from a cupboard, Claudia waited for the water to boil and remarked, 'And apart from that, young Mister Tait is new to the office. He' still learning the job.'

'Wonderful!' cracked Annie. 'So that's it. They've left me to carry the can as usual. An armed surveillance operation, I presume, and I'm left wet nursing everything else. Who's the target, Claudia? I'm guessing they have a suspect to follow.'

'I am instructed by Chief Inspector Churchill,' declared Claudia haughtily, 'To offer you his sincere apologies since he has been out most of the night arranging observation points for the banks. He has asked me to remind you that he has every confidence in your abilities to run the division with Detective Constable Tait and refers you to his mobile number should you have any queries.'

'Wow!' countered Annie with a curious scowl. 'What a spiel. Where did he get that from I wonder?'

Passing a newspaper across the desk, Claudia suggested, 'Have you seen today's front page, inspector?'

Seizing the Chronicle, Annie scanned the headlines and replied, 'Interesting, but not all of our banks have vaults. But hey, that explains everything. The chief constable is on the job and Davies and Barney are obviously up to their necks in it. When can we expect them back from London?'

'Later this morning, I suggest, inspector. Maybe this afternoon, who knows! They stayed overnight apparently,' revealed Claudia. 'Although knowing Chief Inspector King like I do one would never suggest setting your clock by him. He'll come back when he's good and ready that one. Mark my words, inspector. If he gets the bit between his teeth, well...'

Pouring coffee for the pair, Annie surmised, 'So, just me then.'

'Quite!' replied Claudia.

'Priorities, Claudia,' revealed Annie sugaring their coffee. She poured milk and took a sip. 'I need to step up to the plate as they say. What else is happening and where's Mark Tait?'

'The phones have never stopped ringing,' advised Claudia. 'I've routed the calls and done my best to pick them all up from here and take messages, pass them to Tom downstairs, and generally tried to keep on top of things without losing a grip, so far.'

'Well done, Claudia. Thank you. You should have called me earlier. I would have been in at eight had I known.'

'Oh, I'm used to things like this, inspector. This place grows on you after a while and you just get on with it. One day the office will burn down and we'll just reach for the fire extinguisher and carry on as if nothing had happened. But wouldn't you have thought Chief Inspector Churchill would have enlisted help from the uniform section?'

'Mmm...' remarked Annie. 'Did Chief Inspector Churchill leave his briefing notes anywhere, Claudia? I presume he briefed everyone?'

'Not that I'm aware of, inspector. Should he have?'

223

'When firearms are involved, yes,' counselled Annie. 'Everyone needs to know precisely where each other is and what to do if something goes wrong. And then there's rules of engagement, arcs of fire, line of fine, and all that gun stuff, they go on about. Weapon capability and who is carrying what.'

'Oh dear, I just type, make coffee and answer the telephones, inspector,' said Claudia. 'But it must be correct. I mean, he is in charge, isn't he?'

'Well, it's too late now, Claudia. What about Mark?'

'Oh sorry,' apologised Claudia, 'He's gone to a shop break-in on the main street.'

'Harbour Lane?'

'Yes, where else?' asked Claudia puzzled.

'On the same street as the bank job, Claudia! That's what else! Never mind, it's not your fault. When a firearms job goes down there's a tendency to control police movements into and out of the area. Too many police wander into firearms incidents without knowing what's going on. It's like a danger zone and the zone needs to be controlled by the fist of God!'

'God's in London with Sir Thomas and Barney,' offered Claudia sarcastically.

'Don't I know it,' sighed Annie.

Claudia passed Inspector Rock a slip of paper which contained details of the burglary locations and remarked, 'Actually, there's been three burglaries. I wrote them down… Here…' and then she stood up and approached a plant on the windowsill.

'Three!' exploded Annie reading the message. 'Three burglaries on the same street in one night? No way!'

Claudia concentrated on feeding a smidgen of water to her precious amaryllis before returning to her desk and replying, 'Well, I can assure you…'

'Yes, I'm sorry, Claudia. I didn't mean it like that,' answered Annie who then took a long drink of coffee. 'God, that's good strong caffeine and I think it might be a long day by the looks of things. Okay, if that's it I'll go and give Mark a hand. Three breaks in one night is not good for the crime figures and Davies will go mad if we're not chasing them up. Anything else boiling?'

'Nothing that won't keep, inspector,' suggested Claudia. 'Uniform are dealing with more than their fair share.'

There was a gentle thud against a window in the outer office that spooked Annie who shuddered, 'What the hell was that?'

Concentrating solely on her computer keyboard Claudia replied, 'Window cleaner!' Without looking up, her fingers scampered across the black and whites as she remarked, 'Once a month. It must be that time! I'll show your status as out on enquiries with Constable Tait, shall I?'

'Great! Please do! A window cleaner nearly makes me jump out my skin and I'm back to dealing with street crime.'

'Inspector....' admonished Claudia.

'I'm on my way,' admitted Annie. 'Harbour Lane, here I come!'

The telephone rang and was swiftly answered by Claudia who listened before advising, 'Of course, Chief Inspector King, I'll make sure the vehicle is circulated to all patrols including the surveillance team... Inspector Rock is here.... Yes, just a moment... Inspector Rock!'

Claudia shoved the hand piece though the air towards Annie who accepted it with a brief grin.

'Guv?' Annie queried. 'Where are you?'

'Annie, I'm in a country house on the outskirts of London. We've had a full English breakfast and a pot of piping hot coffee and I'm watching television and talking to detectives in Amsterdam on a video link.'

'Ahh tough, guv,' cracked Annie. 'I wouldn't put up with it if I were you. Bet it doesn't beat Bill's bacon butties at the Anchor?'

'Good point,' chuckled Davies. 'Look, we're on to something, Annie. We've just tied Conor O'Keeffe into another murder in Amsterdam. It's untelevised, not caught on CCTV, but the DNA from the victim matches him and there's a stolen motor bike outstanding. I'm sure O'Keeffe did the murder and used the victim's bike to make his escape. He could be anywhere in Europe but if he is in England he might still be riding it. Chief Superintendent Jessop is placing an 'All Ports Watch' on the motor bike and circulating Conor O'Keeffe's photo to all ports officers. It's in cyberspace now. I want you to be sure the surveillance team has details of the motor bike and photos of the suspect.'

'Will do, guv. Anything else?'

'He's armed and dangerous and needs to be dealt with accordingly,' advised Davies.

'Hey, I'm on the case,' replied Annie.

Claudia slipped Annie another piece of paper.

'Red Harley Davidson stolen Amsterdam, owned by murder victim, registration number...,' read Annie. 'Dutch plates.. Conor O'Keeffe wanted... Got it... Leave it with me..... Television? You nothing else better to do, chief inspector? Which soap you watching?'

'Well, if I told you I was watching a bank of TV screens showing both shootings and a ton of historic data from Dublin, Amsterdam, and elsewhere, you wouldn't believe it, would you, Annie?'

'Probably not,' replied Annie. 'No chess then?'

'Wait one,' explained Davies into the 'phone. He turned and spoke to Barney, 'Screen three, Dublin, Barney. The killing there, zoom in on the female victim. She's trying to say something.'

Barney nodded, nibbled into a slice of toast, slurped a mug of coffee, and adjusted the controls.

'The victim is Siofra O'Sullivan, I'm on it,' replied Barney.

'Sorry, Annie,' offered Davies on the 'phone. 'Just trying to get to grips with everything that's going on. Yeah, Mister Jessop has circulated the bike to the Ports so we should have a stop on it unless it's already through, of course.'

Al Jessop confirmed with a thumbs up.

Annie asked, 'You watching horse racing, guv?'

Davies cracked, 'This call is being monitored!'

'I'm gone!' giggled Annie. The line went dead and with a spin on her heel she turned but then went full circle and said, 'Claudia, have you just circulated those details on the radio net?

'Of course,' replied Claudia. 'Chief Inspector King so instructed.'

'They're right. You really do run the nick don't you!' suggested Annie.

'Of course,' concurred Claudia. 'Is your status correct, inspector? Or do you want me to change it?'

Spinning round again, Annie Rock was gone from the office. She snatched a quick glimpse of the window cleaner, smiled mischievously, and stepped down the stairs two at a time intending to join Mark Tait at the scene of a crime in Harbour Lane.

Skipping across the tarmac, she shelved the idea of driving to the scene. No, she decided to walk.

Meanwhile, Claudia tapped away on a keyboard, a dozen telephones rang waiting to be answered, and a window cleaner whistled quietly to himself as he wiped bird droppings from the second storey office block window ledge and carefully stepped down from his ladder to ground level.

In a country house on the outskirts of London, Davies cradled the telephone deep in thought as

Barney studied a television screen and awaited the arrival of more colleagues for a second opinion.

Not all shop windows in Harbour Lane were highly polished surfaces that caused the casual shopper to stop and admire their image in the reflection. Some were hidden by hardboard.

Behind one cut of hardboard, a slender hand rested casually on the butt of a pistol and then restlessly slid down the leather holster almost impatient; or was it perhaps nerves? It was hard to tell.

The hardboard protected the plate glass window of a temporarily boarded up three storey department store which awaited new owners, a new lease, and rejuvenation. But that wasn't surprising since it was located on Crillsea's Harbour Lane: the main street. And it was near the crossroads controlled by the traffic lights, opposite Crillsea's most prestigious bank.

Shoppers strolling along the footpath didn't realise there was a small hole drilled into the hardboard covering the window. Indeed, close inspection revealed that a knot of wood had been pushed through and lay on the floor between the wood and the glass. A drill had merely enlarged the hole, ever so slightly.

There was a slight cough from an armed surveillance officer behind the window in the shop. He and his colleague lay in wait, keeping watch and listening vigilantly to an ear piece linked to a radio system. One of the officers depressed a transmission switch on his radio and said, 'The Shop has eyes on the target premises and all is quiet.'

'Roger Shop from Premier,' radioed Felix.

On a stretch of barren land at the rear of the row of shops a blacked-out Transit van was parked. There were three more uniformed police waiting. They were armed with Glock semi-automatic pistols. One of the officers eased his firearm to the side when he radioed, 'Roger that, Premier... Red team in position.'

'Roger Red team!' from Felix.

And in a lane adjacent to Harbour Lane sat two Crillsea detectives. Drumming his fingers on the steering wheel of his squad car, Felix turned to Terrence Webster and asked, 'See anything, Webby?'

'No, sir,' replied Detective Constable Terrence Webster. 'Well, nothing out of place so far.'

A mobile 'phone rang.

'Could be bad information, I suppose,' offered Felix answering his 'phone. 'Yes, I'm Churchill..... Yes.... Look...'

Turning to Webby, Felix offered a half smile and then spoke into the 'phone. 'It's not convenient at the moment but I'll get back to you before the end of the week...' Felix turned his head slightly shielding the conversation and instructed, 'Just let it lie for the moment and go with the.... err... go with the order I placed this morning. I'll settle at the end of the week....' There was a pause whilst he seemed to take instruction and then he finished with, 'Yes, I promise...'

Snapping his 'phone shut, Felix revealed, 'Nothing important. It'll keep.'

Webby feigned disinterest as vehicles trundled slowly through the town centre and traffic lights played stop and go whilst a posse of armed officers surrounded the bank.

'All units, Crillsea,' blared the radio.

Felix's nimble fingers rushed to the volume control to soothe the noise from the set and prevent the sound escaping into the surrounding area.

'All units, Crillsea.... Stolen Amsterdam. a red Harley Davidson motor cycle...'

'Quality!' cracked Webby. 'A bike and a half that one And, come to think of it, I can't recall ever been asked to look for a bike stolen from the Netherlands .'

Felix scribbled down the number and then engaged the surveillance channel with, 'Premier to all eyes, keep a look out for a red Harley Davidson stolen Amsterdam, Dutch plates, may be connected with this operation. All eyes acknowledge.'

'There's one,' cracked Webby pointing to a vehicle as the surveillance team began to roll through their acknowledgements. 'Nah, it's red alright but it's a Honda... Sorry.'

A red Honda motor cycle carrying two riders drove passed the end of the road and turned off towards the harbour.

'Yeah, fishermen!' declared Webby when he realised one of the men had a couple of rods slung across his back.

'At least you saw it,' offered Felix. And then he transmitted, 'All eyes, all eyes, keep a sharp look out.'

The radio settled down and the wait grew into a long period of restless movement.

Meanwhile, Crillsea went about its business. There were postmen delivering mail, drivers carrying new supplies into shops, taxi drivers plying their trade dropping off and picking up passengers, and every now and again a motor bike would pass through the crossroads opposite the bank and a buzz of excitement would fill the air waves for a moment or two. There was nothing out of place in Crillsea town centre this morning, and the town hall clock, high and out of sight, lazily tolled the beginning of a new hour.

Daily routines were the order of the day for Annie Rock and Mark Tait as they too went about their regular practices of trying to detect comparatively minor crime in the area. They'd met, discussed the break-ins Mark was investigating, and then split up to make enquiries in the street. Now Annie was a block away from Mark with about ten shop doorways between them.

Walking towards the traffic lights and the bank, Annie pushed digits into her mobile, and waited for Mark to respond.

A red Harley Davidson motor bike on GB plates rounded the corner and stopped outside the bank.

There was a slide of a hand down a leather holster behind a piece of hardboard and a colleague cautioned, 'Take it easy. Deep breaths and don't forget the safety switch.'

'What's my line of fire?' a voice enquired.

'Just concentrate on the street ahead and worry about that later,' came the reply.

In the lane, Felix switched on the ignition of his car and throbbed the accelerator in anticipation, perhaps boredom.

Mark Tait crossed the busy street and answered his 'phone acknowledging Annie.

A Royal mail van pulled up outside a post box close to the bank. The middle-aged balding driver swung the door closed behind him and sauntered towards the bank hauling a sack of mail over his right shoulder.

Propping his Harley up onto its stand, the motor cyclist surveyed the street around him. With his black visor down across his face and wearing a set of one-piece black leathers, he looked like an alien of some kind; maybe even out of place as his eyes seemed to penetrate every nook and corner of the street. Tilting the wing mirror slightly, he studied himself in the reflection

'All eyes,' rattled the radio. 'This is Shop and we've got a live one in leathers outside the bank. He's a tall cool looking guy. Oh, maybe six three, I would say, and he's quite broad. His eyes are on stalks and he's looking all over the place. Stand by!'

Felix returned, 'Roger from Premier... All eyes we have a possible outside the target. Stand by!'

Then an old lady, perhaps in her seventies, bent down with her heavily laden shopping bags, and, aided by a gnarled walking stick, struggled across the road oblivious to the blaring traffic and a nearby pedestrian crossing.

With a ladder on the roof and a logo on the side, a window cleaner's van meandered down the road, gave way to the elderly lady and her shopping bags, and parked in a lay by outside the bank.

Simultaneously, a dark blue van arrived at the scene and a uniformed security guard abandoned his vehicle and made for the bank entrance. Held low by his side was a strong box that swung easily and lightly as he stepped onto the footpath and paused, waiting for the pedestrian traffic to clear the way for him.

'Stand by, all eyes,' transmitted Felix. 'Stand by, all eyes. We have a red Harley at the scene. British plates and the rider is in black leathers. He's a possible!'

Inside the bank, two more armed officers lay in wait. They were both wearing plain clothes. One sat at a desk behind the counter close to the bank vault; the other sat in the public area of the bank filling in an application form of some kind at an empty desk. They both heard Felix's radio transmission and waited amidst a gathering crowd of customers queuing at the counter.

Behind the hardboard, a finger depressed a radio transmitter and offered, 'This is Shop! Eyeball at the shop has a red Harley Davidson on the park and black leathers entering the building. I designate the subject *black black* Stand by, stand by, we have *black black* entering the target premises.'

'He'll have to take that crash helmet off when he goes inside,' remarked Webby to Felix.

'All eyes, I have control,' radioed Felix nodding in agreement. 'Suspect is in black leathers designated *black black*. All eyes stand by. Counter Clerk report.'

An officer inside the bank sat near the counter turned casually and engaged a motor cyclist wearing black leathers and a crash helmet. The surveillance officer depressed a hidden radio switch and coolly advised, 'This is Counter Clerk, I have eyeball on the subject. Clear the air.'

'All eyes, clear the air,' repeated Felix. 'Clear the air! Counter Clerk has control!'

The radio waves went silent when the motor cyclist entered the bank followed by a royal mail man, a bank security guard, and a little old lady struggling with her shopping bags.

And passing by all the time were a mixture of shoppers, customers, business people, and tourists filtering in and out of the area.

Cameras fixed to the bank security system angled and twitched slightly as they recorded the images of the customers coming and going, and recorded the movements of the motor cyclist as he reached inside his leathers.

Outside on the street, Annie asked, 'Mark! You listening to the radio?'

'Yeah,' acknowledged Mark Tait. 'I'll make for the bank.'

'No,' ordered Annie. 'Let the guns look after it. They're in control. Hold and wait.'

'I'll go closer,' replied Mark. 'I don't see our people.'

'No, stand fast!' cried Annie, concerned. 'Back off! It might be absolutely nothing.'

Inside the bank the motor cyclist joined a queue and withdrew a slip of paper from inside his leathers, and the postman meandered in with his bag of letters whistling and smiling and saying to the counter staff, 'Morning all!'

On the wasteland nearby, the engine of a blacked-out Transit van suddenly fired and then settled to idle as if ready to move at the slightest notice.

In Harbour Lane, the elderly lady with her shopping bags seemed to be having trouble climbing the steps into the bank and heard the soft voice of the security guard when he said, 'Can I help you, madam?'

'No, no, no,' she resisted.

'Oh, I insist,' countered the guard placing his hand on her elbow and guiding her up the steps. 'Here, let me help you. It's all part of the job.'

Inside the bank, the motor cyclist shuffled towards the counter where a young girl, wearing the a smile and the bank's uniform, sat dispensing cash and pleasantries in equal abundance. She eased forward and signalled those in the queue to move to one side as she attracted the motor cyclist's attention. 'Excuse me, sir,' she advised. 'You'll need to remove your headgear, sir. It's company policy I'm afraid.'

A CCTV camera tilted again, panned and zoomed as it policed the bank's marble concourse.

A bag of mail landed on a nearby counter with a final heave and a burst of laughter from a postman, 'I swear to God Almighty this bag gets heavier every day. Have your customers never heard of email?' Shaking his head, he pushed the bag along the counter towards the door into an internal office and announced, 'Sorry, ladies, I need a signature as usual.'

A clerk smiled and accompanied her demeanour with the words, 'Wait one, please, sir.'

The motor cyclist seemed not to hear and the bank clerk eased forward and repeated, 'I'll need to call security, sir, if you don't remove your helmet. I'm sorry. Perhaps you didn't hear me correctly?'

Suddenly stepping forward, the motor cyclist delved again into his leathers to the consternation of two plain clothes officers inside the bank.

'Counter Clerk has the eye,' whispered one of the officers into his radio. 'Come closer.... Come closer....'

Felix snatched his radio from its holding on the dashboard and yelled, 'Is it going down?'

'Stand by... Stand by...'

Felix radioed, 'Red team move to yellow prepare to deploy front and rear... Shop hold and wait... Premier will do a walk in...'

'A walk in?' queried Webby in the passenger seat. 'You don't mean...?'

'They need help in there. Let's go,' responded Felix crashing into first gear and weaving the car out of the lane. 'And we'll take closer order, young Webster. Besides that, I'll stretch my legs.'

Inside the bank a little old lady with a walking stick laboured gradually towards the counter with the kind assistance of a security guard and a crooked walking stick.

'Security?' exclaimed the girl behind the counter. 'That was quick. I've a customer wearing a crash helmet and I'm reluctant....'

The security guard grasped the problem immediately, swivelled round, and rattled, 'Oy, you. The helmet! Take it off! Understood?'

The motor cyclist began to slowly remove his helmet as he looked round behind him.

'No, you. Don't look round. Just take your helmet off.'

'Non comprende!' replied a Spanish accent, and then in a twist of broken English offered, 'Please, I'm losing my self and needing to be finding Tevington that is close by the sea.'

The security guard pointed to his own head and gestured the motor cyclist to remove his headgear saying, *'Si.... Ah Gracias, signor, muchas gracias senor.'*

The Spanish motor cyclist finally understood.

A helmet was removed and a radio transmitter was quietly depressed followed by the words, 'Hold... Hold.... False alarm... All clear.'

Retransmitting, 'Hold! All eyes hold to stand by,' Felix glanced at Webby and said, 'We'll still take a stretch of the legs though.'

Felix's mobile rang and he answered it gingerly. A second or two went by before he snarled, 'Not now. Give me time. I'll sort it today.'

Closing the 'phone with a *snap,* Felix offered a smile to Webby and said, 'Just a friend. It'll keep.'

'Some friend! Obviously not police, boss?' queried Webby.

'No, obviously not,' snapped Felix. 'What's it to you?'

Allowing his eyebrows to rise slightly, Webby offered a faint smile and tightened his seat belt.

Inside the bank, the security guard guided the lady with the shopping bags towards an internal door inside the building and engaged the bank clerk advising, 'This lady needs some medical care. She seems very ill. Can you open up and let me in?'

'I don't think we can,' replied the counter clerk. 'It's not usual. I mean, it's not usually the done thing. You people just slide the box over the counter and through the hatch and we slide it back when we're done.'

'Unless it's a big consignment,' suggested the guard.

'Err, no disrespect, guv,' interjected the postman. 'But I was here first and all I need is a signature and I'll be gone. So if you could just...' The postman produced a pen and a receipt book and offered it across the counter. There were no takers.

The security guard glanced scornfully at the mail man and instructed the bank clerk, 'Get the manager then, young lady. He knows me personally and apart from that...' He gestured to the elderly woman... 'She needs a doctor and he...' gesturing the postman... 'Can wait in line.'

A bank clerk's mind went into disarray.

'And I did just solve your problem even though it was just a little one,' suggested the guard with a charming smile.

Grinning politely, almost reserved, she offered, 'Okay, it might be best if I get Mister Rumsden, the manager.'

She turned away as an elderly lady dropped her shopping bags and cracked the guard's shin with her walking stick. 'Get your hands off me, young man. Just who do you think you are? I can manage without all this fuss!'

'Oh dear,' remarked the guard. 'You know, you look awfully pale. Perhaps you should take a seat.'

A walking stick lashed out again.

'Ouch!' cried the guard. 'That one hurt, you bitch!'

'Steady on, mate,' cautioned the postman stepping forward to intervene. 'No need to bully her. She's an old lady for God's sake.'

Suddenly the bank guard held up the strong box in his hand, pushed the postman away and cried, 'Back off!'

Plump, muddle-aged and wearing a dark pinstripe suit, Mister Rumsden arrived and promptly intervened with, 'Hey, I am the manager. What seems to be the trouble? What on earth is going on?

'I've come for the memory stick,' declared the guard.

'Pardon?' replied Mister Rumsden.

'The constellation!' urged the guard.

'I've no idea what you're talking about,' responded Rumsden.

'Let me through into the vault, Mister Rumsden. Head office want the memory stick under lock and key in London tonight.'

'Look, I really don't know what you're talking about I'm afraid,' disclosed a mendacious Mister Rumsden looking over his shoulder to try and attract the surveillance officer who was seated close to the vault.

'Then can I suggest you let me through and we'll both ring Head office and sort this out. It's just a two minute job. Put the stick in the cashbox and I'm gone, okay?'

Rumsden continued his deceit querying, 'Where did you get that uniform? You're not our usual contact!'

Pushing his way between the pair, the postman cheekily raised his receipt book and pen and broadcast, 'Look, if you can both keep your quarrelling until I'm gone that would be great. Just sign on the dotted line, Mister Rumsden, and I'm out of here.'

Whack! A crooked gnarled walking stick struck the guards' bone again.

'I don't like you,' yelled the shopping bag lady.

'Enough!' shrieked the guard. It was as if he had dropped his mask when he reverted to his native accent and said, 'Sure that's enough, so it is!'

'You're Irish!' cracked the surprised female bank clerk abruptly. 'Well, I never!'

'So you are,' acknowledged the bank manager flurrying his jacket lapels.

Close to the bank vault one of the surveillance officers radioed, 'Premier, do a walk in please. Looks like an argument developing near the counter and I don't want to blow my cover.'

'Roger! Premier attending,' replied Felix. 'Stand by, all eyes.'

Mark Tait intervened and offered, 'Inspector Rock, I can take that.'

'Who's that calling?' asked Felix. 'Tait? Get off this channel!'

Annie Rock radioed, 'Mark! Get out of there.'

Inside the bank, the security guard twisted an Irish tongue and insisted, 'Look, just let me in, why don't you? I'll take the memory stick and then I'm gone, so I am.'

Mr Rumsden scowled and said, 'Security! You're not Security. Who the devil are you?'

The female bank clerk moved behind her manager and discreetly pressed an alarm button situated on the underside of the counter.

Raising the strong box high, his arm outstretched, the security guard warned, 'I'm the man who's going to blow you all to kingdom come if I don't get that memory stick, so I am. There's a bomb in this box and if I let go of the handle it will detonate. Now get me the memory stick. Now!'

In Crillsea police station, a red light suddenly shone from a panel fixed to a wall in the control room.

Linda, a civilian clerk, lowered her headset briefly, swivelled in her chair, and said, 'Inspector Edwards, there's a personal attack alarm activated inside the bank in Harbour Lane. The alarm has been triggered from behind the counter which means...'

'I know what it means,' replied Edwards. 'Thanks, Linda. Log the time and push the response plan onto the screen.'

There was a rattle of fingers across the keyboard and Linda responded, 'I thought there was an operation ongoing there?'

Twenty five years of policing everything from a garden fete to a political party conference kicked in and caused Edwards to set down his pen and papers, scratch his nose, and deliver, 'Channel Six! Surveillance Channel. I have control!'

A digital map of the bank, the surrounding area, and Crillsea town centre appeared on the screen alongside a list of options to be considered by the control room commander.

Edwards leaned forward and hit a switch opening a radio channel to Felix Churchill. 'Command calling Premier... Calling Premier,' announced Edwards. 'Personal attack alarm sounding at your target. Situation required. Respond, over!'

'Premier responding! Last known a couple of minutes ago was a false alarm with good intent. I am attending scene to confirm. Standby!'

Considering the matter thoughtfully, Inspector Edwards relaxed into his leather swivel chair, scratched his nose, and asked, 'Linda, what time do you have for the alarm activation?'

'About thirty seconds ago,' replied the clerk checking her computer log.

'Thanks! Where's Annie Rock? What's her status?'

Interrogating her computer screen, Linda answered, 'Harbour Lane, burglary enquiries. She's on the same street, sir,'

Edwards fingered more buttons on the console and radioed, 'Command calling Inspector Rock... Personal attack alarm sounding Crillsea bank, Harbour Lane.... Attend as back up and report.... Possible false alarm... Repeat possible false alarm!'

Responding to the call, Annie transmitted, 'Roger, Command. Attending!'

Edwards radioed, 'I'm raising the level to amber until I have confirmation, understood?'

'Roger!' responded Annie.

Sighing, Edwards shook his head, and said, 'An alarm! Is it false, is it a joke or is it real? Hey, do we ever know?'

A row of lights flickered across his computer console as Edwards quietly instructed, 'Linda, I got a brand new detective chief inspector running an armed surveillance operation and according to the computer log, he's driving a car. He should be a passenger somewhere concentrating on the job, not on his driving. I'm calling an amber code on this one until we know more. Punch it up on the screen and follow the instructions.'

'Will do, sir' replied Linda. Hitting the keyboard, she radioed, 'All units, Crillsea, code amber, Crillsea bank..... Code amber!'

'Where's Davies King? Is he still absent?' enquired Edwards

There were further keyboard taps before Linda acknowledged with, 'Deployed to London, no return time, sir. There's a mobile number for him.'

'Wonderful!' sighed Edwards. 'At least we've got Annie and the firearms team. Linda, I don't like the time differential here. Ring the town. I want a defensive line at all major egress points just in case we're not dealing with a false alarm.'

'I'm following the plan, sir. Tango cars?'

'Yes! Traffic and anything else we've got out there.'

There was a crackle of static and a voice from the radio suddenly blurted loudly 'Code red! Crillsea bank! Code red!'

Inspector Edwards snatched the radio, swore under his breath, and radioed, 'Confirm, Premier! Code red Crillsea bank!'

In the bank, Felix was lying on the ground with the robber driving his foot into his shoulder blades and Felix Churchill's stomach pressed hard into the marble concourse with his hand outstretched trying to reach for a dislodged radio.

A uniformed security guard was holding a strong box outstretched in one hand whilst pointing a handgun into the face of a struggling crippled old lady who supported herself on a crooked walking stick.

There was a startled white shroud of terror on her face worsened only when the security guard glared into the eyes of the bank manager and threatened, 'You got five seconds or she gets it first, then him,' indicating Felix lying on the floor, 'And then you. The memory stick. Now or I'll blow this place into the good Pope's backyard, so I will.'

'I haven't got any memory stick,' revealed Mister Rumsden. 'I've heard the news but I haven't got the memory stick. It's not here.'

Detective Constable Webster stood close by and counselled, 'Take it easy now. I'm sure we can work this out without all this fuss.'

A scowl grew from the guard's face and burnt into Webby's eyes.

'Armed police! Freeze!'

The security guard turned slightly whilst pointing his gun directly into the old lady's face. The long smooth cylinder fixed to the barrel of the gun revealed the robber was using a silencer of some kind. The guard glimpsed towards a plain clothes detective standing by the counter crouched slightly with his handgun stretched out in front of him.

'Armed police! Freeze!' snapped another detective behind the counter close to the bank vault. 'Drop your weapon.'

Chuckling the guard replied, 'You won't shoot me. I'll drill this woman's head out before you even take the slack into the trigger.'

'I mean it,' countered the detective. The barrel of his gun waivered slightly as he spoke.

'You're bluffing and you know it,' said the security guard coldly. 'My advice to you is to lower your gun because I'm the one with the bead on the woman and a bomb in my hand…. And do you know something? If I don't get what I came for in the next thirty seconds we're all going to kingdom come.'

The detective's gun barrel shook.

Webby directed his speech to the armed surveillance officer when he declared, 'The bank is surrounded. He's going nowhere.' Then Webby offered to the guard, 'We can work this out you know.'

The guard's hand slashed through the air like a scythe. Pointing his gun straight towards Webby, he warned, 'You too! On your knees. Now!'

There was a gun slicing through the air from Webby to the old lady and back to the bank manager when the guard repeated, 'Now or one of these goes down!'

Webby knelt to the floor and felt a foot push him to the ground. His cheek slapped into the marble with a noisy *thud*.

Then the postman tried to retrieve his sack from the counter but suddenly heard an intimidating voice shout, 'And as for you, Mister Postie,' threatened the security guard. There was another *thud* when the handle of a gun smashed into the postman's skull and he fell to the ground, out of the game.

'Now then, Mister Rumsden,' said the guard bullying the bank manager. 'Open the vault and get me the stick.'

Barely audible sirens invaded the ear from afar when Rumsden offered, 'Just a moment. I need...'

'Now,' insisted the guard waving a bomb in his hand. 'If I let go of this handle you'll end up on top of the town hall clock, so you will.

Rumsden opened the safe and pulled out a few sacks and yelled, 'We don't have any memory stick. I don't know what you're talking about. Here, take this and go!'

A shot rang out muzzled only by the suppressor fitted to the gun and the woodwork behind the manager's head splintered in the explosion.

'The next one will be in your head!' threatened the guard.

'Okay, okay!' surrendered Rumsden. 'It's not in the vault. It's in the safe.'

The guard grasped the money bags and barked, 'Get the memory stick! You're running out of time and my hand is itching something terrible, so it is.' He swung the strong box loosely as a warning.

Webby whispered, 'Is that sirens?'

Felix stretched a hand out towards a radio which was transmitting a female voice, 'Code red, Crillsea bank. Tango one zero attend Tevington By-pass.' His fingers caught onto the edge of the radio and he began to claw it back towards him as the voice transmitted, 'Tango five seven attend Harbour Lane North. Tango Six Two take Harbour Lane South. Red team deploy. Firearms officers on scene... Exercise caution and...'

The guard's foot reached out and his toe hooked the radio towards him. He bent down, snatched the radio from the floor, and smirked at Felix. Turning, he walked towards the female bank clerk and caught sight of the alarm button fixed to the edge of the desk.

'You naughty girl,' laughed the guard.

She tried to bury herself into the marble when the guard approached and told her, 'Lucky this time.'

Suddenly, with a lengthy stride or two, the guard was out of the door and into the street with a gun tucked inside his belt and a strong box, a tiny memory stick, and three bags of money in his hands.

But waiting to greet him were an orchestra of sirens and a glut of blue flashing lights. The noise grew to a crescendo as the surrounding streets filled with police cars tightening the net.

Out of the blue, Mark Tait turned the corner and shouted, 'Oy, stand fast. Police!'

Throwing the strong box towards Mark, the guard snatched the gun from his belt as a group of armed police officers emerged from a shop opposite the bank and a Transit van bounced over wasteland and raced towards the scene.

Shielding his face with his hands, Mark brushed away the strong box which careered through the air and crashed onto the road.

Across the road, Annie shouted, 'No! No! Get back, Mark!'

Felix Churchill ran from the bank shouting, 'Take him down!'

Sprinting like a cheetah, Mark Tait threw himself towards the bank robber. There was a tussle and a wrestle and the two men rolled over and over in the gutter with the guard's gun dislodged from his hand and bank notes escaping from a canvas bag.

A fist flew and connected with a sickening crunch on bone and then there was a cry of pain and anguish followed by a kick and another flurry of fists.

Then there were more bank notes soaring into the air and hovering above the scene of two men rolling on the ground.

Two shots rang out when the security guard momentarily broke free and double tapped a couple of bullets into Mark Tait's chest from close range.

There was a terrifying scream from Mark Tait when the guard watched him drop to the ground like a lifeless sack of potatoes.

'Stand still, armed police,' filled the air as officers simultaneously emerged from the bank, the Transit van, and a shop.

'Freeze, armed police!'

'Stand still, armed police!'

'Halt or I'll fire!'

It was totally uncontrolled bedlam when the security guard dismissed the cries and spun round.

The passenger door of the window cleaner's van parked in the lay-by outside the bank opened and the security guard threw himself into the vehicle. With a squeal of tyres, the vehicle accelerated into the main road with the ladders bouncing from the roof and rattling onto the ground spilling and rolling in all directions.

And immediately Felix Churchill's plan misfired and laid itself bare. The officers couldn't shoot at the fleeing robber. They were pointing their guns at each other from opposite sides of the street. They were all caught in the cross fire.

Seconds later, the traffic lights changed to red but the window cleaner's van charged through the junction and mounted the pavement scattering a dozen pedestrians in the process. And it was travelling against the flow of traffic.

There was a rush of officers in the mayhem that followed as guns were raised and pointed amid shouts of 'Police stop!'

'Stop or I'll shoot!'

Abruptly followed by cries of, 'Watch your background!'

'Down! Get down!'

'Hold your fire!'

'Background! Watch your background!'

And then it was suddenly and eerily silent with no-one having taken a shot and Mark Tait lying on the cold concrete haemorrhaging from his chest cavity whilst a window cleaner's van hurtled at speed down the narrow street against the one-way system.

The stillness was broken with a horn blaring and tyres squealing as the van careered down the pavement, knocked over a dustbin, and regained the road surface.

'Mark! Mark!' cried Annie Rock crashing down to tend the wounded officer.

'No! Goddamn you, Mark Tait. No!' cried Annie Rock.

As Annie Rock tended to her colleague and a dozen officers forlornly chased a disappearing getaway vehicle, Felix Churchill casually bent down and surreptitiously retrieved a canvas bank bag full of money.

Mark Tait's mind floated away. He painfully flickered an eyelid and tried to utter a word.

'What? Tell me,' responded Annie bending close to his mouth.

'Cold, I'm real cold,' whispered Mark. 'I... I... '

'Shush... You're going to be alright,' offered Annie. Removing her jacket, she folded it into a large pad and pressed it into his chest to try and stem the blood. 'You're going to be alright, Mark. Just lie still. Rest.'

Mark Tait's eyes flickered one more time and then closed as he drifted away to who knows where with the painful whispered words, 'Cold, so cold.'

Stuffing the ill-gotten gains inside his jacket, Felix Churchill was quietly gone from the footpath with the smell of cordite fresh in his nostrils and a woman grappling with her radio.

'Ambulance required! Code Black,' screeched Annie Rock into her radio. 'Code Black... Shots fired! Officer down!'

Chapter Fourteen
~ ~ ~

Thursday.
The Secret Intelligence Service, London.

The secret squirrels were gathering for a morning feast on the lawn but even they twitched their ears at the sound of footsteps treading heavily in the corridor within.

The odour of hot fresh coffee wafted towards his nostrils and tried to compete with the cold, bitter streak invading the house and chilling the air. Davies King heard a low distant chatter from the workforce accompanied only by the gentle tap of keyboards and the low ring of an occasional telephone. His footsteps grew louder and then he barged through the door and stormed into the Operations Room, marched straight up to Admiral Crow and barked, 'Why is the memory stick so bloody important?'

'I beg your pardon,' answered the admiral taken aback by the unexpected outburst.

'You heard, admiral,' snapped Davies. 'The memory stick! It's something more than a memory stick, isn't it! Or are you trying to tell me it's only secret is your holiday snaps?'

'Yes,' offered Admiral Crow. 'I'm truly sorry to hear the news from Crillsea but I told you yesterday, the memory stick contains plans to assassinate the Royal family.'

There was a trio following Davies King: a late trio. But Barney, Al Jessop, and Sir Thomas rushed in behind with the chief leading the way imploring, 'Steady on, Davies. I'll deal with this.'

'Just a simple answer to a simple question, admiral. That's all,' declared Davies ignoring the chief.

Commander Pape sidled close to Admiral Crow and said, 'I sense you are upset, wouldn't you know it, chief inspector.'

'If you say that one more time....'

'DAVIES!' yelled Barney.

Spinning on his heel, Davies stepped quickly to the window and looked out across the lawn watching the squirrels. 'Well,' he muttered. 'Crillsea is my patch. Mark Tait is my man and I'd rather be in Crillsea than here right now. How do you expect me to feel?'

There was no reply offered but Davies said, 'I have to keep my mind on the job whatever else is going on. So some answers to some questions might help.'

Admiral Crow and Commander Pape exchanged looks but Sir Thomas pushed forward and announced, 'Chief Inspector King has a point, gentlemen. Yesterday I was called to this room where Sergeant Barnes and Chief Inspector King revealed to me the product of CCTV images streamed into your headquarters from Dublin, Amsterdam and elsewhere.'

'Oh! I see,' remarked Commander Pape. 'Why on earth did you find it necessary to personally attend this enquiry, Sir Thomas? Surely we have sufficient staff to enable our investigation?'

'But not sufficient intelligence,' offered Al Jessop.

'Intelligence?' queried Admiral Crow.

'Sergeant Barnes!' invited Sir Thomas.

Barney stepped forward and said, 'As a result of intelligence we received from you yesterday afternoon regarding plans to assassinate the Royal Family, we arranged for the placement of the memory stick we had recovered into the only bank in Crillsea that actually has a bank vault. As you know we then fed the media with a story designed to draw in our suspect and bring him out into the open. We needed to know if he was in England or still on the continent. Armed surveillance officers were covertly deployed to the scene.'

'Not a decision taken lightly I assure you,' divulged a scowling Sir Thomas.

Admiral Crow offered the slightest nod of his head in acknowledgement.

'Barney! Continue!' instructed Sir Thomas playing with his beard thoughtfully.

Running a hand across the remain of his thin locks, Barney remarked, 'We hoped to pick someone up acting suspiciously in the area, maybe trying a break in, perhaps having a ganders at the bank layout. You know, casing the joint as the Yanks say.'

'I gotcha,' acknowledged Brandon setting up a television screen.

'We circulated a motor bike which was stolen from Amsterdam and is still outstanding. Evidence points to the fact that Conor O'Keeffe is in possession of the bike. We hoped to find him and the bike together,' informed Barney, 'We did not expect a daylight robbery within hours of the Crillsea Chronicle hitting the streets. The town has been turned into a shooting gallery and…'

'Where is this taking us?' probed Commander Pape.

Turning from the bay window, Davies asked, 'What is the constellation, gentlemen?'

'I beg your pardon!' exclaimed Commander Pape banging his walking stick onto the floor angrily.

'Oh you can bang your stick all day, commander,' affirmed Davies. 'Admiral, the constellation?'

There was no reply from the admiral merely a cold stare in return.

'Please?' implored Davies.

Admiral Crow raised an index finger to his lips and narrowed his black velvety eyes.

'Oh yes! Of course,' remarked Davies. 'The mysterious resourcefulness of the SIS. Secrecy! The key ingredient to the defence of the nation but also a cloak for all things clandestine. And we are not in the know are we, admiral? It's a need to know, isn't it, admiral? And we don't need to know, do we?'

The admiral shook his head.

'Your problem,' revealed Davies, 'Is that I know, or at least I think I know. But I want you to tell me what the hell is going on!'

'You're very good at bluffing, chief inspector,' offered the admiral.

'Brandon!' remarked Davies.

Brandon Douglas switched on a television set, smiled, and declared, 'Take your seats and enjoy the show. There'll be popcorn when the lights come up, folks.'

After a few moments, Davies lowered the volume on the television and said, 'When the woman is shot dead on the bridge in Dublin she mouths a sentence or two to a man we now know as Callum Reece. He is the man killed by Conor O'Keefe at the flower market in Amsterdam. I asked Detective Chief Superintendent Jessop if he could supply a lip reader. Mister Jessop!'

'A lip reader,' laughed Commander Pape. 'Oh, this gets sillier by the minute!'

'I'll put it this way,' signified Jessop. 'I haven't reached the pinnacle of my career leading the Met's Flying Squad without learning a thing or two about criminal investigation. Sir Thomas.... Are you going to tell them or shall I?'

Sir Thomas ignored Commander Pape and looked deep into the eye of Admiral Crow.

The admiral felt the chief's laser burning itself into his eye sockets when Sir Thomas revealed, 'Admiral, this has nothing to do with any plans to assassinate our beloved Royal Family.'

Admiral Crow nodded slowly in agreement.

'Davies...' offered Sir Thomas. 'You are senior investigating officer in this matter. I'll have an update from your team now if you please.'

Davies nodded towards Al Jessop.

Al Jessop fidgeted unnecessarily with his tie but coolly informed, 'I engaged a lip reader from London. Siofra O'Sullivan, the woman killed on O'Connell Bridge, utters her last words. They were, *The Dutchman, tell the Baron the Dutchman has got the constellation.*'

There was a look of mild bewilderment on the admiral's face.

'What's more,' revealed Davies.' Speaking with officers from Crillsea this morning, I now know that our bank robber specifically demanded the constellation from the bank manager. It's your move, Admiral Crow.'

'Fascinating,' replied the admiral, and then he challenged Davies somewhat by offering, 'Astronomy or pie in the sky?'

Lifting a white queen from the chess board, Davies moved it deep into the heart of a row of black pawns which he scattered across the table with the flick of his fingers. He declared, 'I believe we are talking about the Eurion Constellation, admiral.'

The admiral's eyes rose to meet Davies's eyes before he replied, 'I believe you have me in check, Chief Inspector Davies!'

'It has to be the Eurion Constellation, admiral. But I might settle for a stalemate if you come clean for once in your life. Your problem is that I read a lot; usually in Crillsea library. On the side of the memory stick we recovered in Crillsea there's a pattern: a design which matches the Eurion constellation. No more false flag operations, admiral. I've no more time for deceit at any level.'

'Very well!' decided Admiral Crow. 'So be it!'

Commander Pape went blue in the face and advised in the most sternest of tones, 'Admiral! I will not stand idly by and allow this. I will not permit you to contravene the Official Secrets Act!' Then he tapped his walking stick on the carpeted floor.

Immediately, two stewards appeared in the room and seemed to wait for their orders from the commander.

Admiral Crow held his hand towards the two stewards and then extended his index finger towards them, controlling their movement, bidding them to remain static with the simple solid use of one digit.

Twisting slowly towards the commander, Admiral Crow said, 'Commander, I am the Official Secrets Act!' And then with a deliberate touch of sarcasm, he added 'Wouldn't you know it!' Walking into the centre of the room, the admiral announced, 'Indeed, I have the responsibility to each and every person living in this great nation of ours to ensure the safety of British subjects at home and abroad and to preserve our national interests accordingly. Now commander, I'll thank you to shut up and sit down. We have our backs to the wall. The whole world is about to collapse and you're worried about the bloody Official Secrets Act!'

'Forgive me, gentlemen,' intervened Sir Thomas. 'Admiral, we're never going to get anywhere like this.'

'I agree!' replied the admiral.

'Who is the baron?' probed Davies.

'He's a rogue, chief inspector,' responded Admiral Crow.

'Oh no, that's it. It's all over,' remarked Commander Pape. The Service is destroyed. It's...'

'It's time you remembered that you are my assistant, commander,' cracked Admiral Crow interjecting.

'And?' enquired Davies.

Admiral Crow glanced at the two stewards and splayed his fingers open wide. Immediately, they gently and politely ushered people from the room leaving only Al Jessop, the men from Crillsea, Brandon Douglas, and the admiral and commander in the room.

Admiral Crow casually approached the bay window, looked out into the garden, and spoke towards the squirrels on the lawn.

'Do you know what Sigint is, gentlemen?' enquired the admiral with his back to the ensemble.

'Signal intelligence,' replied Barney. 'From a wireless or telephone interception.'

Admiral Crow nodded thoughtfully, looked out towards the lawn, and divulged, 'Many years ago we ran an operation against a terrorist group in the Republic of Ireland. We turned one of their Quartermasters and convinced her to work for us in return for regular payments of money, a new identity in the event of compromise, and a huge pay off at the conclusion of events.'

Davies stepped closer to Admiral Crow's shoulder to share his view as the admiral continued, 'She agreed and over the course of many years saved countless hundreds of lives in the process. We recovered explosives and firearms. The operation was a huge success.'

'But she was the lady murdered on O'Connell Bridge?' suggested Davies.

'Yes,' replied the admiral. 'Siofra O'Sullivan!'

'Who recruited her?' asked Davies.

'Our man, Mansfield de Courtenay Baron! We refer to him as the Baron. He's a very experienced senior field intelligence officer. Indeed, some of his peer group would describe as number three in our Service.'

'Number three?' queried Davies. 'Why, that would make him one of the most powerful men in the UK would it not? In matters of security, I mean, admiral?'

'Yes, and it is a proposition that I do not entertain lightly at this time, chief inspector,' simmered Admiral Crow.

'Mmm...' considered Davies. 'This Siofra lady must have had good connections in the organisation?' quizzed Davies.

'Indeed so! Her main contacts were at Brigade Command level.'

'That would make me think Callum Reece and Conor O'Keeffe were brigade commanders, admiral,' revealed Davies.

'Your chess is good, chief inspector,' responded Admiral Crow twisting from the window. 'And in respect of Callum Reece, you are correct. We called him the Lighthouse Keeper.'

'And Conor O'Keeffe?' delved Davies

'Was merely a soldier in the Irish Republican Army... But a good one. A killer! And an extremely effective one!'

'And the Sigint?' queried Barney close to the two men.

Chuckling in a bizarre sort of way, Admiral Crow revealed, 'All I can say is that the operation was compromised. When Siofra's usefulness had run its course we relocated her to Japan under a false identity. She went to work with a computer software firm and, unbeknown to us, met a Dutchman working for the same firm.'

'The Dutchman on the bridge?' queried Brandon Douglas.

'Precisely! We did not know it then but the Dutchman is, or rather was, a man called Yan Luka. He is a member of the Yakuza: a criminal organisation based in Japan.'

Brandon nodded and revealed, 'Yeah! I heard about them. They make the Triads look like choir boys.'

'Japan?' queried Davies. 'The same place you'd relocated Siofra!' remarked Davies.

'Unfortunately, yes,' replied the admiral.

'Admiral! I must insist on your silence,' instructed Commander Pape. 'You've told them far too much.'

Admiral Crow sighed and replied, 'I know, but we need to get to the bottom of it all, commander, and we're not getting anywhere playing hide and seek. Now then, I was saying...'

'Japan!' remarked Sir Thomas.

'This is our problem, gentlemen. The Baron ran Siofra as an agent, relocated her to Japan with a new identity, enticed her back when she discovered the software, told her she would be safe from PIRA, and is the brains behind recovering the memory stick into the possession of British intelligence for the British Government.'

'That explains a lot, sir,' complimented Davies. 'Is it as stupidly simple as number three wanting to be number two?'

Admiral Crow slowly shook his head and offered, 'I wish it were that simply, chief inspector. Sadly, the Baron left our service two days prior to Siofra returning to Dublin.'

'You mean he really is a rogue?' enquired Davies. 'I don't understand why you have painted him a rogue, sir.'

'After the peace process took off in Ireland, the Baron approached Conor and Callum. Both men were recruited when hostilities subsided,' explained the admiral. 'It was simple expediency and a good way for us to monitor the peace process.'

'I see,' admitted Davies. 'It appears that your Baron is not only resourceful but also a very brave man.'

'Agreed!' remarked the admiral.

'I presume both these men joined you?' asked Al Jessop.

'Yes, both alluded to the recruitment for money and future long term lifestyle changes in the years ahead. A financially sponsored retirement, I suppose you might call it. However, our intelligence source, Sigint, revealed that the Baron contacted Callum to ensure there was no PIRA interest in Siofra, and that it was safe for her to return to the fold from Japan.'

'Then she's murdered on the bridge in Dublin,' noted Barney.

'Shortly after her murder, the Baron rang the Garda to tell them Conor was the killer,' explained the admiral. 'This was, of course, incorrect. We know now that Yan Luka, the Dutchman, killed Siofra. We also know that Callum rang Conor to tell him that he would be suspected of Siofra's murder because of events in years gone by. It's common knowledge in the circles our agents move in that Siofra was a tout and fed us Conor's active service unit many years ago. Conor never forgave her for that. But that is an aside in some ways since these two telephone calls, undoubtedly contrived by the Baron, had the importance of unleashing the killer Conor O'Keeffe.'

'Hence,' suggested Davies. 'Conor O'Keefe followed Callum Reece to Amsterdam, I presume, and in order to recover the memory stick?'

Admiral Crow nodded in agreement.

'Are you alleging,' suggested Davies, 'That the Baron set one of your agents up against the other, admiral?'

'That is precisely what he did,' agreed Admiral Crow.

'And the Dutchman?' probed Al Jessop.

'Yan Luka,' explained the admiral, 'Was employed by the Japanese company for whom Siofra worked. He was sent to recover the memory stick for the company but we know that he is a Yakuza hit man, an assassin, and the kind of man who might have sold the product to the highest bidder.'

'Well, I'll be,' popped Bandon. 'Which is precisely where the Yakuza come in,' concluded Brandon Douglas.

'Correct!' admitted Admiral Crow engaging Brandon more closely but speaking directly to the gathering. 'The Dutchman is merely an assassin for the Japanese crime syndicate. The fact that he worked at the same company as Siofra is purely circumstantial, merely a twist of fate. We are convinced that the Baron enlisted Callum to go to Amsterdam to recover the memory stick from the Dutchman in the full knowledge that Conor O'Keeffe would pursue him. You can get a flight to Amsterdam from the UK just about every hour of the day since it is the hub of European travel. Put simply, chief inspector, our man, the Baron, is an expert in his field. He knows his people backwards. It is his function in life to determine everything possible there is to know about his subject: his target. That includes their likely reaction to any course of given events. The Baron is a master class in the field of counter espionage.'

Davies exchanged concerned looks with Barney and his team.

'Looking at Brandon's television footage,' continued the admiral. 'It is obvious Conor witnessed the murderous recovery on behalf of the Baron. You see, we know that only the Baron has the password for the device. The Baron set everything up so that it looked like Conor went in pursuit of Callum so as to give the impression of an IRA fall out and a power struggle within the organisation. But actually, gentlemen,' concluded the admiral. 'The Baron merely wants to keep himself clean until the device is back in his hands in England where he can dispose of either one of the men who return.'

'Advanced chess!' cracked Davies playfully fingering a chess piece. 'Maybe it's time I went back to Crillsea?'

Brandon chuckled and quipped, 'Played checkers, never chess.'

'You should try it some time,' suggested Davies.

'Yeah, maybe I'll take you up on that one day, Davies.'

A mobile 'phone rang in Sir Thomas's pocket and he moved away to answer it out of earshot of the others.

Admiral Crow continued, 'I've made it a habit not to play games in the manner of my profession, chief inspector,' revealed Admiral Crow. 'Indeed, there are times when in order to win, one needs to set the rules of the game yourself. Don't you agree?'

'Depends!' acknowledged Davies.

'I don't know whether the Baron plays checkers or chess but so far he's doing very well,' offered the admiral. 'He's removed Callum Reece, is likely to delete Conor O'Keefe when the time is right, plays by his own rules, and presumably now has the memory stick.'

'Oh yes, the mysterious magical memory stick. What is that all about?' quizzed Brandon. 'Is it something from outer space? What do you think, Davies? A fantasy, is it? Mystical, mysterious, or just plumb crazy out of this world?'

'Interesting,' remarked Davies acknowledging Brandon. 'If I understand you correctly, Admiral Crow, we can all assume that the man dressed as the security guard at the bank was indeed, Conor O'Keeffe. And, if I'm not mistaken, I believe the driver of the getaway van - the window cleaner's van that is - was probably this man you call the Baron.'

'I would go with that, chief inspector,' answered Admiral Crow. 'Yes, I think that will prove to be the case.'

'Mansfield de Courtenay Baron, if I heard correctly,' reminded Davies. 'We'll need a full description, photograph, that kind of thing, admiral. But it occurs to me that we have linked Conor O'Keeffe to the murder of a young lady whose body was found in a flat in Amsterdam. Her motor bike was stolen and is still outstanding.'

'I believe you are correct to suspect Conor of that murder, chief inspector,' agreed Admiral Crow. 'And leave the photograph and description of the Baron with me. I'll arrange for a portfolio to be delivered to you within the hour.'

'Thank you, sir,' replied Davies. Turning to Al Jessop, Davies requested, 'Mister Jessop, can I leave you with spearheading the motor bike side of the enquiry? We need to find it!'

Jessop replied, 'No problem, Davies. But it does make me wonder why if the Baron and O'Keefe did the bank job yesterday, why didn't they use the motor bike as a getaway vehicle. It would have made better sense than a window cleaner's van.'

'Maybe O'Keefe ditched the bike,' suggested Barney.

'Do you always think like criminals?' asked Commander Pape.

'Only when we're playing chess,' replied Davies.

Back in Crillsea, slender fingers smoothed over the black and white tabs of a keyboard and an Irish voice softly declared, 'You were right, so you were. We've been duped. This is a blank memory stick. Look, see for yourself.'

The Baron clicked on the icon and confirmed they'd been had. 'It's a long time since I met a player like this man,' he declared. 'Conor, this man is very clever. By now, he knows who we are and he will soon know where we are.'

'Do you want me to finish him?'

'There's no point, my friend,' replied the Baron. 'No point at all. And he's not the reason we came to Crillsea. No! But we shall play the game my way from now on.'

Conor nodded and smiled whilst the Baron set aside his computer and rummaged for a mini TV set.

'Now that's clever, sir, so it is,' cracked Conor. 'That is a card up the sleeve in the back room of a Dublin pub, so it is.'

'But not the only one,' chuckled the Baron. 'And I don't play cards either. I only play solitaire and I never lose.'

The forefinger and thumb of his right hand gently turned the dial, gently tuned in to the frequency, and eventually zeroed in on their target.

'Well, well, so that's what you were doing!' observed Conor.

The squirrels were midway between the copse and the bay window playing on the lawn as the conference continued.

Suddenly, the chief voiced, 'Oh no!' and then spun on his heel whilst adjusting the telephone at his ear. He shook his head sadly.

Glancing at Davies, Barney suggested, 'Mark Tait?'

'What's the latest?' asked Al Jessop.

'I think we're about to find out,' remarked Davies. 'Excuse me, admiral. Just one moment, please.'

The admiral nodded and Davies approached Sir Thomas.

'How bad, sir?' enquired Davies.

'Mark Tait lives,' responded Sir Thomas with an ear to the 'phone. 'Just!'

'Thank God for that,' replied Davies. 'How bad is he?'

'Not good,' replied Sir Thomas. 'Heavy blood loss and obviously severe trauma; but it looks as if it could go either way. Apparently the bullets tore into his upper shoulder narrowly missing his heart and the vital organs. A bloody mess and it will take time provided he has the strength to make a fight of it'

'Let's hope so,' suggested Davies.

'He's young and strong,' noted Barney. 'Let's hope he makes it.'

Sir Thomas spoke into the 'phone instructing, 'Inspector Rock in headmaster like style, 'Make sure we are doing all we can for Mrs. Tait. I want a car and driver placed at her disposal with immediate affect and I want you to organise some flowers from me personally, and the constabulary separately, to be delivered to Mrs. Tait and the hospital. It's the least we can do in the circumstances.'

Davies nodded appreciatively as the chief stepped away again and delivered a list of welfare requirements to Annie. Eventually, he turned and handed his 'phone to Davies saying, 'Inspector Rock for you, Davies.'

Taking the 'phone, Davies acknowledged with, 'Thank you, sir... Annie?'

Listening, Davies occasionally responded with, 'Still unconscious.... I don't care that he won't see the flowers if he's unconscious, Annie. I want him to see them when he wakes up, and he will wake up because I will order him to bloody well waken up... Yes, good idea, Annie. Get Claudia on the flowers and fruit job and send something from the office and myself... Payment?... Claudia will sort that out.... Leave it with her...'

A steward entered the room pushing a trolley upon which were the makings of boiled water and coffee or tea. There was a slow but measured rush to the aroma.'

Sir Thomas removed a large square handkerchief from his pocket and began to mop his brow.

Tilting his head towards the chief, Davies engaged Barney who responded with, 'Iced water, sir? Do you know, it's awfully hot in here. Iced water all round might be good for all of us!'

'I'll arrange it,' offered Commander Pape. 'At least iced water isn't contravening the Official Secrets Act.'

Barney acknowledged Commander Pape with, 'Correct, commander, ice tends to freeze all known bugs!'

Commander Pape threw an askew glance at Barney as he whispered into a steward's ear.

Sir Thomas smiled, returned his handkerchief to its hiding place, and interacted with, 'Very kind of you both. Very kind! I don't know what came over me there.'

There was a concerned look from Al Jessop when he saw a trickle of perspiration making its way down the chief's temple.

Eyeing Al Jessop, Barney slowly shook his head causing Jessop to relax somewhat.

Meanwhile, Davies continued his telephonic spiel.

'Tell me what more you've found out about the bank job, Annie. And then tell me why Felix Churchill isn't talking to me on this 'phone!'

Barney shook his head and pursed his lips as he helped himself to coffee and then handed Davies a cup.

'Webby says what? Felix was plagued with personal telephone calls during the operation! What's going on there then?'

Sir Thomas checked his wristwatch and remarked, 'You'll be out of credit in a few moments, Davies.'

A steward arrived carrying a jug of iced water and some glasses. Sir Thomas helped himself and took a large mouthful to cool down.

'There's money missing from the bank, Annie,' continued Davies. 'But it's not money that was stolen from the bank. Is that what you're saying?'

The chief was about to raise another glass to his lips but he lowered his drink and said, 'What? There's been a mistake there surely, Davies?'

'Yeah, CCTV! Good idea, Annie. Where's Chief Inspector Churchill?'

There were cold looks of anguish as the ensemble listened to the telephone conversation.

'We'll be back as soon as possible, Annie. Meanwhile, if that's the allegation, seize the CCTV inside and outside the bank and study it,' instructed Davies. 'I want to know what happened on Harbour Lane, okay?.... Yes... Yes... Okay!'

Davies snapped the 'phone shut and returned it to Sir Thomas.

'Do we have yet another rogue?' enquired Admiral Crow dispassionately.

'You tell me, admiral,' suggested Davies, eye to eye with the Head of the British Secret Service. 'I'd love to know myself. But at this moment, it's a need to know; okay?'

'Oh, I'm sorry, chief inspector,' cracked the admiral grinning widely. 'Listening to your conversation, I presumed someone had stolen some money, that's all. I just wondered to myself if it was the day of the rogues.'

Smiling politely, Davies glanced firstly at the chief and then the admiral before responding, 'Yes, there is some money missing from the bank but it's far too soon to draw conclusions on why money is missing. Apparently, some of the cash blew away down the street and it's being counted now. I believe we should move on and let things develop, gentlemen. Can we get back to our conversation?'

'Of course,' remarked the admiral. 'Where were we?'

Al Jessop suggested, 'You were just about to tell us about this mysterious thing everyone seems to be calling the Eurion Constellation.'

'So I was,' acknowledged Admiral Crow. 'Chief Inspector, it's your move.'

Accepting the veiled challenge to his self-professed investigative skills, Davies began, 'I did some research in Crillsea library some time ago. But let's start with the memory stick, shall we?' He moved through the throng speaking. 'It appears the reason why we are all here is because of a memory stick. For those who aren't too sure what that is, it's a Universal Serial Bus - a connector - or if I can computer speak for a moment, it's a computer device which has a flash memory drive that can save a copy of important files so if something happens to the files on the computer there is a safe copy on the flash drive. Because the memory stick is the size of your thumb you can transport files between computers and take information from one area to another very conveniently The average size of one these things is one or two Gigabytes.'

'And the Eurion Constellation?' queried Admiral Crow.

Davies made his way deliberately through the small gathering. When he reached the American CIA man, Davies stated, 'Brandon can tell us that. Can't you, Brandon?'

'I don't know what you mean,' offered Brandon trying to force a smile but suddenly caught on the back foot.

'That's why you're here, Brandon. You're CIA. You're here to represent the American government.'

'Well, yes, I'm a field officer and I...'

'You're here to safeguard the dollar, Brandon,' suggested Davies forcefully. 'You're here because you know all about the Eurion Constellation. Am I right?'

'Okay, okay!' admitted Brandon. 'I'm not trying to be secretive about this. But yeah I do know all there is to know about the Eurion Constellation; even if I say so myself.'

'Except the password!' mentioned Admiral Crow.

'Good God!' sighed Sir Thomas. 'Will someone please tell me what the hell the Eurion Constellation is?'

'Brandon?' challenged Davies. 'They brought you back out of retirement for a reason and it wasn't just to play television producer.'

'Okay!' replied the CIA man. 'They brought me back because I was a Treasury agent attached to the CIA! Okay? Is that okay? You Brits just don't seem to trust anyone do you?'

'With good reason,' intervened Sir Thomas sternly.

'Go on then, Brandon,' suggested Davies. It was almost an order. 'Put us out of our misery!'

There was a sigh from the American but then he found his voice and explained, 'The Eurion Constellation is a pattern of symbols found on a number of banknote designs. It's been around since the mid nineties and that's the problem. We're still using nineties technology in the twenty first century.'

'And what relevance is that?' enquired Sir Thomas thumping his chest to prevent a coughing bout before he mopped his brow again.

'The computer industry deliberately added the symbols to help software detect the presence of a banknote in a digital image,' declared Brandon. 'The software blocks the user from reproducing banknotes. It prevents counterfeiting that's all.'

'You mean counterfeiting using colour photocopiers,' asked Barney.

Brandon nodded in agreement and continued, 'The name *Eurion Constellation* was coined in 2002 when an experiment with a colour photocopier refused to reproduce banknotes. The word is derived from a mix of the Euro currency and Orion: a heavenly constellation in the night sky that is of similar shape to the symbols.'

'Which is how I found out about it in Crillsea library,' remarked Davies. 'I had the memory stick in my hands and there was a design on the sides. I searched through the astronomy books and found a tiny reference on one page about the Orion constellation. That page led me to the Eurion issue. The design is very similar to the Orion constellation. But then with a hint of sarcasm, Davies added, 'Brandon, you have us all enthralled. Do continue.'

Throwing a glance at Admiral Crow, Brendan divulged, 'The technical details of the software are kept Top Secret by the inventors and the users.'

Davies moved in between the admiral and the CIA man and challenged with, 'A historic patent application suggests that the pattern and detection system were designed by a Japanese electronics company.'

'Japan!' declared Al Jessop. 'Now we seem to be getting somewhere. But I don't understand why this thing is all that important.'

'Allow me, gentlemen,' remarked Admiral Crow. 'It's as simple as this. The latest colour photo-copying machines are a major feat of technological know-how. Moreover, gentlemen, the rather large commercial copiers are extremely expensive. Some of them run into thousands of pounds to buy, but they will not copy many of the world's banknotes; such as the British pound, the Euro. American and Canadian dollars, the South African Rand, as well a Chinese and Japanese currency... etc ... etc... Oh yes, we're talking of virtually every currency in the world, gentlemen. You see a mechanism built into these machines decides what a banknote is and searches for a simple geometric pattern. The pattern is the Eurion Constellation and it consists of five 1 mm large circles that appears on the notes and can be easily detected and tested for the presence of the characteristic constellation.'

'So that's why people can't really copy banknotes from these fancy printers that everyone has access to nowadays,' noted Barney.

'Precisely, sergeant,' cracked Admiral Crow. 'Indeed, fierce competition in the inkjet printer market has made domestic digital colour printers so cheap and the print quality so high that a £100 printer can produce fake banknotes that pass for the real thing in the dim light of a bar or nightclub.'

'Oh, yes, we get the odd one of those dropped in the West End clubs,' revealed Al Jessop. 'Not a lot we can do about it I'm afraid. And it's small money you see. Not worth chasing around for a couple of twenty pound notes in some cranky bar down a back street in Soho.'

'That's where I come in,' revealed Brandon enthusiastically. 'You see, the global banknote trade is enormous. Did you know that about one hundred and sixty billion banknotes were printed last year? And that figure is still growing.'

Davies suggested, 'I thought *Chip and Pin* was taking over?'

'Yeah,' complimented Barney. 'There's talk of doing away with cheque books because these *Chip and Pin* cards and electronic bank transfers are making the use of real cash in hand money less fashionable. And it's cheaper and quicker to use electronics rather than real money.'

'Oh, be that as it may,' answered Brandon, 'You're talking in the main about the UK and, to some degree, America and Canada. The western currency systems, if you want. But the reality is places like China, Japan, Asia, and the emerging countries of a global economic system are increasing the demand for hard money - cash in hand stuff as Barney here calls it.'

'Who prints the money?' asked Sir Thomas.

Answering, Brandon disclosed, 'Over eighty percent of the world's banknotes are printed by state-owned enterprises. Many countries, like Britain, America, Russia and China, will not allow their notes to be printed abroad. So banknotes in these countries are printed inside those countries and nowhere else.'

'Which seems to make good sense as far as national security is concerned,' imparted Admiral Crow. 'Can you imagine having our currency system compromised?'

'American dollars are printed at two federal government-owned sites, in Washington DC and Fort Worth, Texas,' explained Brandon. 'But there is no international body for the regulation of currency issue, which means there is nothing to stop companies printing money for the so-called rogue states like Syria or North Korea.'

'And the same goes for emerging states like Somaliland or Western Sahara,' conceded Admiral Crow. 'Countries which are not yet universally recognised.'

Sir Thomas puzzled, 'I thought these banknotes had lines in them... You know, erm...'

'Security threads?' offered Brandon. 'These rogue states with questionable leaders could quite easily copy our currency if they had the right equipment and the technical knowledge. That's why we use security threads. It's not just about stopping Jack the Lad from copying a few hundred dollar bills to treat the girlfriend.'

'Yes, that's what I was thinking of,' admitted Sir Thomas. 'Security threads!'

'Well, chief,' disclosed Brandon. 'Bank notes are manufactured using special security paper as well using security threads and holography to defeat the counterfeiters.'

'I see,' acknowledged Sir Thomas. 'Counterfeiting has always been a major problem for policing.'

From his perch close to the bay window, Davies King studied the squirrels scurrying towards the far off copse and reflected, 'Nothing worse than holding something in your hand and then realising it's dud.'

'It's happened to you too, Davies,' asked Brandon.

Davies smiled in a detached sort of way and offered, 'Counterfeiting is a lot harder nowadays, Brandon.'

'Yeah,' agreed Brandon. 'Some of the banknotes are made from cotton fibre and linen rag nowadays. One way to prevent banknotes from being counterfeited by commercial copiers is by using very fine detail and security marks in the design to prevent them from being copied. We place specially arranged dots on the notes. The dots are called the Eurion Constellation. The pattern of circles is able to be digitally identified using an electronic technique from the Counterfeit Deterrence System.'

'And there begins our problem,' announced Admiral Crow. 'Siofra, our agent killed on O'Connell Bridge, was working for a Japanese electronics software company working on the Counterfeit Deterrence System.'

'What's that?' enquired Sir Thomas.

'It's a system which is built into these scanners and copiers at the time of their manufacture. It's an electronic scanner that reads the shape of the dots in the Eurion Constellation. The software blocks anyone from reproducing banknotes to prevent counterfeiting using colour photocopiers. It's the same software that scans your banknotes when the shop assistant puts it under the scanner to check it.'

'And so the memory stick that we are chasing, and the Baron has stolen, contains the Eurion Constellation?' surmised Sir Thomas.

'Something like that,' agreed Admiral Crow.

'Nah, I don't buy that,' declared Davies.

'Me neither,' concurred Al Jessop.

'If it's such a problem, all that needs to be done is the reconfiguration of the constellation,' suggested Barney. 'You should be able to reproduce the constellation's design from the original programme. Surely that's what needs to be done?'

'Ordinarily,' agreed Brandon.

'Except this time,' suggested Davies. 'I suspect there's more to it than that. Wouldn't you say?'

'Two things, chief inspector,' confirmed Brandon. 'How do we go about recalling the world's currency? Secondly, the original computer programme for the Eurion was destroyed by Siofra. It can be rebuilt but that will take time. More worrying for us all is that she also destroyed a new programme she had access to. The memory stick in possession of the Baron carries the electronic capability of recognizing the Eurion Constellation and configuring a response to counter the counterfeit deterrence system and allow any notes to be printed in a manner specified by the software.'

Davies suggested, 'That sounds like one of those high tech warfare systems that attacks the computerised system controlling a weapon. A counter electronic warfare system is challenged by a counter-counter electronic system!'

'That's one way of looking at it,' acknowledged Brandon.

'If I understand this correctly,' probed Jessop. 'You mean the system would confuse a printer or a scanner into believing that the note is not a counterfeit? It counters the counterfeit deterrence system!'

'Exactly, chief superintendent,' acknowledged Admiral Crow. 'The software in the memory stick, which we know is password protected, allows the operator to print their own notes with their own version of the Eurion Constellation in the full and precise knowledge that counterfeit deterrence systems will not identify the governmental issue of the Eurion Constellation and will actually approve their counterfeited notes because the technology fools the deterrence system.'

'The cyberspace war!' suggested Barney.

'Now we know why Mossad are here!' revealed Al Jessop.

'It's a licence to print money throughout the world,' declared Davies.

There was a silence in the room only broken by the soft murmur of electricity emanating from the television and the clink of the last dissolving ice cubes wallowing in Sir Thomas's glass.

'Add to this the ability to transfer the protocol to *Chip and Pin* and credit cards and you will soon grasp why this matter does not only affect national security,' admitted Admiral Crow. 'Oh no! The theft of the memory stick threatens the very fabric of our global economic system since the technology imprinted in the software has the capability to convince any scanner or checking device that things are alright. It's electronically telling the counterfeit deterrence system that it's reading itself so it must be alright. And yes, that's why the Israelis and the rest of our international colleagues are here.'

'But Mossad?' queried Sir Thomas.

'Has a scorpion under every rock in the desert, Sir Thomas,' admitted the admiral. 'And at times like this, we need to turn all the rocks over in all the deserts.'

Al Jessop stroked his chin thoughtfully and confided, 'I could sell that system to any criminal organisation or rogue government in the world for literally billions of pounds if I had the contacts. It beggars belief. I mean, I could use it in my computer at home and print off a couple of thousands of pounds in half an hour.'

'Or dollars!' sniped Brandon.

Jessop threw his hands up in acknowledgement and conceded, 'Or you could feed it into a government printing system and print millions in a day. In fact, millions of any currency by the sound of it.'

'You've got it in one!' confirmed the admiral. 'And the Baron has numerous contacts in many spheres of operation. Indeed, he is something of a cryptologist.'

'Can he play chess, admiral?' enquired Davies.

'I don't know, but he can hack into most things if he needs to.'

'Did he hack into the CCTV system covering O'Connell Bridge in Dublin?' quizzed Davies.

'Undoubtedly!' agreed the admiral. 'From our office I am informed by our computer boffins.'

'Thank you for that, admiral,' said Davies.

Thinking aloud, Al Jessop mused, 'The Forgery and Counterfeiting Act, 1981!'

'What on earth are you on about?' enquired Sir Thomas.

'Oh nothing really,' replied Jessop. 'Are you familiar with the legislation, sir?'

'Not since I was a young detective more years ago than I care to remember. Why? What's on your mind?'

'Section one!' remarked Al Jessop. 'Section one tells me that it's an offence to make a counterfeit of a currency note or of a protected coin, intending that he or another shall pass or tender it as genuine, or for a person to make a counterfeit of a currency note or of a protected coin without lawful authority or excuse.'

'Well, that's alright then,' remarked Sir Thomas.

'Not really, sir,' quipped Al Jessop. 'How would we ever prove a bank note was a forgery when the device we use to determine whether or not a banknote is a forgery is, in itself, a forgery?'

There was an almost resigned chuckle at Jessop's remark but then Sir Thomas muttered, 'The Eurion Constellation, well I never! They've got us over a barrel, haven't they!'

There was a look of disbelief on the faces of the gathering followed by the dawning reality they were likely to face a major attack on the world's financial system when Sir Thomas declared, 'We're looking straight into the eye of a global economic disaster that could change the entire world order!'

'It's down to us now,' remarked the admiral. 'Historically, it's known that in the infant days of our Navy British ships would enter French and Spanish ports under a false flag. Once inside the harbour walls they would destroy the enemy. May I say, Chief Inspector King, that you're false flag operation intending to draw the Baron to Crillsea by the use of media and subterfuge obviously worked. But on this occasion he escaped, and he escaped with the software in question!'

'Fascinating!' declared Davies. It goes to show that you should never presume that everything is what it seems to be. But now we have a motive, admiral - pure unadulterated greed from a man who has placed his own desires before that of his country. We know who they are - the Baron and Conor O'Keeffe: a British Secret Service officer and a born-again terrorist. And I'm going back to Crillsea because that's where the last piece of this jigsaw was played!'

'I'm with you,' confirmed Al Jessop.

Turning to Commander Pape, Davies cracked, 'Commander, whilst we're away, make sure you feed the squirrels.'

There was a chink of an ice cube when Sir Thomas drained the bottom of his glass and slammed it on the table with, 'Crillsea!'

*

Chapter Fifteen

~ ~ ~

Friday.
Crillsea.

Barney was first into the office with the files and a stack of paperwork from London.

'Where's Davies?' he asked Claudia.

Looking at the clock, Claudia replied, 'Seven thirty in the morning, Sergeant Barnes! Goodness me! Chief Inspector King will be in the gym at this time of day, I suspect. He usually manages an hour each morning before work.'

'Well, Claudia, I couldn't sleep. Such a lot to do today. The chief and Davies wrote down a list of this, that and the other, to make enquiries about as we drove back last night. The Head of the Flying Squad and a couple of his guys are moving in for a while as well. I've fixed them up with extra 'phone lines in the office. The engineers will be along very shortly.'

'Does the chief inspector know?' enquired Claudia.

'Which chief inspector is that, Claudia, Davies King or Felix Churchill? Last I heard, Felix was missing. Absent without leave apparently!'

'Quite, Sergeant Barnes,' acknowledged Claudia. 'Mister Churchill was missing for a short time but he returned late yesterday afternoon with a large amount of money that everyone seems to think was originally missing from the bank.'

'Ah, the missing bank money,' quipped Barney. 'Not the money stolen by the robbers but the money missing from the cash that was stolen by the robbers.'

'Yes, that's correct, sergeant,' confirmed Claudia.

'Thank God for that,' remarked Barney. 'But are you seriously telling me Felix Churchill took all day yesterday picking up money from Harbour Lane that had been blown away in the bank raid?'

'No, I am not,' revealed Claudia 'Inspector Rock will fill you in, I'm sure.'

Annie Rock appeared in the corridor and headed straight for the office.

Claudia continued, 'All I know is that Chief Inspector Churchill went straight to the hospital after the raid to enquire about Constable Tait. On his return, he was diverted to meet an important informant. That is the reason why he was late. You know, it's completely wrong to accuse a man of something when you have no evidence. Indeed, I'm led to believe everything is above board in that respect. Why shouldn't it be, Sergeant Barnes?'

'Oh, no reason, Claudia. No reason at all. Look I'm going to book Chief Superintendent Al Jessop and his team into the Anchor and then I'll be back.'

'You may find Chief Inspector King there shortly, sergeant. If he doesn't breakfast in the canteen downstairs, he'll be in the restaurant area of the Anchor having a bite to eat before the day starts. Busy day planned is it, sergeant?'

'We're going to sweep every piece of accommodation in the Crillsea area today,.' revealed Barney. 'We think our men are here sleeping on us.'

'That's a lot of telephone calls in a tourist area, sergeant. Crillsea, Crillsea Meadows, Tevington and all points along the coast. It will take you most of the day and probably all night to complete that task properly.'

'Yes, hence the early start!' quipped Barney

'Surely these criminals will have made their escape long ago,' suggested Claudia. 'It wouldn't take too much to evade a couple of road blocks in this town. It's not as if we have a hundred police cars on every street corner, is it?'

'Davies thinks they may be lying low until the heat has died down, that's all, Claudia. He thinks they are smarter than the average and instead of making a run for it, they've got their head down somewhere, waiting for things to blow over. As far as we know, no other motor vehicle has been stolen from Crillsea and the window cleaner's van they used is still outstanding. So, they might still be here according to out illustrious leader.'

'Who am I to argue with our leader,' cracked Claudia. 'Except to say, of course, that he is has been known to be wrong in the past.'

Annie walked into the office and announced, 'I'm on your side with that one, Claudia. The baddies had plenty of time to escape Indian territory yet the guvnor seems to think they are close by. Look, I'm arranging to brief everyone this morning so where's the kettle? I need caffeine! Once that's over, I'm going to see how Mark is getting on at the hospital.'

Claudia reached across from her keyboard and flicked a switch on the wall socket.

High on Crillsea Meadows, close to the cliffs that overlooked the crashing angry sea, two men occupied a remote holiday cottage and they were plotting the future over a full English breakfast.

The Baron's 'phone rang.

'Who's that 'phoning at this time of day?' asked a puzzled Conor chasing the remnants of a fried egg around his plate.

'A friend,' replied the Baron smiling. 'Quiet now!'

Tucking away his last fork full, the Baron slid his plate to one side, flipped open the cell phone, and announced, 'Brogans Bookmakers, how can I help?'

'There was a long period wherein only the sound of muffled breathing could be heard and then a voice declared, 'It's Churchill Felix Churchill!'

Glimpsing sideways at Conor, the Baron nodded and spoke into the cell phone, 'Thank you for ringing me back at last, Mister Churchill. I need to discuss your account urgently.'

'Who is this? Are you Mister Brogan?' enquired Felix.

'A friend or an enemy,' replied the Baron. 'It's your decision.'

'Very funny! Listen up, I'm on my way to work in five minutes time,' explained Felix. 'I got all your messages and I don't want you bothering me at work again. Do you understand me?'

'Bothering you at work, Mister Churchill?' queried the Baron. 'You know why we bother you at work, Mister Churchill. Indeed, you know what we want and we want it sooner rather than later,' explained the Baron.

'I don't like your tone,' challenged Felix.

'I don't like your debt,' retaliated the Baron.

There was a short pause before Felix responded, 'Okay, I understand. I'll get you the money. I've managed to get some of it already.'

'How much have you got?' asked the Baron.

'About ten grand but I can get more if you give me time.'

'Who is this guy?' whispered Conor.

The Baron covered the mouthpiece of the telephone and told Conor, 'I intercepted his Bookies 'phone. He thinks he's talking to his bookmaker. It's the man in charge of the police division. I'm just about to put him in my pocket.'

'You intercepted his 'phone...'

'Tricks of the trade! I used a signal intercept.'

Smiling, Conor sat down to listen to the conversation.

'Ten thousand pounds isn't much when you owe close on a hundred thousand, Mister Churchill,' suggested the Baron.

'A hundred thousand! No way!' snapped Felix.

'I'm afraid it's a hundred thousand when you add the interest, Mister Churchill. Why don't you come down to the office and we'll discuss it properly.'

'No, I can't do that,' revealed Felix. 'That's a non starter. I can't be seen to be...'

'In trouble?' suggested the Baron intervening sharply.

Amusement crossed Conor's face.

'I'll stick with the 'phone. Look can I pay you back at a grand a month?'

'No!' snapped the Baron, cold and complete, final in his tone.

Conor reached across to a table and poured two Bushmills Irish whiskeys. He slid one to the Baron and waited for Felix to respond.

'How much do you want a month to clear this debt?' asked Felix.

'I'm a reasonable man, Mister Churchill,' indicated the Baron. 'Something else might do!'

'Something else?'

'Yes, something you have and I want,' revealed the Baron.

'What would that be?' requested Felix suspiciously.

'A memory stick!'

'What do you mean a memory stick?'

'It's in the newspaper,' offered the Baron. 'And I am aware of its true value. I make it my business to know of such things, Mister Churchill.' There was a silent pause on the telephone before the Baron continued, 'You have been a foolish man, Mister Churchill, but I am not unreasonable and seek only to rectify this debt to our mutual satisfaction.' The silence continued for a moment. 'Well?'

'No I couldn't!' came the reply.

'In that case, I'm sorry you can't consider my offer. I'll have to take it up with your employer and possibly apply to the civil court for a detachment of earnings order from your salary, Mister Churchill. Good bye and thank you for calling.'

The Baron ended the conversation and snapped the phone shut.

'That was stupid, so it was,' quipped Conor. 'You had him on the hook there.'

'Bit early for whiskey isn't it?'

'Just a wee nip to keep the cold out, so it is,' replied Conor.

Savouring his whiskey, the Baron replied, 'And when the 'phone rings again, I'll reel him in. Why don't you stack the dishwasher while we're waiting?'

Watching a dead telephone, Conor replied, 'Yeah, I'll do that but I don't share your optimism. The man can't be stupid and he could lead us into a trap if he took the bait.'

The Baron sneaked a peep through the window. 'Lovely view of the sea, Conor. Quite lovely! But I haven't time to stand and stare, as they say. Give me a hand with these boxes.'

Hoisting a series of containers onto the table, the Baron carefully unpacked them and began to assemble the contents.

'Funny shopping spree you went on,' remarked Conor. 'Is there anything I can do?'

'Yeah,' decided the Baron. 'When the time comes for me to collect the memory stick, you're going to stay here and look after this little lot.'

'I'd be better with you, so I would,' responded Conor. 'You'll need another pair of eyes and protection or do you just want me to watch television?'

'No, I need you here listening and watching,' recommended the Baron. 'Do you know what this is?'

'No idea,' replied Conor.

The Baron continued to connect two laptops together by a length of grey cable, then he fed another cable to various pieces of equipment on the table before he ran a yellow Ethernet cable from one of the laptops into a telephone socket in the corner of the room.

'What are you doing?' enquired Conor.

'Making a shield!' chuckled the Baron mischievously.

'You've lost me,' remarked Conor.

The Baron explained, 'This piece of kit gives us an extra ear and another eye. One of the laptops link to a wireless receiver which carries the signal to a device that recognises encrypted data. That piece of kit deciphers the encryption into plain language.'

'Cool!' remarked Conor.

'The language then prints onto your laptop screen but the signal is monitored and shows on the underlying map where the radio signal is coming from. Here, watch!'

Fingers tapped onto the black and whites and revealed a map of the region.

'Shield?' queried Conor.

'Yeah, a shield,' confirmed the Baron. 'It's a fairly bog-standard electronic shield that I've just thrown over Crillsea, Crillsea Meadows and Tevington. It's not as strong as I would like and it's a bit unstable because the equipment isn't state of the art. But it will keep us safe for a while. Why don't you play with it?'

'Bog standard!' quipped Conor. 'What can you do with the real stuff?'

The Baron declined an answer but gestured with his hands for Conor to try out the equipment.

Accepting the invitation, Conor soon picked up the finer points of basic technology and said, 'I'm looking into an office from a window and at the same time I'm listening to all these radio calls. Who is it?'

'Who is our enemy, Conor?'

'The police!' responded Conor.

'Exactly!'

Conor trailed a finger over the mouse pad and watched the cursor move across a map. He turned a dial slightly and listened to a radio message...

'Charlie one, traffic accident junction Crillsea Manor Place with Old Harbour Lane! Minor injuries, two cars, ambulance attending. Charlie One attend and deal!'

'Roger control from Charlie One... E.T.A. three minutes.

'That's the police, so it is. It's the police network!'

'Correct!' replied the Baron pointing to the equipment he had arranged. 'Decrypted! You can watch them here, listen to them there, and...' The Baron turned a switch from off to on and declared, 'And you can listen to the mobile network here. If it's in the ether over Crillsea, it's mine.'

Shaking his head in disbelief, Conor said, 'It's a listening station, a bloody listening station, so it is!'

'Not quite, but all we need today,' acknowledged the Baron.

The 'phone burst into life and began ringing again.

'Brogans!' answered the Baron

'If I do what you want is it over?' asked Felix on the 'phone.

'Ahh, is that Mister Churchill again?' posed the Baron.

'You know it is,' replied Felix.

'Listen to me, Mister Churchill. I am really quite an honourable man but you will have realised that you owe me one hundred thousand pounds. I can destroy you and your career with one telephone call. Now listen carefully and it can all be over.'

'I don't have the memory stick,' declared Felix.

The Baron grimaced and continued, 'Yet you, above all others, will know where it is, Mister Churchill.'

'Yes... Yes, I do.... But I can't get into the safe. I don't have the keys.'

'But you can get the keys, can't you, Mister Churchill?'

Whispering, Conor advised Felix, 'Tell him to bring the damn thing to you. What are you waiting for?'

Closing his palm over the mouthpiece, the Baron said, 'Sit down and leave this to me. I know what I'm doing. I used to do this for a living. Understand?'

Resigning a nod, Conor heaved a sigh of relief and took a sip of his Bushmills. He looked out from the front window of the cottage and watched the winding road that climbed up towards them and no further. The sky was blue and dotted with a dozen seagulls or more dancing between the clouds. But Conor didn't care for the seagulls or the rolling clouds. He smiled, rested his feet on the end of the table, and listened to the Baron twist the knife into a bent policeman's gut.

Meanwhile, in a gymnasium in Crillsea, Davies King was in workout mode when he pounded the punch bag with a series of lefts and rights. Then he dodged, shadow boxed his reflection in the mirror, and swivelled back to the leather throwing his fists into the body of the punch bag hanging from the wall.

The door burst open and a figure walked in wearing a cleaner than clean, never been worn before, track suit.

Turning towards the intrusion, Davies remarked, 'Good God! Harry Reynolds, what on earth are you doing here?'

'Came to see you, Mister King, that's all.'

'What, dressed like that? Where's the snazzy suit and kipper tie, Mister Big Shot?'

'Ha ha, very funny, Mister King,' responded Harry making his way towards a treadmill. 'I'll have you know I've been properly inducted into the gym and am proficient in all the equipment here.'

'Yeah, and how many stone you trying to lose?' enquired Davies.

'My body is a temple, Mister King.'

Harry mounted a treadmill, whacked the start button, and began jogging.

Dropping his arms, Davies tugged his boxing gloves off and leaned across the front of the treadmill saying, 'Good to see you, Harry, what have you got for me?'

'I heard about the policeman being shot, Mister King,' declared Harry labouring right from the start of proceedings. 'It's not right. Definitely not right.'

A second later, Harry's tracksuit top lay on the floor.

'Yeah, nasty,' winced Davies. 'Some vest you got there. Runners Club United logo, wow!

'No need to be personal, Mister King. Just a fancy I took that's all. How is your man?'

'I'm going up to see him later this morning, Harry, but I'm not sure they'll let me in. What you heard?'

'Town's full of the talk, Mister King. It's not local. From away, mark my words. London, Birmingham, Manchester maybe. Big city boys, I would say.'

Harry suddenly found a second wind and began thundering into the treadmill at some speed.

'Did you read the Chronicle, Harry?'

'Sure did,' replied Harry. 'I guess you know who it is you're looking for then?'

'Maybe,' reacted Davies cautiously. 'But I always try to keep an open mind.'

'I came to help, Mister King. Some of us in the business think it's not right - shooting a policeman - that's why I came to find out what you need to know.'

Stepping towards a locker, Davies removed a towel from within and began wiping sweat from his brow and his arms.

'You never cease to amaze me, Harry.'

'It's to do with the plant you bought from the market, isn't it, Mister King. I'm the cause of it all.'

'Don't be stupid, Harry,' cracked Davies looking over his shoulder. 'You didn't know the memory stick was there.'

'No,' acknowledged Harry. 'And you didn't realise how important it was. I'm not stupid, Mister King. Memory sticks and your big chief landing some international task force job. Murders left, right and centre, Dublin to Amsterdam and all points in between, I daresay. No, I want to help, that's all. It's my fault you found the bloody memory stick in the first place. If you hadn't found it your man wouldn't be lying in a hospital bed fighting for his life. It's my fault. I helped put him there!'

Davies lowered his towel, thought for a moment, then slung the towel across his shoulders before suggesting, 'You know something don't you?'

'No,' snapped Harry. 'But I can find your men quicker than you could ever imagine.'

'Your little network of...'

'Market traders, shall we say?' suggested Harry, upping the speed of the treadmill to a steady pace.

Considering the offer for a moment, Davies knew he might spend hours on a telephone checking places where the Baron and Conor might be holed up. And he reckoned it would take an army of men to scroll through the 'phone book ringing all the accommodation sites on the south coast of England.

Nodding, Davies finally revealed, 'Two men: one distinctively Irish, the other distinctively English. The Irishman is lower middle class; the Englishman is upper class, Eton educated. They're both moving into their middle age. I think they'll be travelling together but I can't be certain.'

'South or north of the border?' quizzed Harry.

'What do you mean?'

'The Irishman, Dublin or Belfast?'

'Dublin accent,' replied Davies.

'I'll see what I can do,' announced Harry.

There was a slight judder in the treadmill when Davies reached across and slammed the emergency stop on the treadmill.

Harry crashed into the hand barrier and slumped onto the treadmill deck. Davies snapped 'What's in it for you, Harry? Why the sudden interest in memory sticks that you know sweet nothing about?'

Regaining his feet and his composure, Harry remarked, 'All's fair in love and war but a shooting like that at point blank range is neither and stopping the treadmill like that wasn't bloody necessary.'

'I've a lot to do and I'm short on time, Harry.'

Shaking his head, Harry replied, 'I'll put my people to work. Meanwhile, Mister King, I'd look in Crillsea Meadows or down by the harbour if I were you. According to the Chronicle, they made their getaway in a window cleaner's van. They've either got clean away in the van, ditched it for another set of wheels, or bedded down somewhere close until the heat dies down. Is that correct?'

'Which do you think, Harry?' probed Davies.

'They're still here!'

'Why do you say that?' quizzed Davies.

'Because you're still here and I've known you to long, that's why, and you always follow the money, Mister King.'

Chuckling for a moment, Davies remarked, 'Talk to me, Harry.'

Switching on the treadmill again, Harry began a slow jog whilst explaining, 'If I was on the run in this area I'd want to be miles from anyone else or right under your nose. The first is hard to find and the other is so close you won't even think of looking there. Has your man got a boat? How about an aircraft, a helicopter? You can look in the fancy hotels and the bed and breakfasts at

Tevington if you want, but if you think like a man on the run you might be closer to getting him.'

'That's my problem, Harry. He's not on the run. I think he's hanging around to have another go.'

'You need to think like a criminal to catch him, Mister King.'

'Yeah maybe,' said Davies.

But deep down inside, Davies King thought to himself, that's my problem. These men aren't ordinary criminals. They don't think like crooks. They're in a different class to your average tea leaf. A different class in every way you could think, Harry Reynolds.

Fifteen minutes later, a fully dressed Davies King sporting his smart new leather jacket strolled into the Anchor to devour a continental breakfast.

Midway through hot coffee, fruit juice and a croissant, Al Jessop swaggered in and announced, 'I'm back!'

'Didn't know you'd gone!' cracked Davies. 'You get moved in alright?'

'No problem, thanks to Barney. Nice place, clean, tidy, just what we need, Davies,' offered Jessop.

His mobile 'phone rang and was answered abruptly with, 'Jessop!'

Big Al stepped away to find better reception, or was it privacy, as Davies waved an acknowledgement to Bill Baxter, the licensee. 'Spot on, Bill. Lovely, thank you!'

'Well, you did say health was important, Mister King, so my good lady wife Brenda ditched the fry up for sparrow food.'

'Ha ha,' responded Davies. 'I'm on a diet, Bill.'

'Again?'

'Yes, again,' interjected Barney appearing in the bar. 'And don't we know it. He'll be after a personal trainer next.'

'Mmm... What a good idea,' mused Davies.

'Davies,' remarked Barney. 'Archie Campbell apparently put six pints of mild on your slate last night.'

'What! How do you know that?' asked Davies.

'Bill tipped me the wink,' replied Barney looking to Bill for some form of back-up.

'That's right, Mister King,' acknowledged Bill. 'Archie said it was something to do with the dog track and...'

'That's fine,' quipped Davies cutting in smartly. 'That's fine, Bill. Leave it on the slate. I'll sort it. Typical, Archie, the soul of discretion, but no more until I see him.'

Tapping the end of his nose with his finger, Bill acknowledged with, 'Leave it with me, Mister King. Leave it with me!'

'Dog track?' queried Barney.

'Later,' replied Davies. 'Sit down, Barney, help yourself to coffee. We need a list.'

'I made a start,' offered Barney. 'A check list!'

'Go on!'

'Hotels, bed and breakfast, youth hostels, holiday rentals, estate agents, lettings, local newspaper adverts. Right along the south coast, say no more than one hours drive from Crillsea.'

'Sound great, Barney. Run it past Annie and then make a start.'

'I already have. Annie's up to the task and don't we know it. She's sending Webby down to help and then she'll join us when she's finished up at the hospital. She's gone to see Mark Tait and she's hoping to get a statement from him if he's well enough.'

'Annie Rock is two steps ahead of me as usual, Barney. That's what I should have done first thing instead of going to the gym,' replied Davies.

'You can't be everywhere, Davies. Going to be a busy day and we need all the help we can get.'

'Just one thing,' advised Davies.

'What's that?'

'I want the harbour area nearby done first - house to house - Webby and one other to do it; our team only. And then I want Crillsea Meadows turned over on the 'phone. It's too rural and widespread and we can crack most of that area on the blower. Pull the Tevvies in and get them to do the same in Tevington and along the coast there. Al Jessop's men will help in whatever way you want. Bang a couple of their lads on the 'phone and get cracking. Put them onto hire car firms, planes, boats, taxis and trains. Bus movements even! If two men have moved together in the last twenty four hours through this division I want to know. Al's squad will be ideal for that. The Met never let go once you feed them a bone. I want as much done on the 'phone as possible. It's too big an area to send troops out. Get onto the Special Branch and the Counter Terrorist Command. I want to know if there's new movements in or out of the area over the last week that we should know about. This Conor O'Keefe might have family living on us for all we know. Check it out, Barney, please.'

'What about SIS and the Admiral's secret squirrels?' suggested Barney. 'The same could be said of the Baron. I mean this super sleuth spy of theirs has to have friends and family somewhere.'

'Good point! Admiral Crow and Commander Pape will be here this morning with some technical equipment apparently so we can follow that line up too. Hey, Barney, we need to try and flush these two crooks out. I want to take a look at the CCTV from the bank and stuff like that as well going up to the hospital!'

'Consider it done,' acknowledged Barney scribbling a note and wrestling with his mobile 'phone. 'You seem so sure they are still on our patch.'

'I think they're close, that's all,' offered Davies.

'I'm on it,' cracked Barney shifting away.

'I think the chess might be off tonight,' suggested Bill from behind the bar. 'I can see you're set for a busy one.'

'Yeah, looks like it, Bill,' agreed Davies. 'Time will tell!'

'Claudia rang by the way,' advised Bill. 'She told me the chief is looking for you and he'll be in the office about ten or so if you've a mind.'

'And what did you tell her?'

'That you were busy briefing Barney, Davies.'

'Sound! Thanks, Bill.'

Snapping his 'phone shut, Al Jessop slid onto a seat next to Davies and quipped, 'Typical, I'm here and it's all going down in Ilford.'

'What! The Baron is in Ilford?' quizzed Davies surprised.

'No, that was one of my informants. There's a job going down at eleven this morning in Ilford High Street and he's my man. It's my shout?'

'There's no way you can get back to London for that one. What do you want?' ventured Davies.

'Your office and a direct video link to my ops room. I'll do a video brief. My number two is going to have to carry the ticket on this one.'

Punching the buttons on his mobile, Davies replied, 'I'll get on it now, sir.'

'Oh! It's sir now, is it, Davies, something you ate?'

Smiling, Davies hooked up with Claudia and said, 'Claudia! Good morning to you! We're on our way to the office. We'll be there in fifteen minutes. I want you to set up a video link from my office to Mister Jessop's Flying Squad office as soon as possible.

And a gallon of coffee from the canteen if you please. If the chief asks, I'm on the way.'

Listening to Claudia's reply, Davies's eyebrows rose as he asked of Al Jessop, 'Anything else, sir?'

'Direct link to the Met's Command Centre, I want a map of Ilford High Street on a computer screen for me to plan it out?'

Nodding in agreement, Davies continued, 'And a direct link to New Scotland Yard Command and Control Centre if you can, Claudia. I want a map of Ilford High Street on the screen when I get there.'

Davies listened and finished with, 'Claudia, I don't know what I'd do without you.'

'That was quick!' acknowledged Jessop.

'Come on, let's go, sir. Claudia is Claudia. She'll have it all laid out by the time we get there. She'll even tell you where to sit for the camera.'

The two men stood to leave the bar, Jessop fishing for his mobile again and Davies stowing his away.

'Bill, breakfast on the tab. I'll catch you tonight for chess, all being well.'

Sighing aloud, Bill polished an imagined spot from the bar top, reached for his note book, and watched the front door of the Anchor close behind the two detectives.

'No chess tonight, Davies,' remarked Bill to no-one specific. 'You're going to be one busy man today by the sound of it.'

They were striding out full pelt along the footpath by the harbour wall with Al Jessop issuing orders on his mobile to his sergeant in London.

'It's a blag on a security van delivering cash to the bank on Ilford High Street, Jim. One driver and three hoods - total four to take down - all with shooters. Sawn offs, I'm told. Eleven o'clock this morning in a dark blue Transit van.

It's Geordie Joe's mob. He's down from Newcastle again meeting up with his brothers from Brixton. I want three ten man teams with the DI taking ground control and Superintendent Howard in command and control. I want you to lead the strike team. I'll authorise firearms. Issue each officer with their handgun and thirty rounds. One Viking shotgun per team but designate Rickie and Phil as unique carriers with multiple slugs. I want them to plug the Transit's engine block from close quarters and put the vehicle out of action!'

There was a pause as Jessop quickened his step and listened for a moment.

The tide crashed over the wall in front of the two men and Davies snagged hold of Jessop's arm and saved him from a drenching.

Jessop continued, 'Command and Control to monitor all Transits into the street by CCTV and declare a red zone when the play begins. No unarmed officers in the game.... No, I don't want anyone inside the bank; no-one at the front door, and a uniform firearms team acting as an outer cordon to close in when the hoods are on the plot. Got that?'

Davies pointed to his left and the two men crossed the road dodging traffic before arriving safely on the opposite pavement.

'Under vests to be worn, yes,' agreed Jessop. 'Diced head gear to be carried and worn for the hit. Ballistic shields on scene. I want your team to take them out in the car without the hoods touching the pavement. Take the windows out, block the engine, kill the tyres, secure the street.'

'Ouch!' muttered Davies.

'I know, it's my decision,' agreed Jessop. 'Jim, I'll be in the DCI's office in Crillsea in ten minutes. I want the team gathered for a recorded briefing to be used in court proceedings in the event that anything goes wrong. I want the firearms commander to issue rules of engagement; lethal force procedures and suchlike..... Busy?... No, it's a quiet day by the seaside, Jim. We're just going for ice-cream and candy floss. I'll be in touch in ten.'

Jessop snapped his 'phone shut and said, 'Right about now my sergeant is knocking on my second in command's door and,' he looked at his wristwatch, 'Yep, the balloon has just gone up.'

'The beauty of a squad geared completely to responding instantly to a major crime lead,' remarked Davies.

'That's the plan. There's always a team on standby and you can bet your life they'll be geared up for this in no time at all.'

'We should have had you in command here for the bank job,' suggested Davies.

'Your man, Felix, has done all the courses, hasn't he? Even the table tops! He should know what it's all about, Davies, surely.'

'Nice guy, Felix,' confided Davies. 'In some ways that is. On the other hand the reality is that all the qualifications and contacts in the world count for zilch if you can't make the right decision at the right time.'

'Only if you get caught out, Davies,' cracked Jessop.

'And you're in danger of that, aren't you Al?'

'It goes with the job doesn't it?' responded Jessop.

'No, I mean the snout who passed you the information. Is he close to the team?'

'He might have been in the team if I hadn't put my oar in and persuaded him to get out,' replied Jessop. 'No, he's safe. He might have been the driver once!'

'So you're taking a chance, Al?' suggested Davies. 'If Geordie Joe and his cronies suspect him, they might just do a dry run today to test him out.'

'That was last week, I'm told,' advised Jessop. 'It went down well and the job's on for today. At least, that's what my man says.'

'But you've only got your man's word for it,' challenged Davies. 'On the word of a shady informant you're going to close down Ilford High Street, put at least two slugs into a Transit van's engine block, blow the tyres out, and smash the windscreen to smithereens in order to take them down before they can out of the van!'

'Got it one, Davies. This is London! It's my city! I knew you should have joined us in the Squad. Just tell me when you want in and we'll find a space for you!'

'Thanks, Al, but I'll have to start calling you sir again and that just wouldn't do,' chuckled Davies.'

They walked on with the harbour disappearing behind them and Crillsea police station coming into view.

'What happens if it's another dry run in Ilford, Al? What happens if you blow the van to kingdom come and they haven't got a pea-shooter between them? What happens if Geordie Joe is using your man to make a fool out of you? The media will have a field day and the top brass will be all over you. Suddenly you're the villain and the Geordie Joes of the world have taken down a top cop just because they rumbled one of your informants.'

'Life's not easy, Davies,' cracked Al Jessop. 'Maybe that's what's on Felix Churchill's mind. Life in general.'

A mobile 'phone rang. Davies snatched it from his jacket and held it to his ear.

'Have you told the chief?' asked Davies into the 'phone.

A double-decker bus went passed and noise intervened.

When it went quiet again, Davies quietly closed the 'phone and said, 'That was Annie at the hospital. Mark Tait died half an hour ago!'

There was only silence as the two men treaded carefully across the tarmac towards the front door. Eventually, Al Jessop pulled Davies back by the arm and remarked, 'I don't know how to say sorry at times like this, Davies. My immediate thoughts are with his family.'

Davies looked away trying to hide a pained expression.

Jessop revealed, 'Never could find the right words but in the short time between breakfast and now I've got a major armed robbery on my plate and you've got what is now a murder enquiry to lead.'

'I know,' acknowledged Davies.

'Oh, you'll lift the tab on that one because it's your division and he's your man,' suggested Jessop.

'I will! No-one will stop me!'

'Just remember this, Davies,' advised Jessop. 'They'll be on their bellies in there. No-one likes it when a colleague falls. They'll be collecting for his widow before lunch time and the media will be all over anyone who knew the slightest thing about young Mark Tait. Some gook inside will be wanting a quiet moment of remembrance; some idiot will be opening a book on who gets his job, and his best friends will be trying hard not to shed a tear. Work? Forget work because these guys have just lost one of their own and they're in the gutter. Unconsciously, some of them will down tools today because that's the way the job is and they'll just want to shut up shop and tell the world to sod off. And somewhere in there will be a hard core wanting to tear the living daylights out of the man who pulled the trigger.'

Davies followed every word.

'Now when we walk into this building,' said Jessop. 'The whole world is going to come down on you and the talk will only be of Mark Tait.'

'I know,' agreed Davies. 'I put him on CID. He's my man!'

'He was your man, Davies. Not any more. He's dead and the man who killed him is on the run. Today, you've got to be a leader as well as a manager. Today we catch a killer. Tomorrow, we'll remember Mark Tait.'

Davies King looked directly into Al Jessop's eyes. It was a cold dispassionate moment before Davies acknowledged, 'That's why you're a leader of men Al! Because you can prioritise.'

'And so can you,' quipped Jessop.

Davies stood thinking of Mark Tait and looking at the front door of Crillsea police station.

Al Jessop pushed the door ajar and held it open for Davies saying, 'This is your time, Davies. Lift them off their knees and lead them!'

Davies King slipped the 'phone into his pocket, pushed the door open, and stepped into a police station in mourning.

Annie Rock was handing out jobs, supervising the shift, managing the people, and making sure the job was being done.

Taking two pieces of adhesive tack she placed a photograph of one Conor O'Keeffe on the whiteboard next to an image of the man depicted as the baron.

'Make sure you know these faces,' Annie advised sternly. 'Burn them into that brain of yours and take copies from the pile at the door on your way out. When the chief inspector says, they're still here, still on our patch, still in our hair, then our job is to find them. Today Not tomorrow. Come on guys and gals, let's go to work. You've got the jobs, you've got your lists, make it happen because no-one else will.'

Davies King walked in with Al Jessop and saw the commotion, felt the activity, sensed the atmosphere sharp in the air.

Turning to Al Jessop, Davies remarked, 'You were saying, sir?'

'Okay, Davies. It might be my London but it sure looks like you own Crillsea good and proper.'

Smiling, Davies surveyed the workers bustling and hustling from the 'phones to the books to the computer screens and back again.

'Today, it's their Crillsea, Mister Jessop. Not mine!'

Al Jessop nodded and declared, 'Game on!'

Down in Crillsea market the place was alive with people shopping, searching for a good bargain, and trying hard to make the pennies and the pounds go as far as possible.

Hard at work doing the job he loved best, Harry Reynolds was giving it a loud voice when he cried, 'Roll up! Roll up! Come on now, don't be shy. Three for thirty pounds and it's a bargain. Come on, my lucky people. You won't get better this side of Tevington, that's for sure.'

'What's so special about them?' asked a rather large lady wearing an old fashioned mackintosh and a paisley pattern headscarf.

'Special!' declared Harry. 'Here, she wants to know 'special'. Here, I'll tell you, missus. Three for thirty pounds! Yeah! Three pans for thirty pounds, that's what. Frying pan, milk pan, sauce pan! What more do you want then?'

'Teflon coated?' she yelled above the noise of the market.

'Teflon coated? You betcha,' cried Harry. 'Teflon coated, double layered, anti burn, anti corrosive, non stick latest technology. Here lady, three for twenty five quid. It's my birthday and I need to move 'em quick before the police arrive. Know what I mean? Nudge, nudge, wink, wink! Come on now. It's a bargain, so it is.'

'Knock off, is it, Harry?' the lady ventured.'

'Do me a favour, missus, do I look like a criminal?'

'Yes!' she yelled to the delight of the gathering crowd.

'Okay, three for twenty quid and no questions asked!'

'Go on then!' she responded. 'I'll have some of that.'

A middle-aged man wearing a cloth cap and an old blue anorak quietly approached and beckoned Harry to one side.

'Here we go!' cried Harry. 'It's my solicitor in disguise. Excuse me, one and all. There's a warrant out for these pans! Here, Elsie, this lady here wants three for twenty quid. Make sure she gets the pans and you get the cash before they close us down and no sauce, missus.'

Harry stepped away and handed the job over to his assistant, Elsie.

'Bless ya, Harry,' laughed the lady shopper and then promptly handed over two crisp ten pound notes to Elsie in exchange for three brand new sparkling pans.

'You need to be careful what you say,' said the man in the cap and blue anorak. 'Sometimes your sales pitch is too close for comfort, Harry me boy!'

'Alright, Pete, good to see ya, son. What's the score then?'

Pete checked over his shoulder, squared away his cloth cap and guided Harry to a quieter area.

'You looking for two guys, Harry?'

'Sure am, Pete. How do you know?'

'You put the word out and I picked it up at Benny's cafe.'

'Oh, I see. What you got then?'

'Computer shop in Tevington, couple of days ago, Harry.'

'And?'

'One Irish, funny eyes apparently, and an English geezer with a posh type accent. Not like us. Maybe educated in London, definitely got a few bob in his pocket.'

'How do you know this, Pete?'

'Just talk, Harry. The London chap bought a load of computer stuff from the shop. You know, geeky stuff like wireless receivers and lap tops with external hard drives and suchlike.'

'Oh my God!' replied Harry. 'Computer geeks by the sound of it. External hard drives and such. How much they spend then?'

'About five grand!'

Harry gasped and said, 'No wonder you guys picked them up. Got an address?'

'Depends on what you're trading?'

'Never change, do you, Pete! If it's good, I'll see you right. Can you take couple of hundred watches in a weeks time?'

'Watches? Never had watches for ages. Good are they?'

'Oh yeah, good!' cracked Harry. 'Bankrupt stock, good stuff. No word of a lie, my son. Normally fived hundred quid but to you, Pete, special price - two hundred and fifty! What do you say, Pete, deal?'

Pete considered for a moment and then asked, 'Straight up, Harry! I mean straight up and straight as a die?'

'Oh yeah, they're clean, Pete. Worth a bob or two, I can tell you. There's a grand in this for you if you can move them to the right boys. It's all good stuff. Coming in from France clean as a whistle!'

Pete nodded and agreed, 'Yeah, okay, that's a deal then. Crillsea Meadows, Harry. Up on the cliffs near Windy Brow Point.'

'Oh, yeah. I know it. Holiday cottages!' declared Harry. 'About twenty of them strung out along the cliff top there like pearls on a string. Bloody hundreds of holiday gaffs stuck up on the Meadows. Damn tourists, can't move for them.'

'In one, Harry. Problem is I don't know which one they're in! Must be off. Got a batch of watches coming in next week. Need to move them on at a profit. Be good, Harry! Be good!'

'Bless ya, Pete. You take care now. I won't let you down.'

The man in the blue anorak and cloth cap was gone from the market stall, swallowed into the crowd, and gone from Crillsea market.

Harry swivelled round and pulled his mobile from his pocket.

No signal, he thought checking the face.

'Elsie,' queried Harry. 'Keep banging them pans out will you, my love. I need to make a phone call.'

'No problem, Harry. Come on ladies and gents,' she cried. 'Get yer pans here, three for thirty quid!'

Turning his collar up, Harry Reynolds stepped away from the market stall and threaded his way through the crowd towards the nearest telephone kiosk

Crashing against the harbour wall, an inbound tide thundered into the concrete and seemed to echo in Terry Webster's ears as he made his way towards the harbourmaster's office.

His mobile rang and he dodged beneath the canopy of a bus shelter in order to respond and keep dry.

'Webby!' he snapped. 'Oh, it's you, sarge! Bad news about Mark. You heard, I presume?'

'Yeah, not good, very sad! We'll catch up later but the chase is on and we need to close this one fast before we lift a glass to the man. Look are you at the harbour yet, Webby?' asked Barney.

'Ten minutes maybe but it'll take an hour or so to check yesterdays movements against what's in the marina today.'

'Good!' replied Barney on the 'phone. 'I'll send some help down shortly. How many vessels are there to check, do you think?'

'A couple of hundred at least, I would say,' replied Webby. 'And the tide is starting to come in so that's going to muddy the picture because there's a few putting out to sea now.'

'Okay, stick at it and keep in touch.'

'Will do!' responded Webby closing his 'phone, making for the vessels at anchorage ahead, and a harbour master's office in the distance.

Elsewhere, three floors up at Crillsea police station, oblivious to the rest of the world, Claudia struggled to hold back the tears as she tried to focus a television screen linked to a computer and hook up some kind of Skype video conferencing set up with London.

Moments later, Sir Thomas Daniels hobbled painfully down the corridor and remarked to Claudia, 'Terrible news, Claudia. Absolutely heartbreaking! We've lost one of our own and he's irreplaceable. It's devastating!'

'I know,' agreed Claudia. 'Are you alright, Sir Thomas? You look a little pale. Can I get you a glass of water or a cup of tea? Coffee perhaps?'

'I'm fine,' countered Sir Thomas. 'Hot day, that's all and just a little upset at the news. Indeed, everyone seems mortified. Last night it seemed as if he was going to make it and then this morning...'

'I know,' replied Claudia. 'Life is so very precious, isn't it. One minute all is well and the next minute...'

Moving to the rear of a television screen, Claudia finished hooking up the video relay to the Flying Squad.

Brushing a bead of sweat trickling from his forehead, Sir Thomas fumbled for a handkerchief, mopped his brow, and tried to stem the rising temperature before revising his decision. 'Yes, well maybe a glass of water... Yes, just a cold one, I think.'

Down by the market, Harry Reynolds was waiting to use a public telephone and he was impatient.

Tapping on the window, he leaned against the glass and announced, 'Come on, mate. My wife's having a baby!'

The man inside the kiosk revealed his back as he turned away into the kiosk and Harry swore beneath his breath.

Meanwhile, Terry Webster knocked on the door of the harbourmaster's office down by the marina and then entered.

'Hi there,' he said producing his warrant card for inspection. 'Detective Constable Terry Webster, Crillsea CID. I don't know if you remember me but...'

'I remember you Mister Webster,' revealed the harbourmaster. 'What can I do for you this time?'

'Looking for two guys in a boat possibly. An Irishman and an Englishman and recently just arrived. Well, some time this week we think. Can you help?'

The harbourmaster flicked over the pages in a huge leather register and responded, 'Well, this book carries the details of the paid anchors and this one...' The harbourmaster reached behind to the top of a filing cabinet and said, 'And this one is the daily tide turners as I call them. Only a few hundred. What's the name of the vessel?'

'Ahh!' cracked Webby. 'That's the problem, I don't know.'

'In that case we'd best go and speak to some of the local fishermen down at the fish quay. They'll know what's new in this week.'

'Where's that?' enquired Webby'

The harbourmaster stood up and looked out into the marina saying, 'Out there passed all the fancy yachts and the rich tourists with their weekend boats and summer sails. What's it all about, young man?'

On a television screen in Crillsea police station the image of Ilford High Street flickered on and off before eventually stabilising and an audience drew near.

'Okay, I have the High Street on screen. The link is good. Well done! I've nothing more to tell you. That's it. Is everyone happy? Any questions?' asked Al Jessop.

The screen image reverted to a squad room and a gathering of detectives with one man dressed in jeans, roll neck sweater and a jacket stepping forward.

'Hey, Mister Jessop,' cried the detective. 'I've got ground control as from now. Have you got screen control?'

'Yeah, yeah, yeah,' remarked Al Jessop. 'Very funny, Jim. Yes. I'll watch the telly while you guys do the work. All happy? Off you go and good hunting!'

'And you,' from the television screen. 'Buckle up and head on out, gals and guys. It's off to work we go. Hi ho hi ho, it's off to work we go!'

'Funny that,' remarked Davies watching the screen, 'I always thought your people were normal but now I'm not so sure.'

Turning his head slightly, Jessop replied, 'Normal! That is normal to them. They're just crazy that's all.'

'Thought so,' cracked Davies. 'Yeah, crazy!'

'Oh, new boats is it?' enquired Sam, a weathered old fisherman tending his nets. 'New boats yesterday, is it? Or new boats today?'

'Either,' responded Webby patiently.

'You see,' said the fisherman, 'Yesterday were a good day and we wuz out most of the day on the tide but today... Well, today isn't like yesterday. I mean yesterday we didn't see any new boats, did we, Alfie?'

'Nope!' said Alfie sitting nearby. 'Nope!'

'And today?' enquired Webby.

'Talking to you today, Mister Webster. Mind you this morning...'

'What about this morning?' probed Webby.

'This morning we wuz out, but didn't see no boats, did we, Alfie?'

'Nope!' articulated Alfie. 'Nope!'

'Mind you, I can tell you all about the boats I saw the day afore yesterday. Lots of boats came in then from the regatta up Tevington way. You remember, Alfie?'

'Nope!' replied Alfie. 'Nope!'

The harbourmaster engaged Terry Webster with a smile and advised, 'Well, I'll leave you with it, shall I? These chaps seem to know everything that's going on!'

The harbourmaster pulled away and Webby said to his two man audience, 'Let's start with the regatta at Tevington then. Were you fishing up that way?'

'Nope!' replied Alfie. 'Nope!'

Webby shook his head but then heard the reply, 'He wasn't, but I was.'

A long morning might be on the cards, thought Webby.

'Okay, let's make a start then, Sam,' announced Webby. 'At the regatta at Tevington, is it?'

'Aye!' replied Alfie. 'Aye!'

The rear basement door of Crillsea police station closed quietly behind the dark figure of Felix Churchill.

He stood listening for a moment and then took his first step onto the concrete staircase leading to the Criminal Investigation Department

On the third floor, Al Jessop, proud and resplendent as usual in his pinstripe suit set off by a flourishing handkerchief poking from a breast pocket, felt a tinge of what might have been either jealous excitement or subtle envy when a dark coloured Ford

Transit moved slowly into sight from the bottom right hand corner of the television screen.

'Here we go, gentlemen,' revealed Jessop.

'You think so?' remarked Sir Thomas.

'Could be,' mentioned Davies.

'They've clicked onto that one early, gentlemen. That's my men in front and behind the Transit,' explained Jessop.'

'Red Ford and blue Renault?' queried Davies.

'Yeah, that's right,' replied Jessop. 'Davies, we need better sound.'

A door opened and closed and revealed Annie Rock dressed in a denim suit of jeans and jacket finished off with a colourful scarf.

'Just in time, Annie,' revealed Davies leaning forward to adjust the volume switch.'

The television screen played out a real life drama.

'Charlie One on the approach into the High Street, stand by.'

'Zulu Zulu, I am in the bus shelter with an eyeball on the approach... I need the air... Come back...'

'Charlie One, go Zulu Zulu!'

'Zulu Zulu.... Wait... Wait.... Wait.... Yes, Zulu Zulu confirms it's the Geordie Joe team. Geordie is driving. his brother is in the passenger seat. Repeat, I have a positive identity call on the driver as Geordie Joe. A.K.A George Joseph Stewart... Designated Target One... Also confirm Joseph Frederick Stewart, brother, is in the front passenger seat... Designated Target Two... I designate the Transit as Bandit One... Over.'

'Roger Zulu Zulu.... Target One and Target Two in Bandit One... Acknowledged.... I have control... Stand by!'

'Is he going to take them now?' asked Davies King?

'Watch!' cracked Jessop. 'There should be four targets but only two mentioned so far.'

Annie observed proceedings keenly offering, 'Who's in the back?'

The show played on.

'Charlie One I have control... Stand by.... Charlie One Bandit One is slowing watching the bank, checking the streets. Bandit One is slowing, he's slowing.... Charlie one stand by all teams.'

The television screen flickered again and then showed the Transit van pull to a standstill opposite the bank.

'Charlie One... Executive Action Bandit One Wait... I have control.... Wait.... Wait... Wait.... This is Charlie One I have control.... All teams..... STRIKE... STRIKE... STRIKE...'

The rear passengers of a red Ford saloon car emerged from their vehicle, turned to face the front of the Ford Transit van, drew double barrelled shotguns from their charge and let loose a slug each into the front engine block of the Ford Transit.

The engine died instantly.

Simultaneously, a leather-jacketed clad youth ran from a nearby bus shelter carrying a sledge hammer which he wielded into the Transit's windscreen. At the same time that the windscreen exploded in a shower of glass, the two rear passengers of the blue Renault bounded from their vehicle and ran to the rear of the Transit. One of the plain clothes detectives jumped up and smashed the rear blacked-out window with a hammer whilst the other detective stepped onto the rear bumper and inserted a stun grenade into the rear passenger compartment through the resultant hole. Both men dropped, covered their ears, and hit the ground whilst a plain coloured squad car suddenly drew line abreast with the Transit and discharged its contents of armed plain clothes police onto the street.

There was a huge explosion of sound, smoke and mayhem when the assault took place.

It was all over within two minutes.

Four men lay bundled and handcuffed on the pavement before one of the detectives, wearing a flak jacket and black and white diced cap, reached into the front of the Transit and returned with his findings. He held to the camera high, four balaclavas and a couple of shotguns. Carefully, and in full view of the camera, he broke the shotgun and watched two big red cartridges fly out of the barrels and onto the pavement.

Triumphantly, he approached the camera and mouthed, *'Result!'*

'Coffee?'

Turning to greet Claudia, Al Jessop remarked, 'How kind, thank you, Claudia.'

'You're welcome,' smiled Claudia.

'Intergalactic!' said Davies. 'The Flying Squad in action!'

'Practice makes perfect, Davies,' replied Jessop tasting his coffee. 'And that's the way we take them out whenever we can!'

'Bet you're glad they were armed,' offered the chief.

'Not half,' chuckled Jessop. 'If you take them out like that then the world thinks you're wonderful because you've prevented an armed robbery and possible serious injury to someone who might have got in the way. If you take them out like that and they're not armed then everyone crucifies you. Sometimes it's a no win.'

'But if you don't play, you'll neither win nor lose,' observed Davies.

'Precisely!' said Jessop. 'Great coffee. Absolutely great?'

'Charges?' asked Sir Thomas.

'Top of the head?' suggested Jessop. 'Probably conspiracy to rob, going equipped to steal, unlawful possession of firearms, loaded firearms in a public place. Enough to put them away for a long time - Maybe a few things, actually. It will depend on all the evidence when it's assembled. They didn't rob the bank so there's no robbery charge as such, but everything else fits.'

'Agreed!' revelled Sir Thomas decisively. 'Congratulations, chief superintendent. Well done, indeed.'

'Thank you, sir,' acknowledged Jessop.

Shaking hands with Al Jessop, Davies offered, 'Well done, sir. I'm pleased it worked out for you in the way that it did. Job well done and no-one hurt.'

The chief laid his cup and saucer down on a nearby desk and enquired, 'Davies, can I use your telephone? I need to make a private call to the Tait family.' He checked his wristwatch and added, 'And I had arranged to call round about this time! I would like to go and visit them but only when they feel it is appropriate.'

'Of course, sir,' answered Davies.

The chief made his way down the corridor towards Davies King's office. He seemed to be hobbling and sweating profusely at the same time.

'Is he alright?' asked Jessop.

'I can't crowd him, Al,' suggested Davies. 'I'll check if he's not back in five minutes.'

The telephone rang on a desk and Annie took the call.

'He's busy,' she revealed. 'Yes, I'll give him a message. Who shall I say is calling?'

Felix Churchill was on his hands and knees delving into Davies King's safe when Sir Thomas Daniels stumbled and challenged, 'Chief Inspector Churchill! What on earth are you doing here?'

'I was just...' Felix couldn't find the words. 'I was getting something for Mister King and...'

'I think not, Felix,' responded the chief. 'That's his private safe. No-one is allowed in there. What are you up to?'

'Oh, I'm just looking for some files, that's all!'

'Files?' quizzed Sir Thomas. 'Files, indeed and what's this about the money and the bank yesterday. One moment money is missing then it's not. What do you know about it? You were there weren't you?'

'I was in charge, yes!'

'Precisely!' cracked the chief. 'So you'd best start explaining to me what happened yesterday and what on earth you are doing today. Fifteen minutes and I'll see you in my office! Understood?'

Ignored, Sir Thomas moved closer and bent down to look in the safe. 'Good God! The memory stick! You...'

'Back away, old man,' threatened Felix. 'You're too old to stop me and I don't need you any more. Now back away!'

Holding his ground, Sir Thomas tried to push the safe door closed as he yelled, 'Where did you get those keys?'

Felix rammed his foot into the space and pushed the chief away. 'It's mine now. The memory stick is mine.'

The chief constable stumbled backwards and hit his head on a radiator aligned to the wall.

Reaching into the safe, Felix pushed aside an inscribed chess clock and a pair of dumbbells. He grabbed a memory stick lying on the floor of the safe and turned back towards Sir Thomas saying, 'I've got this now. I don't need you anymore and I don't need this stupid bloody job. Understand?'

'Have you flipped?' suggested Sir Thomas.

But before Felix could answer, a volcano exploded on the chief's brow when a gush of perspiration seemed to ooze relentlessly from his skin. Sir Thomas reached for his forehead and then tried to regain his feet.

Felix moved past him making for the door but Sir Thomas grabbed his ankle and dragged him back towards the safe shouting, 'Davies! Claudia! Get in here, now!'

Grappling to free himself, Felix eventually thumped Sir Thomas hitting him on the neck and managing to break free. Pocketing the memory stick, he slammed the safe door shout, pushed Sir Thomas against the wall again and made for the door.

As Davies burst into his office, Felix Churchill bundled past into the corridor and set off at speed.

Within seconds he was turning into the stair case with Annie Rock ten yards behind him shouting, 'Felix!'

In the office, Sir Thomas cried, 'Davies, he's got the constellation. He's stolen the memory stick. Get him!'

Davies shouted, 'Al, Claudia, he's got the constellation. Stop him! Annie! Stop him, Annie!'

But then Davies bent down and cradled Sir Thomas in his arms and noticed how hard the chief was breathing.

'No, oh no you don't, Tom,' yelled Davies watching the chief's chest rise and fall.

And then the dam broke and sweat just rolled and rolled like a waterfall from his brow. Tom's heart thundered and his skin grew a pale deathly grey when deep inside his chest something gave and a valve stuck in the wrong place.

Moaning, Tom was trying to say something but suddenly Davies couldn't hear him and he bent down close to his ear.

'Helen... Helen...' whispered Tom. 'Tell her, she was the only...'

'Shh...' answered Davies. 'You can tell her yourself.'

'No, I think not, my dear friend,' muttered Tom. 'I'm going. I know. I feel it... I... I... Why is it cold again?'

Davies scramble to the pulse, weak and falling, and sought a sign that Tom was recovering but he could only watch as life ebbed away from his dear friend, his mentor, his early day companion and life long pal, his....

'No, Tom... We're on the train in New Street, Birmingham and the chess pieces are on the board. I've got the train tickets, remember? We're going up north to investigate a murder and you've just got the beers in. You're white and it's your move. Where you going to put your Queen? Come on you keep telling me you want to beat me for once. This is your chance. What's your move?'

'Davies...' uttered the chief... 'Davies...'

'What, Tom? I'm here. I'm always here for you...'

'Get him, Davies. You've got to get him....'

The chief was going.

'You've got to get the constellation back, Davies. My last order..... My last...'

'Tom, the Lord Lieutenant can't make the Commendation Ceremony. You're going to have to do the presentation. Now get yourself into shape and make it happen.... Come on, Tom... Tom!'

Davies cradled him, held him close, watched his eyes close, felt the hair from Tom's beard tickle his forearm, and felt his pulse grow weaker.

A tear formed in the corner of his eye and Davies rocked Tom back and forth in his arms saying, 'Come back.... It's your turn to play. It's your move.'

Al Jessop appeared at the door, pulled a mobile from his pocket and punched 999 into the keypad.

'Ambulance! Now!' yelled Jessop.

Elsewhere in the police station, Annie Rock was bounding two at a time down the stairs in pursuit of Felix who was pulling away from her.

Eventually, out of breath but with tireless legs, crashing into a wall, Felix regained his balance and forced the fire escape into the car park.

'Stop him!' screeched Annie.

Archie Campbell, soft cap on his head and snuff box in hand, was strolling along the nearby footpath when he heard Annie shout. When Felix pelted past at speed, Archie stretched out a leg and tripped him up.

Tumbling over and over, Felix cannoned into the base of a lamp standard before rolling away and setting off again with Annie only a yard behind.

A black Range Rover with blacked-out windows arrived at the entrance of the car park and screeched to a halt.

Brandon Douglas and Admiral Crow jumped from the vehicle to hear Annie Rock yelling, 'Police! Stop thief! Stop that man!'

Without further ado, Brandon Douglas stooped low, hunched down, and delivered a haymaker of a right hander into the solar plexus area of Felix Churchill.

Felix wheezed out loud, doubled up into a foetal position, and gave up the escape as Annie Rock leapt on top of him and produced a set of handcuffs from her belt.

'You're nicked!' She shouted. 'I don't know why you're nicked, chief inspector, but you're nicked because the boss told me to nick you. You have the right to moan all day, Chief Inspector Churchill. You have the right to sack me if I'm wrong. You have the right to throw your guts all over the avenue from that punch, and you have the right to clean it up afterwards. But don't you ever... Do you hear.... Don't you ever run away from me again!'

'I take it you're on our side?' suggested Brandon Douglas.

'Rock! Annie Rock!' she replied with her knee firmly pressing into Felix Churchill's back. 'And you are?'

'I'm CIA and he's SIS,' snapped Brandon.

'In that case, get your butt over here and lend a hand,' snapped Annie. 'Or are you not up to the job?'

Brandon bent down to help apply the handcuffs but Admiral Crow saw a piece of metal drop from Felix's pocket. It was shining on the pavement and he bent down to examine his find.

'A memory stick!' declared the admiral collecting the article from the pavement. 'It fell from this chap's pocket. Well, welcome back into lawful possession my dear constellation.'

Minutes grew and the clock ticked on with Crillsea police station plunged into despair for the second time in the same day. But the investigation was still live and it was Davies King's job to keep the shoulder to the proverbial millstone.

'Admiral, there's something you should know,' explained Davies in his office moments later. 'The chief authorised me to bug Felix's mobile 'phone. I've just downloaded the recording from the interception unit,' explained Davies. 'It looks as if Felix has been talking to the Baron. Indeed, the calls we intercepted and recorded rather confirm that Churchill was in debt to a bookmakers in town to the tune of one hundred thousand pounds. I'm guessing your favourite cryptologist intercepted Felix Churchill's 'phone and posed as the bookmaker.'

'Don't tell me, chief inspector,' intervened Admiral Crow. 'And in return for dropping the debt and keeping his name out of any possible scandal or stigma, the Baron offered Felix Churchill a deal he couldn't refuse.'

'That's right,' confirmed Davies. 'The Baron blackmailed Felix into stealing the memory stick from the safe in exchange for ripping up the debt.'

'And Felix didn't realise he was being duped,' replied the admiral. 'Silly thing is the debt would have come back to haunt Felix. Or did the Baron recruit Felix into his team? Will we ever get to know?'

'You can imagine the conversation, can't you, admiral? I'll drop the debt in return for the constellation on the memory stick!' qualified Davies.

'Check!' snapped the admiral. 'And I'm presuming the baron thought your man Churchill was the head of the crime section in Crillsea and not you.'

'How do you make that out?' asked Davies.

'Because the Chronicle reveals Felix Churchill is in charge of the Crillsea bank enquiry. There's no mention of you, chief inspector.'

'You mean, your man made a mistake.'

'Yes, he's slipping,' said the admiral.

'Good job the chief authorised me to bug Felix Churchill's 'phone.'

'Oh, by the way,' suggested Admiral Crow. 'Talking about telephone bugs I brought this along, just in case.'

Brandon Douglas removed a black plastic device, perhaps the size of a chocolate bar, from an inside pocket and offered, 'May I do the honours, admiral?'

'But of course,' chuckled Admiral Crow.

'What's that?' asked Davies

'TSCM!' revealed Brandon. 'Technical surveillance counter measures!'

'Or to put it into layman's terms, chief inspector,' revealed Admiral Crow, 'A device that we use to ensure we are not being bugged by our enemies.'

'You're having a laugh, admiral,' suggested Davies. 'Only the chief and I are allowed to bug telephones here and then you wouldn't believe the number of forms we have to fill in and....'

'How fares, Sir Thomas, chief inspector?' enquired Admiral Crow.

'The chief was taken to hospital with a suspected heart attack brought on by a condition of brucellosis, admiral. That's all we know at the moment.'

'Oh dear!' expressed the admiral.

'I'm getting something,' declared Brandon.

'What?' asked Admiral Crow.

The monitor on the device flashed red and Brandon turned and moved until the flashing became more regular and became constant. Brandon stood perfectly still at the window and announced, 'Well, I'll be... Look here, Davies. Someone has been cooking your goose!'

'What do you mean?' enquired Davies.

'Whatever has been said in this office is been listened to elsewhere,' revealed Brandon.

'Where's the bug?' asked Admiral Crow.

Brandon quipped, 'I guess that's it outside on the window ledge. Look I can see it from here. A small transmitter with a tiny inbuilt aerial has been fixed to the window sill. It's very common in our world. We call it a *one time drop!*'

'The window cleaner the other day!' realised Claudia

'Annie bound into the office with, 'Boss, your man 'phoned five minutes ago before I got stuck with Felix. Your man has a lead on two men. One Irish, one English, sounds like our targets.'

'Where?' snapped Davies.

'Crillsea Meadows, Windy Brow Point!'

Standing abruptly, Davies ordered, 'Get Barney and the boys, let's go!'

Shaking her head, Annie suggested, 'How about a slow considered approach... Surveillance!'

Davies glanced at the admiral, then Brandon, and then the technical surveillance counter measures constantly showing a red light.

'Not any more, Annie. They've been cheating. They're probably listening to us right now.'

'Damn!'

'Come on! Close the town down and block the road from Crillsea Meadows. It's our only chance to catch them,' cried Davies.

There was a rush of activity as the radios blurted out messages; officers ran for their cars, blue lights, sirens, and hastily created road blocks. But twenty minutes later,

Davies, Barney and Annie stood in deserted cottage on Crillsea Meadows close to Windy Brow Point.

The cupboard was bare.

Leafing through some papers lying on the table, Barney found a brochure for a holiday letting agency. He rang the number, asked the questions, heard the answers and closed the call.

'Davies, the Baron and Conor booked into this place a couple of days ago. One of them apparently arrived in Crillsea on a boat: The Serpent's Head. Webby is at the harbour now.'

'I'm on it,' snapped Annie banging digits into her 'phone.

Down by the harbour, the sea was as choppy as ever and still crashing over the fragile wall.

'Yeah, the berth is empty,' shouted Webby into his 'phone. 'Apparently the Serpent's Head put out to sea on the tide about thirty minutes ago. We need a search at sea from the Navy and the Air Force!'

*

Chapter Sixteen
~ ~ ~

Crillsea Meadows.
The Funeral

It was a grey day with a lack of sunshine and an absence of deep blue sky. There was just an unwelcome chill in the breeze and a slow measured movement of cloud across the sun.

The iron gates stood open and held back, locked to a rusting hook embedded in the tarmac. The black tarmac was smooth and unbroken on the long slender drive towards the chapel. Only a soft crunch could be heard when the leather of a shoe caught the debris close to the kerb before stepping onto the grass track that led uphill to the place of worship.

He had told Elsie, his wife, that in the event of his passing he wanted to look out over Crillsea Meadows towards the cliffs, where he had served the community, and then beyond towards the horizon deep and afar away.

And it was to the chapel on the hill, near the cliffs, in Crillsea Meadows, they had flocked to respect his calling and to celebrate his life.

The motor cycles came first with their white bulbous fairings, sparkling panniers, Battenberg signage, and blue lights flashing one last time. And their headlights full into the daylight.

They were followed by a solitary police car close behind escorting the cortege.

Then a man dressed in morning suit walked alone with his top hat in one hand and an ebony walking stick held aloft in the other. The ebony was finished off at the top with a fine handle of silver glinting in the sun.

He led the silent procession up the tarmac drive with its gravel on either side bounded by the grass and the footpath lined with people

So quiet, were the people.

Lined in twos and threes, occasionally just a sole haphazard figure making into the queue, and then the uniforms, blue.

White gloves, helmets, and row upon row of blue police uniforms gathered in line to pay their respects to their friend and their leader.

One hearse, one coffin, and a thousand brothers and sisters, sons and daughters, and a family within a family.

For that was the nature of the police family.

Rank and status immaterial at the time of death and not so relevant at the celebration of a life lived.

He held again his walking stick high; his black ebony stick with its silver top, and he lowered it as they neared the door.

There was a salute to the man and his family in mourning. Not a lone salute but a salute by hundreds as the ebony walking stick fell downwards at some unseen pre-determined signal.

The cortege passed by and stopped at the entrance to the chapel door.

More uniforms, all ranks, stepped forward by family selection and drew out the coffin from the vehicle.

Mourners gathered behind the cortege and the music from within sounded and heralded a welcome.

They stepped forward into legend, into history, into a never to be forgotten tale of a man in uniform who died in the line of duty serving his country, living his calling.

One who died a hero tackling a violent gunman.

Hero!

Sir Tom Daniels felt a chill cold breeze meandering its way through the graveyard when later they all stepped away from the chapel on the hill and Helen guided his wheelchair to a waiting car.

He had survived his heart attack and needed to rest in the weeks ahead. He waved to his men; he smiled to friends, he held tight the hand of Elsie Tait: wife of Mark, now a widow.

Helen paused, paid respects, and moved on pushing the wheel chair and denying Davies King such a privilege.

They had buried their dead.

It was what they did with honour and they did it well.

In the afternoon, Admiral Crow visited the police station and found Claudia in the outer office of Davies King.

'Is he in?' enquired the admiral.

'No, admiral. He's taken the afternoon off following the funeral. I think you may find him in the Anchor. It's been a difficult time for him and he's never been able to grieve for Mark properly. He's looking for his own space and time in his own way. That is the way of Mister King. He chose to focus on the investigation and I think he may now regret not giving enough time to the last hours of Detective Constable Tait. My Mister King is a remarkable man, Admiral Crow. He is a man amongst men and, as a result, carries that mantle with him.'

'Of course, I'm sorry... I should have realised...'

'Can I help?'

'No, I doubt it, but thank you, Claudia.'

She smiled politely and he turned to go but then faltered and said, 'Claudia, behind every such man there lies a wonderful woman. Are you and Mister King...'

'No!'

'I do not mean to be personal, Claudia, but my observations and enquiries within this building indicate you are a truly remarkable woman. Perhaps you are a woman amongst women, shall we say!'

'That is kind of you, admiral.'

'Claudia, I took the memory stick back to London. It was the wrong one. It didn't have the Eurion Constellation on it. I don't suppose that means anything to you?'

'Not a lot, admiral, no!'

'I thought not. I need to find your chief inspector as soon as possible, Claudia. It looks as if he night be in trouble. In fact this memory stick just keeps getting everyone into trouble. I may need to talk to you again soon.'

'Memory stick?' queried Claudia standing to tend her plants on the window sill.

'Yes, memory stick,' confirmed Admiral Crow.

'He told me not to tell anyone, admiral, but I think it's time I told you in view of what you've said.'

'What? Who?'

'Mister King, admiral. He told me not to tell anyone and that I had to use my personal judgement in the days and weeks ahead. Mister King told me that I could only speak of this with either yourself or Sir Thomas Daniels, the chief constable. In the event that neither of you were present, I was to tell Detective Sergeant Barnes in one month's time.'

'What did he tell you to say?'

'That he'd hidden the original memory stick in the base of the amaryllis; the other two were false flag operations. He said you would know what that meant.'

Claudia lifted the amaryllis from the sill and tapped the side of the pot until the plant shuffled out.

'He hid it in there some time ago,' she said. 'He told me everyone would be looking for it and we had to trust no-one.'

Admiral Crow approached and sifted through the pot and realised that the memory stick had been secreted in the base of the pot beneath the plant. 'Well, I never,' he offered. 'Why didn't you speak out sooner?'

'Oh, I couldn't do that, admiral. Chief Inspector King told me not to tell anyone until circumstances were right and I had made my mind up on people. So I didn't.'

'And you trusted him?'

'Well, yes. It is Chief Inspector King we are talking about, admiral.'

'Of course,' answered Admiral Crow. 'The Anchor, you say?'

'Indeed,' revealed Claudia.

Out by the harbour a man walked and then stood firm looking out to sea defying the elements as they crashed into the wall beneath him.

The sea was wild today, thought Davies. And the surf gathered and rolled again crashing into the sea wall.

'I was told I would find you here,' said a voice.

Davies recognised the tones and replied, 'Who told you?'

'Claudia! Bill! Archie! They said you wanted time to yourself.'

'It's a day for burying memories, that's all, admiral,' revealed Davies. 'A time to start again and decide that one day I shall find the men responsible for the murder of Detective Constable Mark Tait and hang them out to dry. Your global economics and cyberspace attack falls second to the cold blooded murder of one of my men however important your priorities may be.'

'Naive!'

'Agreed!' responded Davies. 'But then when you attack a policeman, admiral, you don't attack one of us. You attack all of us.

'Agreed!' responded Admiral Crow.

'Your Baron and Conor O'Keeffe are well and truly on my board now, admiral. Where they disappeared to is a mystery but I shall find them one day. Believe me, Admiral Crow. Our problem is that they will still think that we have the software relevant to the Eurion Constellation in our possession. We need to trick the Baron and Conor and pull them into our lair before we behead the serpent that they are. This is not the end, Admiral Crow. It is the beginning.'

'Davies, I have a problem,' declared the admiral.

Still standing looking out to the horizon, Davies withdrew a memory stick from the pocket of his leather jacket and said, 'The Eurion Constellation by any chance?'

'Correct!' replied the admiral. 'Is that the one?'

'Oh yes,' answered Davies. 'This one has the constellation inscribed on the outer casing. It's the one alright. It's never been out of my possession since the moment I realised what it was.'

Davies held tight the stick and held it for inspection.

'Which was quite some time ago?' ventured the admiral.

'Yes, it seems a life time ago now,' revealed Davies. 'Or is it Mark's life gone and Tom's life shortened?'

'Difficult!' suggested the admiral.

'Not for me,' remarked Davies. 'I am intent on revenge.'

'I need the constellation, Davies,' ordered the admiral with his hand outstretched. 'Or rather, Her Majesty's Government needs the technology.'

'They can make the old one up again, can't they?.

'The old one, yes! It will take a few months but they'll produce the old system again. They'll never be able to produce the one you have in your hand. It's unique. It's the only one of its kind.'

'Thought so!' declared Davies.

Davies held high the memory stick with the Eurion Constellation embedded deep inside its software. Then he closed his hand around it and crushed it tight using all the strength his gym days could muster. The plastic casing cracked first and then splintered pushing out the metal tongue that fit into a computer port. Davies's thumb felt the metal tongue, pushed, and bent it, and crushed it again until the device crumbled in his fist.

Then Davies took a step back and hurled the memory stick and its contents into the water below.

The memory stick, in all its broken pieces, headed into the sea.

It was as if the ocean reached up to devour the device, envelop it, hide it, secrete it beneath its waters. The memory stick was gone, hidden, thrown and hurled against the sea wall with all the power of a raging ocean; the innards destroyed by the deep salt of the sea, rusting, corroding, destroying the Eurion Constellation and the dangerous technology that had been there.

'Best place for it,' revealed Davies. 'Now no-one will kill for it and no-one can have it.'

'The Baron will not be an easy adversary for you, chief inspector,' declared the admiral. 'He is a very powerful man who could severely embarrass the government and M16 if he ever spilled the beans on our operations in some parts of the world. Sometimes we have to do things in one part of the globe to influence events in another. It is not an easy role but we do our best to protect our nation from its unseen enemies. The world thinks we live in peace but actually we wage a war against our enemies every day. It is a war that we fight for our freedom and the freedom of our friends. It is a war we fight to preserve our nation. It is an unreported quiet war.'

'I understand that,' replied Davies.

'Your adversary knows no boundaries in the war that he has fought. He considers himself invincible.'

'And I too,' quipped Davies.

'But in the scheme of things, the Baron is dispensable.'

'You think so?' queried Davies.

'Chief Inspector, some things are best left to lie. Let others write history, I say. We must prepare for and safeguard the future of our nation. The Baron is yesterday. The important thing is that the Eurion Constellation has not fallen into enemy hands. Indeed, you seem to be the last to have seen it and I seem to be the last to have seen the Baron.'

'Some things are best left to lie, admiral.'

'So be it, chief inspector.'

'I shall find these men!'

'And behead the Serpent?' asked the admiral.

'So be it, admiral,' announced Davies.

They looked to the sea beneath and the horizon beyond before Davies asked, 'Chess is a difficult game, admiral. Some of the pieces are very powerful; much more powerful than others. The pawns, like myself, for example, can sometimes cause big problems for the powerful pieces. Don't you agree?'

The Admiral considered and returned, 'Yes!'

Davies asked, 'Do you play chess admiral?'

'Only with the best,' replied the admiral.

'Would you play chess against me, Admiral Crow?'

The admiral turned away from the sea and looked inland before replying, 'Mister King, it would be an honour... An absolute honour...'

Turning, they strolled towards the light of the Anchor pub some distance off.

'Black or white?' enquired Davies.

Admiral Crow smiled and commented, 'We have choices?'

Elsewhere, 'The Serpent's Head' put into the harbour and slowly negotiated the final stages of the berth.

'Another day?' remarked Conor.

'Another day!' replied the Baron.

* * *

Printed in Great Britain
by Amazon